SCARECROW BLEEDS

BLEEDS FOR LIFE
BOOK THREE

RIK JONES

This book is dedicated to the two strongest women in my life.

In loving memory of whom I got my creativity from,

my mother, Mary Arnette Jones,

and

to my loving wife, Debbie,

for always being patient and supportive.

Thank you both, with love.

Chapter 1

October 27, 1945
4:30am
Burn's Property, 15 Miles from Windsor Hospital,
Middle Tennessee

BURN QUIETLY EASES THE door shut and turns on his front porch light to look out over the patchy fog. It was quiet and serene as the clouds were sparse, and the dark trees created patterned shadows in the moonlight.

It is about an hour before dawn, the time Burn usually leaves in the morning for the hospital to relieve the night help, Mitchell. His hand clutches a small brown paper bag as his sharp eyes scan the plowed fields. The sight of the long straight rows of the last of the tomatoes, green beans, and sweet corn brings a slight grin to his light scruffy, bearded face. His mind stows away a reminder to tell his boys to plow over the summer crops during the next cold spell.

Wearing worn cotton slacks, a thick woolly buttoned shirt, and a Carhartt jacket, he bounds down the six wide wooden steps. He'd left the top of his shirt undone, revealing his red faded long johns. His heavy work shoes hit the moist ground, leaving nary a footprint on the well packed soil.

As he starts his two-tone older model Ford truck and eases it down his bumpy drive, he looks out over the open field to the left of his drive. His grin transforms into a wide smile at the sight of the hilled rows of potatoes with fresh straw mulch covering the heaps. Other rows held worn plants of beans, squash, and cucumbers. As he travels over 100 yards along the gentle slope, he wonders if he has forgotten any chore that he hasn't directed his farm hands to do in his absence. He hoped not.

His short drive to the main road passes the planting fields, and on one side of the roadway is an abundance of pine and oak trees. The underbrush is a heavy thicket with briars and enough cover to provide shelter for deer. The deer love the acorns, and Burn's family loves the venison.

But the other side of the road reveals trees with blackened trunks, where a fire was set earlier in season to burn off the majority of the underbrush. Several trees are felled every so often and small cords of firewood are stacked by each empty stump.

His eyes follow the headlight beams as they bounce down towards the main dirt road. A three-strand barbed-wire fence is smartly stretched between selected trees on the burned side to follow the old worn roadbed.

His mind is preparing for another trying day at the mental hospital. Canine's behavior and the other patients make each day stressful and unpredictable. But the powers and spirits inside the four walls give him a bit of comfort and security.

He has lived in this area for his whole life, 50 years now. As a kid, he barely remembers public school. Partially because he barely attended and spent most of his time at home working on the farm.

But his ties are tight to the Windsor Hospital, and to J.B., because he was one of the first in Chatham Hill to bury his father (many years ago) in their hillside cemetery.

As he slows his speed to merge onto the main road, his eyes scan the land in both directions. He has a better chance to see a farmer's tractor than a car or truck this far out, but his eyes catch a glimpse of a mound of trash piled up in the middle of his drive. He stomps hard on his brakes and the truck slides several feet to a stop. Loose dust and dirt form a plume that passes his front window.

He raises up in his seat to look out over the dashboard. His eyes try to focus through his headlight beams past the fog and dust, but his lights are too high because of the slope of the road. He locks his parking brake and opens his door. He imagines it is a dog's or calves' remains. As he rounds his opened door, he sees clothes on a small, feeble body. He slowly approaches what is revealed to be what is left of Lester, his old friend.

Burn can only identify him from his thread bare skirt and torn trouser cuffs. The same clothes he last saw him in when he told one of his hands to take him to the remote shed. His eyes squint, trying to see more closely, but the darkness is too thick. He retrieves a flashlight from behind his seat and flips a switch to shine a beam on the lifeless body.

Burn kneels down. He sees the tire tracks in a straight, deliberate line towards Lester's head. The skin and hair is torn away to expose the skull. It is cracked from the weight of the truck traveling over his head. A trail of blood splashes away from where Lester's head should be. He is pretty much decapitated.

Burn turns away as flies continue to swarm around the congealed remains of the neck. But as his flashlight beam serpentines away from the body, Burn catches sight of a dirt circle drawn in the wet dirt from last night's rain shower, obviously drawn by someone's finger. His eyes focus into the middle of the six-inch diameter circle. He fixates on three irregular pieces of what must surely be Lester's teeth. His anger grows as he comes to the realization that someone has deliberately disposed of his body here.

He flips the flashlight onto his truck seat, as he recklessly jambs the column shifter into reverse. He stomps the gas. The truck shoots back quickly as he turns the steering wheel hard. The Ford turns into the underbrush, and he floors the gas pedal as the rust spotted truck accelerates up the road.

Burn's eyes are incensed as his truck steams full speed towards his two-story wood frame house. It is smartly kept and everything in its place. His truck speeds past his house about 100 feet to the next one-story frame house resting alongside his own.

Before his Ford even slides to a stop, Burn is exiting his truck. He shouts loudly as his fist shakes the door fiercely, banging several times. "CROCE...CROCE...IT'S BURN." A commotion is heard inside as someone hustles to get to the door.

A 30-year-old black man wearing just boxer shorts, swings the door open holding a pistol. He's six feet tall with a muscular physique and short, kept hair.

"Croce, trouble at the main road..." Burn struggles to spit out the words, "Lester's dead, we got to make a run. Get the keys to your truck, and I'll wake Gant. Then you two meet me at the main road." Before Croce can answer, Burn is down the steps and heading around the corner. Croce watches for a moment and closes the door.

There are five other houses or sheds or barns arranged on a diagonal to Burn's house, parallel with each other and separated by about a stone's throw. Burn hustles to the third house.

BANG! BANG! BANG!

Burn waits a moment. The door cracks. "GANT!" Burn scrutinizes the sleepy eyes outlined in the cracked door. "Trouble at the main road. Get dressed NOW and meet Croce at his truck. Hurry! Hurry! Hurry!" The door creaks closed and there are some loud noises from the other side of the door.

Burn goes to a small storage shed between some of the houses. He gets his keys and unlocks the door. The door swings open and he retrieves a 100-foot-long rope. It is neatly wrapped in a circle. It's an old braided 1-inch rope smudged with grease and oil and dried dirt from where it was used to pull stumps out of the ground. Well past its usefulness.

He tosses the rolled-up rope over his shoulder, locks the shed door, and goes back to his truck. He slings the rope into his truck bed and looks back towards Croce and Gant's houses before driving away. He honks his horn.

~~~

Croce drives his faded green 1930 Ford Model A pickup up behind Burn's truck. Croce steps out as Gant exits the passenger side. Gant is a 24-
~~~

year-old, skinny black man about average height with stringy, long hair. Both men go to the front of Burn's truck and see Lester's body illuminated in the headlights.

Croce sees the body first. "Is that...Lester?"

"What's left of him," Burn admits, moving to Lester's side as Gant turns away. "Croce, let's pick him up and put him in the bed of your truck."

"Pick him up? He'll fall into pieces," Croce protests, but Burn is already crouching down.

"Let's go, we ain't got much time 'til daybreak." The three men lift Lester's skinny body, and gently lay it in the back of the Model A. "You've boys been to the slaughterhouse, right? This ain't much different."

Gant still tries to distance himself, revulsion clouding his features. "I don't pick up the animal just after they slaughter it."

"Hell, you eat the slaughtered animal a week later." Burn rolls his eyes as he steps away from the truck. "Listen, boys, serious now, Lester probably spilled his guts, so trouble is probably headed our way... You know what I mean?"

The boys nod.

Burn observes them, apprehensive, but decides he doesn't have much choice in the matter. "Now, follow me. We've got to hurry."

Chapter 2

October 27, 1945
5:30am
On the road to Major Grisco's House, Chatham Hill,
Middle Tennessee

DANNY'S TRUCK RACES DOWN the road toward his house, his face occupied with a look of horror as his truck sways from side to side. He stands on his brakes as his truck slides to an abrupt stop just missing the bumper of Major's patrol car, the family car, and the mailbox.

But he is still a bit too slow as his front tire unhinges a row of smooth river rocks around his mother's favorite flower bed.

He exits his truck and runs up the front steps, moving faster than the cloud of dust forming in his wake. His mouth is dry from the news he can't wait to tell Major.

It's just minutes before daylight as he slams through the front door.

"MAJOR!" The house is silent except for his panting. He goes to the bottom of the staircase and directs his voice up the steps, "MAJOR! LESTER IS HANGING FROM THE RIVER BRIDGE!"

He pauses a moment as shuffling is heard upstairs. A door squeaks open. Major looks over the banister railing. "What's hanging?"

Danny begins to climb the steps to face Major. "Lester...I think. He ain't got a head, well, he ain't got a neck, really."

Major furrows his brow. "Call Frost at the jail and tell him to meet—"

Elliott's sleepy face appears in his doorway.

Danny continues as if his father had never spoken, not noticing his brother's interest, "—couple of cowboys from the stockyard are going to stop by the station and tell Frost—he should be on the way by now."

Major turns to his bedroom, Ms. Grisco moving out of his way. "Tell me what you know."

"Want me to make coffee?" she offers, but before Major can answer, the phone rings.

"Dammit. I ain't got time. That's the station, Kathleen. Go tell 'em I'm on my way to the bridge."

Slipping on her housecoat, she heads downstairs to do as she's told, her eyes catching on Elliott. "Elliott, back to bed." He jumps at her loud voice, closing the door as she rushes downstairs.

Major starts getting dressed, his son bringing him up to speed. "—Headed to Peppers and when I got to the bridge about three or four cars and trucks were backed up 'cause a tree had blocked the whole road." Major bounds down the steps. Danny continues to talk as he follows, "Well, the stockyard boys had a rope and pulled the tree off the road, and when I drove around the curve, I saw...well, I thought it was one of those clothes dummies they got at the general store."

"A mannequin?" Major leans down to lace up his boots.

"Yeah, I guess. I could tell it was a man by the way he was dressed, but I thought it was a prank of some kind, you know Halloween and the Festival."

Major rolls his eyes. The phone begins ringing again. Major finishes putting his work boots on as the ringing continues. "If he doesn't have a head, how is he hanging?" Danny opens his mouth to answer, but Major holds up a finger to stop him, shouting, "KATHLEEN!" The ringing stops as Major puts his hat and gun belt on.

Kathleen looks around the corner from the kitchen, her face red. "I was taking a piss! That was *another* caller. I told the station you knew about the hanging." The phone rings a third time.

Major starts out the door. "STOP SAYING HANGING!"

Danny is unbothered by the sound of his parents yelling at one another. "Oh, mom, I accidentally ran over a flower or two, sorry."

Her eyes roll to the ceiling. "Daniel, I can't have nothin' nice that you and your father won't tear up." She shakes her head in disgust, disappearing into the kitchen as Danny looks back at his father.

"The rope is tied around his chest."

"Danny, follow me in your truck."

"You don't want—"

"Follow...in *your* truck," Major reiterates.

Major backs out of the drive and speeds towards the main road. The patrol car siren begins to sound just before his tires hit the two-lane paved highway.

~~~

Major pulls the patrol car up onto the pavement. He travels a couple miles when he sees a row of vehicles stopped in the right lane. He slowly eases into the left lane, rounding the cars lined in the curve to see the dangling body in the distance. He slows to examine the tree on the side of the road. Frost has his car in the center of the bridge diagonally across both lanes. A row of vehicles waiting to cross the bridge back up behind him.

He sees the corpse with its feet about 5 or 6 feet above the ground. As he slowly approaches, he notices the rope tied around the man's chest as Danny said. Its end is slung over the steel support and extends 50 plus feet back down near the ground. The rope has bunched up in a ball where it goes over the steel support because of the body being pulled up.

As he climbs out of the car his eyes scan the rope to see it tied to the handrail across where Frost was parked. Danny's truck quickly drives up near the bridge and slides to a quick stop just off the pavement near Major.

Major jumps a bit because of Danny's close proximity. His shoulders raise as his eyes slowly turn to Danny. "Son, back that truck up where the traffic is and don't let anyone come any further until I say so!"
~~~

Danny's shoulder's fall, but he does as he is told, his father's eyes watching the entire process, ensuring Danny is with the general public before retrieving a department-issue flashlight from his glove box.

He walks toward Frost and they stand about ten feet away from the body, the fog making it difficult for anyone other than the two police men to see. He studies the head, which is twisted sideways to reveal some of his skull. Dried blood is covering what's left of Lester's shirt, front and back.

Frost breaks the silence first. "That's Lester alright." The frail body slowly twists in the slight breeze. "Who'd do that to an old drunk? He ain't got no enemies...right?"

Major shakes his head. "I can make out his skull...thought I heard rumor the county guys had tips where Lester was, and I was expecting to see him alive in a day or so."

"The county guys? I don't know about that. I got a call to the photographer, should be here—"

Major interrupts. "Cut him down when the ambulance arrives. I don't want the public to watch him swing in the wind."

"Yes sir," Frost agrees as the sound of the siren gets closer. "I'll go move and direct them by."

"What did the cowboys say at the station to ya'?" Major's eyes remain focused on the corpse.

"They drove up, and a tree was laid across the road, so they moved it with a rope and found the body."

"They say if they saw another truck or anybody?"

"No sir, they didn't say."

Major scratches his chin. "Go by after we get the body out of here and ask them again...you know what I mean—make 'em remember." Frost turns to walk away, and Major speaks louder. "—and get the names and numbers of all those cars backed up and see if they saw any truck as they drove up, not just here but a mile or so away. See if they remember anyone they passed before the bridge. And make 'em think about it, you know, scare it out of them. I got to know, and someone's got to have seen something."

The ambulance eases by Frost's patrol car, stopping a few feet back from the body. Major issues directions the minute the personnel step from the vehicle. "Don't touch the body until I say so."

They nod as Major walks back to Frost. As he nears, a black plain car drives up next to Frost's patrol car. A wiry, 30-year-old with glasses, a white pressed shirt, and dark slacks steps out, camera in hand. "Called for some pictures?"

Major doesn't wait for Frost, giving his own directions to the camera man. "Yeah, Robert, get some pictures of this knot and how it's tied. It looks different...and get pictures of the body and hurry, I want him down now—Go, I don't have all day." Robert's camera flashes as he takes a couple of photos of the knot and the body at all angles.

The two officers continue to examine the rope. "That rope is frayed, in three or four places and got black spots...Where's Cutter?"

"He comes in at noon."

"Looks like grease all over it, like it's seen better days. I'd like to ease Lester down without damaging the rope."

Frost nods. "You say something about the county guys over in Madison?"

Major looks at Frost. "Just a rumor." His eyes remain shuttered.

"You want me to—"

Major cuts him off. "No, I must have heard something wrong."

Frost doesn't say anything more, but apprehension clouds his features at his boss' words.

Major watches Robert take the final pictures. He motions Frost to come closer. "You see the tree that fell across the road around the curve?"

"No, didn't get a good look at it, sir."

"That tree has been dead for four or five months. It was dragged across the road intentionally by the fellows that strung up Lester." Frost nods as he listens and records in his memory for later.

As Robert finishes, Major eyes the photographer. "Got enough pictures?" He nods and Major waves one of the ambulance workers over. "Listen, we are going to ease him down easy—the rope is bad but I want to try and save it whole, okay?" Frost nods and begins to leverage the rope with one of the ambulance workers as Major undoes the knot. "Little more." Major twists and grunts. He finally unties the knot. "Alright, ease him down…" They begin to ease their grip. "Slowly…"

The rope snapped in two where it went over the steel support directly over Lester's body. Major looks toward the ambulance drivers, but they have just jumped back from Lester's body, hitting the ground. Major could tell Lester's legs turned in an unnatural direction. There's a camera flash.

He sighs in defeat and yells towards the medical personnel, "Alright, get him to the coroner, he's all yours." The two men lay the gurney down and untangle Lester's legs. They get him on the cushioned mat. Robert flashes several more pictures of Lester on the gurney.

Major calls from a distance. "I want the rope—lay it to the side." One of the medics nods while the other begins unwrapping it from what remains of Lester.

Frost passes the patrol cars and goes to the first car in line, Major preoccupied with collecting the rope, looping in in his grasp. As soon as the corpse is free of the rope, a white sheet is pulled over the body. Major watches as they load it into the ambulance, the continued fog giving the scene an eerie feeling.

"Robert!" Major calls over his shoulder, the photographer pausing his picture taking. "Robert, listen," Major leans in so closely that Robert begins to lean back up, a grimace on his face. "You work for the county, right?"

"No sir, just a freelancer…kind of whoever hires me."

Major's eyebrow raises. "Frost called you, right?"

"Yes, sir."

"Listen, my department hired you so if I see any of those pictures in the newspaper or any place other than my office I'll personally handcuff you and take you out to your *last* darkroom, you hear? I got a shovel in my trunk right there—" Major points to his open trunk, the ream of rope tucked in next to the shovel. "See it? Right there." Robert nods, struggling to swallow. "I'll get you to dig a hole out near the swamp and bury your camera, and your glasses, and that clean pressed white shirt—"

A bead of sweat rolls over Robert's lip.

Major's hat brim is pushing on Roberts's forehead. "—And your sweet smelling little wife won't see you *ever* again. She's the black hair, tight-figured girl that wears those dainty hats and gets that sweet sway when she walks down near the diner in town, right?" Robert nods nervously. "You understand how important those pictures and negatives are to me?"

"Yes, sir."

Major slams his trunk closed, Robert flinches at the sound.

Major steps back and points towards the traffic. "Go around that curve and get a couple of pictures or two of that log someone dragged across the road, can you do that for me?" Robert's head shakes emphatically. "My department and your pretty wife would both appreciate that." Robert turns without a word, and hustles back towards his car.

Major waits for him to drive by before returning to his own vehicle and backing it out of its spot. He turns his attention away from the bridge back toward his house. As he slowly approaches his son, who has taken control of the traffic, he slows his vehicle. "Danny, you remember anything else you haven't told me already?"

"No, sir... That was Lester, right?"

Major doesn't answer his question. "And the cowboys were the first vehicle to see the body?"

"Yes, sir."

"Alright, tell everyone that the road is clear, and you can go to work. You ain't been telling anybody what you saw, have you?" Danny looks down at the ground, his lips pressed in a thin line. Major groans, "What have I told you about snitches?"

"Yes, sir, I know."

"Tell Nina and Jeremy why you are late, and no one else."

"Yes, sir."

"How are they?" Major asks as an afterthought, as he genuinely doesn't care about the pair that runs the general store.

"She runs the place, and Jeremy coughs all the time now."

"Might drop by to see them later."

"I'll be in and out today."

Major looks perturbed. "I'll drop by to see them, not you." Danny's face falls. "Now, get to work, go on."

Major eases off the brake, his patrol car lurching forward, his eyes watching his son through the rearview mirror as he heads home. It was time to ask the county boys some questions.

~~~

Major stops in front of his house. Kathleen watches from the living room window, sipping her coffee, her eyes drawn to her damaged flower bed. Her husband walks in the door and begins to remove his shoes.

"Was it like Danny said?" Her voice trembles.

"I'm afraid so."

"You want a coffee?"

His eyes drift to the phone. "Yeah, let me make a quick phone call first."

Major waits until she disappears into the kitchen to turn the rotary dial. "This is Major, it's important, get your boss on the phone." He pauses a moment, listening. "I know how early it is, put the old man on, now." Kathleen returns to the room, setting the cup of coffee on the side table.

"It's too damn early." Mr. Sweet's voice is heavy with sleep.

"Lester's dead." Major pauses. Mr. Sweet doesn't say a word. "Someone hung his body from the River Bridge. We just—"

Click. The phone goes dead.
~~~

Chapter 3

TODAY IT IS BENJAMIN'S job to run the front desk at the hospital. While it isn't his favorite job (he preferred accounting) it did give him time to read the newspaper. As his eyes skim down the black and white pages, Benjamin methodically moves a red lollipop in and out of his mouth.

There's an ad about the November 6th election and the names of the two candidates. One of the articles is about Robert Fields, the acting D.A. of Coweta County and assistant to Mr. Fitzgerald, another about Adam Kieffer, though in terms of size, it fails in comparison. Mr. Kieffer's picture is twice the size of Mr. Fields. Mr. Fields is a quiet and unassuming gentleman, which is good for working behind the scenes, but for a politician, it's not a good trait at all.

Benjamin shakes his head thinking the small-town gentleman versus the big city lawyer from Virginia may not be a fair fight. As he gazes at the newcomer's picture and reads the list of his titles and accomplishments, he thinks Mr. Kieffer's smile and confident frame has him set dead ahead of Mr. Field.

Although he is supposed to be paying attention to the comings and goings through the hospital front doors, Benjamin is fully engrossed in his paper. At least it's a quiet day in the hospital and, besides the sound of the nurses passing through the doors to the back room, silence fills the lobby.

Annie Mae emerges from the back room, her eyes settling on Benjamin and the dozen lollipop sticks strewn across the counter desktop. As she passes through the waiting room to her office she says, "Benjamin, how long have you been here? I see you found the candy..."

Benjamin doesn't say anything as he watches Annie Mae walk into her office and sit down behind the desk, the door wide open. Once she is seated, he says, "Fifteen minutes or so...who brought the candy?"

"Burn did. You know he's got several children living on his farm...said it was left over." Annie Mae glances down at the papers on her desk, sorting through them as she converses with Benjamin.

"I didn't know that. Have you been out to the farm?"

"He's got several acres and a bunch of tenant houses. He supports a lot of people."

Benjamin looks up from the paper, tucking it under his arm, and walks to the doorway. "Really? What do they all do?"

"Well, I can't say for sure. Burn likes his secrecy."

"You can tell me," Benjamin insists.

"No." She pauses for a moment, considering. "No. I can, but I won't." She notices the paper tucked under Benjamin's arm. "What's the news?"

He looks at the folded paper. "Oh, the whole paper is stuff about the festival. Rides for the kids, ponies, food contests, fireworks and all the sponsors. They got all their names in large print..."

"Will you come in here for a moment...and close the door behind you."

Benjamin does as he's told. "I saw Danny at Peppers yesterday when I picked up the paper," he says once the door is closed.

Annie Mae stops what she is doing and looks at him for more info.

Benjamin continues, "I spoke to him briefly, and I talked him into letting me run his Friday delivery to Yaphank so I can bring Cass and Silva back with me. I guess I invited them to the Harvest Festival and to ride Glory."

"And the Peppers said it was okay?" Annie Mae's eyebrows are raised high on her forehead.

"Oh, yeah."

"And? What else?" she prods.

"That's it, just setting the hook."

She knew what he meant as she had already filled Benjamin in on her and Sadie Blue's plan. "This isn't going to bother you, is it?" she asked, referring to the part of the plan that Benjamin was assigned to execute.

"No, ma'am. I'm kind of looking forward to seeing him in pain. What's it supposed to do anyway?"

"It won't take long to see results...and it's gory." Annie Mae grimaces even as she keeps her explanation brief.

"Gory? I'm ready to see what gory looks like."

Annie Mae doesn't like the grin that spreads across Benjamin's face as he says the words. "Don't pretend like you're enjoying this."

"Yes, ma'am, I won't pretend," Benjamin promises.

Annie Mae goes to her filing cabinet and opens the second drawer as Benjamin changes the subject. "Mr. Strickland and Stephen do a great job with reporting all the news in the area from livestock reports to socialites, wedding news from here to Madison. He makes the newspaper business sound pretty interesting."

"Every business sounds good to you."

He nods eagerly in agreement. "I think I would like to pick his brain one day."

"Benjamin, shut up a minute and come over here." He folds the paper up once again and sticks it in his pocket.

He looks into the filing cabinet as Annie Mae points to a medium-sized light blue glass medicine bottle wedged between some folders. "That's it?" he asks.

"Yeah, it's not quite full, but she says he's got to take at least half to do the trick since he's a big man."

"Sadie?" Annie Mae stares at him, letting her silence be the answer. "Okay, I've got an idea how I'm going to work this."

"I hope so. You've only got that one night."

"I got some help."

"Help?"

"A girl."

"Don't get anybody else involved," Annie Mae pleads in disbelief. She hadn't realized that Benjamin had brought anyone else into their plan.

"Don't worry, no one will find out," he assures her.

"I hope so, you could be putting her in danger," Annie Mae cautions her youngest grandson.

"Oh, I told Danny about a girl that was asking me about him."

"I don't want to know." Annie Mae holds up her hand. "Just don't get anybody else hurt."

"Yes ma'am. I'm going to leave the bottle—"

"No, take the bottle now and hide it at the house somewhere," Annie Mae insists, enclosing the bottle in her fist and holding it out to Benjamin.

"Now? I was going to say 'hi' to Amber, and after that J.B. and I were going to get the books in order. He wanted to do it today 'cause that lawyer is coming tomorrow."

Annie Mae thinks for a moment. "Okay, go hide it now, then go see Amber. I didn't know you and J.B. had something scheduled. He doesn't tell me about such things anymore…"

"I told Amber yesterday she could drive me around and show me what she's learned."

"Lunchtime. You can see her after you and J.B. get the books straightened out," Annie Mae states as Benjamin finally reaches up to take the bottle from her outstretched hand. He slides the bottle into his pocket and begins to leave the office without another word.

Annie Mae watches as Benjamin throws the newspaper from his pocket onto the lobby counter before exiting the main doors of the hospital.

As soon as he is out of sight, she turns and locks her office before heading through the double doors to the back of the hospital.

Ms. Elvie approaches with a serious look on her face. "Everything running okay this morning?" Annie Mae asks her.

"Yeah, everything's normal. But my mind has been in tatters since last night...I couldn't sleep."

Annie Mae takes her by the arm, and they go to the surgery room, closing the door behind them.

"What's the matter?" Annie Mae asks.

Ms. Elvie's eyes look somber. "Do you remember before when you told me you saw a vision of Paulene?"

"Yeah. It was just a short one, like a flash."

"Tell me everything about it again, because Victoria told me last night that Amber told her to watch Paulene and not the fire...and she wouldn't tell her any more."

Annie Mae eyebrows rise. "I don't know. I didn't see anything about a fire."

Ms. Elvie's eyes search Annie Mae's face for answers. "Well, how about let's get Amber in here to give some answers, 'cause we are talking about my baby, and my nerves are on edge and I'm about to break."

Annie Mae wishes she could help, but she too has many unanswered questions about her vision which she tries to explain, "Ms. Elvie, now my vision was only a flash like a photograph. I saw the— Do you really want to hear this?"

Ms. Elvie reaches up and physically grabs Annie Mae's uniform by the lapels, her hands curling into a fist. "Yes, goddamn it! Tell me everything."

Annie Mae sighs, shaking her head before continuing, "I saw the body of Paulene draped across a firewood pile face down...that's it...I don't know where, or when, or anything else. I swear."

Ms. Elvie takes a step back in shock, her hands dropping Annie Mae's lapel. "Dead?"

Annie Mae searches for words to soften the blow. "Maybe unconscious? Or asleep?"

It's too late however, because Ms. Elvie is beyond consolation from the few words Annie Mae provided. "Please, please, call Amber, please. I need to hear everything she can tell me."

Watching her friend fall apart, Annie Mae knows she has to agree, and she does, before walking out the door. Ms. Elvie collapses into a chair, putting her face in her hands.

Annie Mae returns a few minutes later, Amber just a few steps behind her.

Amber sees Ms. Elvie hunched over in despair. "What do you want me to say?" she hisses to her grandmother.

Ms. Elvie raises her face from her hands, tears glistening on her cheeks. "The truth, dear...the truth, please."

Amber looks at Annie Mae before turning back to Ms. Elvie and recounting her dream. "I'll tell you my dream." She takes a deep breath. "At the start, I saw a shadow grab Paulene from behind and then she vanished. It all happened quickly, like a scene in a motion picture... The fire was like in the distance, and that's it."

Ms. Elvie stands on shaking legs pointing an accusing finger at both women. "You both told me something that has crumbled my world. I don't know what to do. I can't sleep and watch my daughter all the time or just desert her and simply forget what you have told me." Her voice has a note of hopelessness woven through the words.

Annie Mae sighs. "Where is she now?"

"Cebo is with her today. She's safe now, but if something happens to her, you two will have blame on your hands... At least tell me, will she live?" Annie Mae drops her head as Amber bites her lip. "Ms. Mae, tell me..."

"It was just a picture. That's all I can tell you."

"You both will have blood on your hands...as if you hurt her yourselves," Ms. Elvie threatens a second time.

"You can't mean that," Amber pleads, tears glistening in her own eyes at Ms. Elvie's obvious pain.

Ms. Elvie looks directly at Amber's eyes and says with authority, "Yes I do!" She nods as if to reassure herself. "Yes I do." She says a second time with less venom before a dizzy feeling comes over her. "I'm tired...I would like to lay down for a moment"

"You can lay in my bed," Amber volunteers, motioning to the hospital bed where she has been spending her nights.

Ms. Elvie waves her off. "No, just an empty bed in the hospital will do, and just for a few moments."

Annie Mae and Amber watch as Ms. Elvie leaves the room into the main part of the hospital. Once she is out of earshot, Annie Mae turns to Amber. "I thought we were helping."

"Maybe we are, maybe something we say can change the future," Amber says hopefully.

"You keep dreaming, child...keep dreaming." She pats Amber's hands. "Let's get back to work and maybe carry some of her load the rest of the day."

Amber nods and heads back to work as Annie Mae makes her way to the front of the hospital.

Chapter 4

October 28, 1945
11:00am
Windsor Hospital, Chatham Hill, Middle Tennessee

J UST AS ANNIE MAE is making her way back to her office, she sees Benjamin enter the hospital, making a beeline for J.B.'s door. He reaches the door, but stops and waits for a moment before twisting the knob and entering.

Annie Mae decides to do the same, crossing the room and twisting the knob to step into her husband's office. "You two getting ready for the lawyer's tomorrow?" Benjamin's voice reaches her ears as she closes the door behind her.

"I talked with Truman's lawyer on the phone a few days ago." J.B. replies, his voice filled with tension. "He wants money, a large sum of money."

"So you're figuring out how much we have? How much does he want?"

"He didn't really say, so I too would like to know how much we've got."

"Did you get a lawyer?" Annie Mae asks, keeping an eye on Benjamin out of the corner of her eye and the boy begins flipping through an accounting ledger.

J.B. drops his head. "Weston's referred us to a lawyer," He checks the name on one of the many papers on his desk, "A Mr. Hixson, from Nashville."

"Nashville, sounds expensive," she replies.

"He can't make it tomorrow, but he has been in touch with Truman's family lawyer."

"If our lawyer isn't going to be here, why is he coming?" Annie Mae asks, confused.

"He's bringing an investigator and—" J.B. tries to finish his thought, "I guess he's got a report from Major. Weston says we need a civil lawyer that deals with litigations, he says he's good and will be well worth his fee."

"Fee... Can we afford all this?" Annie Mae asks as her husband pulls the ledger from Benjamin's hands.

J.B. looks up earnestly from the open ledger to Annie Mae. "I hope so. I hope we can survive."

"Survive? Our lawyer says they have a good case against us." Annie Mae drops her head.

"I'll leave it with—" She turns back to J.B. "—What about that deaf kid from up Richmond?"

J.B. answers without looking up this time. "Oh, I talked to his father last week and told him to delay until Hal gets back. Maybe he can come around the first of December."

"Yeah, I told him the price. I tripled the start fee and monthly fee and he didn't bat an eye, so that might help us with the finances for sure," Annie Mae says as she turns to leave the office. "Good luck." She closes the door behind her.

Annie Mae hesitates but eases through the next set of doors. She sees Weston with his cart giving medication to the patients. Rein is talking with Jennifer while sitting on her bed. She approaches Burn, who is bringing Mr. Solomon back from the bath. He's clean and freshly clothed. "Burn, when you finish walking Mr. Solomon I need to talk to you."

"I walked him before his bath," Burn replies as he helps Mr. Solomon into bed.

"He's definitely worn out," Annie Mae observes as Burn tucks Mr. Solomon in, before following her to the back of the hospital near the gate which overlooks Canine's lodgings.

Once she is sure they are out of earshot of the rest of the staff, Annie Mae begins, "I appreciate all you do for us, Bernard. Without you and Weston we could not handle things around here."

He nods his head in agreement. "Yes, ma'am. I've been here so long it's just second nature to me."

"Well, Weston's leaving around the end of year, and David is useless, so J.B. and I have been thinking about asking Cebo to join us on staff, but we wanted your feedback since he'd be helping you mostly."

Burn thinks for a moment before answering, "I think he would be a good addition to the staff. He's trustworthy, got a strong back, and Hal trained him to be a hard worker. When you thinking about hiring him?"

"Soon, to get him in and get David out."

"Why's David even still here?" Burn asks.

"With his injury, J.B. said the lawyer said it would be favorable if we didn't fire him but let him work his way out," Annie Mae explains.

"Okay, I guess I see some rationale to that."

"One other thing," Annie Mae pauses, "You know tomorrow morning Truman's lawyer is coming by with an investigator, I've heard, and they may want to question you." She slows her words. "Tell them the truth."

"A madman went crazy, broke through his straps, and bit Truman around the neck until Cutter shot him. That's it, short and sweet, nothing that he had not done before," Burn replies, his voice even and firm.

Annie Mae's voice is laden with concern. "That's the problem, since he did it before and we had the paperwork when he came in, they are going to say that we should have anticipated his behavior."

"Do you want me to tell them the man changed into a wolf and chewed his neck off?"

Annie Mae holds up her hand. "No, no, let's stick with the first story. But what if Cutter tells the truth?"

Burn hesitates. "The people will think he's crazy, so I think his story might be close to ours."

"I don't know, that's why I'm a little weary." They both pause, thinking over the event. "Well, we'll see tomorrow. They may ask about David."

"I don't know about him…probably…" He trails off, not sure what to say.

"Just letting you know." Annie Mae changes the subject. "I see all the candy you brought in…getting ready for the fun? I know the kids will love it. Are all your kids coming to the Harvest Festival this weekend?"

Burn laughs. "You know they will."

Annie Mae replies, "I might sneak into town to visit some old friends."

Burn responds, "Maybe you should. You don't get to see anybody new, unless they're hurt or sick."

Annie Mae is happy Burn is offering some news. "You going to be in the middle of it all?"

He shrugs. "I really don't know. This is a big day for my kin. We'll be from one end of the town to the other."

"Okay, if I see ya', I'll say hello," she finishes, just as Sadie emerges from the laundry room. Noticing her, Annie Mae says a quick goodbye. "See you this weekend."

Burn keeps the smile on his face as she walks away. Even though he is muttering, "I hope not…I hope not," under his breath.

Sadie takes that as her cue to walk up to Annie Mae. "Sadie, I talked to Benjamin…it sounds a lot more dangerous than I anticipated."

Sadie nods. "I'll start my plan and finish it before the festivities this weekend."

Annie Mae whispers, "Plan?"

Sadie mumbles just loud enough, "I'll make a doll that I learned from New Orleans."

"A doll… Does it work?" Annie Mae is curious because she had never heard of such magic before.

"It did in Orleans. That red piece of handkerchief I got will fit in its back pocket just fine." Her eyes look into the distance. "It'll do the trick...don't worry about Benjamin. Daniel won't have a chance." Sadie cracks a confident smile.

"Good." Annie Mae says before the two women part ways, both heading back to their hospital duties.

Chapter 5

October 28, 1945
1:00pm
Windsor Hospital, Chatham Hill, Middle Tennessee

BURN POLISHES OFF THE last bite of the sandwich Amber made for him, crumpling the paper with his left hand. It's a quiet, sunny afternoon, the beams of sun illuminating his face from his position on the front porch. There is almost no noise, beyond the sound of Weston puffing a cigarette on the other side of the porch.

Burn studies the young man, who is wearing a sweater with jeans, his book propped firmly on the bottom rung of the porch rail.

"I heard you're leaving soon," he asks the young intern, breaking the afternoon peace.

"End of the year or so."

"Well, you've been a great help to the hospital. J.B., and Annie Mae, Elvie, and me, we really appreciate what you have done here for the last, what, over a year, I guess."

"Yeah…15 months or so." He takes another puff before looking at the older man. "The lawyer's coming tomorrow. What are you going to say about Canine?"

Burn shifts his weight, the chair creaking. "My guess is Cutter's going to say he's half human and half animal—he's in a cage for good reason."

"Hm. What about his powers?"

"Say..." Burn starts to close his eyes, "...you heard about split personalities, right? You tell them the medical jargon and I'll tell 'em...the other..." Burn's words fade, his breath deepening. Moments pass as Weston contemplates the stories.

Weston continues, "What about blood and him turning into a...dog...or wolf?" When Burn doesn't answer, Weston turns toward him, finding him asleep.

He takes his last toke and flips the butt down in front of the vehicles parked in the lot. The butt bounces before coming to rest in its final landing spot among the sea of other butts he has tossed there. "Two, four, eight, twelve, fifteen, twenty." His counting stops as he quickly realizes there are more than one hundred, and that's just the butts he can see.

With a grimace, he makes his way down the steps and begins collecting them, only to find he can't carry them all. Glancing at Burn, he uses his foot to brush sand over the ones that remain.

When he looks up again, Rein is there, studying him. He blushes.

"You can't fool me. I saw what you're doing, cleaning up your mess." Weston looks up at Rein's grin. As he ascends the steps, she holds out a small brown bag. "Here, put them in here."

He eyes the bag.

"Burn brought the candy in it yesterday," she explains as he dumps the contents of his hands inside. "That's a lot of cigaret—"

Weston closes up the bag and sets it down by the stair post. "Tell ya', this nightlife has got me doing crazy things."

"Crazy or stupid? What's your girlfriend going to say when you get back?"

He shrugs, his gaze not meeting hers. "The letters are getting farther and farther apart...I think she's moved on."

"I doubt that. She'll be fine."

Weston thinks for a moment. "I don't know about that."

Rein puts her arm around his midsection and gives him a quick side hug and a smile. "Maybe you need to change your nightlife, it doesn't seem to be helping ya'."

He smiles, throwing his right arm around her shoulder to give her a reciprocal hug back. Her head leans in as a reflex to his chest for a brief second. He breathes her scent in, his breath hitching.

The sound of Burn rustling in his chair breaks the tension, both of them breaking the hug to look at the sleeping man.

"Have you changed your hair? You look different," he asks, his eyes on her dark tendrils.

Rein reaches up to touch the ends of her hair. "Amber, cut a couple inches off and brushed it back differently. She's learned to cook now and I'm teaching her how to cut hair—you like it?"

He studies her. "It looks good."

"Thanks," Rein says, noticing the way his eyes remain on her face for far longer than it takes to observe her hair.

Weston finally turns away to look out over the fields. "She seems to be happy living with Sadie."

"You're right, both are thrilled. Sadie seems rejuvenated, like she got a new daughter. They work the same hours now, so Amber brings her back and forth."

"I guess Hal will love that. I notice she and Ms. Mae don't talk so much anymore."

"I noticed that too," Rein pauses, her mind shifting to her adoptive grandmother. "Maybe it's the stress of Truman's death, the lawyers, and running this place and her attitude with Major."

"As an almost doctor, if she doesn't slow down and take it easy—well, I got J.B. to prescribe some pills to help her ease her stress."

"For real?"

Weston nods. "Maybe the holidays will bring Annie Mae and Amber closer together."

Rein folds her arms across her chest as the cool breeze shoots across the porch. "Maybe the holidays will bring us all closer together. Anyway, I got to get back inside to see Jennifer, I promised her a story."

"Oh, that reminds me, I've read your comments about Jennifer and have talked to J.B. about her advances."

Rein squeals and grabs Weston's hands with hers. "You have? And what is the prognosis?" Realizing how forward she is, she releases his hands just as quickly as she grabs them.

Weston is quiet for a moment, his mind focusing on where her hand had been gripping his. "She is talking more regularly about her sister and her mom, maybe try and get her to write?"

"Like a story?"

"Yeah! And maybe see how far back she remembers in her childhood or what her dreams are."

Rein looks a bit puzzled. "Her dreams...like at night?"

"No, like the future." His eyes find hers briefly before he turns his gaze away. "You're so optimistic. See if you can get her talking about what she thinks will happen when she leaves here."

Rein's shoulders slump. "Sometimes people aren't happy talking about the future."

Weston's lips twist as he realizes the effect of his words. "Teach her about love."

Rein's eyes splash with excitement. "Love?"

"Yeah, emotions."

"I'm not the person—"

Weston looks into her eyes and takes her hands like he had done before. "Yes, yes, you're the perfect person to teach her that."

Rein's eyes widened again.

"It may take some time for a person to learn about love, but just don't give up on your patient, okay?"

"I'll try...I guess I've got plenty of time." She bites her lip.

Weston nods. "I'll be here for you."

Rein turns to go inside, thinking of everything Weston said.

"Wait, Rein..." She turns around. "I'm a little concerned about my parents, and the problems I have put on them."

Rein offers a smile. "If you want someone to talk to, I'm your girl."

Weston's heart jolts and he blurts out, "Did you get a chance to look at the university brochures?"

Her smile turns immediately to a smirk. "You remember what I just said about people talking about the future? That's something for later, much later."

Weston's mouth opens and closes silently as he can't think of a response. Seeing his dilemma, Rein opens the lobby door, shouts emerging from within. She turns back to the sleeping assistant, "BURN!" Burn awakens with a snort, rising slowly from his seat. Rein points inside the hospital, "They need you." He throws his hand up and takes a step towards the door, Rein following behind.

More shouts come from the back room, and she quickly retraces her steps to where Weston still stands on the porch. "Dr. Galloway, you are needed also."

He grabs the brown paper bag, tossing it in the lobby trash as he follows her, coming to stand next to Burn in the lobby, who is still rubbing sleep out of his eyes. "I guess we're all needed. Did we finish talking about what to say tomorrow?"

"We did, split personalities."

Burn's eyebrows furrow. "Oh yeah."

Weston watches as Burn heads into the back room, his mind flashing back to his conversation with Rein and the words he wanted to say, but couldn't get them out in her presence. "I think we're all needed. That's why I've stayed around so long, I guess."

Chapter 6

October 28, 1945
2:00pm
Windsor Hospital, Chatham Hill, Middle Tennessee

MAJOR'S PATROL CAR EVER so slowly creaks down the dirt drive. Even the dust is unaware of the approaching car, remaining still as he parks in front of the hospital. Major exits his car, slips on his hat, adjusts his gun belt and lumbers up the steps.

Major closes the door behind him as he enters the lobby. It is quiet. He sees Annie Mae's office door closed and no one is in the nurse's locker area. So he takes a few steps and puts his big face into one of the glass portals of the double swinging doors, peering into the world behind them. His eyes sway from side to side watching the commotion of the working hospital. Annie Mae catches sight of Major's round face and bashes through the left side of the door, her face red. "What are you doing here?"

Major steps back, unperturbed. "Business. Need to see Bernard on the front porch for some questions."

"About what? He's working pretty hard," she snaps, her eyes drifting to the closed door she just exited.

"None of your business. I'm working pretty hard too. I can come inside and get him and we can go to the station for the questions."

Annie Mae narrows her eyes, but disappears back through the doors, presumably to collect Burn. Major waits, his face calm, but his muscles remain tense, his feet fighting distance apart—just in case.

Burn steps into the lobby, and Major's hand shifts lower, to where his bully stick is tucked into his belt.

Burn speaks first. "What's this about, Sheriff?"

Annie Mae pushes open the door behind Burn, watching the altercation through the crack.

"Hadn't talked to ya' since the medicine cabinet fiasco and I got to talk to you about some recent events." His eyes drift to Annie Mae. "Alone."

Burn doesn't seem to notice her eyes on his back, his own glance not straying from Major.

"Let's go out on the front porch so we can talk freely. We've got lots to talk about." Major puts his hand on his holstered gun, his head tilting toward the door.

"Do tell. Maybe you can question me right here."

Major takes one step closer to Burn. "We need to get some fresh air and air out our differences...just a little chat."

Burn's eyes turn to Annie Mae, and he gives her a nod. She eases the door shut and disappears quickly into the back of the hospital.

"Lead the way." Burn falls into step behind Major, but at the door, Major holds it open, motioning for Burn to move in front of him.

As Burn steps out onto the porch, Major closes the door behind him.

Before Burn can turn back around, Major grabs his arms, spinning him until his chest is pressed against the hospital wall, Major's baton shoved into his spine. Burn doesn't move.

Major begins his search, patting Burn's arms and waist for weapons, but he comes away empty handed. Burn shifts his weight, and Major releases him. "Let's sit down and I'll say my piece, and then I'll be on my way." Major points to the rocking chairs.

Burn walks towards the chairs checking behind him to ensure Major isn't going to sucker punch him. He gets to the chair and instead of sitting, moves to stand behind the chair. His hands rest on the knobs of the chairs. "What you got to say to me?"

Major studies Burn. Leaning on his lessons from his army days, he continues to stare until Burn relents and blinks. Burn observes Major's stance, debating whether or not he could gain the upper hand. His eyes also calculate the distance to his truck, where a gun is waiting.

"Lester's dead...and I know you had something to do with it."

Burn presses his lips together. "I didn't have anything to do with his death...just his travels."

Major crosses his arms and sets his feet at the ready, "I think I can prove otherwise...you see I talked with Nina at Peppers yesterday morning and a couple of your workers stopped by for gas and coffee early Saturday morning...about the time Lester was hanging."

Weston pops open the hospital front doors. "Burn, you need a hand? I can be a witness..."

Burn throws his hand in the air towards Weston. "No...no...I got this. Check back in five minutes and see if I'm still alive."

"I'll watch from the window," Weston replies, letting the door swing shut behind him.

Burn turns his attention back to Major, his head tilted to the side. "My workers are out early every morning making deliveries so that don't prove nothin'."

"We about to vote in a new District Attorney in a week or so. He might have something to say about the evidence that I give him."

"Are you talking about one of Sweet's old used-up lawyers?"

Major steps back a half step and unfolds his arms. "Politicians know everybody one way or another...he might go easy on ya' if you and Mr. Sweet can just talk and be on the same team. The partnership might save some of your kin folks lives."

Burn takes a step closer to Major. "Listen up...don't threaten me...I've lived around here my whole life...and while you went off to play army, I got plenty of connections from Madison..." Burn pauses a moment to let his words sink in, "...like a little birdie told me that Lester was in your custody Friday..."

Major raises his eyebrows.

The corners of Burn's mouth turn up in a smirk. "Your name has been in the newspapers more than the end of World War II...so don't think this new District Attorney's going to scare me..." Burn points his finger at Major, "...I live closer to Madison than you do...and I ain't talking about miles." Burn calmly sits down in the rocking chair and begins to rock.

Major puts his foot in front of the end of the rocker, forcing Burn to stop his rocking motion, "We don't want any bloodshed around here. So, let's save some lives with a talk...that can't hurt." Burn isn't engaged. He looks out over the barren field, towards Hal's in the distance.

Major speaks softly with a little compassion. "I know it was heart-breaking to lose an old friend like Lester. His scrawny little body all crumpled up in a knot. Bad way to go. You think?"

Major's eyes study Burn's face for a reaction. Burn's head slowly turns, "I see why you're here now. Lester must have said he was a friend of mine and you two jackasses put two and two together." Burn isn't fazed. He continues, "Listen, I know you think you two sons of a bitches have discovered a gold mine, but listen, Sheriff...don't be in the shaft when it collapses."

This time, Burn does smirk, his own foot nudging Major's out of the way so he can start rocking once again, "Tell your boss, no. I ain't got nothin' to talk to him..."

"Listen, Bernard." With the forceful sound of his name, Burn's eyes focus on Major's voice with disdain. "Sweet demands a meet...We can do it at the jail or on the road between here and your homestead. He don't want you killed, but for me...I won't miss a breath if you're gone. You really ain't got no choice."

"Listen, Robert,... or Bob...by." Burn says to Major with more force than Major said Bernard. "I've got plenty of choices. You got guns but I got friends here at the hospital that's got my back." Burn points his thumb behind him towards the inside of the hospital. "The power of loyalty and it's a power you can't see or beat. And you know what? I know where you live, too."

Major's eyes freeze a moment as he realizes Burn is correct. Burn balls up. "So go tell your boss I expect some peace and quiet."

Major is confused. "What the hell, you've lived around here long enough that you may have 'em inside fooled, but you ain't got me fooled. I've had you figured out since we were kids and you should know there ain't no such thing as peace and quiet around here."

Burn shrugs. "Tell Sweet, there won't be any bloodshed unless he starts it... Maybe he'll understand that."

Burn stands and faces Major. Major, "He doesn't understand no."

The sheriff doesn't say anything, his teeth grinding behind his lips. Burn turns to go back into the hospital.

When he's almost back inside, Major calls after him, "Oh, forgot to mention I found out you knew both the Hick's girls." Burn stops abruptly. Major stands and steps closer to Burn's back. "Gemma...the poor girl that was raped and murdered...and her sister...she said you used to give them candy...and she thought of you as a friend."

Knowing he had hit a nerve, Major continues his path, walking around Burn to stand in front of him and look him straight in the eye. "Imagine that...you were their friend, Bernard."

Burn's face remains stoic. "Yeah, I knew 'em both...I'm a black man and imagine that, I knew those black girls." He puts his hands on his hips. "I deliver supplies in every direction, and me and my boys are in every pig path from the other side of Madison to the other side of kingdom come, so do with that what you like."

Burn begins to walk away again and Major watches him go. "Oh, by the way, there might be another girl or two killed in the surrounding counties that the Feds are looking into...so they might want to talk to you someday soon...probably ask me to drive them out to your place and ask you a few questions about that."

Burn stops and turns. "You come onto my place, you better bring some help with ya'." He pauses a moment. "Let me know when you'll be coming, so my lawyer from Madison can be there."

Major smirks, "Oh, I'll bring plenty of help. I suggest you keep your family close...Lord, only knows how many you got . What a dozen or so now? So many...so many beautiful girls."

Burn steps toward Major, "Hope your women folk don't end up like Lester."

Weston eases the door open. "Need any help out here?"

The two men stare at each other, not responding to Weston. It's Burn who once again caves first. "I gots to get back to work, 'stead of wasting my time talking to the lawman that's supposed to be protecting us all." Burn pushes past Weston and reenters the hospital, leaving the intern to watch Major as he walks off the porch and back to his car.

Chapter 7

October 29, 1945
10:00am
Windsor Hospital, Chatham Hill, Middle Tennessee

IT'S QUIET AS WESTON exits the hospital onto the front porch, making his way down the steps toward the river. It's a brisk morning with light gusts of wind ruffling his hair and clothes as he lights up a cigarette and inhales.

He does a few stretches to loosen his muscles between puffs, groaning at how tight some of them are. Enjoying the cigarette and the cool morning air, Weston takes a glance around, his eyes coming to rest on David sitting in a parked car in the hospital lot, not moving.

Weston walks up to the car, noticing the front window is down a crack, so he addresses David, "Are you coming in today? Burn needs your help."

David's voice is muddled as he replies, "He always needs my help." He doesn't even glance in Weston's direction, his facial expression remaining stoic.

Weston watches him, his eyes evaluating the man who is just a few years younger than himself, but different and immature in every way.

David never makes eye contact with Weston, keeping his eyes straight ahead as he stares off into the distance. Weston becomes angrier the longer he sits there when he should be inside helping Burn and Ms. Elvie.

Moments later, an expensive car bursts into view as it makes its way down the drive. Dust billows behind it and Weston sees Cheddar's tan furry body chasing it from behind. The vehicle comes to a stop in the parking lot, as does Cheddar, and he takes a seat right by the driver's door, clearly hoping for some pets.

Weston observes as a man wearing a brown suit and matching fedora hat emerges from the car. He's of average height, albeit overweight, with a mustache. The passenger steps out as well. He is wearing a tweed herringbone suit with thin lapels, a loosely tied tie, and holstered gun resting on his hip. Weston watches as David finally exits his car and meanders towards the newly parked car. He has to hide his smile as Cheddar tries to jump up on the man with the gun. He gently nudges the happy dog away.

It's as this happens that Weston notices there is a third man in the car, who is still seated in the back seat. The man peers out his window, but appears to be afraid of dogs, and eyes Cheddar with apprehension in his eyes.

David sees the man's predicament and picks up his pace so he can grab Cheddar by the collar and direct him back to the main house. The dog, however, doesn't like being manhandled and struggles in David's grip toward the car.

"Cheddar, go home," David commands.

Cheddar takes a couple steps toward the Windsor house and stops, looking back as the back seat passenger steps out, clad in a black three-piece suit with a silk handkerchief and a dangling gold chain attached to a pocket watch. He is carrying a leather satchel that Weston knows likely cost more than a month of his wages. As the three men assemble, David introduces himself to the man in the three-piece suit and Weston notices that something about the driver looks familiar, but he can't quite place where he has seen him before.

Weston continues his vigil as the men make their way toward the door of the hospital, taking note of the fact that Cheddar keeps his distance and doesn't try to approach the trio again.

Two of the men glance at Weston and give him a nod on their way up the stairs. David, noticeably, keeps his gaze forward, not even sparing him a glance.

Weston watches Cheddar slowly climb the steps until he comes to his side. He reaches down to pet him. "Cheddar...things are going to be changing soon. Winter is almost here, a snow or two will fall and...I'm leaving soon after." He stands and takes a last drag of his cigarette before tossing the butt in front of Burns' truck. "Amber's leaving," He looks out over the fields, "Rein's leaving too, and a year or two later Benjamin will probably be traveling the world. Don't tell anybody I said this—" He looks at Cheddar, the dog's eyes trained on him as if he truly was listening, "—I don't think the hospital will survive with all the young people leaving," Weston pauses, "and I'll deny I said that if you tell." He rubs Cheddar's head once more and heads inside.

The trio of men are still in the lobby when Weston enters, the man carrying the gun currently arguing with Annie Mae.

"Sir, you simply can't take a gun into a room with unstable patients, no matter who you are," Annie Mae insists.

The man pulls out a badge. "I'm telling you that carrying a gun is my right."

"I understand that," Annie Mae pleads, "But the individuals in there are dangerous and you bringing in a gun could hurt all of us."

The man sighs. "How about I take all my bullets out and leave my suit buttoned?"

"Sir, with all due respect you have no idea—"

The lawyer cuts Annie Mae off. "He's a man of the law. He's allowed to have his gun. The way I see it, he is being nice by leaving the bullets here. He could go in as is."

Annie Mae sighs. "Alright I suppose emptying the bullets will be sufficient."

The gunman quickly pulls the gun out of his holster, emptying the bullets into Annie Mae's outstretched hand. As soon as the gun is empty, she places the bullets out of sight under the counter before noticing that Weston has joined them.

"This is our intern from Boston University Medical School, Mr. Weston Galloway." Annie Mae paints a smile on her face as she motions to Weston.

The men all begin to introduce themselves, their voices overlapping. Weston holds his hands up. "I'm sorry, but I've been petting the dog, and I need to wash my hands. If you will excuse me, I'll greet you in the back."

Now that Weston is seeing the men up close, he realizes that he's seen the driver before, at Jernigan's. He doesn't remember what job the man had at the restaurant, but he knows that no one at Jernigan's goes out and about without some sort of weapon—meaning it was likely that he, too, had a gun beneath his jacket.

With a shake of his head, he leaves to wash his hands just as Annie Mae asks David to get some chairs and bring them to the area near Canine's cage.

The driver watches as the group of men and Annie Mae leave the entry and head to the back, and as soon as they are out of sight, he grabs three lollipops and two bubble gums from the dish on the counter and puts them in his pocket, except for one lollipop which he unwraps and puts in his mouth.

Wrapper in hand, he looks around the room for a trash can, until he finds one behind the counter. His eyes catch on the newspaper on the counter, so he decides to sit in the seat behind the counter and read.

Meanwhile, Weston washes his hands quickly in the bathroom, and as he opens the door to exit, he runs into the chest of the man who was arguing with Annie Mae about his gun. The two look at each other for a moment, and then he introduces himself. "Mr. Galloway, my name is Ethan Mueller."

"Nice to meet you," Weston replies as he moves out of the way so Ethan can enter the washroom.

As Weston walks away, Ethan steps into the bathroom, closing the door behind him and switching the lock. He efficiently loads his gun with three bullets from his front suit pocket before returning it to his holster and putting the strap over the hammer. He washes his hands, buttons his suit jacket, and leaves to join the others.

While he was in the bathroom, David had set up four chairs which were now arranged in a semicircle looking into Canine's cage. Annie Mae and J.B. sit in two of the chairs while Burn, Weston, and David remain standing.

The lawyer's eyes connect with Weston's, and before sitting down he sets his binder on a cot and extends his large palm to Weston. "My name is Daniel Hightower from Nashville."

"Yes sir, nice to meet you," Weston replies.

Mr. Hightower heads over to the fence surrounding Canine, reaching his hand out to shake it to test its sturdiness. He observes over Canine sleeping in his cot. "Is this the location of Mr. Singletary on the day of the attack?"

"Yes, and that cot there—" J.B. points, "—is where Mr. Truman was."

"Both were strapped down?" Mr. Hightower asks.

"Yes," J.B. affirms.

Burn tosses the torn straps from the incident on the cot beside J.B. "These were the straps."

Ethan picks one up and Mr. Hightower looks at the other. Ethan is aghast. "No way."

"You would think not, but he did," Burn assures him.

"They must have been defective. He couldn't have done that...could he Ethan?" Mr. Hightower's voice is filled with doubt.

"I don't see how he—" Ethan tries to say but he is cut off by Annie Mae.

"He did, tore right through them."

"Can I take these as evidence?"

J.B. and Annie Mae look at each other but before they can reply, Weston speaks up. "Maybe you should get them from the sheriff."

Mr. Hightower looks at Weston. "Ethan, call..." Hightower picks up one of his papers from the cot, "...a Major Grisco and let's go through the proper chain of command." He looks at Ethan. "We'll get them from him. Now, did a photographer come last week?"

Annie Mae shakes her head. "No...no one stopped by."

"Well, I'll talk to your lawyer so we can get the same photos."

Hightower looks at the paper a second time. "Was Mr. Singletary under sedation?"

"Yes, he was," Annie Mae assures him.

"Did you administer the dosage?"

"Yes, I did."

Hightower looks at the paper yet again. "From the hospital's medicine lock up?"

Weston cuts in. "Ms. Mae, before you answer that maybe you should consult your lawyer."

All of the individuals in the room look at Weston with differing degrees of interest. Annie Mae slowly turns away from Weston, deciding to respond to Mr. Hightower, "Well, yes, we obviously got it from our medicine cabinet."

Weston lowers his head. He doesn't like the direction this questioning is going in.

"Well, we have a police report that states the official hospital drug cabinet was installed incorrectly and a person or persons may be able to get to the contents without unlocking the cabinet doors." Mr. Hightower looks around at the room, "Also there are several names that had ample opportunity to compromise said cabinet. This is a signed report from Major Grisco covering everything I just said. Does anybody want to comment?"

Nobody moves.

Weston drops his head. "Mr. Hightower, I believe that the Windsor Hospital staff would like our attorneys present during any further questioning. In fact, I think we should stop right now."

"That's your prerogative, but we will have to get depositions from each of you before trial, and whether someone participates now or not is up to them, not you."

J.B. stands and walks towards Weston. Annie Mae's mouth is hanging open. "Trial?"

Chapter 8

October 29, 1945
10:20am
Windsor Hospital, Chatham Hill, Middle Tennessee

I WAS HOPING NOT TO take this to trial, but if you all refuse to answer questions, then we will probably have no choice." Mr. Hightower's eyes move around the room until they land on David. "You all know Mr. David Larson, and I just want you to know that he has obtained me as his attorney also to obtain compensation for pain and suffering and emotional distress." He pulls out another paper. "David, while we're here, where did your incident occur?" David points to the floor. "Right where you are standing?" David nods. "And who witnessed your attack?"

"Weston was holding one of Mary's arms and I was holding the other arm, and she bit a chunk of skin out of my arm. I've been wearing a bandage for at least two weeks."

"Do any of you have any comments that you would like to offer Mr. Galloway?"

A chorus of "Not really" fills the room.

Mr. Hightower smirks before continuing his questioning, "And who administered Mary's medication?"

Weston raises his hand. "I did. She received the normal allotted dosage."

Mr. Hightower peers up to Weston. "Maybe normal was not sufficient?"

"I believe it was," he replies.

Mr. Hightower says with a slight grin, "I'm sure you would."

J.B. looks at David. "Why are you still working here?" Everyone can tell by the look on his face he feels angry and betrayed. "I think you need to leave with your attorney and not come back."

Mr. Hightower is unfazed. "I'm not your attorney, Mr. Windsor, but I would advise that you not be hasty in terminating my client."

Annie Mae just shakes her head. "You're fired, David. Get out and don't come back, do you hear?"

David has his mouth slightly open. He takes a deep breath and takes a step back.

Weston chimes in to try and calm the situation. "J.B., you might not want to fire him today. Mr. Hightower is probably right."

J.B. doesn't listen. "Mr. Hightower, I believe you need to pack your papers and get out."

"I will but I request that I be allowed to make a few notes and check out this—" He looks at another paper, "—Mary."

Annie Mae stands and points to Mary, "You want to interview Mary? The yelling old lady that calls for her dead brother to come get her and take her home daily Mary?" Annie Mae carries on, "Are you sure you want to talk to her?"

Mr. Hightower isn't bothered. "I would like to see her, and also the whereabouts of this medicine cabinet."

Annie Mae walks away and stops in front of David. "If your daddy was alive things would be going a lot different today, wouldn't they?" She gives David a stare. "I got to get back to work. I'm needed."

Mr. Hightower ignores Annie Mae's words and turns to David. "Is your arm healed completely yet?"

"No, it got infected."

Hightower looks at J.B. "I guess you have given your attorney all the patients medications in question."

J.B. begrudgingly nods before his attention zeroes in on David. "Come back later for your last pay."

Mr. Hightower shakes his head. "This is unfortunate that he is being fired today. But I would like a copy of David's payroll records also."

J.B. nods to Annie Mae and Mrs. Elvie. Mr. Hightower turns to look at Weston as the next question leaves his mouth, "Mr. Galloway, you were the attending physician when David was attacked?"

"I believe I need to have an attorney present before I say another word." Weston presses his lips together in a thin line.

"Have it your way, Mr. Galloway." Hightower begins packing his papers away, except one he keeps out and looks at it. "Mr. Weston Galloway, son to Mr. Edward Galloway, a banker and foreign goods exporter, and Susannah Galloway, or Sunny, an artwork curator and collector—"

Weston interrupts. "Why are you reading my background? You seem to know me very well."

Hightower steps closer to Weston. "I know your family at least. I'm sure you know that individuals can be liable if he or she was negligent in causing an accident." Weston's anger grows at his words. "A certain brownstone in Beacon Hill. You can't hide money, son." Weston turns away but Mr. Hightower continues. "I advise you to talk to your daddy. He'll know a good attorney for you." Weston says nothing as Hightower puts his papers away and closes his satchel.

Mr. Hightower walks by Weston with Ethan close on his heels. They walk to David, and he points towards the medicine cabinet. They all follow David.

Weston contemplates what has occurred the last few moments. His mind races. Was he negligent? Did he, J.B., or Annie Mae give Mary her last dosage? He knew his name would be on the lawsuit because of his family but he didn't think the lawyer would take it this far.

Weston watches as David tells J.B. to unlock his office. J.B. reluctantly gets his keys from his pocket as Mr. Hightower and Ethan are waiting. He unlocks the door, and they enter the office. David stands just outside, but when he sees Weston looking at him, he heads for the front office, his anger growing.

As the two men enter the front room, the driver stands from his spot behind the desk as Weston bolts through the door. He is itching for a fight, but he turns to the driver to ask a question. "You work at Jernigan's. I've seen you around."

The driver lays the paper back where he found it. "I know who you are and where you're staying. You're the rich kid driving the Maserati."

Weston points to the closed door. "Why are you driving them around?"

The driver unbuckles his jacket. He doesn't want to answer but relents. "They came in on the train and since David has ties to Jernigan's, we just thought we'd help."

"You mean Jasper," Weston snaps.

The driver's ears perk up. "Maybe we just wait for our guests and enjoy the peace and quiet."

Weston eyes track his movements as the gunman slides his hand nearer to the opening in his jacket. Weston turns to David. "David, I would say nice working with you...but I won't lie."

The driver notices that David is scared of Weston. "Hey kid, tell him whatever you want, he can't do nothing. His hands are tied. You can even tell him off if you want, I'll be your witness."

David understands what the driver is saying but keeps his mouth closed, feeling that it isn't the right time to confront Weston just yet.

The driver pats the newspaper. "I didn't see your name in the paper today, Mr. Galloway, but I bet your name will be on the front page in a week or two. What do you think? You and the hospital will be famous and all them women will be all over you with all the publicity..."

Weston steps toward David, who flinches. He rolls his eyes at the other man's timidness and exits out the door. "I need a smoke."

The driver continues as if he was still standing there. "Yeah, you'll be famous for sure—"

His words are cut off as the door closes behind Weston.

Chapter 9

October 30, 1945
10:30am
Windsor Hospital Laundry Room, Chatham Hill,
Middle Tennessee

I APPRECIATE YOU COOKING for Trevor and me last night. It was too much. You don't have—"

Amber interrupts. "Sadie, it's the least I can do for you letting me stay at your house. The fellowship with you and your son was the most I have talked to anyone in a long time. It was, how would Rein say it...very therapeutic."

A grin spreads across Sadie's face, ear to ear, as she takes notice of Amber's happiness. Sadie's hand continues moving as she places a bundle of towels in the washer. "Like I have said before, you and Stephen are welcome to stay at my home as long as you like."

Amber shakes her head, her smile remaining in place. "Now when Stephen gets his first paycheck from the newspaper, we are going to start paying you rent, you hear Sadie Blue?"

Sadie spins around to argue, "Now, Ms. Amber—"

"I insist." Her gaze softens. "Sadie, now I don't insist much at all, let me have my way on this one time...okay?"

Sadie relents and agrees. "I won't know how to act having money come in from..." She pauses searching for the right word, "...family."

Amber is folding the sheets coming out of one of the two dryers sitting side by side, her mind drifting to Sadie Blue's home. "Trevor has finished the inside of your house so sublimely."

"Now, child, don't go spewing words out I don't know the meaning of."

"I mean if I close the door in the hallway, it's like we have our own little apartment...he's so smart," Amber finishes her statement before realizing Sadie's question. "Oh, Sadie, you know what it means. Trevor has spoiled us here at the hospital and you at your house. He fixes everything."

"We are lucky," Sadie comments, a bit embarrassed of the praise on her son's behalf.

"Not lucky, blessed. We are blessed to have Trevor's talent right here at our fingertips. I don't think Stephen can even fix a flat tire."

Sadie nearly drops her towel, but catches it at the last moment. "Now, Amber, you know a man of faith can fix more important things to worry about than a tire."

Amber's shoulders slump.

Sadie shakes her head. "Now, we ain't going to have these mood swings. Not under my roof."

Amber stops folding. "I've told Stephen, so I want you to know. The congregation at Piney Grove has pretty much distanced themselves from Stephen and me. I pass people in town, and they don't speak to me anymore. They don't ask about Stephen. I try to talk to them, but you can tell they just want to get away." Sadie opens her mouth to speak, but Amber continues, "The only people from our church that will carry on a conversation with me are Hannah from the diner and Justin from the trucking company. And that's 'cause I see him in town and at Peppers." She blinks furiously, trying to hide her pending tears.

Sadie approaches her and takes her hand. "Ms. Amber, you know as well as I do, when God closes a door, he's got a reason, and you know he's got a plan bigger than you can imagine." Amber doesn't say anything.

Sadie wracks her brain for something to say to cheer the girl up. "Amber, you are coming to my church with me this Sunday! Do you understand? Get your prettiest dress and shoes and I am going to show you what preaching and singing is all about. Okay? Now it's my turn to insist."

"Well, if you insist...then yes, ma'am." Amber's mood begins to shift at her words.

"My church is different. You'll see. We got singers with beautiful voices and music—music that will make your toes start tapping and your heart start rejoicing. We ain't no quiet church. We rejoice out loud. We scream and shout so the Lord can hear us. I know it's only Tuesday, but you better start getting ready now."

Amber starts to wriggle in her seat in excitement. "Yes, ma'am. I'll be ready."

"Now get them sheets folded and start thinking about lunch for the patients."

"Yes ma'am...." Amber taps her chin as she thinks. "How about chicken pot pie and sweet corn?"

Sadie shakes her head. "Now Ms. Windsor, that's too complicated for right now, let's boil some chicken and have some green beans for lunch."

"I'll make enough pot pie and sweet corn for everybody for supper," Amber says.

"That's my girl." Amber finishes folding the last towel. "Now when Hal gets back into town, he needs to start bringing over some of your furniture."

Amber shrugs. "I don't want any of my stuff from my room. It's kind of being used right now."

Sadie is confused by her comment. "Being used? Like Rein's using it?"

"No, like I don't want to ever see it again."

Sadie approaches Amber and puts her arm around her. "Oh, okay."

"I promise one day I'll explain, but not today." Amber returns Sadie's hug.

"Maybe the piano though...and a few clothes... Will you help me to get the clothes?"

"Yes, ma'am, you just say when."

The two women stand to fold the larger sheets. "When are you going to see Stephen again?"

"Tomorrow morning after breakfast."

"Tell him I said hello and that I love him and pray for him everyday."

Amber beams at the thought of her fiancé. "I will, but the deputies told me last week that next Tuesday a new district attorney was going to be elected, and Stephen would get out quicker if he was elected... Whatever that means, I don't understand. They told me to come vote but I want Stephen to go with me."

"I understand, but I don't know all the information that goes into voting."

"I see a few signs at Peppers and in town...it's too confusing for me...I just want my fiancé out of jail."

"I do too, sweetheart... I do too."

Amber moves the sheets to their place on a shelf. "That's the last sheet. Do you need any more help before I go start the chicken?"

"No, I will help as soon as I finish rounding up the laundry."

Amber moves toward the door. "Remember, I'm leaving to pick up Paulene from school. I'll take her to your house, and you're sure that it's okay to have Paulene at your house until I bring her home before supper?"

Sadie nears Amber. "Yes, Lord, I know Ms. Elvie is worried sick about Paulene and you keeping her is the best news that her and Cebo could have hoped for."

Amber nods. "My dream and Annie Mae's vision has her about to pull her hair out. I wished she'd never found out..." She trails off, knowing deep down there was no alternative.

"Well, she did. We can't change that."

Amber walks to the kitchen and begins preparing the chicken. Cebo sticks his head through the door. "Ms. Windsor, you need any help?"

Her whole demeanor brightens at the sound of his voice. "Why Cebo, have you started working here today?"

"Yes, ma'am, I have." He moves toward her, looking over her shoulder.

"Well, we need another strong man with helpful hands around here." Cebo turns to close the kitchen door, but Amber stops him.

"Mr. Driver, let's leave the door open."

"Cebo, ma'am, just Cebo, no need to call me nothing special."

Amber raises her eyebrows. "I don't believe that Mr. Driver—" His eyes flash at her words, "—I mean, Cebo. We usually crack open that window right there." She points to a window up high. "It gets a breeze through here to help with the heat."

As he proceeds to open the window, he says, "Ms. Mae and Burn say for me to help everybody today so I can be a team player."

Giving Cebo a once over, Amber asks, "Well, have you worked in a kitchen?"

"My wife is Ms. Elvie, what do you think?"

"Well, there's a brown bag full of green beans, you can start snapping the beans and I'll start shucking the corn. I've just started the chicken boiling, see where I set the dial."

He focuses his eyes on the dial. "Just past straight down for about 25 minutes or so?"

Amber is impressed. "That's right. Boiled chicken and green beans for lunch with some biscuits."

"Oh, I love me some biscuits and butter."

"The butter is the best part," Amber agrees.

"Oh, you're telling the truth about that, Ms. Windsor."

"Amber, Cebo, you call me Amber," she corrects him, thinking how he corrected her.

"Oh, no ma'am, it's Ms. Windsor, til the end of time."

Amber shakes her head as she adds the beans to the water. "I insist, Cebo."

"You can insist all day long, but you'll always be Ms. Windsor to me." He turns his attention back to the stove.

Amber watches him, impressed. "Who have you worked with so far this morning?"

Cebo scratches his chin as he begins to list them off. "Mr. Willis, Mr. Weston, and Ms. Mae. They have all directed me on what they expect from me, hope I won't disappoint."

"Mr. Driver, I'm sure we all will be pleased with your help, have each one told or shown you the dangers around the hospital?" she inquired, thinking about the pit.

"Yes, they have. Bernard told me things twice, so I was sure to remember."

"Heed his words like you would from the Lord himself." There is a moment of silence as both study each other's eyes.

"Are you trying to scare me, Ms. Driver?" Cebo asks.

Amber's stare continues. "All the way to your soul, Ulysses." Amber looks away as Cebo takes a deep gulp, understanding filling his gaze.

Chapter 10

October 30, 1945
10:45am
Windsor Hospital Kitchen, Chatham Hill, Middle Tennessee

AMBER GETS THE CORN from the fridge and opens a drawer with a lock on it. "Well, there aren't many dangers, just stuff you need to know to stay out of trouble. The sharp knives are in this drawer, and I mean sharp, you know, Hal and Cebo sharp, if you get cut then Ms. Elvie will tend to ya'."

"Oh, we can't have that."

"Eating utensils are in this drawer, meats are in the freezer provided by Hal and Cebo..." She points and he cracks a grin again.

"Most of the workers have coffee for breakfast, you do make coffee?" She looks at him but continues on without waiting for an answer. "I hope you do, or you probably won't work out. Coffee keeps everybody happy if you keep a fresh cup ready." Amber cracks a smile. "Breakfast 8:30 to 9:00, lunch 12:00 to 12:30 and dinner 5:30 to 6:00, times vary by what's going on."

"I got it." Cebo dips his chin.

Amber stands at the same table as Cebo and begins to cut the kernels from the cob into a bowl. Her eyes catch on one drawer she forgot to describe. "Oh, in this drawer—" She goes to a side desk and opens it, getting out a notebook and pencil. She shows him both, "—when Burn brings in a bag of produce or vegetables, he'll set them here, that morning when he comes in," She opens the notebook, "Write what it is in this column and how much in this column, and date it." She points as he watches. He nods as she closes the notebook and places it back on the desk. She closes the drawer. "He turns in a bill weekly. It's just a check, for J.B. and Benjamin."

"Benjamin, how so?" Cebo is surprised.

"He's good with numbers, he keeps things straight." Cebo nods and goes back to the green beans.

Amber spins around, ensuring she had mentioned everything in the kitchen. "That's about it. You know Haven?"

"Yes, ma'am."

"She's doing dinner each night this week, so you'll meet her." She returns to shucking the corn, before a question she forgot before bubbles up. "One last thing, Cebo. What is Hal going to say when he gets back about losing you?"

Cebo twists his lips as he answers, "J.B. told me that winter is coming, and the family is focusing more on the hospital than the farm."

"My advice, Cebo, tell Hal that Annie Mae and J.B. told you to stay inside the hospital walls and that Hal will tend to the outside chores."

"I don't see that happening," Cebo replies, knowing how big Hal was on farm work.

"Mr. Driver, I insist you tell Hal you work at the hospital now."

"Well, if you insist."

"I do." He nods.

"Now," Amber takes a deep breath before broaching the next subject. "What do I need to know about Paulene, before I pick her up this afternoon?"

"Try and get her to do her homework, if you can. She'll try and make any excuse to not do it; she'd rather talk, anything to get your attention."

"I like to talk. We'll get along just fine," Amber replies

Amber thinks about things they can do as Cebo is talking. "Does she like to cook?"

"I'm not sure. You can ask her, though." Cebo moves to rest a hand on Amber's shoulder. "We sure appreciate you doing this for us."

Amber smiles. "Listen, Mr. Driver, I miss talking to Stephen, Rein, Annie Mae, Ms. Elvie, anybody anymore. I hope you don't mind, but I'm going to talk Paulene to death. When I bring her home, she'll be wore out."

Cebo isn't so sure about that, but he encourages Amber anyway. "I hope so...it'll be nice for her to have a big sister to talk to."

"Um..." Amber starts, thinking about Victoria, Paulene's actual sister.

Cebo didn't need magic to see where Amber's thoughts were going. "Her real sister don't spend as much time with her anymore, 'cause of her work."

"I'm sorry to hear that, but she could at least wake her and give her a kiss when she gets home."

Cebo's jaw locks. "Well, she could if she didn't smell like cigarettes and beer or whatever."

Amber realizes she hit a nerve, and thinks carefully before replying, "Sadie asked me to come to her church this Sunday for a visit. That's your church, right?"

"Yes, it is, we would be happy for you to join us."

"Will you be there this Sunday?" Amber presses.

His eyes raise and he looks confused. "I don't know, will I be there Sunday?"

Amber isn't sure whether or not Annie Mae and J.B. planned to ask him to work Sunday, so she says, "If I have something to say about it, you will be there."

"Now, Ms. Windsor, I don't want to get you in any trouble."

Amber doesn't miss a beat, heading out the hallway and down to where Annie Mae is with a patient. She taps her on the shoulder. "Ms. Mae, I would like a word with you."

Annie Mae doesn't look up from the patient as she responds. "Yes, I've only got a minute."

She finishes her task and then follows Amber into the hall. Amber barely waits for her to stop walking before she starts gabbing, "I have been invited to Sadie's church Sunday, and I told her 'yes'."

"Beulah?" Annie Mae's eyes widened.

Amber shuffles her feet. "I guess so..."

"Okay, you seem to be making bigger decisions, that's good. You have my permission to go. You seem to be more headstrong these days."

Amber wrinkles her nose at the comment. "What's that supposed to mean?"

"Nothing, sweetheart. Is that it?"

"No, I've been talking with Cebo in the kitchen and asked him if he was going to be there, but he wasn't sure." She clasps her hands in front of her, hoping Annie Mae will listen to her plea.

"He's taking David's chores, so he has Sunday morning off. I'll talk to him about his hours."

A smile begins to creep in. She exhales. "Good, we'll go as one big happy family."

Annie Mae's frown deepens at the comment about 'happy family.' "Now Ms. Elvie needs to be here Sunday morning."

The smile falls from Amber's face. "Oh, no, that can't be."

"She's scheduled to work this Sunday and with the shift in staff for the festival, she needs to be here." Her answer is firm.

"Why does anybody need to be here? It's Sunday morning?" Amber whines.

Annie Mae crosses her arms. "Ms. Parsons, this is a hospital, these patients don't know it's Sunday."

"Ms. Parsons?" A bead of sweat grows on Amber's forehead at the sound of Stephen's name attached to her. "Is there anything you could do so she could be off?"

"No, it worked out that way and she was okay with it. You seem to be the only one objecting actually. One of the responsibilities of an adult is to accept the things you cannot change."

Amber's blood begins to boil. "I see what you're doing. We don't talk much anymore, adults have responsibilities, you say 'accept things you cannot change', you say 'we've grown apart'." She pauses. "You say all this like you're my family, but you know we've grown apart since I turned sixteen and you allowed it."

Annie Mae recoils like she's been hit.

This doesn't faze Amber, and she continues her tirade, "You know what I'm talking about. You were supposed to protect me, you and your husband were supposed to protect me." She shakes her head in disdain. "What happened, Ms. Mae, what goddamn happened?"

J.B. and Burn turn the corner, and Annie Mae takes a step back.

"You used to be my precious granddaughter, but I feel like you have a new family now and have abandoned your old one," Annie Mae says with just as much vinegar as the words Amber threw at her.

Amber doesn't back down, however, and crosses her arms over her chest. "My family is the ones who love me." Without waiting for an answer, she spins around and stomps back to the kitchen, Cebo still where she left him.

"Was any of that about me?"

Amber smiles sweetly. "Looks like I'll join your family at church this Sunday morning...except for Ms. Elvie."

Chapter 11

October 31, 1945
1:00pm
Windsor Hospital, Chatham Hill, Middle Tennessee

AMBER DRIVES STEPHEN'S VEHICLE past the burnt hickory towards Pepper's store. It's been over a year since the lightning bolt hit that tree and disintegrated the top half of the tree, boring a black hole to the bottom of its roots. The black, hollow tree trunk had since become firmer, like a rock. On a windy day the faint scent of char could still be scented on the air, as if it were still smoldering.

Amber speeds past, oblivious to the tree, her mind focused on her boyfriend, Stephen. Her gift of sight would never lie to her, and she knew they had a positive future coming their way.

Unfortunately for her eager heart, the gas gauge ticks near empty, and she knows it's probably better to stop by the General Store for a splash. Besides, seeing Nina and Jeremy was always a good feeling. She stops at the intersection by the store, looking both ways before pressing the gas and nosing into the parking lot.

She pulls the car up to the pump, gathers her tan purse, and heads into the store, her brown shoes clicking on the worn porch boards.

Jeremy, who was on his way out, meets her halfway.

"Good afternoon, Jeremy, how are you?" She offers him a sweet smile, brushing the skirt of her tan dress.

He wipes his hands with a smudged rag, coughing as he approaches. "Amber, I would say I was fine, but I'd be lying."

Amber stops in her tracks. "I'm sorry, Nina said last week J.B. had given you some pills to help with the cough."

"Fill it up?" Amber nods in affirmation. "You got it." He starts filling up the tank. "The pills help with the cough, but it's my lungs... I went to the doctor over in Madison, he gave me some syrup. It tastes awful and I don't think it's much different than whiskey."

"I'm sorry."

"Supposed to stop the cough, it doesn't. I'll just live with it...if you call it living." He taps the nozzle, the rushing sound of gasoline reaching Amber's ears. "I quit drinking over 10 years ago...come to find out I may have to start drinking again to feel better."

"Now, Mr. Pepper, the doctor didn't tell you that." Amber scolds.

"No, that's my own diagnosis."

"I'd rather trust the doctors," she says pointedly, her gaze on Jeremy's bended form.

He finishes filling and closes the tank. "At my age, I don't have time to believe in any of their remedies." He turns to head up the steps to the store, Amber following along.

Nina emerges from the back room, smiling at the sight of Amber.

"Got to go to the back, tell her it's a dollar and 60 cents," he tells Amber, before disappearing into the back room himself.

"I'll pray for you, Mr. Pepper," she calls after him. He doesn't answer.

"Good afternoon, Amber," Nina greets her, taking one look at how she is dressed, "Going to see your beau?"

"Yes, ma'am. Is Jeremy hearing okay?"

"No, I thought he was just ignoring me, but his hearing is fading in his right ear, but just the same, he only hears half of what I tell him...so I figure he's grateful for that."

"I told him I'd pray for him, would you let him know?"

"Sure will, he's got to turn the right way though." Nina lets out a breath, and moves behind the register.

"One dollar and 60 cents of gas and some black shoe polish." Nina raises her eyebrows but collects the polish all the same. "Got invited to Beulah by Ms. Sadie Sunday morning. Got to get my shoes nice and shiny," Amber explains.

"Oh, you sure do...Beulah, you say?" Amber nods and leans toward, as if she is about to share a secret.

"Listen, Jeremy says that the doctor in Madison hasn't helped him much with the cough...Will he be okay?"

Nina leans back, debating. "He doesn't know the whole truth." Tears gather in her eyes as she looks to the doorway where her husband disappeared. "He may not have long to live...maybe a month."

"Oh, my God!" Amber nearly drops her purse at the admission. "Did the doctor say that?"

"No, they're too vague."

"Then how do you know?"

"Well, the note had instructions."

"The note?"

Nina takes a deep breath. "Yeah, I found a small, folded paper in my safe maybe fifteen years ago...pencil's kind of faded now, but..."

Amber tilts her head in confusion, trying to make sense of what Nina is saying. "Fifteen years? The note tells you when Jeremy's going to...pass?"

"Well, the instructions had to come from *your* family. I think it was there maybe three to four years before I found it." Her emphasis on the word sounds like an accusation to Amber.

"My family?"

"Or one of your relatives, ask your brother or sister. I guess one of you dropped it in the slot on the side and it got into some papers we rarely look at." She lets out a huff. "I've seen the goings on at your house. I don't want you to say a word about this to anyone, you hear?"

Amber's lip quivers, unsure what to make of the accusations flung her way.

"Jeremy lives with aches and pains all day now, but the nights are even worse..." A tear forms and travels down Nina's cheek. "We've got to probably sell this place and...and...move away." Amber embraces Nina, the two women stand like that for several minutes.

When they finally break the embrace, Nina steps back, furiously wiping away tears.

"Nina, if you need me to come over and give you some company one night...or any time, call Sadie's place. I'll be glad to do it," Amber offers, her heart breaking at the sight of Nina so upset.

"Okay, I'll remember. You just keep dreaming, hon, I hope the note is wrong...but I doubt it."

"Yes, ma'am," Amber replies, reaching into her purse for a tissue and discreetly dabbing her eyes as Nina punches numbers into the cash register.

"One dollar, 60 cents gas and 29 cents for shoe polish for a total of...$1.89. Want me to put it on your account?"

Amber hesitates at the question. "No...no, I would like to pay it right now." She opens her purse and pulls out two dollar bills and hands them to Nina.

"You know, I moved out of my room at Annie Mae's and now I'm living with Sadie in a back apartment," Amber hedges.

"I didn't know you had moved." Nina's voice remains flat.

"As of right now, I'm going to pay my own way. Just remember that," Amber insists, grabbing the polish tin and turning toward the door. "I better get to the jail and see Stephen."

"Don't forget your prayers and I hope your next dream will ease my mind," Nina calls after her.

"Yes, ma'am." Amber opens the door, but Nina calls out a second time.

"Words of advice, don't forget to eat a good breakfast Sunday morning before the service."

Amber's eyebrows draw together at her words, but she nods before closing the door and making her way back to the car. As she climbs in and puts the key in the ignition, her eyes catch on Pepper's truck parked on the side of the store. She squints, trying to see if Danny is inside, but she can't make out the driver's seat with the glare from the windshield.

She pulls away from the pump and onto the road, toward the jail. She's halfway there when she notices a truck approaching in her rearview mirror. Pepper's truck.

Her palms start to become clammy, her mind racing. She pulls her car to the side of the paved road, off the shoulder and onto the grassy dirt. Her eyes watch Pepper's truck stop in the same manner as her car, just a few hundred feet behind her.

Panic sets in. Knowing she doesn't want to be caught unaware again, she climbs out of the car, opening the trunk and grabs the tire iron she knew Stephen always kept there. It is heavy in her hand.

She stands on the pavement to the side of her car. The tire iron is in plain view of Pepper's truck, but whoever is inside doesn't move. She wipes the moisture from her forehead with the back of her hand. She stands there for several minutes, but there is no movement from the truck. Not knowing what else to do, she climbs back into her car, setting the tire iron on the passenger seat.

When she pulls onto the road, Pepper's truck does the same. Amber slows...the truck slows. Amber wonders if it's Danny behind the wheel. She speeds up, as does the truck, the distance between them closing rapidly.

Her eyes flicker to the road, which is open, and when she glances in the mirror again, Pepper's truck is still gaining on the distance between them. Without hesitation, she presses her foot down firmly, the car accelerating.

She doesn't slow until the road curves, but then she is forced to ease up. She's only had her license for a couple of weeks, and the speed is making her nervous.

When she finishes the turn, her eyes return to the rearview mirror to find Pepper's truck nearly on her bumper. In a moment of desperation, she reaches for the tire iron, setting it on the dashboard.

River Bridge is directly ahead, and she knows the jail is just around the next bend. She can make it.

She zooms past the bridge and through the turn, the tires squealing, her hands white-knuckled in their grip on the wheel. Her heart is pounding in her ears. There is a truck heading her way.

Panicked, she presses on the gas, her car veering into the other lane, but she quickly realizes her mistake, correcting the steering wheel to veer back into her lane, just missing the oncoming truck.

Once back in her lane, her eyes find the mirror again, only to find Pepper's truck is no longer behind her. Focusing back on the road ahead, her breathing still staggering in fear, Amber forces herself to calm down, lest she start hyperventilating behind the wheel.

She turns around the bend, the jail coming into view. She slows down, nosing the car into the jail parking lot, pulling the car up to the spot right by the door. As she climbs out, she looks over her shoulder, just to be sure, but the truck is nowhere to be seen.

Just in case, she grabs the tire iron from the dash before rushing through the jail door, her eyes settling on Frost, who is sitting behind the desk, eyes wide.

CLANG! She drops the tire iron onto the top of his counter as he takes in her disheveled appearance.

Amber takes a deep breath. "I'm here to see Stephen Parsons."

Chapter 12

October 31, 1945
1:30pm
County Jail, Chatham Hill, Middle Tennessee

ADRENALINE STILL COURSING THROUGH her veins, Amber decides it's better to cool down before seeing her betrothed. Although Frost waves her past to go to the visitor's room where she usually waits to see Stephen, she turns right short of that door, pushing open the door marked 'Restroom' instead.

Closing the door behind her, she flips on the light, eyeing the toilet warily. It clearly hasn't been cleaned in an age, dust and hairs crowding the surface. She wrinkles her nose. "I would rather use the bathroom outside behind a bush than to sit on that lid," she whispers to herself, choosing instead to head toward the sink for a splash of water.

The sink isn't in any better condition, the spigot rusted and crusty, the white stopper dangling by a chain that won't last another decade. Someone even left a drinking glass by the cold handle, causing Amber to scoff in disgust at all the diseases which were likely just waiting to spread.

Mustering her courage, she flips on the cold water, letting it run for a moment, before wetting a paper towel under the flow and dabbing her face.

The paper towel wasn't her first choice, but there weren't any other options in the dismal bathroom.

She wets the towel a second time, checking her face in the mirror. Once the paper towel is nearly disintegrated, she tosses it into the overflowing wastebasket near her feet. Trying to avoid the paper towels littering the floor, she moves on her toes back to the door.

As she reenters the hallway, she spots Frost watching her from the lobby.

"Are you ready?"

At his words, Amber realizes she is still shaking slightly and needs another moment. "May I sit and gather myself?"

"Sure, gather all you want, just give us five minutes to get the prisoner ready," he replies as he stands and heads for the cells.

"Thanks." Not knowing where else to wait, Amber heads back into the lobby, choosing a chair in the corner and leaning back against the wall. She crosses her legs and lets out a loud breath. Not sure what else to do to calm her nerves, she closes her eyes and focuses on her breathing. Pretty soon, she's drifting off to sleep.

She's inside a church, sunlight peering in through the windows along the walls and by the altar, illuminating the interior. She looks up to see the back of the wooden pews all lined up, the colors of the stained-glass windows dancing on the wood. She starts walking down the center aisle, her eyes perusing the biblical scenes outlined in stained glass. Turning her attention back to where she is walking, she notices she is walking on a bed of flower petals.

She is jolted back to the present when she feels a hand on her arm. Startled, she scrambles back, only to realize it was Mr. Cutter, who had sat down next to her and touched her arm to wake her.

"Why, Mr. Cutter, you startled me," Amber shrieks, which in turn startles Cutter and they both chuckle.

"Sorry, I should have made a noise or something as I approached."

Amber brushes off his apology. "No, I must have fallen asleep. I'm sorry."

"It's okay, you reminded me of Maria."

"I do?" Amber raises her eyebrow before realizing she should ask after the policeman's daughter to be polite. "How is she?"

"Like a wild horse that can't be tamed. It's boys, boys, and oh, she's going to try and get her driver's test next week."

"That's good."

"No, that's bad."

"Why's that?" Amber asks, confused, as she thought a driver's test was a good thing.

"Well, because of the boys. It'll be harder to keep up with her." Cutter sighs, standing up.

"I know she'll be careful and pick the right one," Amber says, trying to quell his fears.

"In due time I hope."

"Benjamin has been talking to her lately," Amber tells him, remembering the last conversation they had.

"Benjamin?" Cutter rubs his chin, "Now that you mention it, I do hear his name often when she's talking with her schoolmates on the phone."

"Well, I trust him to make the right decision about girls, after all, they are still quite young." Amber stands from her chair for Cutter to lead her back.

"I trust him too... Say, I know you're here to talk with Parsons, but can I say one thing real quick?"

"Sure, you can," Amber replies, sitting back down.

His tone changes. "It's my mother, remember when you were attack—" His voice breaks and he has to take a deep breath before continuing, "I spoke to Ms. Mae about my mother at that time—she mentioned something about her...a while back." His voice breaks again. "She's gotten to the point where she...I mean, we might need your Care Center soon."

Amber reaches up and takes Cutter's hand. "I'm so sorry."

Cutter, overcome with emotion, continues as if she hadn't spoken, "I lost my father 2 years ago, and I check on her, my wife checks, Maria, the neighbors, everybody checks—" He sniffles, holding back tears, "—

anyway, could you get the doc or Ms. Mae to give me an idea of the cost of the care? She's got the land and house along the river that we need to sell anyway, she can't keep it up, so we've got to the point that we're going to let the Lord take care of things from here."

Amber pats his hand. "Yes, he knows best. I will do that for you."

He looks up. "Maybe the first of the new week would be nice?"

"For the price or the care?" She tilts her head to the side and wrinkles her nose.

"The price..." He clarifies. "I'll talk to the doctor and my wife about when we'll need the care."

"Okay."

He offers a forced grin and motions to the back room. "Well, you've come here for some time with your...well, Stephen. Let me go get things ready for your visit."

He leads Amber down to the visitation room, pushing open the door and waving her in. It's a small room outfitted with a table and a lone chair on each side. "Now, listen, Ms. Windsor, during the visit I must ask you to refrain from...this will not be a—" He fights the words, unsure how to say what he needs to say.

Amber, however, knows exactly what it is he wants to specify, "Yes sir, no inappropriate touching, I understand. Stephen's a man of God, after all."

"Isn't he?" Cutter closes the door, leaving Amber alone in the room.

~~~

When the door creaks open again, it's Stephen, his eyes quickly coming alight when they spot Amber. Without thinking, he runs across the room, allowing the door to fall shut behind him as he pulls her into an embrace. Amber's hands go around his neck, and their lips meet in a kiss.

KNOCK! KNOCK! KNOCK!

Amber pauses the kiss for a moment, "Yes sir, nothing inappropriate, I know!" she calls through the door.

She kisses Stephen for a few moments more, before breaking away to
~~~

rearrange the furniture in the room so the chairs are facing each other, and the table is pushed to the side. Just as she finishes, Cutter pushes open the door to check in.

His eyebrows raise at the moved furniture, but he doesn't say anything, simply pulling the door closed behind him. When it snicks shut, Stephen reaches for Amber's hands, clasping them in his.

"I've missed you," Amber whispers, her eyes gazing into his. "I think of you all the time."

"Sweetheart, it's killing me to know that I am wasting time away from you, but I promise I'll make it up to you as soon as I get out," Stephen whispers back, unable to take his own eyes off of her beauty.

She leans into his shirt and smells his neck, before leaning in to kiss it. Stephen groans. "Now, Amber, you need to stop, there is only so much I can take." She doesn't stop, and Stephen groans a second time.

"Do you want to marry me?" she asks, her voice breathy.

Stephen cups her face in his hands and looks lovingly into her eyes. "Amber, I love you. Will you marry me and make me the happiest man alive?"

"Yes, oh, yes. I've even dreamed of the church we'll get married in and—"

Stephen cuts her off. "The church...pray tell, where?"

Amber taps her chin with her finger, trying to think of where her dream took place. "I don't know, I just saw it in a dream in the lobby. I don't know where the church is."

He kisses her again. "That's okay. We've got time to figure that out." Between kisses, he starts to explain, "A week and a half, my lawyer said, as soon as the election was over with. I should be released."

Amber stops, pulling back. "Election? I don't understand, but I'll be there as soon as you're out. I have a home and bed ready for us now to start a family together, and I can drive us home if need be." She smiles and kisses him again.

"Where's our home going to be?" he asks.

Amber quickly tells him all about how she had moved in with Sadie Blue, her face alight with excitement. Stephen's energy doesn't match hers, but he nods in agreement all the same. Their lips meet again as Amber's hands shift to the buttons on Stephen's pants, her cheeks heating at the bulge she feels there. Feeling daring, she begins to unbutton them, but Stephen pushes her hands away.

"No, no, no, we are not going to start our lives together like this... Not in a jail."

Amber doesn't seem to hear him as she stands to shift her dress, Stephen's eyes drawn to her white skin. As his words register, she pauses, "But, Stephen, I'm on fire. I love you and I think about you all day."

Stephen stands, pushing Amber's dress down and embracing her. "I know, my dear, but good things come to those who wait." They stand like that silently for a few moments until Stephen speaks again. "I have a gift for you."

Her eyes widen and she pulls back from the hug. "A gift, in here, how?"

"Not how, you're supposed to ask what."

"Okay," she acquiesces, "What?"

"It's a secret. Mr. Strickland has it at the newspaper office in town, you'll have to drop by and ask him for your gift. We've talked about it, and he knows to look out for you."

Amber grins with excitement. "Mr. Strickland has been so nice to you with the visits and all."

Stephen nods in agreement. "He said he's holding my job for me until I get out... Has he written anything in the newspaper about you or the attack?"

Amber looks at the closed door for a moment before responding, "I was out of it and don't remember the first week. I haven't read the papers at all since... Maybe I should, people have been...unfriendly lately."

"I'm just glad they caught the guy, Major said he was killed running out of town."

"Yeah, he was...I've got to come up with a gift for you," she says, changing the subject.

"You have already given me your gift, your love, our home...and that I can call you my fiancé." They both embrace again.

"I don't know what your gift is yet, but thank you—" There is a knock at the door and moments later Cutter pokes his head in.

"Time's up."

"Let me say goodbye," Stephen says to Cutter, who pulls the door shut once more. Stephen looks back at Amber. "So my congregation is gone, I'm unemployed and—"

Amber puts her finger on his lips to cut him off. "Listen to me, Mr. Parsons, you are a newspaper reporter now, that's your job, I'll talk to Mr. Strickland when I get my gift, and we'll get things straight." He nods in appreciation. "Another thing, I've got some secrets, some you need to know and others you don't. I'll reveal them as needed."

At her words, Stephen takes a step back, "Amber, you're scaring me."

"I'll explain later, okay?"

"Okay," he agrees, grinning.

"Why are you smiling like that?"

"You're just acting all grown up all of a sudden and I kind of want to tear your clothes off."

Amber blushes, but shakes her head. "Sorry, Mr. Parsons, it's too late for that now, you missed your chance." He takes a step toward her, sweeping her up in an aggressive kiss, she squeals in delight. There are two brief knocks on the metal door.

When they come up for air, she asks, "When do you want me to visit you again?"

He thinks for a moment before responding. "Let's say a week from today, the Wednesday after the election. Hopefully, my lawyer will know something by then." Stephen opens the door wider and exits the room, Amber on his heels.

"It's a date," she promises, her eyes turning to Cutter, who is waiting in the hall. "I need a word with you shortly."

Cutter nods before escorting Stephen through the steel door at the end of the hall.

Amber fixes the furniture in the visiting room in the meantime, before returning to the hall to wait for Cutter.

When he reappears, he comes to stand next to Amber, waiting for her to say something.

"Cutter, can I trust you to keep a secret?"

"Yes, ma'am...to a point. I am still a police officer."

She nods in understanding. "You have seen *things* at the hospital that are hard to explain—"

He rolls his eyes and steps his feet apart to take a more dominant stance. "Yes, I have. It's hard to explain is an understatement."

"The lawyers for Truman came Monday to the hospital and must have spoken with you the last couple of days, did you offer an explanation? And if so, was it graphically detailed or more...broad, shall we say? Basically, what I'm asking is, did you keep the secret?"

He chooses his words carefully. "As a lawman, I'm supposed to ask the questions, but let's say I offered an explanation that was *humanly* probable."

Amber nods affirmatively. "I've never spoken about my attacker, and do you know why?"

"You didn't see him or were struck on the head and your memory—"

She interrupts. "No, he threatened to kill members of my family." Confusion clouds his eyes. "As we know, the authorities have solved the case, that's good, but if someone threatened Maria or your wife or your mother—" His eyebrows jump. "—for you to keep quiet, what would you do?" Cutter's shoulders fall as he realizes what she is saying. "Cutter, after this election, my fiancé will be released in a timely manner and with my case closed, hopefully your department will let my family handle things as we would like...discreetly...like you and your mother, we are going to let the Lord take care of things from there..."

"Yes, ma'am," he agrees.

"Good." She makes her way to the lobby, Cutter following silently. As she reaches the front counter she turns around to say, "And I know Benjamin and Maria will work things out without any trouble."

Before she can push open the door, Cutter looks around and concludes, "Danny is involved in some way."

Amber freezes in her steps and she slowly turns. "What about Danny?"

"I heard Danny's name when Maria was talking with Benjamin."

Amber lets out a gasp, "I'll talk to Benjamin."

Cutter puts his hands up. "No, don't say nothing to Benjamin or Maria. They will know I was listening to her private conversation."

"Okay," Amber lets out a breath. "I guess you're right, but you need to keep an eye on Maria—for her safety...that Danny, I don't really trust him...do you understand what I mean?"

"I sure do."

"I hope so. Good day, again." She grabs the tire iron from the counter, waving it at Frost, her voice a whisper. "Keep an eye on him. I don't trust him either."

Cutter nods, watching as Amber makes her way out the door.

Frost doesn't seem to notice the exchange, turning to the next page in his newspaper.

Chapter 13

October 31, 1945
3:00pm
On the Road, Outskirts of Chatham Hill, Middle Tennessee

TIRE IRON RESTING ON the seat beside her, Amber heads to the school to pick up Paulene as she promised, the truck rocking as she crosses the washboard-like dirt road on the way there. Although she couldn't have been in the jail longer than an hour, traffic has shifted in her absence, making everything seem different than it was before.

The elementary school is situated directly next to the high school, surrounded by a grove of trees. The lot is crowded with vehicles as she turns in, pick-up time for the students who don't walk home well underway.

As she inches the car forward through the packed lot, she eyes the many students beginning their walk home. Some of the parents couldn't afford to pick up their children by car, and assumed they would be okay walking. Amber and her siblings had been one of those families just the previous year. Although she had walked home herself many times, Amber couldn't help but think the parents of the walking children were naive to not worry about their kids. After all, a killer had been on the loose for several months now, though he hasn't taken a new victim in several weeks.

She nudges her car to the front, Paulene spotting her and running forward to yank open the door.

Her face falls at the sight of Amber. "Hello, Amber."

Trying to cheer her up, Amber replies, "Well, hello, Ms. Driver. How was your day today?"

She giggles as she gets in. "You know my name is Paulene. My mom is Ms. Driver."

She slams the door and Amber noses the vehicle back toward the road. "Okay, Paulene, you remember a short time ago we used to walk this road, now we're driving this road?"

"Yeah, I remember."

"Let's talk like we did back then, like friends, okay?"

"Okay," Paulene agrees, but then her eyes spot the tire iron. "What's this?"

"Thought I might be having some trouble this morning with my tires, but they seem to be good." Amber takes the iron from her hands and sets it on the dashboard. As her eyes turn back toward the road, she sees what Paulene has set on the seat. "What're these?"

"English and math books," Paulene replies, looking out the window.

"Homework?"

Paulene nods, not seeming all that invested in doing the homework she'd been assigned. Amber pulls the car over in the shade of a large tree. She points. "Paulene, where's that path going to... the river?"

Paulene scoots up in the seat and looks out. "That's Jackson—"

"Know their last names?"

Paulene bites her lip, thinking. "I think...Stiles and Wain...or something, I don't know it's long..."

Amber's eyes track the kids who disappear into the woods. "How far are their houses?"

"I'm not so good at distances."

"If Pepper's store is a mile from here, how far would you say it is?"

Paulene tilts her head to the side. "I guess a little less...Is something wrong?"

Amber's smile falls, but she quickly adjusts her expression to hide it from Paulene. "No, nothing's wrong, you know, I don't think I should worry about everybody else's problems, do you?"

Paulene shakes her head. "I think you should let God worry about them."

The truck fills with silence as both girls descend into their thoughts.

It's Amber who eventually breaks it. "You know what I'm going to do? I'm going to make a list of questions to ask God when I get to heaven." Paulene doesn't say anything. "When I go through the pearly gates...are you going to heaven too, Paulene?"

"Mama and Daddy said I was, the preacher said so and said I got saved."

Amber cracks a grin. "That's good." She looks back at the road as the truck again rocks over the bumpy road, her teeth grit in concentration. "So today we got homework and cooking dinner, which should we do first?"

"Ma usually brings supper home for us."

"Let's finish the homework and then we'll do something special," Amber suggests.

"Something special? Sounds fun." A grin grows across Paulene's face.

"Oh, it is, there's washing the dishes or the clothes, sweeping the floors, or beating the rug clean, or dust—"

Her grin stops growing and she crosses her arms over her chest. "I don't call that special."

Amber looks at Paulene out of the corner of her eye. "You don't? What do you think special is?"

Paulene's lips curl as she thinks of an answer. "Maybe riding Glory, going to Pepper's for candy, or downtown for chocolate or ice cream...or reading stories." She pauses for a breath, "Benjamin invited me to Hal's tomorrow morning to ride Glory. Victoria is supposed to take me, we are supposed to meet a friend of his from Yaphank."

"Really? Isn't tomorrow a school day?" Amber inquires.

"School's out tomorrow 'cause of the Festival."

"Oh."

Amber had completely forgotten about the festival, her mind flashing back to years prior and the crowds that had gathered in their small town. Folks came from all around to enjoy the food, carnival games, and rides. And this year there were supposed to be fireworks.

Deep in thought, Amber drives on autopilot to Sadie's house, swerving around the potholes in the driveway. Pulling to a stop, she grabs her purse and climbs from the car, Paulene grabbing her books and doing the same.

The two girls make their way up the steps and Amber digs in her purse for the key.

"Good golly, this porch is longer than my house." Paulene sets the books at her feet.

Amber unlocks the door, as Paulene sprints down to one of the rockers. She climbs in and begins rocking vigorously back and forth.

"Be careful, don't turn it over. I wouldn't want you to get hurt on day one."

Paulene stops her motion, and the chair comes to a stop. She climbs down and grabs her schoolbooks, following Amber inside. "We can sit in them and talk after we finish your homework."

Setting her purse down by the door, Amber's eyes are immediately drawn to the piano in the middle of the room and her eyes well with tears.

"Why are you crying?" Paulene asks, looking between Amber and the piano, eyes filled with confusion.

"This wasn't here when I left this morning." She opens the cover, and Paulene starts tapping the keys randomly with her finger.

Amber caresses the piano. "Would you like me to teach you to play?"

Paulene freezes. "Do you know how to play?"

Amber sits properly and begins playing a church hymn that Paulene recognizes. Amber plays a full verse, Paulene noticing Amber's scar on her throat. "That was beautiful."

"Thank you, I haven't played in a while." Amber flips through the few sheets of music on her stand.

"How did you get that spot on your neck?"

Amber's jaw tightens and she begins to stack the sheet music.

"What...did I say something wrong?" Paulene's voice quivers. "I'm sorry...momma says I say stuff that's wrong, whatever that means."

Amber places her hands on top of Paulene's clenched hands. "Someone hurt me badly," she explains. "I try to hide my scar." Amber pulls her dress top up a bit.

"It's a beautiful scar," Paulene promises in the way only a child can. "Was it a boy?"

Amber hesitates a moment. "Yes, yes, it was."

"Men are pigs."

Amber chuckles and holds her hand out for Paulene. "Let's go to the kitchen and get something to drink."

Paulene takes her hand. "You sure do a lot of hand holding."

"Victoria doesn't hold your hand?" she asks, curious as to why the woman she finds so sweet is apparently not sweet with her younger sister.

"Not unless we're crossing the street or something. Mama holds my hand all the time."

"That's nice. Is Victoria happy living at home?"

Paulene thinks quietly for a moment. "No, I've heard Victoria say that living at home is harder than a preacher's dick."

Amber jumps, whirling on the young girl, her face clouded with shock. "Paulene, you take that back!"

Paulene is unperturbed. "How am I going to take it back?"

"That's not appropriate. Ms. Elvie would wash your mouth out with soap if she heard you say that."

Paulene shrugs. "That's what Victoria says."

"Don't say that again."

"I thought you said we were friends. Can't I talk to you like friends?" Paulene's shoulders slump and Amber quickly back tracks, trying to make Paulene understand.

"Sure, but that's a bad word. It's a man's private parts." Amber points on herself. "Don't say that word again...please."

"Yes, ma'am," Paulene agrees, dejected.

"Get your books and we'll do your homework on the kitchen table."

Paulene returns to the living room and Amber calls after her, "You want milk or water?"

"Water."

"Good choice." Amber begins to fill two glasses. "There should be a notepad and pencil in the top drawer. I can help you with your sums if you'll pull it out for me."

Paulene searches the first top drawer. It's mostly cloth napkins, but her eyes catch sight of a leg of a doll. Paulene lifts the cloth and pulls out the doll. She holds it out to Amber. "What's this?"

Amber's eyes widen and she quickly sets the glasses down and grabs the doll, squeezing it. "I expect it's a gift or a hobby of Sadie's."

"Can I have it? It's kind of cute with the button eyes and red handkerchief in its back pocket." Paulene's eyes are hopeful, but Amber shakes her head.

"No. It's Sadie's. We'll put it back and not say anything. We may ruin a surprise for someone so let's keep this a secret to only ourselves. Okay?"

"Sure." Amber studies the details of the doll, before tucking it back in the drawer and pushing it closed. "Let's check here." She opens the second top drawer and pulls out the pad and pencil before taking a seat at the table next to Paulene. "Alright let's get started, shall we?"

Paulene agrees and opens her book to the page she had been assigned in class, copying the sums and completing them as Amber watches. A couple of sums in, Amber stands from the table. "Okay, now you keep working while I go to my room and change clothes."

As Amber leaves the room, Paulene flips the page to continue working, biting her lip as she does the calculations. It doesn't take long before she finishes the page, setting down the pad and waiting for Amber to return.

She sits patiently at first, but as several minutes pass, she begins to get bored, rising from the table to follow the direction Amber had headed. She passes two rooms filled with dark bedroom furniture, but no Amber. As she is checking the second room, she hears a sound at the end of the hallway, jumping as she turns to look.

Luckily, it's just Amber poking her head out of the room she hadn't reached yet.

"Let me show you my room." Amber offers to show her inside. Paulene follows, her wide eyes taking in all the details.

The room has a full-sized bed, similar to the two rooms she passed, a dresser, an armoire with a mirror, and a desk with a padded chair.

"And my bathroom is through that door." Amber points, Paulene's eyes following the motion. "That's a tour of my room." Paulene observes the pictures hanging on the wall and the two small windows with curtains. "Let's go finish your homework and make those lists of questions to ask God, shall we?"

They make their way back to the kitchen, re-settling at the table. Amber checks over Paulene's math homework, while Paulene pens a list of questions to ask God. "Your penmanship is great."

"Momma says that too," Paulene says with a smile, her eyes spotting the barn in Sadie's backyard through the kitchen window. "Do they have any horses in that barn out back?"

Amber shakes her head, her eyes still skimming the math problems. "No, Trevor, her son, does all his carpentry back there. It's kind of a workshop. I'm sure it's locked up, but maybe I'll see if I can get the keys and ask if he doesn't mind us looking at his stuff." She pauses for a moment. "He also built those rocking chairs on the front porch."

Paulene's eyes widened. "He did? Maybe him and Cebo, and Mr. Hal can build us another room onto my house, the size of yours, when they get a chance."

Amber shakes her head and changes the subject. "Let's get back to your homework, okay?"

Chapter 14

November 2, 1945
12:00pm
Pepper's Truck, On the Road to Yaphank, Middle Tennessee

BENJAMIN IS DRIVING AT a steady pace in Pepper's truck, on his way home from Yaphank. Silva is in the passenger's seat, watching out the window as the countryside rolls by, with Cass tucked in the middle between them. It's cramped, but Silva's excitement is infectious, bringing a smile to Benjamin's face as she alternates sticking her head out of the window and pulling it back in to tell Benjamin and Cass about something she saw. Their overnight bag rests on the cab floor between them.

"How often do you get into town?" Benjamin asks Cass as he slows the truck down to take a bend in the road.

"About every other Saturday," she answers.

"You got a car or truck?" Benjamin turns the wheel into another bend.

"Yeah," Silva interrupts, her head inside the truck for the moment. "Mom calls it 'skippy'!"

"Skippy?" Benjamin raises his eyebrows. "'Cause it goes so fast?"

Cass smiles. "No, because the first few times we drove it, it would jump and miss. My mom used to give all our cars names." Cass looks out of the corner of her eye at Benjamin. "Roddy lets us use that car parked outside of his garage. It's Lucy's, but she doesn't drive it much lately. Roddy, he's a great mechanic—always working on something."

"I could tell by all the tools in his garage," Benjamin replies. "How is Roddy—his arm?"

Silva's head is once again outside of the car as Cass answers, "He was in a sling for two weeks or so, but he's out of it now and doing better. He says it aches in cold weather."

"How's London?" Benjamin asks, and the car fills with silence.

"We haven't seen her lately…" Cass answers at last. "They went to stay with Micki's grandfather."

"So Micki doesn't live with her mother?"

"Not anymore, she's gone to the top of the hill," Silva interjects.

Benjamin remembers that top of the hill reference before when London was born. Before he can ask more about it, Cass abruptly taps Silva's thigh with the back of her hand and Silva turns from the window and sits down in the seat.

After a few minutes of silence, Benjamin decides it's time for a subject change. "Isn't Burn's last name, Willis?"

"It is."

"Is that your dad?" Benjamin asks, finally putting two and two together.

Cassidy puts her arm around Silva and pulls her close. "I thought you would figure it out once you saw my name on the diplomas on the wall at the hospital."

"I know about where Burn lives but I have never been to his house," Benjamin explains. "He's so private and he never talks about…well, never talks really at all. So do you want to visit—"

Cass interrupts loudly, "NO, we are going to ride horses and go to the festival and go home."

Benjamin raises his eyebrows in surprise. "You might run into him at the festival."

"Oh, I'm sure…he loves kids," Cass replies, her voice full of attitude. Benjamin realizes he better change the subject.

"Have you ridden a horse before?" Benjamin asks Silva.

Silva springs out from under Cass's arm. She looks at Cass for an answer. "You have, but you were too young to remember."

"I can still ride, can't I?" Silva asks, her eyes wide.

"Sure, you might need some help. It kinda depends on the horse," Cass explains.

"Oh, Glory is gentle and loves kids. Matthew is four and he rides him with no trouble."

"Will he be there?" Cass asks.

"No, he lives near Houston, but I invited a girl about your age named Paulene to come ride. She's ridden before and maybe you can be friends."

The excitement on Silva's face is unmistakable as she brightens at the idea of a friend to play with. She's so giddy, it's hard for Benjamin to look away as he maneuvers the truck over one of the last roads that separates them from the farm, the canopy of trees casting a shadow as they pass through.

As they get closer, passing the field where Hal and Benjamin shot the wolves, a thought comes to the front of his mind. "I haven't done anything with that information you showed me a while back. I...uhh..."

Cass nods in understanding. "I understand...you need to be *sure* who you tell 'cause you could get *yourself* in trouble...and *us* too."

Silva stares at Benjamin, upset that he hasn't told anyone as she thought he would. "You got to do *something*," she pleads.

Benjamin can see her desperation. "I've got someone in mind, but I got to be sure."

"I understand," Cass replies as they turn over the rickety bridge.

Silva picks her feet up off the floorboard of the truck. "Mom!" she yells.

Cass smiles and lifts her feet off the floorboard.

"Superstitious? I usually just hold my breath," Benjamin says with a smile.

Silva rolls her eyes. "If you don't hold your feet up, you'll never meet your true love or get married—"

Benjamin raises his eyebrows and interrupts, "Never heard that."

"—or you'll die young," she finishes.

Benjamin holds his feet up to humor her and the truck slows to almost a stop.

"Benjamin…go, go, go."

Benjamin chuckles as he presses his foot back down on the gas pedal and the truck lurches, making its way across the bridge once more. Silva giggles too.

Benjamin turns down the drive to Hal's house. As they near, they see Glory trotting around the fence outside the barn. "Rein must already be here. Glory's out of the barn."

Cass and Silva both twist their bodies and crane their necks to see if they can spot Rein in the corral. Benjamin's eyes zero in on his sister as she is walking toward Paulene, who is sitting on the wooden fence surrounding the field. Benjamin points her out to Silva and Cass. "My sister Rein is here and so is Paulene."

A smile grows across Silva's face as Benjamin stops the truck and rolls the window down. "We're going to the house and unlōad," he calls, pointing to the house.

Rein nods. Silva takes the opportunity to open the door of the truck, hop out, and run around the vehicle to where Rein is standing. Benjamin and Cass both laugh at her obvious impatience.

Benjamin continues to the front of Hal's house and parks by Hal's truck. Cass grabs her satchel as they both exit. Benjamin offers to carry it, but she doesn't seem to notice and makes her way up the steps with it slung over her shoulder. She waits for Benjamin to unlock the door as she looks around the farm.

"All the bedrooms are upstairs," Benjamin explains as they walk in the door.

She drops the satchel on the bottom step. "Can I walk around and see the downstairs?"

"Of course," Benjamin replies, watching as she drifts into the living room.

Elegant curtains inhabit every window, paintings hang on the walls, and kids' pictures are on the mantle. She swings around the dining room and looks out the back window to see Silva talking to Rein and Paulene. "What's Hal's wife's name?"

"Julie."

"Julie has good taste."

Benjamin is confused. "What do you mean?"

"You can tell she has been brought up proper. She's got everything in its place."

Benjamin nods as the two of them head for the kitchen.

"Can I get a drink of water?"

Benjamin hurries to retrieve a glass from the cupboard, filling it at the sink. He hands it to her and she drinks. "Do you want to see upstairs?" he asks as she empties the glass.

"Maybe later. I'm going outside to check on the girls."

She fills the glass a second time before carrying it out the back door and down the wooden steps. Benjamin is not far behind.

"How come you and Paulene aren't in school today?" Cass asks over her shoulder.

"They closed school today because of the Festival. They do it every year. It's a big day for Chatham Hill, you know."

"That worked out for all of us, didn't it?" Cass says.

Benjamin smiles. "Are you going to ride?"

"I might...Silva, come here for a minute," Cass calls, as she notices that Rein and Paulene are both dressed in old clothes ideal for riding. She hands the glass of water to Silva, watching as she takes a few gulps. "Drink it all," she insists, and Silva finishes it off.

Once she is done, Rein begins explaining how to saddle Glory. Cass watches, curious herself, taking note of the scratches on Glory's back.

"How did he get the scars on his back?" She points to the scars as she asks.

"From a wolf pack. He was trapped in the corral, poor thing. He used to be skittish but not anymore."

"Hm." Cass isn't so sure about that, but she doesn't say anything. Out of the corner of her eye she notices Benjamin edging toward the house. "Do you have something else to do?"

"Well, to tell the truth, I have to run a few more errands for Peppers. It was part of the deal, but I'll bring back supper from the hospital," he answers.

"Sure, that would be great. Do you need Rein to come?"

"No. I'll manage on my own."

Cass nods. "Okay. I'll see you later on then."

He picks up the glass on his way to the house. "Rein, Paulene, do you need any water?"

Paulene replies with, "No sir," at the same time that Rein calls, "I'm fine."

"Okay then." Benjamin gives them a wave with his free hand before disappearing into the house.

Chapter 15

November 2, 1945
1:00pm
Hal's House, Chatham Hill, Middle Tennessee

REIN FINISHES SADDLING GLORY. "Let's let Paulene take the first spin around the corral, just so Glory can get used to things."

Silva is practically vibrating with excitement and frowns at Rein's announcement.

"Silva, you can ride with Paulene the next trip around," Cass assures her, placing her hand on Silva's shoulder.

"Okay," she agrees as Rein helps Paulene get on Glory and pats the horse so he begins a slow trot.

"She looks pretty comfortable," Cass observes.

Rein nods. "She's ridden the horse for some time now. Glory and her have a bond." As the words leave her mouth Paulene nudges Glory, and he picks up the pace.

Benjamin honks as he passes by in the truck and Cass and Rein wave as Cass says, "You can tell."

"I feel good about letting the two ride together. I'll walk beside her until she gets to know them," Rein reassures Cass. "Did I hear you wanted to ride?"

"Maybe later. I had to plow fields with a mule when I was their age, so I haven't ridden them as much as worked 'em."

Before Rein can say anything else, Paulene and Glory have finished their lap and come to a stop beside Rein. Silva came and stood in front of Glory. Rein presses some feed into her open palm. "Put your hand out and let him eat the oats." Silva does as she is told. "Now let him smell you." Then she pets Glory's neck, motioning for Silva to do the same. "Just stand there for a moment and stroke him. He likes that."

As the girls are petting Glory, Cass takes notice of the necklace Paulene is wearing. "Paulene, what's that around your neck?"

"It's a necklace. Benjamin gave it to me to keep me safe."

Rein holds her hand in front of her mouth and whispers to Cass, "Benjamin gave it to her months ago. I can't believe she still wears it. He made it out of a piece of metal along the roadside we were walking and a leather strap. She was having a bad day and, well, that gift brightened up her day."

Cass smiles. "He does seem to have that effect on people."

Rein cups her palms together and crouches down, instructing Silva on how to use her hand to step up onto Glory. Silva executes Rein's instructions perfectly, swinging up on the saddle behind Paulene, looping her arms around the other girl's waist to keep herself secure.

"You ready?" Rein asks.

Silva nods.

Rein walks around the horse to ensure the girls are secure before whispering to Paulene, "Paulene, keep it slow, dear."

"Yes, ma'am."

Rein nods and with a small kick, the girls and Glory begin their loop. Rein watches, slowly backing up so she is next to Cass once again. "Paulene will ride until the sun goes down. She's ridden Glory more than anyone."

"Hal is your uncle?" Cass asks, her eyes also trained on the girls.

"Yeah, he's kind of the foreman of the whole ranch. He does whatever anybody needs. He's handy to have around and kind of like a father to us."

"What happened to your father? If you don't mind me asking?"

Rein pauses, thinking on how much she should share. "He and my mother left us when we were just kids. I really don't remember them, just as well because they did some bad things when they left. Annie Mae is my grandmother and has raised us since. J.B. married her after we were born."

"I'm sorry." Cass feels bad that she asked. The two women watch the girls as Glory gallops around.

"Does your family live in Yaphank?" Rein asks.

"I don't remember my mom at all. She died when I was a kid, but my dad—" She pauses, "—my dad is kind of like yours. He did some bad things and kind of let me—me and Silva just got each other. I don't like remembering either."

"I understand."

Rein puts out her hand to stop Glory as the girls draw near. "Paulene, you get off and let Silva ride around a few times by herself." Paulene jumps down as Rein helps Silva slide up into the saddle and put her feet in the stirrups. "Cass, you and Paulene walk around with Glory, unless you want to go with me and clean out the stalls and get her hay down?"

"That does sound like fun," Cass says jokingly.

Both girls scream that they want to ride. Rein laughs. "Okay...okay, I'll be in the barn."

Rein heads to the barn alone and gets to work throwing hay bales down from the rafters. As she finishes and slowly climbs down the ladder, she happens to look up underneath the loft boards. Her eye catches some stuff hanging on rusty nails on the wall. There's a weight and a long irregular piece of metal. She has never noticed them before.

"What could that be?" She says out loud to the empty barn, mentally running over the possibilities in her mind. "To weigh cotton bales, maybe?" She nods, agreeing with herself as her eyes catch an old cast iron frying pan.

The shape and size look familiar. "No way," she whispers as she looks around the barn for a way to get even closer. Finding no ladder or step stool, she begins to pile bales on top of one another.

With two in place, she begins to climb. The bales are wobbly and it takes all she can to sturdy herself and keep her balance. She reaches up, her fingertips barely brushing the pan. Still not high enough. Rising on her toes, she pinches her fingers around the bottom of the pan and unhooks it from the nail.

She lowers it down and flips it over, her eyes wide. The pan has RAW and VD etched on the bottom. Just as she is trying to wrap her head around what she's found and how it got here, in Hal's barn, the top bale wobbles and she begins to lose her balance.

Suddenly, she is airborne, but the fall is short, and the top bale topples over just in time to break her fall as the pan clatters to the floor a few feet away.

It takes a moment for Rein to catch her breath before she is able to crawl over to the pan. How had Hal gotten it here? Where had he found it?

Rein studies the pan a few more moments before the pieces of the puzzle click into place. The fireplace had to be a time portal just like Annie Mae claimed.

As soon as she realizes this, she also realizes she has to put it back on the nail otherwise Hal will know something is amiss. Wondering why she didn't think of it before, Rein decides to use her magic to put it back.

She sets the pan on the hay bale and takes a step back, trying to visualize her magic floating it up to the nail. It takes a few moments, but Rein is successful, the pan falling into place on the nail with a light 'clink.'

Rein quickly exits the barn, wondering if she should mention this to anyone. But as she makes her way back to the girls, she realizes that she can't risk telling anyone about this. It will have to be her secret.

Chapter 16

November 2, 1945
3:00pm
Windsor Hospital, Chatham Hill, Middle Tennessee

THE NEXT DAY, AMBER is walking through the hospital after finishing her shift, a smile plastered on her lips, intent on speaking with Mr. Strickland at the Gazette for Stephen's gift, when J.B. suddenly steps into her path.

"Amber, I heard the good news being spread around the hospital about Stephen and you getting married."

The smile falls from Amber's face as she tries to step around him. "Yep, we will be married just as soon as he gets out of jail."

J.B. matches her step, remaining directly in her path. "Congratulations. Things are changing around here. Maybe you'll come home for the holidays?"

Her jaw clenched in defiance. "Doubt it. I will have Stephen's parents, Sadie and Trevor, like a whole new family by then." Again, she moves to step around him. "Sometimes people say they're changing—but they never do."

Amber spots Weston out of the corner of her eye, but when she glances over, though he is looking her way, the bulk of his attention is focused on Jennifer, giving J.B. the opportunity to step in front of her again.

Amber narrows her eyes, "You step in front of me again, I'll put my knee on you where you always liked to touch me. You want to be so talkative...how about telling me about what the lawyers have been talking to you about since we have a standing agreement that needs to be executed."

"The lawyers said they will call next week with a settlement amount, and if that falls through they will file the necessary papers soon after."

Amber tries to hide her smile. "How does it feel that you might be losing your treasured possession?"

"I'll fight for what I think is mine."

Before she could think, Amber was raising her palm, slapping her step-grandfather across the face. The sound was loud enough to draw Weston from Jennifer's side.

Recovering from the shock of being slapped, J.B. reaches out and grabs Amber's upper arms, his grip like steel.

Amber doesn't flinch. "You can't hurt me anymore than you already have."

"Why don't you follow David out the door?" J.B. suggests with malice in his voice.

"I have patients to care for."

"Is everything okay?" Weston interrupts, his eyes darting between Amber and his boss.

J.B. drops his hold, Amber's hands coming up to rub the red marks where his hands had been gripping.

"We were discussing a family matter that's none of your concern," he snaps at Weston.

Weston shakes his head, recognizing the signs of a fight. "You both need to go into your office or at least off the floor to finish your family discussion."

"We're finished. Amber, why don't you go help Weston until you finish your shift?"

Amber's eyes narrow at his suggestion, considering her shift had already ended, but she says nothing, standing next to Weston in silence as J.B. makes his way back to his office.

"Are you alright?" Weston asked as the two of them made their way back to Jennifer's bedside.

"I'm fine," Amber insisted. Weston returned to his task of setting up Jennifer's medicine. Amber offers a remark, "Are you scared?"

Weston replied, "She's scared of voices, noises, being awake, asleep, being alone—"

Amber shakes her head. "I wasn't talking to Jennifer. I was talking to you."

Weston nearly dropped the syringe in his hand as he scrambled to find an answer.

Amber helps him out. "I was talking about everything the lawyers are going to blame you for, Dr. Galloway."

Weston swallows, a slight tremor in his movements. "I've told my father everything that is going down. He recommends that I see what the settlement offer is."

Amber's eyes were focused on Jennifer as she replied, "I suggest you get your own lawyer and look after your own best interest." Done with that conversation, Amber switches gears turning to the young patient. "Jennifer, Rein said that you like to go outside and sit on the porch, is that right?"

Jennifer blinks.

Amber tries again. "Jennifer, would you like to go outside now?"

Letting out a breath, Weston turns away from Jennifer, watching as Ms. Elvie enters the patient area. When he turns back to Jennifer, Amber is helping her out of bed.

Jennifer's legs are shaky, but Amber is patient, allowing her to lean and coaching her step by step as they make their way toward the porch. They pass Ms. Elvie, who raises an eyebrow.

"I thought you had to leave, Amber?"

"I do," Amber agreed, not making eye contact with Ms. Elvie, "But Jennifer's got to get out of here too."

Not one to argue, she falls in step with the two women, her mind drifting to the things her young daughter had told her that morning. "Paulene had a wonderful time with you yesterday, thank you."

"I love her, she is so smart and I enjoy her company." Amber pauses to help Jennifer over a loose floorboard. When she rights herself again, she continues, "I got less people to talk to now, so it works pretty well." Both ladies go through the set of double swinging doors and into the lobby with Ms. Elvie in tow.

Amber turns back to Paulene's mother. "Let me get her outside on the porch and to the first rocking chair."

"Alright I'll speak with you later," Ms. Elvie replies, disappearing into the kitchen.

Jennifer and Amber continue their slow movements out onto the porch and up to the first rocking chair, Jennifer sinking into it with an exhausted sigh.

Still holding on to her shoulder, Amber says, "Jennifer, each day we are going to go a little farther, do you understand?"

Jennifer nods her head slowly up and down.

Proud of her development, Amber adds, "Tomorrow, when I get time, I'm going to my room at my old house and get you some of my old clothes. They will fit you perfectly. I have some pants and shirts and shoes....and we are going to get you back talking."

Jennifer doesn't say anything.

"Actually," she beams, "Let's start now. Jennifer, say I love you."

Jennifer's lips begin to move, but she struggles to form sounds, only air passing through her lips. Closing her mouth, she swallows, then tries again. "I love...I..." she stutters, gasping for breath.

"You got this," Amber presses.

"I love...I..." A tear rolls down her cheek, perspiration breaking out on her forehead.

Amber places Jennifer's hand over her heart. "I love you."

Jennifer tries a third time, this time shortening the syllables to save her breath. "I... love... u..." Amber smiles ear to ear and kisses her cheek. She is so excited she gets on her knees and hugs Jennifer around the neck. A moment passes and an amazing thing happens... Jennifer hugs her back.

So happy about her progress with the young woman, Amber doesn't notice that Weston has joined them on the porch until he is helping Jennifer from her seat. "Ladies, I think that's enough for today."

Amber's shoulders fall at the interruption, but she can see the surprise and pride in Weston's irises. She had done well today.

Weston helps Jennifer into the wheelchair that Amber hadn't noticed him rolling out onto the porch, and he pushes Jennifer back into the lobby, past Ms. Elvie, tears shining in her eyes.

"What—Did you hear me?"

Ms. Elvie nods. "Why, yes, from this window in the lobby. It was beautiful."

Pride swells in Amber's chest as she follows Weston and Jennifer back to her bed. Jennifer tries to speak again, but all that comes out is a garbled, "U."

Patting the young woman on the hand, Amber promises she will be back tomorrow.

"You better get going. Downtown might be getting busy at this time of day, with the Festival tomorrow," Weston says, breaking her focus.

Amber relaxes and smiles at Jennifer as she sees her eyes drifting closed. "I'm going to sit here until she nods off."

"Okay. I'm going to note on Jennifer's chart the progress you have made today."

"Thank you, Dr. Galloway," Amber replies with a smile, her eyes trained on Jennifer as she drifts off to sleep.

"I'm not a doctor yet, Ms. Windsor."

"You are to me."

Chapter 17

FINALLY FINISHED WITH HER shift, Amber says a quick good-bye to Weston before changing out of her uniform into her clothes. Not wanting to linger and in a rush to find out about her gift, she simply waves goodbye to Ms. Elvie before heading out to Stephen's car.

Driving into town, Amber's mind flashes back to her scary encounter with the truck the day before, wanting to get to the bottom of things, she raises her foot from the gas as she passes Pepper's, her eyes spotting two trucks. One with Pepper's printed on the side in dark letters, the other is Danny's personal truck which he had been gifted by his father.

Her heart drops into her stomach, her foot prepared to stomp down on the gas.

But, after looking for another moment, she realizes that a third truck is present, Justin's Trucking Company, and it is backed up to the loading dock—meaning Danny was likely too busy to follow her.

Leaning out the open window and letting the wind whip though her hair, Amber smiles as she passes through the town, preparation for the festival well underway. Banners are being strung, and advertisements posted to every pole. There are even some larger trucks in the distance, filled with metal beams and lights—the carnival rides waiting to be assembled.

Among all the items for the festival, political signs also run rampant. Kieffers' and Fields' faces were plastered on every other window or door.

Struggling to find a spot among the crowded streets, Amber almost hits a pedestrian but stops just in time. Trying to remain calm, Amber lets out a breath and swings into what has to be the last open space near The Hill Gazette. As she climbs from the car, she sends up a silent prayer that Mr. Strickland didn't see her close call with the pedestrian.

Amber hustles underneath the large wooden sign toward the door, nearly hitting it with her face when it doesn't open as she expects. Confused, she steps back, twisting the knob repeatedly, but it doesn't budge—the door is locked.

Trying again not to panic, Amber steps to the side to peer into the darkened interior, spotting a man behind one of the machines. When he raises his head and spots Amber, he quickly rushes to the door, unlocking it and pulling it open.

"Mr. Strickland?" Amber asks as she enters the darkened interior.

As Mr. Strickland places his hand on Amber to steady her, he chuckles. "Young lady, you about bent the door."

Panicked, Amber turns to look at the door. "Did I break it?"

"No, I think the door won this time but let me know you're coming next time and I'll leave the door open." He motions to one of the few wooden chairs in the lobby. Amber takes a seat.

"I'm sorry, Mr. Strickland, but I was so determined to get here before you left."

"Child, I got so much work to do I'll be here late to finish pamphlets, the newspaper, and sales ads for the stores." He lets out a long gasp as he sits beside Amber. "Got any news for me? You know that's my specialty."

"Stephen proposed to me Wednesday when I visited him in jail," she offers, not knowing what else to mention.

He smiles. "That's great. Congratulations, you've landed a hard worker and a good man."

"Thank you so much." Amber dabs at the sweat on her face with a handkerchief. Mr. Strickland, "Can I put it on the front page?"

She thinks for a moment. "Don't think it's worth going there." His face breaks into a smile afterward. "You pay and I'll make it the headline." She smiles as she realizes he was joking about his first comment.

"Anything I can do to help around here?" Her eyes peruse the mess of blocks, ink, and paper scattered over every visible surface.

"Hm..." He rubs his chin. "You can help run these pamphlets through the printer." She follows him behind the counter, waiting for directions. "I need 50 of these and 100 of these. The ink is already loaded, so move this crank back and forth with each paper to print it."

"Yes, sir. I'm your girl."

"The ink will be wet so don't touch the printed parts." She nods in understanding. "I'm just around the corner at the big press doing the daily paper if you got any questions."

He comes back with a sturdy leather apron gripped in his outstretched hand. "Here put this on to keep your clothes from getting smudged." He slips the loop over her head and helps her with the strings. She ties them into a bow.

She inserts the first blank page, turning the crank as he had shown her. The machine spits out the page, completed. She sets it to the side. As she does so, the flow of air above her head catches her attention. "What's above our heads?"

"Oh, mostly storage, old files and boxes of business stuff," he calls back and Amber puts a second blank page into the machine. "I'll be glad when Stephen gets out and comes back to work. Or do you think he'll go back to preaching?"

"Oh, I told him Wednesday that he's coming back to work here as soon as possible, that's one thing I wanted you to be assured of today. I told him he's a full-time newspaper man now. Can we depend on that?" When he doesn't answer, she tries again. "Mr. Strickland, will you give me your word?"

"Yes, ma'am, you have my word," he says, his voice a bit more hesitant than Amber would have liked.

For a while, the sound of the machines fills the room: the thumping from the larger machine Mr. Strickland is using, and the creaking of the smaller machine operated by Amber. After a bit, Mr. Strickland pauses, the room becoming much more silent than it had been before.

"Tell me about your family," she says, her voice demure.

He faces her, breathing in deeply before replying, "My wife passed away five years ago. Got one son that's somewhere up North. Ain't heard a word from him since the funeral. And don't expect to. He's got anger problems that I don't understand. My sister died two years ago, and my brother could go anytime. They keep to themselves. I'll get a call one day with the news...but I'm alone and expect to be until I die. Why do you ask?" He looks at her, searching for comfort, "I've told you about my family. You seem strong enough now to talk about yours?"

She shrugs, feeding in the next paper. "You know my story, everyone in town does. Mom and dad dumped us on grandma and left. Grandpa got murdered...so Rein and Benjamin are all I have left. You know Sadie Blue?"

He nods.

"She's my new mama." He raises his eyebrow, confused by the admission. "I've been really thinking hard and...I've got a short list for my new father—well, really just one person I got my eye on right now." She cuts her eyes to him. "You're sweet, kind, and caring, and I know I can trust you. Can we get to know each other better?"

Mr. Strickland's eyes swell. "I always wanted a daughter." He smiles.

She steps towards him and embraces him, and he hugs her back. They stand like that for a few moments.

"Can you tell me who really hurt you? Off the record?"

Amber swallows stepping back from the embrace, not saying anything at first, but then, "Danny Boy cut me and tried to rape me, and he threatened my family. But he'll get what's coming to him. So don't worry about me or my family." Her eyes filled with tears. "He broke into the Care Center and threatened to kill Rein or Benjamin if I speak about him...I've been afraid ever since." Mr. Strickland struggles to find a reply, and he is saved from embarrassment when Amber changes the subject. "Have you ever been threatened?"

His head tilts to the side as he questions how much he should reveal to her. "Yes, yes, I have... back in the old days when I was writing stories about your mama and daddy."

Her eyes widen in shock. "My family threatened you?" He nods affirmatively. "Oh, my God, I'm so sorry."

"It was a long time ago. It scared me for a time, but I had help to deal with it."

"Who?"

"That's a story for another day," he insists. "Oh, I've got a present for you. One moment..."

Her mood immediately shifts at the words as Mr. Strickland dips around the corner, her eyes switching from sad to eager.

He reappears with a guitar case. He sets it on the counter and looks at Amber. "This is from Stephen."

Aghast, Amber opens the case and sees a shiny wooden acoustic guitar. She brushes her hand over it lovingly. She hugs Mr. Strickland again.

"I could get used to this," he jokes and she kisses him on the cheek.

"Thank you, oh so much."

"There is some sheet music in the bottom there and pages with chords and such. Stephen says you are a wonderful singer. I would love to hear you, one day."

"For you, Mr. Strickland, I'll sing anytime you want." She beams, already digging in the case for the music.

"Amber, please call me, Joseph."

"Jesus's dad?"

He laughs. "I don't think I'd go that far."

"I'll call you Joe...maybe Uncle Joe."

The corner of his lip turns up, but the smile doesn't quite meet his eyes. "That would be nice."

"I tell you what," She puts a hand on his arm, "When Stephen gets out, you get to come to Sadie's house and have dinner with us some nights."

"Alright," he agrees.

Amber steps back toward the printer. "We've got lots of work to do, maybe I can go to work down here as soon as I'm finished at the hospital every day."

He starts up the press again, yelling over the noise, "You got news about the hospital?"

She pauses her cranking a moment. "I'll let you know in due time, Uncle Joe."

"Yes ma'am, I can always use a pretty face in sales."

"Sales?" Amber nearly drops the crank at the words.

"Yeah, somebody got to talk to the customers and get more advertising, and you've got a way with words."

She smiles at his compliment as she stacks her finished pages in separate nicely stacked piles. "I'm so excited about the guitar and learning to play."

Chapter 18

S ILVA AND CASS ARE snuggled together in Hal and Julie's bed. In her sleep, Cass pulls the blanket tighter around her shoulders to block out the cold air that is leaking in through the window panes. Fog obscures the natural light which would otherwise pour into the room from beyond the misty pane.

Down the hall, Benjamin also sleeps peacefully in Jacob's old room. The bed is a bit too small, and, as a result, his bare feet and legs are sticking out over the edge. The sheets are sufficiently wrinkled, as they are the same sheets he has been sleeping in all week.

Silva is the first to wake, so warm in the cocoon of blankets with her mother. She sits up and slides the sheets back before deciding to go to the bathroom.

As her bare feet hit the floor, she sees the tiny mouse scurry behind the dresser. She lets out a blood-curdling scream that jolts both Benjamin and Cass awake. Benjamin jumps to his feet and runs down the hallway, bursting into the master bedroom. The door flings open so hard and wide that it barely stays on its hinges. He flips the wall switch, and the room is immediately bathed in brightness.

Cass is standing by the bed in a long men's nightshirt with only her panties underneath and Silva is in her thick pajamas pointing to the dresser. "Silva, what's wrong?" she asks, turning to see Benjamin standing in the doorway in nothing but his sleeping pants.

"A mouse, ma'am. There's a mouse behind the dresser and it ran under that closet door."

Benjamin goes to the bathroom and grabs a broom from the closet there. He comes back and begins searching the room for the mouse.

Silva hangs on to Cass on the other side of the room as Benjamin looks in the closet floor and around the shoeboxes stacked inside. He gets down on his hands and knees and gazes at the empty corners of the closet by the door. He has a death grip on the broom, ready to strike if he sees its little gray head. He pushes the boxes toward the center of the closet and a couple of boxes flip over. Banking account statements, records, and large numbers catch his eye on some of the papers. He pushes all the boxes around until he's satisfied the mouse is not in one of them.

It's nowhere to be found. He does notice a hole in the corner of the closet, however, and suspects the menace may have slipped through. "No mouse, I think he squeezed through this crack. Do you want to see?"

Cass shakes her head. "No, no, just fill up the hole."

Benjamin has an idea, and he retrieves the toothpaste from the bathroom, using it to plug the hole. "That should do it for now."

"It'll eat the toothpaste...and come out," Silva says, her voice clouded with fear.

"No. I happen to know mice don't like this flavor," Benjamin assures her.

"What flavor is it?" she asks.

Benjamin looks at the tube. He reads, "Original."

"Liar."

"Trust me. The mouse is gone for a while. You screamed so loud he probably left the house and he's probably in the barn by now."

Cass begins to giggle and then laugh. "That was a loud scream."

"Loud? Rein will probably call in a minute and see if everything's okay." Benjamin laughs along with Cass.

Silva watches Benjamin and Cass laugh, crossing her arms at their insinuations.

Benjamin stops his laughing, his eyes drawn to Cass's legs, which are on full display in the short nightshirt she is wearing. His eyes follow them, noticing he can see her panties. His eyes continue to trail upwards until they meet Cass's eyes and he quickly looks away with a "Sorry."

Cass doesn't say anything, but she steps back away from the door, goes to the bed, and covers her bare bottom half with the bedsheets.

Trying to think of a way to diffuse the awkward situation, Benjamin begins to pick up the folded papers off the closet floor and he sees large numbers and dollar signs. Curiosity getting the better of him, he opens up a couple of the papers and sees 'Madison National Bank' and large numbers. As large as $12,000 and $22,000. He stops and looks at another box with similar numbers of $1,800 and $2,400.

"Are you still looking for the mouse?" Cass' voice interrupts his snooping.

"Yeah, I don't see him," he mumbles, focused on the papers in front of him. He looks at the dates. Some are from six years ago while others are just from last year. He looks in a couple other boxes and sees one date from over 12 years earlier and another from 15 years before. The papers have a header with the name Wells Fargo Bank & Union Trust Company from New York City.

Realizing that he's getting into dangerous territory, he starts trying to put the papers back like he found them. But he notices quickly that he doesn't really know how they were organized and that Hal will definitely know.

"Listen, I need you both to do me a favor. You trusted me with a secret, now I need your help." Cass' nods as she takes notice of Benjamin's muscles which are clearly visible without his shirt. "I know Hal didn't want me to see those papers in those boxes. But I did. I need you to tell him that if he ever asks you, that Cass got in the closet and scattered those boxes—not me."

Cass doesn't move her eyes from where they are focused on Benjamin's torso. "Okay. I'll do it. I'll tell him I scattered the boxes."

"Okay, that's the story, you screamed and you got into the closet looking for the mouse."

"Okay, I think you better leave," Cass says. Really she would rather Benjamin stay, but she knows she can't with Silva there. "We need to go back to sleep, Silva, it's too early for you to get up. Go to the bathroom."

"I don't need to now," Silva says with a yawn as she crawls back into bed.

Benjamin turns to the door. "Let's try to get a couple more hours of sleep. It's going to be a long day." He stops and his eyes meet hers. "Oh, I've got to go pick up some workers and take them to work at the hospital. I'll be back 'bout the time you'll get up."

Cass nods and watches him leave. He turns the light off on his way out.

Silva and Cass slide under the sheets. "Ma'am, that mouse scared me. I'm glad Benjamin was here."

"I'm glad Benjamin was here too." Cass turns over and caresses Silva's back. As she begins to drift off into dreamland her mind goes to another time, one when she was enveloped in a man's arms...

~~~

An hour later, Benjamin climbs the porch steps and unlocks Hal's front door. His eyes are immediately drawn to the fireplace where there's a small fire, before drifting to Cass who is sipping coffee with her knees curled under her on the couch. She's wearing jeans and a shirt with tails tied in a knot in front, her bare feet poking out from the ends of the frayed jeans. "There's a little coffee in the pot if you want some," she offers.

He removes his jacket and lays it over the easy chair back. "Yeah, I need something to take the chill off."

Benjamin makes his way to the kitchen and pours the remainder of the coffee in his cup. It's half full. "Did you get enough?" Cass calls from the couch.
~~~

"Yeah. It's the perfect amount." He sinks down next to Cass and takes a sip.

"Did you get everybody to work?"

"I did. The help is going to be scarce today because everybody's going to the Festival," Benjamin replies.

"Are they going to be alright?"

He sips again before answering, "I think so. The workers are kinda taking shifts, so they'll be fine." He had been avoiding eye contact but now he can no longer resist, and his eyes come to rest on hers. "This morning was a little hectic."

"I'd say so. Silva scared me good, and you bolted in there like a true hero."

"Well, I don't know about a hero. She scared me too," Benjamin admits as Cass drains her cup. Benjamin watches her intently. "I figured we could head downtown after 12 sometime for a hot dog, and they got rides, and games, and...well, I don't have any plans until then."

"Oh, Silva and I are going to have guests this morning."

"What do you mean?" Benjamin asks, surprised.

"Paulene and her sister, Victoria, are coming this morning and riding Glory until noon and we'll clean up and head downtown after that."

"Sounds like you got everything organized. Now Victoria works late nights so early for her could be noon." Benjamin warns, as he's known Victoria for long enough not to expect her to be on time.

Cass looks at Benjamin with confidence. "Paulene assured me she would be here this morning."

Benjamin tilts his head to the side. "Okay...we'll see."

"Glory is so gentle, but stout," Cass observes, her eyes drifting to the window where the area where the girls rode yesterday is visible.

"He's gentle, but feisty," Benjamin cautions her, taking another sip of his coffee.

"When I rode him, I gave him a kick and he took off like a rocket."

"Well, yesterday was all girls. He loves the women. He can smell their affection and demeanor."

"Oh, I know he does. He did great all day and he tired us all out." Cass' admiration shines through in her voice.

"That's good. Only got one horse."

Chapter 19

November 3, 1945
7:30am
Outskirts of Chatham Hill Township, Middle Tennessee

MAJOR PRESSES HIS FOOT down on the gas, causing his patrol car to lurch on the dirt road, the two patrol cars in his wake adjusting their speed in response. Frost, who was half-asleep on the window, jolts awake.

"We got a search warrant for his property, his buildings, and any individuals occupying these premises?" he says to the man in the back seat.

Special Agent Charles Webber is wearing a collared shirt, brown slacks, leather boots, and glasses. He also has a holstered handgun draped inside his leather jacket. His eyes connect with Major's in the rearview mirror. "That's correct."

"We're going to have about twelve adults and six to eight, hell who knows, ten kids under the age of fifteen, supposedly."

"That's fine, we'll herd them into a searched area and my men know where to look, their hiding places, underground spaces, we got an idea what we're looking for...shine and the still..." He takes a breath, "And any evidence of all the young girl murders."

Major's eyes peruse his outfit, noticing there isn't a speck of dust anywhere on his person. "You don't look like you're ready to do any searching."

"I'm here to make sure the warrant is carried out. If there's anything to find, my men will find it," Webber replies, unperturbed by Major's obvious doubt.

Major slaps Frost with his back hand on the upper arm. Frost nearly jumps out of his seat. "It's going to be a beautiful day."

Frost narrows his eyes but turns his attention back to the road just in time. "That's one of their trucks right there." He points as Croce and Gant's truck is pulling out of Burn's drive onto the main road. Major puts on his lights and intercepts the vehicle, forcing the truck to come to a stop. Croce pulls the truck off to the side of the road.

"We don't have any authority to search a vehicle not on the property," Webber interjects. "You and your men stay in the cars. We'll handle this." S.A. Webber opens the back door, steps out, and waves his men in the following cars to unload.

Major and Frost, not keen on missing the action, step out of their vehicle and walk along opposite sides of the truck, taking note of the crates and boxes of fruits and vegetables occupying the truck bed.

"What's the problem, officer?" Croce cracks open the driver's door.

Gant is quiet as Frost approaches his side with a shotgun at the ready.

"Both you fellas, step out of the truck and put your hands on the hood," Major commands. "You carrying any guns?"

"Got a pistol under the front seat," Croce informs him as he climbs out of the car.

Gant is moving more slowly and Frost quickly loses his patience, grabbing him by the shirt and pushing him up against the truck.

The officers take their time frisking the two men. When finished, Major turns to Frost. "Watch 'em both." Frost nods and points his shotgun in their direction.

Major flicks on his flashlight, shining it through the cab and behind the seats. It doesn't take him long to find the gun, and he snaps it open. Major flips the barrel open, ejects the bullets onto the dusty ground, and closes it again. Flipping it closed he hands it to Webber. He motions back to an agent. "Log this in." The agent takes the gun and scribbles a note in his booklet. Major, "Check the cab, still need to look in the bed."

Webber nods to his agents, who immediately jump in the back and begin sliding the crates haphazardly around in the truck bed. Watching with the side of his face pressed to the cab, Croce cringes. "Hey, hey, all them boxes are measured and ready to be delivered."

Major slips a piece of paper out of his front shirt pocket. He flashes it at Croce. "Lookie here, got a warrant."

The agents continue shifting the boxes and baskets around to look at the truck bed. One of the agents takes notice of what is underneath them. "It's got a couple of metal plates attached to the bed." Croce, "This truck has got so many rusty holes in the bed... it's got three or four plates underneath."

S.A. Webber shakes his head, "Nothing found in the baskets or produce?"

"Nothing yet," the men reply.

"That's enough for now, then." The agents jump down from the bed of the truck and go back to their cars.

"What ya' looking for?" Croce asks Major.

Major grits his teeth before spitting his answer, "We're looking for two men with your descriptions that were seen hoisting a drunk up on the River Bridge...and they were seen buying cups of coffee at Peppers just moments later."

"That's just where we're headed," Croce says, his voice firm and steady.

Major looks at Gant. "You got anything to add?"

Gant quietly shakes his head.

"Maybe we'll haul your asses down to jail and see if you might shed some light on what you know...you may not talk now, but you'll talk one day. Soon."

"Maybe we need to call our attorney... What about my gun?" Croce asks, his eyes on the metal in Webber's hands.

S.A. Webber holds it out to Croce. His eyes briefly find Major's before he turns and walks away.

Disappointed, Major turns to Frost. "Let's go. Our day is just starting."

Releasing the two men, but leaving their items in disarray, Major and Frost make their way to the main house with two black cars following them. When they get close, Burn steps out onto the porch, clothed only in long underwear.

"Sheriff, is that you?" he calls, rubbing the last bit of sleep out of his eyes.

It's S.A. Webber who calls back, "Bernard Willis, this is Special Agent Webber with the Department of Treasury. We have a warrant to search your property and buildings and persons. I need you to please escort all the individuals out of all the buildings so we may search the premises."

Burn's eyebrows raise, his eyes evaluating the group of men currently on his lawn. "Damn, Sheriff, you brought all these agents from the State of Tennessee just to see me, my family and my crops? Did you bring us any coffee?" The agents don't take kindly to Burn's joke, pushing past him and into the house, their hands all resting on their guns. "The missus ain't straightened up the house. So I hope you know it's a mess."

The men don't reply, so Burn makes his way down the steps toward Webber. "Can I see the warrant?"

Webber obliges. He lets Burn read a moment then asks, "We need keys to all these buildings?"

Taking notice of the sledgehammer by the agent's side, Burn quickly relents. "I'll get the keys, let me get dressed." As he heads back into the house, two men peel in after him, presumably to keep an eye on him as he dresses.

Never one to wait patiently, Webber splits his remaining agents into groups, sending them to the outbuildings on Burn's property.

Major watches as two men walk to the edge of the bluffs, look over, and then begin their searches of each house. Many of the houses are roughly hewn, set up on blocks to create a natural crawl space underneath. As one man slides below, out of sight, the other begins waking up the residents of each structure. "Get dressed, we need to search the premises."

Croce's wife exits one house with two barely dressed young children in tow, one dangling from each hand, nearly stumbling in her haste.

Burn returns with a bunch of keys, handing them to Webber.

"Which one is to the shed?" Major asks, impatience spreading through his features. Burn holds out a single key, which Major quickly snatches, motioning for Frost to follow.

Pushing open the wood plank door, his eyes crawl over all the contents, but he quickly realizes there is nothing illegal. His shoulders slump.

Burn, who followed the two men, laughs. "You didn't think it was my honey hole, did ya'?"

Not one to be discouraged, Major narrows his eyes on a rope hanging from the rafters in the shed, taking a step to get a closer look. "Looky here! Burn, this looks like the same type of rope tied around Lester."

Burns crosses his arms over his broad chest. "You let Lester be."

"Why Bernie, I didn't know you cared so much for your customers." Without missing a beat, Major leans outside the shed and motions for Frost and Webber to join him.

"Yes, sir?" Frost asks.

Major motions to the rope, taking note of another one deeper in the shed. "I want those two ropes put in the back of my car."

Webber looks confused. "Why these?"

"They're eerily similar to the one used in a hanging we had on the River Bridge a few days ago." Webber holds the first rope as Frost reaches for the other.

Webber inspects the rope. "It's greasy in spots."

Burn's watches from a few steps back. "Easier to get a tighter grab on tree stumps and such, helps the ropes last longer."

"These ropes match the one from the bridge," Major surmises and motions to Frost. "Put the ropes in my trunk. Keep your cuffs ready though."

Webber continues his own search, shuffling aside tools, tractor parts, and hay, but there is no sign of moonshine.

Major, unsatisfied, heads to the other shed on the property, but his eyes catch on something on the edge of the bluff on the way there. Stepping closer, he sees an apparatus that resembles a tripod.

Upon closer inspection, he realizes it is some sort of pulley.

"What we got here, Bernard?"

Chapter 20

November 3, 1945
8:00am
Outskirts of Chatham Hill Township, Middle Tennessee

WEBBER, WHO HAD BEEN following Major, makes his own observations as Burn answers, "Old power line support. It was where we used to get power to Yaphank before the power company put in the new lines." He points to a pole down the slope, a power pole and line stretched to another metal brace 50 feet down the bluff.

Webber looks over the edge. "How do you keep all these kids from falling?"

Burn shrugs. "They've been taught right."

Webber doesn't say anything more, instead he walks along the bluff, leaning down to toss a few stones over the edge.

Major returns to the second shed, Burn looking over his shoulder. "Pretty clean, right?"

Major doesn't reply to the verbal jab, instead returning to the front of the main house and his patrol car, his eyes catching on the large number of black women gathered on the front porch. The group consisted of an assortment of ages: school kids, teenagers, and those in their early 20's.

They're standing there with their kids, and a few young black men.

"Which one of you is Burn's wife?" he calls.

"That's none of your business," Burn snaps.

"Maybe it is. You've got a very young group of kids here. I know a man like you has got to have...urges."

Burn ignores Major's insinuation. "Let's get in the house and start putting these back to normal."

Major doesn't move. "This ain't normal, big man, this ain't normal at all. Maybe we need to search this house again." Burn and Major stand across from each other on the porch, their eyes narrowed, their stances widened.

They are distracted from their almost-brawl when Webber calls from the bluff, "Sheriff, I need to see you for a moment!"

Major lumbers over wiping his brow with a bandana. When he reaches Webber, he sees a small rock in the palm of his hand.

"Listen, Sheriff, I've done this a long time and I'm going to tell you what we are going to find here." Major holds his breath. "Nothing...besides maybe a pint jar or two. This ain't the mother load...you know where the still is?"

Major doesn't answer and Webber throws the stone out over the cliff edge. Major watches it float out and drop out of sight.

"You got to have fresh water like a stream or creek or a spigot flowing out of any of a hundred crevasses on the side of this bluff." Major eyes drop. "How many miles of mountainside we got from the fields we passed to the next main pass?"

Major voice cracks. "Thirty miles or so."

Webber nods his head. "That's where the still is. You would have to have fifty men a week or two to search all of them hollers for 30 miles."

Major thinks for a moment, his eyes crawling the landscape. "Okay, I understand what you're saying. There's a guy down there in the bottoms that probably knows..." Major's voice fades, "...but he ain't very friendly. There really ain't no law to speak of down there."

Webber looks perturbed. "Look, my guys aren't coming back up here. If you got a guy down there, then I expect you and him to handle it. Do not call us back out here. But if you insist, you got to go way over my head. Do you understand?"

"Yes, sir," Major agrees.

"I guess you've been stopping shine runners and searching their cars not to find anything, right?" Major nods. "That's because they've been pulling the shine up that pulley—" he points at the shed, "—with the ropes and running it out up here. Now he knows you know, so he'll move the tripod around now. So you got thirty more miles to patrol. Good luck, Sheriff." He turns and walks away, calling back over his shoulder, "We're just about finished."

Major stares over the edge of the bluff for a minute, his body mirroring his disappointment. The only sound is the creaking of a rocking chair on the porch. Major turns to find Burn there, rocking, a smug look dancing on his features.

"Voices sure do carry around here, Sheriff."

Not happy about being bested, Major rushes after Webber. "Wait." Webber steps to the side. "I got a murderer that has killed three young pre-teens or more, and I would like for us to search that one house for any evidence one more time."

Webber blinks slowly. "My guys searched the house and found nothing that pertains to moonshine or murdered girls."

Major pleads, "Just that one house, I'll—"

Webber interrupts, "You'll have to get another warrant for another day. Listen, we found some glass jars and containers in one of the houses' backrooms and some stacked in boxes in the back shed. But they were empty. We found plenty of stacks and piles of girls' clothes. You can't expect us to find a miracle. Do 'ya? So we are going to pack up and head back to Nashville. I'll send you a report. You'll get it in a week or so. If you want additional help, I'll jot my boss's name and number down on a page in the front. You let him know."

Major agrees, watching as the agents and Webber return to their vehicles, Frost standing next to their patrol car. Then, he approaches Burn, still sitting in the rocker, who has a big smile on his face.

"I would like to search your house again. This time personally."

Burn stands and leans against a wood post as Major nears. "Do you need my permission?"

"Not really."

"Well, you don't have my permission."

Major turns and signals Frost to come. "Watch my back," he hisses and Frost nods. Burn follows them inside, not saying anything. "Where's your room?"

Burn replies with a smile. "I sleep in all of them."

"I bet you do." Major doesn't entertain his gloating, focusing his energy instead on scouring the house, his flashlight landing on several pictures of young girls.

Burn calls to one of the girls on the porch. "Collette, go watch the sheriff and be sure he don't break...or steal anything."

The 12-year-old curly haired, black girl passes Frost at the bottom of the steps and follows Major as he checks each bedroom.

"Which room does Bernard sleep in?"

She points.

Major follows her finger to find a large room with an unmade bed, light filtering through the sheer curtains on the windows. He crosses the room in three large steps and digs through the dresser, followed by a chair draped with clothes.

Burn's calls from downstairs, "Be sure he doesn't mess with my wallet!"

Colette obeys, crossing the room to snatch the wallet. Major, "Let me see that. Colette relents. Major slowly checks every paper and pocket of his wallet. He hands it back to the watching girl. She stashes it in a drawer.

Major stops her to dig through the drawer.

"What are you looking for?"

Major decides to try a different tactic. "Do you ever go help your parents deliver vegetables to other houses?"

"Yes."

"Do you know Gemma Hicks or her sister, Shane?"

She hesitates and ever so slightly nods no.

"You don't?" he presses. "Has any of your family disappeared lately?"

She takes a step back as Major continues, "I'm looking for something that someone would hide."

Her head tilts to the side. "I hide stuff under my bed and in my closet all the time."

Before Major can reply, Burn sticks his head in the door. "Colette, is my wallet safe?"

"Yes sir, I put it in the drawer." She points.

"What's he been doing?"

"Looking for something."

Annoyed at how this entire search is going, Major pushes past Collette to exit the room.

"Do you want to look under the bed?" she asks innocently.

Burn chuckles as Major walks by. "Under the bed...Colette, you'll have to look under the bed for him. If he ever got down that low, he would never get back up."

Major doesn't say anything and begins to make his way down the stairs, finding Frost still waiting for him at the bottom.

"Hey, Major! You want to look in my closet?" Burn calls after him in a taunt.

Major doesn't even turn around. He says to Frost under his breath, "Let's go."

Burn watches Major and Frost climb in their car before yelling, "Kids, let's get ready to go to the Festival." A bunch of cheers ring out from the porch, then Burn yells again toward their car, "Have a great day, Sheriff."

Major and Frost close their doors simultaneously, Major starting the car and speeding off down the lane, dust billowing behind them.

Chapter 21

B ENJAMIN NODS AS SILVA comes loudly down the steps in her riding clothes. "You didn't get enough riding yesterday?"

"No, sir. One more day," Silva says as Cass stands from her seat on the couch and heads for the kitchen. Benjamin follows, his cup gripped tightly in his fist.

"Want some oatmeal or toast and jam?" Benjamin offers.

"Yeah!" Silva replies with enthusiasm. Benjamin pulls out the bread and puts one piece in the toaster just as a heavy knock sounds at the door. Before he can say anything, Silva is up and running toward it.

She yanks it open to reveal a smiling Paulene and Victoria. "Reporting for duty," Victoria says with a wink.

"Come in," Benjamin calls before coming into the front room to introduce everyone. He is interrupted by the sound of the toaster popping. "I'll get that."

"We were just about to have breakfast—well, toast and jam, would you like some?" Cass offers as Benjamin returns to the kitchen.

Paulene nods, following Silva to the kitchen where Benjamin is buttering the first piece of toast. Victoria trails after her sister, with Cass coming back in behind her. Benjamin looks up from what he is doing to notice that Victoria is wearing a long skirt instead of pants. "Victoria, I see you don't plan on riding today."

"Not today. I've gotten used to motorized vehicles, so I'll just watch as Paulene and Silva show me how it's done," Victoria replies, smiling at her sister.

"Cass is a good rider, too," Paulene chimes in.

Benjamin just barely finishes putting on the jam when Silva and Paulene each reach for the single slice. "Silva, you know your manners. Sit down and wait for the next piece," Cass chastises.

The second piece of bread emerges from the toaster and Benjamin adds butter and jam before handing it to Silva. "Would you ladies like some toast?" They both shake their heads.

"What do you do in Yaphank?" Victoria asks Cass, trying to be polite.

"I'm the doctor. I get to see all the sick people."

"Wow. My mom's a nurse, and has been for probably over 20 years now," Victoria explains before turning to look at Silva. "Are you going to be a doctor, too?"

Silva shakes her head. "No, I'm more of an outside person. I'm going to be an explorer. I like hiking the trails and climbing the cliffs and if mom would let me, I'd jump on a raft and ride the river five or six towns down."

"And where would you go then?"

"To a place called 'get the hell outta here'," Silva replies and they all giggle.

"Silva, you and I are a lot alike," Victoria says with a smile.

Her eyes meet Victoria's. "What do you do?"

"Same as you in a way. I work at a social club, and I get together with all my friends around town and try to decide how to get outta town too."

Silva scrunches her eyebrows up, clearly confused by Victoria's words.

Benjamin puts another piece of bread in the toaster. "Cass, do you need me to saddle Glory?"

"No, if you have some errands to do, go right ahead. I think we girls can saddle and ride today all on our own. What do you girls think?"

Silva and Paulene shout with excitement, as they quickly stuff their mouths with the remaining toast on their plates.

As they start to run out the back door, Benjamin calls after them, "Do you want some cold milk to wash it down?"

Silva stops and turns to Benjamin. "That would be nice. Could you bring it out to us after Glory is saddled?"

He throws the folded towel over his arm and says with a British accent, "Yes, my lady, would there be anything else?"

Silva hesitates for a moment. "No, that will be all." Both girls run down the steps and toward the barn.

Cass steps to catch the back screen door before it can slam against the door frame. "Watch for snakes!" The girls slow their running, searching around their feet for snakes.

Cass then turns to Victoria. "Victoria, are you ready to get the day started?"

Victoria makes her way toward Cass, as Benjamin says, "Victoria, Julie's got some boots on the back porch you might want to wear."

Victoria looks down at her nice heels. "Okay, that's probably a good idea, thanks."

"I'll be out shortly. I do have something to do," Benjamin replies before disappearing back into the house.

"No hurry, we got it," Cassidy calls after him as Victoria sits to pull on Julie's boots.

Benjamin watches out the back window as Cass and Victoria walk towards the barn. He wishes he was a bit older...it would allow him to do so much more.

As soon as the women are out of sight, Benjamin runs upstairs to Jacob's old room, past the bed he has been sleeping in, and into the closet. He grabs an old baseball cap from a shelf and turns it over to reveal the blue tinted bottle Annie Mae had given him. He runs back downstairs and sets the bottle on the kitchen table. Moving to the refrigerator, he opens it and retrieves three amber glass bottles from the bottom rack. They are the

Orange Crush drinks Hamel had given him a few days earlier. He leaves one in the back as a spare.

Checking outside the window to ensure the girls are still occupied, he sets them on the table and studies the top of one of the bottles. He needs to somehow get it off but put it back on without damage. Deciding his powers are the best option, he hovers his hand over the bottle, moving it in a swirling motion.

The top twists slightly. He does the motion again.

Pop! The top releases.

Benjamin pours out a few swallows into a glass from the cupboard. He then carefully pours the potion back in the bottle until the liquid level is where it was before. The blue tinted bottle is still half full. He swirls the concoction around to mix it with the orange drink before putting the top on and tapping it firmly with his palm.

Using his fingernail, he scratches the label so he will remember which bottle has the potion, before taking the three bottles to Hal's truck. He pushes the seat forward and sets the bottles and potion behind the driver's seat, wedging some rags and an old towel around them so they won't break.

Satisfied that the drinks are secure, Benjamin jogs back to the kitchen, filling two glasses with chilled milk. He then opens the back door, holding the glasses of milk in one hand and the orange drink in a glass in the other. He walks toward the girls just as they finish saddling Glory.

"That was perfect timing," Cass says as she notices Benjamin approaching.

Benjamin, in his British accent, says, "Your milk as you asked, my ladies."

"It's about time, my servant," Silva jokes back as she takes one of the glasses. Paulene reaches for the other.

The two girls chug the milk quickly before handing the glasses back to Benjamin and jumping on Glory with Paulene mounting first. Within moments, they are off.

Benjamin holds the glass with the orange crush out to Victoria. "Here's a treat. It's an orange drink. Hamel gave me a few bottles last week"

Victoria shakes her head, "No, I'm fine."

Benjamin shrugs and holds it out to Cass. She takes the cup and takes a swig, then another. "That's good. It has a different taste, a little twang." She hands the cup back to Benjamin.

"Paulene seems to have gotten older since yesterday."

Victoria's mouth quirks up in the corner but she doesn't smile. "She thinks she's invincible with that necklace you gave her."

"I'm not going to tell her any different," Benjamin replies.

Victoria thinks for a moment before admitting, "It does give her confidence."

"That's a good thing," Benjamin insists.

Victoria purses her lips before looking at Benjamin out of the corner of her eye and saying, "We'll see."

Chapter 22

November 3, 1945
2:00pm
Hal's Truck, On the Road, Chatham Hill, Middle Tennessee

A FEW HOURS LATER, BENJAMIN, Cass, and Silva are once again in Hal's truck and on their way toward town. Benjamin keeps his eyes on the road except to occasionally look up at the mostly cloudy sky. He had been hoping for some sun today, but the weather hadn't obliged. Silva didn't seem to mind though, as she was still boundless with excitement.

Cass brushes a strand of Silva's hair back, tucking it behind her ear. "I want to thank you again for doing this. As you can see you've made her day."

"Well, you've made my day. I don't see my sisters much anymore. I enjoy spending time with you both and hope you are having a good time," Benjamin replies, looking over to smile at Cass before turning his eyes back to the road.

"I'll have to repay you one day for your kindness."

Benjamin doesn't say anything as they round the last curve. The straight road into town stretching before them, banners strung from every surface the eye can see. The first overhead banner is just past the jail, the letters 'Welcome—Harvest Fall Festival' in bold letters. Another matching sign adorns both the General Store and the bank.

"And when are the fireworks?" Silva asks, her eyes drinking in all the decorations.

"I think 9:00," Benjamin says.

"Hope it doesn't rain," Cass adds, eyeing the clouds herself.

"It might be later tonight," Benjamin grimaces.

The streets are packed, lined on both sides with vehicles of all shapes and sizes. The courthouse parking lot is filling up, but Benjamin notices an older car performing a u-turn in the street up ahead.

Silva points. "There's a spot."

Benjamin presses the gas pedal and heads for the spot. "We got lucky today."

Silva starts trying to pull off her jacket saying, "I'm hot. I don't need a jacket now."

"Well, leave it in the truck. We'll come back and get it later," Cass says, leaning out of the way as Silva pulls her arms out of the sleeves.

Benjamin parks the truck and they all jump out, Silva placing the jacket on the seat as she leaves. The minute her hands are free she begins to move quickly, looking at everything the fair has to offer.

Cass jogs ahead to catch up with Silva. "Young lady, you need to come here. Don't get so far ahead." Silva slows and takes Cass' outstretched hand. Benjamin trails a few steps behind them.

They pass the barricade into the festival, which is one of the few Chatham Hill police cars parked diagonally on the road. Benjamin's eyes immediately land on Cutter, who is patrolling near the edge of town. The street is filled with all types of people, some of who Benjamin has never seen. Some are sitting and eating, with kids running around and playing, and others are walking, seeing all the sights for themselves.

The General Store has a steady stream of people going in and out of the front door, which is propped open to give the tired hinges a break. The bank porch is full of people, obscuring the colorful banners hung on the bank windows. Benjamin's eyes are drawn to the many large banners in front of several buildings. Some have Adam Kieffer plastered on them, while others contain images of his opponent.

As he observes the event, Benjamin's eyes find Cutter again and he wonders whether or not he should mention the shallow graves at Yaphank. Cutter is the only person Benjamin trusts, but he's not sure that it won't get back to those on the force he doesn't trust, like Major. In the end, he decides to think about it, and maybe tell him later.

Benjamin follows the girls as they turn left toward the crowds. The noise level increases, and Benjamin practically has to shout to be heard by Cass and Silva. "Let's get something to eat down by the picnic tables."

They both nod and the trio begin to make their way to the picnic area, which is even more crowded than the street. Cass scans the area before turning to Benjamin. "We're going to the diner and get some food."

Benjamin reaches in his pocket for his wallet, but Cass stops him by putting her hand over his. "I got it. You coming in?"

"No, I'm going to look around. Just get me a hot dog with mustard and onions."

She nods and the two of them disappear into the crowded diner.

The sidewalk is littered with booths selling everything from cotton candy to ice cream cones, and Benjamin struggles to make his way through the throng of kids whose attention is focused on their snacks rather than watching where they are going.

As he makes his way toward the newspaper office, he passes a teenager who is handing out flyers to each individual within arms reach. Benjamin is handed one, which he tucks under his arm as he continues on his path.

When he reaches the newspaper office, he glances in the window to confirm Mr. Strickland is there before pushing open the door and heading inside.

The bell on the door dings, announcing his entrance.

"Good afternoon, Mr. Strickland. Remember me?" he asks, his voice strong.

Mr. Strickland comes out from the counter. "Oh, yes, Benjamin, right? You've gotten thicker in the shoulders and taller, but I never forget a face. How have you been? And your sister?"

"Amber is working at the hospital and doing great," Benjamin replies before diving right into the reason that he is there. "Say I've been reading your newspaper and want to thank you for all you do for the town and talking up this festival, it gets bigger every year."

"Well, thank you for saying that, it means a lot to me."

Benjamin's eyes focus on Mr. Strickland as he sits on a stool. "I would like to travel one day and I would like to be a businessman like you."

Mr. Strickland puffs out his chest in pride. "Would you like a job at the newspaper? You're young and smart."

"I hadn't thought about a job…" His mind stirs. "Maybe this summer? I don't know how to say this but here it goes, I want to know all you know about business."

Mr. Strickland raises an eyebrow. "It took me years to learn. There's no shortcut, son."

"What if I interview you? We could put excerpts in the Gazette. I want to know and I'm sure others want to know too."

He leans back into his chair. "Do you think so?"

"I know you own several papers. You travel between cities, right?" He nods. "Maybe I could chauffeur you and we can talk. I'll do it for free—you can't beat that."

Mr. Strickland leans forward. "I am getting old, and the travel is taking a toll on me. Maybe we can work something out, you let me know when you get out of school."

Benjamin's shoulders drop. "I don't have time for school, I've got too much to do."

"Get all the school you can, while it's free. That's my first piece of advice."

Benjamin knows that Mr. Strickland isn't going to change his view, so he changes the subject. "Yes sir. Have you heard anything about Stephen?"

"I've interviewed Fields, Fitzgerald's assistant, and he tells me his office is pushing his case out until the election Tuesday. His case is pending until the election results."

"Who's going to win the election you think?"

Mr. Strickland taps his chin in thought. "The big money is backing the new kid, Kieffer. Usually the money wins."

"If he wins, Stephen's case will kind of start over, right?"

"No, the evidence isn't changing." Mr. Strickland lets out a long breath, like the air flowing out of a balloon.

Benjamin waits to see if he will say anything else, but as the silence stretches on, he starts to get a bit anxious. "I better go. I got friends to meet." He stands from his chair.

Mr. Strickland reaches out his hand for Benjamin to give him a firm handshake. "First lesson is a good first impression. You've got a good handshake and your eyes are spirited."

"Thank you, sir. I'll be talking with you soon," Benjamin promises before bidding him goodbye and heading out the door back toward the diner, his eyes searching for Cass and Silva.

They aren't on any of the benches, so Benjamin peers into the windows of the diner, but they aren't there either. His eyes begin to skim the crowd, catching on the sight of Elliott who is headed toward the area housing the rides. As he passes, he finally sees Cass and Silva sitting on a bench a ways out, and rushes over to meet them.

"Why are you eating way down here?"

"Didn't seem to be so crowded down here," Cass says as she slides him a hot dog and he takes a big bite before removing a few bills from his pocket. Cass holds up her hands. "I told you that..."

Benjamin slides the bills into Silva's pocket instead. "I know, I know. This is just in case."

"In case of what?" Silva asks, eyes wide.

He looks straight into her eyes. "In case you need it, you got it?"

Cass looks over Silva's shoulder and into the crowd. "See someone you know?" Benjamin asks.

"Too many," she replies sadly as Silva begins to turn her head. Cass snaps at her. "Silva finished eating." Silva turns back to her food, her eyes downcast. Benjamin looks over where she was looking.

His eyes fall on a bench across the street, a large group of kids laughing and running back and forth to a few adults sitting on another bench nearby. "I think I saw Roddy and a few of his kids," Cass informs him.

"How many has he got?"

Silva begins to turn her head again. Cass chastises her a second time, "Silva." Silva turns back to her mother, and she gets a look. Cass doesn't answer Benjamin's question.

Silva finishes off the last few bites from her hands. "Can I have some of that?" She points to the cotton candy.

"Sure, you can." Benjamin smiles. "Use the money I gave you." Silva looks at Cass, who nods her permission. Silva bolts toward the cotton candy stand.

Cass finishes her food. "Did you say you had some friends to see?"

"Yeah, but I—"

Cass interrupts him. "Maybe you need to go and do your thing, and we'll see you in a couple hours."

Benjamin tried to apologize. "I didn't mean to—"

Cass cuts him off again. "There are people here we know. We just need them to keep their distance."

Benjamin can sense that she doesn't want him around. "Okay. I'll go do my thing and you all have fun."

"That's best," Cass says as Silva returns, pink cotton candy clasped in her hands.

"Want some?" she asks Benjamin.

"No, I've got—"

Cass interrupts. "He's got business to tend to." Cass takes Silva's empty hand. "Let's go." Silva looks at Benjamin's face, which is occupied with a smile, as her mother pulls her away.

Benjamin walks in the opposite direction. His curiosity gets the better of him, however, and he circles back around to the benches to find the kids he saw before jumping and laughing with a man in the shadows. He steps towards the shadow and his eyes adjust to see Burn.

Burn is playing tag with some kids, and Benjamin feels his jaw drop at the way they all seem so happy to be around him. Benjamin has never seen Burn smiling and laughing so much. He also notices that Burn is passing out candy and bubble gum from his pockets to every kid that comes within talking distance of him.

Benjamin realizes in the same instant that Cass didn't want Burn to see them. He isn't sure why, or what happened between them, but he knew that if it had been important, Cass would have told him.

He takes one last look at Burn and all the happy children before heading the same direction he saw Cass and Silva head in just a few minutes before.

Benjamin finds the girls without much issue, and begins following them through the grounds, watching them smiling and laughing. They also ride on the rides, play games, and just spend some time sitting and talking.

Watching them lean back on a bench as they chat, Benjamin is reminded of his sisters. They used to just sit and talk like that, whether they were in their living room, or walking to school. But now things have changed, and he feels more distant from his sisters than ever before.

Chapter 23

November 3, 1945
3:00pm
Chatham Hill Township, Middle Tennessee

BENJAMIN IS SO LOST in his thoughts, that he nearly jumps a foot in the air when a hand slaps him on the back. In shock, he spins around to find none other than Roddy looking at him.

"Benjamin...how ya' been?" Roddy smiles.

Benjamin smiles in response. "Great! I see your arm has healed. It was smashed up pretty bad."

"It gives me trouble when the weather changes, but I've gotten used to it." Roddy rolls his shoulder as he answers.

"How's Lucy?"

The smile falls from his face. "They are doing fine."

Benjamin opens his mouth to push for a more detailed answer but then he realizes he better not pry any further, otherwise it could come back to hurt Silva and Cass.

"I got something for ya'—" Roddy says, "—meet me behind the feed and seed in about 30 minutes."

"Okay. What's back there?"

"Just got something for ya'." Roddy turns to leave. "30 minutes," he reiterates.

Benjamin nods in agreement, watching Roddy stalk off before turning back to the bench to find Silva and Cass are no longer there. He does a quick scan of the crowd, but he doesn't see them in any direction.

He walks around for about 15 minutes, but there is no sign of them. As he continues to search, he runs into a couple of girls from school. One of them is Maria, who is wearing a fall dress, her hair woven into a braid, something which suits her.

"How are you girls doing?" Benjamin asks.

The girls' eyes all light up at the sight of Benjamin, all of them wishing he was theirs and tossing envious looks at Maria, who is clearly the best looking of the three.

Benjamin gives Maria a once over. "Maria, that's a beautiful dress, but are you going to be able to ride any rides?"

"You tell me," she says back. "Are we riding any rides? Don't let this dress stop you."

Benjamin shakes his head, a smile on his face. "I tell you what. You wear that dress on any ride, and I'll be right there." All the girls snicker. "Where's Susie?"

"She is around...why?" Maria replies.

"You said she has eyes for Danny Boy," Benjamin says, trying to get the information he needs without revealing why he really wants it.

"That was two weeks ago. She's talked to him since and she hates his guts now."

Benjamin's shoulders slump. But that doesn't stop him from giving Maria a second look up and down. He really wouldn't mind kissing her later. The big question is whether he should wait until the fireworks or try to do it on a ride.

Before he can come to a decision, his eyes catch on Elliott, who is standing with Danny several yards away. "I've got to go. Maria, save me a ride later."

"Okay. The answer might not be the same later," she says sweetly, twirling a piece of hair on her pointer finger as Benjamin walks away.

He isn't quick enough though, and Danny disappears down an alley before he can reach him. Changing plans, he heads for Hal's truck.

When he reaches the truck, he opens the door quickly and flips the seat up. His eyes bug out as he realizes there are only two bottles, not three. Looking around the truck to double check, he also realizes that Silva's jacket is gone. They must've doubled back while he was talking to Roddy or Maria.

"My god," he groans quietly, "I've poisoned the people I love."

Just then, he remembers that he marked the bottles and he quickly lifts them to evaluate them. Bottle one has no scratch on the label, and his heart quickens. He squeezes his eyes closed as he lifts bottle two, opening them to see a telltale scratch across the words.

He pauses a moment to send a quick prayer. Everything is going to be okay.

He grabs the two orange Crush bottles and the blue tinted bottle of potion and slides it into his jacket pocket before turning around to rush to where he last saw Danny.

As he reaches the general store, he sees Cass and Silva sitting on a bench on the sidewalk, sipping the orange crush.

Turning, he resumes his path toward Danny, only to notice Burn eyeing him from where he is leaning up against a store wall.

"I'll give you a dollar for one of those orange pops," Burn calls to him.

Benjamin just nods and waves, pretending he didn't hear him.

Turning down the alley, Benjamin turns in place looking for Danny, only to see his personal truck backed up against the back of a store. Danny is standing with another boy, but backs up as he catches sight of Benjamin.

Benjamin signals him over. "Are you working today?"

Danny reluctantly approaches. "I work all the time. What the hell do you want?"

"Got something for ya'," Benjamin says excitedly.

"Better be a beer or stronger."

"No, just a cold bottle of orange pop. Just a 'thank you' for letting me take your delivery to Yaphank."

Danny looks back at the boys loading something into his truck. He doesn't make a move to take the soda in Benjamin's outstretched hand.

"I insist, I've been carrying these around for a week or so, just for you." Benjamin twists the top off his bottle and takes a long swig. "It's good."

Danny eyes Benjamin's throat as it bobs with his swallow. He's still suspicious.

"If you don't want it, give it to one of your helpers." Benjamin holds the bottle out.

Danny grabs it and in one fluid motion, twists the top off and throws the top to the ground.

He takes a couple of long gulps and swallows. "Dammit, that tastes awful." His head twitches.

"Mine's twangy, too, just swirl it around a bit." Benjamin urges.

He looks at Benjamin's bottle before swirling his own and taking another long swig. He swallows. "That's even worse." He tosses the bottle to the side. It lands on the ground and begins to spill.

"Mine tasted fine, must have been a bad batch," Benjamin insists.

"Get the hell out of here." He waves his arm and turns his back, heading back to his truck.

As Danny walks away, Benjamin retrieves the half bottle and pours the remainder of the bottle out. He then turns to leave, chugging the rest of his soda.

He recalls the meeting with Roddy at the feed and seed and grimaces as he realizes it is past the 30-minute mark. He picks up his pace, tossing the empty soda bottle in the trash before jogging the rest of the way to the feed and seed.

When he arrives, he spots Roddy, leaning against a fence railing. "Glad you could make it."

"Kind of out of the way," Benjamin replies, looking around.

"That's the point. I got people watching me wherever I go."

Roddy slips his hand into his jacket and pulls out a small brown bottle. He hands it to Benjamin. "This is a gift to let you know I appreciate your help in the garage that day."

"But I don't drink—"

Roddy interrupts. "It's 'shine. It'll grow hair on your nuts."

"Well, thanks, I'll try it later," Benjamin hedges.

"Be careful with it. Just don't put it near a fire."

Benjamin still isn't sure about the gift, but he sees how excited Roddy is about it, so he slips it into his pocket. "Thank you, I'll let you know how it goes."

"Enjoy." Roddy gives him a last nod before heading back toward the crowded streets.

Benjamin glances around to be sure he is alone before taking a closer look at the small bottle. He removes the top and smells. His nostrils flare.

"It smells like something that would run Hal's truck," he whispers to himself.

At the same instant, a brilliant idea comes to him.

He knows how to get Danny to drink more of the potion.

Quickly, he runs back over to where he last saw Danny, only to find the alleyway is empty. With a sigh, he turns to head back to the street to see Danny's truck parked behind another store.

Tucking himself back around the side of the building he checks to be sure no one is nearby before retrieving the small blue bottle from his pocket, holding it to the light to see how much is left.

Opening the brown bottle, Benjamin takes a short swig. He immediately bends over and puts his hands on his knees, breathless at the burn in his throat. He decides to pour out just enough to make space for the remaining poison. He hesitates and decides to take another short swig.

Pouring the poison in carefully, Benjamin twists the cap back on the brown bottle, shaking to mix it together. Then, with a satisfied smile, he begins the hunt for Danny.

~~~

The search takes longer than he had anticipated, and with the distraction of Maria, it was now nearing dusk and Benjamin was no closer
~~~

to finding Danny. That was, until he spotted him ducking into an alley delivering supplies to the diner.

Unfortunately for him, Danny hears him coming before he can get close. "Get the hell away from me kid. Leave me alone."

"Sorry about before, but I got some 'shine." Benjamin holds out the brown bottle.

"Shine? Where did you get that?" His eyes are focused on the bottle.

"I got friends." He smirks. "This will clear out your sinuses."

"You try it first."

Benjamin is caught off guard.

"You try it, then I will." Danny insists a second time.

Benjamin mentally searches for an escape but he finds none. He slowly puts the brown bottle to his lips and takes a small swig before holding it out in Danny's direction. It hits his throat like lightning, he coughs. He looks up to see Danny swig on the brown bottle. "Now that is good stuff."

Benjamin is relieved that his plan worked, but the relief is short lived as Danny says, "I ain't drinking alone take another swig with me."

Benjamin grimaces, but accepts the bottle back from Danny, taking another small sip. Danny sees this however, and tilts the bottle so a large amount passes between Benjamin's lips.

Benjamin's eyes roll back into his head, and he has to lean against the building for support.

"I don't like drinking alone."

Benjamin can't answer, his eyes drifting closed of their own accord, his mind going dark.

Chapter 24

November 5, 1945
11:00pm
Mooney's, Outside Chatham Hill Township, Middle Tennessee

WALTER, GOT AN ORDER for table eight ready yet?" Victoria calls as she steps out of the locker room.

"Yeah!" He sets two bowls on the tray. "Oh, here's hot sauce and some crackers."

Victoria studies the ticket. "Two beers," she mumbles and rotates her head on her shoulder, trying to relax.

"These late hours will get to you young kids, one day." Walter chuckles from behind the line.

She smiles and massages her neck with her own hand. "How's your wife working out for ya'?"

"She's dead to me now."

Victoria's eyes widened. "Does everybody know or did you bury her deep enough?"

Walter grins. "No, that stupid old coot took off to her sisters in Tallahassee."

"She coming back?"

"Hell, yeah, it's too hot for her down there. She'll be back someday, dammit."

"Walter, it's a shame she ain't got a sister in Boston." Victoria continues trying to massage her neck.

"That's the God's honest truth, Ms. Driver."

Not having any success relaxing the knot in her neck, she decides to try a different tactic. "Walter, would you be a dear?" Walter nods and steps over and starts massaging her neck. "Walter, you've got some great hands...if you were 30 years younger, and not married, we could go somewhere."

"You're pretty enough even if I was married we could still go somewhere," he jokes.

She steps away and gives Walter a kiss on the cheek. "I bet if your wife kissed you like that she wouldn't run off to Florida."

"Hell, I ain't going to let her get that close."

Victoria picks up the tray and turns to go. "If she comes back into town, let me know, don't sound like Sweet's going to take care of it. I will, I promise."

"I'll hold you to it, Ms. Driver."

Victoria heads out the swinging doors, making a beeline to the bar for the beers. "Seven, two beers," she snaps with a yawn. "Everything okay tonight?"

Seven shrugs. "It's busy as hell, all these soldiers coming back from the war. Sweet's making a killing."

"I was wondering where all the uniforms came from."

"They'll be hot to score and wild as hell tonight." Seven shakes his head and continues with a chuckle, "You better keep your legs crossed, even to pee." He sets the two beers on her tray.

The music coming from the stage crescendos, and Victoria has to admit that Sweet did have good taste in music. The latest hire was a group that had it all, guitar, violin, and piano. They were a rag tag integrated group, but no one seemed to care because the music was perfect for dancing.

Dropping off the food and the beers, she asks the husky men for payment, "That's two bits each." She lays the napkins down and waits for the money.

"Put it on our account," the man on the left says, taking a swig of his beer.

"We don't have accounts around here," Victoria replies, her foot tapping.

The other man lifts his beer, swallowing a large gulp. "Oh, that's got a good taste." His eyes meander up and down Victoria's body. "What time do you get off?"

"That's two bits each," she repeats. The beer taster reaches out and grabs Victoria's arm, she looks down at it, venom in her gaze. "You're new, I guess?"

"Yes, ma'am," the man holding her arm replies.

"Well, I suggest you put your hand in your pocket and let me see some money." Victoria tilts her head to the side, annoyed.

The man makes no move to release his grip. Tobin, one of the largest men in town, takes notice from his position leaning against the wall and walks toward the table. "Any problem here?" he asks Victoria.

Victoria turns and a smile grows across her face. "Tobin, long time no see." Her eyes flick back to the man's hand on her bicep. "Tobin, I would give you a hug, but this gentleman has a hold—" The man releases her arm. "I'd love to catch up with you, but these guys haven't paid so they might be leaving real quick."

Two coins clank on her tray.

Tobin peers over her head at the two men. "Are they good tippers?"

She looks at the money on her tray. "Not really, nothing special."

Tobin looks at the two men a second time, and both rush to pull another coin from their pockets and add to the tray.

Victoria glances back. "Yeah, they are good tippers." Tobin smiles. "You kids need anything else give me a call," Victoria calls over to the table before grabbing Tobin's hand and leading him away. "I've missed you, you never told me you were going away."

"I'm sorry, I did come back several nights after our first encounter, but you never showed." Tobin leans in, his voice hushed.

"Well, tonight we are busy as hell, and I can't talk to you like I want."

"That's okay, just seeing you, and that you remember my name, has made my day. Do you work tomorrow?" Tobin brings his hand to her arm to lightly brush the skin where the man at the table had grabbed on to her.

"Yeah, but I work so late it wouldn't be fair—"

"How about lunch or coffee here before you start work?"

Victoria opens her mouth to reply, but is interrupted by a table calling for service. She looks over and motions that she heard them before turning back to Tobin. "Listen, here is not a good place. There are too many jealous people around."

Tobin's eyebrows furl. "Can we dance tonight?"

Victoria smiles, she loves the word dancing, but she's also got a lot on her mind and quickly taps the bar twice to get Seven's attention, holding up two fingers. He nods.

"Where do you live?" Tobin asks, drawing her attention back to him.

"I live in Chatham Hill. It's—"

He interrupts. "Meet me at the diner... 1:00pm."

Victoria shakes her head. "No, listen, they got a Festival in town. Tonight and tomorrow. How about Monday, same diner, 1:00pm?"

"That sounds great. It's a date," Tobin replies with a smile.

Victoria looks over to see she has a minute more as Seven finishes pouring the two beers. "Where have you been the last six months?"

"Went to Europe for a while. Been back and forth, you know, army stuff."

She looks him over quickly. "You don't look shot up."

"I've been lucky." Seven sets the two beers on her tray, quickly grabbing the two coins for them from her tray.

She turns to go. "See you Monday," she calls, his eyes following her across the floor and into the poker room.

She brushes past several regular patrons, including Slayter, who's been waiting to order. "How about getting me a beer. You know what I like," he says in a low voice.

"I know what you like is to break the rules," Victoria retorts, practically rolling her eyes at his audacious display.

"I'm thirsty. You owe me one."

"I do? Remind me of the favor you have done me."

He quickly searches his mind, clearly making something up. "People have been asking about you."

"They have?" Victoria's voice carries no surprise, just boredom at Slayter's tactics.

"That's the favor. As long as I keep them off your ass, you stay safe."

"I didn't ask for that."

"Mr. Sweet told me to, and 'cause I got this." He folds his jacket back to reveal a holstered gun.

His story is getting more unbelievable by the minute. "Mr. Sweet told you to keep me safe?" She raises her eyebrow.

"He told us all."

"Hm." Victoria brushes an invisible speck of dust from her skirt. "I appreciate you fellows helping me out, but if you want a beer, Seven will have to serve you one right over there. Or wait an hour."

"An hour?"

"Yep." Victoria grins.

Slayter's eyes narrow and he leans in close. "Let me give you a word of advice, girl. Get a gun. Carry a gun. Peoples around here will take you out and rape the shit out of ya' ten times and throw your ass in a ditch. You hear?"

She nods.

"I'm serious about these people asking about you, ain't no joke," he insists.

Victoria is shocked by his words, and not sure what else to say. She gasps, "Let me get you a beer." Slayter smiles.

She returns to the bar, heading right up to Seven and putting her tray down. "Seven beers, four whiskeys, and one shine, oh, and put one of those beers in two of those big coffee cups." He holds out his palm and she drops a few coins.

As she is waiting, Jesse sets her tray beside Victoria and says, "You had any trouble with any of the customers tonight?"

Victoria inspects her fingernails, her voice bored. "I have lots of trouble at work. It's like wrestling with a herd of bears, or whatever you call a bunch of horny guys."

Jesse shakes her head. "They wear me down too." She twirls a small strand of her hair back with her fingers.

Seven empties the dry beer mug with cash and coins into his till and starts putting the order onto Victoria's tray.

The next words out of Jesse's mouth shock Victoria. "You got a gun for protection?" She leans in closer so as not to attract attention. "Listen, a week after I started. Elijah told me he'd protect me, but I learned quick, he's only here for six to seven hours when we work. We're on our own the rest of the time. Two weeks ago, a strange car with their headlights kind of startled me at a road stop. I got the gun out and fired three shots close to their car." Jesse smiles. "They drove right off. Ain't seen the car since. Now be careful, I went to grab it fast one night and grabbed the trigger first and it went off in the car. If someone had been in the back seat, I woulda' shot their legs out from under them—"

Seven empties Jesse's mug into the till, snapping the two women back to the present, Victoria realizing the tray has been ready for a few moments. "Jesse, you're my hero," she says, hoisting the tray off the counter.

"Hero, hell no, they end up dead." Jesse shakes her head, but she is still smiling, "Just remember, shoot first and often."

Victoria repeats her previous loop, dropping off drinks as she goes by until once again she reaches Slayter, who's eyes have been watching her motions hungrily. "Here you go."

Slayter looks at the coffee cups. "You brought me coff..." A smile comes to his face as he grabs up both coffee cups. "I love you, Victoria, have I told you that before?"

"About a hundred times."

"You ain't bothered by me speaking my mind?"

"No, your mind isn't what I'm afraid of." Victoria shakes her head with a smile playing on her lips.

He works up a smile and sips the cup. "Oh, yeah, that's some good coffee."

She leans in, her lips close to his ear. "Listen, you gave me some advice, let me give you some." He sips again but keeps his eyes on hers. "If them dogs ever race at me again. I'll put their asses on the roof, you hear."

He rolls his eyes as she walks away but his lips move anyway. "Yes, ma'am."

Chapter 25

PETE CIRCLES HIS CAR around the building, pulling to a stop in the back. Looking over his shoulder, he backs the car as close to the door as possible, as he was instructed. As soon as the vehicle is stationary, shadows move to make the transfer.

Once that is done, the product is packed into the women's storage room on the opposite wall from the lockers. Roddy and Pete head into the bar, Roddy grabbing a beer while Pete heads directly to Mr. Sweet's office.

He passes the usual patrons, rolling his eyes at some of their antics. Mooney's never changes.

Arriving at the office door, Boots pats him down, Pete smirking as he doesn't find anything. He left his gun in the car for this exact reason.

Elijah cracks his office door and calls him inside, "Pete."

Pete follows the instructions, closing the door behind him, only to back up a step when he notices Slayter is also in the room. This wasn't how the deliveries normally went.

Without any warning, Slayter steps forward and punches him in the gut. Pete doubles over in pain, allowing Slayter to grab the back of his collar and pull him into a chair directly across the desk from Sweet's.

"Pete, we have talked many times...Are you listening?" Pete gasps for air. "Let me know when you can listen." Elijah stands and takes a couple steps towards his personal bar. Pouring himself a short drink into a nice crystal glass, he takes a sip, his eyes on his collection. Boots enters Sweet's office and eases the door shut.

Finally, Pete stops his gasping and nods for Elijah to continue.

Elijah swirls his whiskey. "You see Pete, it's so easy to lose your breath, isn't it Pete? We have chatted many times about different ways we can work this predicament between us out, but we never can come to an agreement." Pete's face is reddening, but Elijah continues without pause, "Pete, you're lucky, I could have gotten my guys to beat you around the face, but you're a good-looking kid so I thought one small thump would get your attention. Did we get your attention?" Pete nods yes.

"Tell Bernard that our business arrangement has changed. We know where you live, your cousin lives and Burn lives. Tell him that the price he charges is going to be cut in half. He supplies the same amount, but we don't want you back up here. We're going to work out a different way to get the 'shine...and if he changes the recipe we'll serve his batch to his good friends around Chatham Hill." Elijah walks around his desk and gets some bills out of his top drawer. "Stand up, Pete." Pete wobbles to his feet. "Per our new agreement, you have given us today's delivery at half price." Pete looks down at the measly number of bills. "Thank you. You can count it later and get back to me if you think I'm short." Pete folds it over and begins to stick it in his front pocket. "Have you got any questions, Pete?"

Pete struggles out a sound, but it comes out more of a cough.

"Did you say trouble, Pete?" Elijah raises his eyebrows, Pete nods. "I hope you weren't threatening me, Pete?"

Pete vigorously shakes his head from side to side.

"I see you're angry, and confused, and your family will retaliate but you see where your family shoots at deer and raccoons, my guys shoot tires on moving vehicles, gas tanks, windshields, houses, power lines, and so many other things. Are you going to remember all we've talked about, Pete?

I hope we can work together, but if not, so be it. My boys are looking for something to do in this cold weather, anyway." With a nod, Slayter and Boots each grab one of Pete's arms and drag him to the door. "Goodbye, Pete. Have a safe trip home."

Just then, Boots punches Pete in the gut again. Pete folds over to the floor, unconscious.

Elijah sighs, his eyes on Pete's unmoving figure. "You didn't hit him on the same side, did you?"

"No, sir, the other side, we're taking turns," Slayter replies.

"That's good, just not the face, he's a looker. You know where he's parked?" They nod. "Search his car. Then get that other brother, or cousin, to drive them both out of here."

The men agree and hoist Pete's arms over each of their shoulders to escort him out of the office and through the bar, Victoria's eyes following their motions. As they approach the back door, she follows.

As they pass through the kitchens, Walter steps directly in front of Victoria. "Not now, Ms. Driver, another time, another place." She tries to step around him, but he blocks her efficiently, stepping to the opposite side as she does the same. "I'm serious," he hisses.

Victoria purses her lips, but knows he is right, turning from their confrontation to head into the locker room. Not sure what else to do, she slams the door, sliding down to sit in front of it, putting her head in her hands.

She groans. "What am I supposed to do?"

~~~

Outside, the two men drop Pete in a heap alongside his car. They signal to someone alongside the building, before murmuring amongst themselves and beginning the destruction of the car.

They tear out everything, tossing items to the ground before taking a knife to the seats. A bottle is found, and it smashes as it is thrown to the ground, the shatter ringing through the chilly night air. A handgun is found under the seat. Slayter hands it to one of their employees.
~~~

Just as they are about to finish their assault, the man they motioned to earlier returns to the porch, Roddy in hand.

The man pushes him to the driver's side door, his eyes on Pete's unmoving form. "Is he alive?"

Slayter watches Boots. "He is right now. Maybe not later, it's up to you."

Boots has taken the keys from Roddy's pocket and uses them to search the trunk, tossing a tire iron and the car jack to the ground. He slams the trunk shut.

Slayter forces Roddy into the driver's seat, tossing the keys at him. "Drive home, don't stop, and don't have a flat." Roddy nods furiously as a pistol is cocked and aimed at his head.

"Get in and drive, make sure Bernard gets the message." The voice isn't from Boots or Slayter. There's a thump in the back seat.

Not wanting to take any chances, Roddy shoves the keys in the ignition, throwing the car into gear, and guns it out of the parking lot as fast as the potholes and other vehicles will let him. He doesn't stop, speeding up when he reaches the road, barreling over the bridge.

Once he is past the wooden slats, he slows, reaching into the back seat. "Pete? Pete, are you okay?" His hand feels a shoulder, but Pete doesn't answer him.

Roddy knows it isn't safe to stop yet, so he speeds back up until he makes the turn onto the main road. Once he is sure he is out of Mr. Sweet's domain, he pulls the car to a stop on the shoulder, climbing out and opening the back door.

Pete is still unconscious, his breath labored due to the crunched-up position he was shoved into the car in. Roddy tries to straighten him up, arranging his friend's arm under his head in hopes it will be a more comfortable position. Once that is done, he sighs, "Let me get us out of here and back to Coweta." He climbs back into the driver's seat and slams the door, dust billowing behind the car as he speeds off into the night.

~~~
~~~

Victoria stays in the locker room for a long time, telling Walter to go away when he knocks a few minutes later. Once it is silent, she goes to her locker, opening it to look at the mirror she hung inside.

Her voice in a whisper, she hisses to her reflection. "I ought to burn this place down and start all over. The people here are ugly and—" She pauses. "Actually, I guess I'll play their game." A smile spreads across her face. "I do like games. Surely, I can outsmart them. It'll just take a little time and a little skill..." She slams the locker door shut with a chuckle, a satisfied grin on her lips.

Chapter 26

November 6, 1945
1:45am
Mooney's Bar, Outside Chatham Hill Township,
Middle Tennessee

VICTORIA ABSENTMINDEDLY REMOVES AN empty beer mug from her tray and wipes it down, thinking of everything that had occurred earlier that night. Distracted by her thoughts, she moves to start wiping down tables, hoping that Jesse has also begun her end of night duties so they can leave at a decent time—considering they had just performed last call.

Torn by her emotions, Victoria finishes cleaning and heads to Mr. Sweet's office, pausing with her hand on the doorknob.

Sweet sees Victoria begin to enter his office as he comes down the stairs. Feeling her resolve strengthen, she finally pushes open the door, her nose filling with the scents of cigar smoke and whiskey. Mr. Sweet is not there.

"Why, Victoria, this is an unexpected treat." Elijah's voice comes from behind her, along the staircase, his hand resting on the banister. "Sit down."

As he enters his office behind Victoria, he motions to one of the chairs. She sits.

Victoria takes note of his appearance. He is wearing a button-down shirt, with the top buttons popped to reveal his dark chest hair.

Victoria struggles to start the conversation. "How is your wrist?"

"You did a number on it. I hope you know it's still tender to the touch," Elijah replies, pulling his sleeve over the still obvious red patch on his wrist. He comes to stand behind her, placing his hands on her shoulders, causing her to jolt in surprise. "It's been a long night, maybe you need some company," he whispers in her ear as he begins to massage her shoulders. His fingers moved expertly through her muscles in a way that Walter's didn't.

She begins to relax, her eyes drifting closed. Without meaning to, she opens her mouth and lets out a moan.

The sound jolts her back to the present, and she stands from the chair and turns to face Elijah. "We need to talk, and I want some answers."

He steps around and sits in the other chair. "Sure, sure, ask away."

Victoria swallows, her throat dry. Spotting a pitcher on a side table, she pours herself a glass of water and tosses it back. Elijah keeps his eyes on her, unblinking.

"What happened to Pete?" she says at last, her voice still sounding rough despite the water.

Elijah shifts in his seat. "Do you know what Pete and Roddy deliver?"

"Yes, I do. I see the crates and boxes stacked in our locker room."

He nods. "Of course you do, I believe, if my memory serves, your first visit with them to this house, they delivered 'shine, and I think you helped them carry it in."

"Maybe, I don't recall. That was so many months ago."

"Your memory is just fine." He smirks. "Pete and I had a business meeting, in which I laid down some rules and he agreed to them."

Victoria tilts her head to the side, sensing the lie in his words. "Why did you have to carry him out?"

"It took a minute for him to agree."

"That's not the way meetings go."

He nonchalantly replies with a flip of his hand, "That's the way I do meetings."

"I guess they won't be back up here anytime soon?"

"It depends on their boss." Elijah rubs a hand down his jaw. "He'll have to decide the easy way or the hard way."

Victoria shakes her head. Elijah doesn't know the way things are, and she tells him so. "You don't understand us country folks. The only way we know is the hard way."

Elijah's gaze hardens. "You have to choose which side you're on."

"I thought I had been doing that with my actions?" she asks, smug.

Elijah holds up his wrist. "What about this?"

She smiles. "That was just a moment of passion, you can't hold that against me."

"I don't forget when it hurts...and this hurts."

Victoria begins to ever so slowly stroll behind Elijah's desk with her eyes circling from the ceiling to the pictures on the walls to every item on his desk.

"I remember as if it were yesterday." His jaw shifts in disdain before he continues, "Oh, it was a special day for me." She spots his shaded globe lamp, pens lined up in a row, and a monthly calendar covered with scribbles.

He watches her sashay around his desk and twirl his chair around like a dancer choreographing her moves. "Why special?" she asks.

He crosses his legs and hands and watches her with a sly smile. "You had a twinkle of conviction in your soul. I could see it."

Her eyes settle on the newspaper on his desk, the front page story about the upcoming election.

Elijah shifts in his seat. "Do you like nice things?" he asks, his eyes dancing with mischief.

She slows her walk, intrigued. "Yes. I enjoy nice things."

He looks at her body swaying. "How about travel? New York, Chicago...I see you're a dancer, strong legs and agile. Maybe Broadway shows, musicals, nice restaurants..."

Her ears perk up. "Oh, I would enjoy going to those."

"If you play your cards right..." he hedges, but Victoria sees right through him.

"You mean if I was your girlfriend?"

His eyes gain a spark which wasn't there before, his eyes looking over her form with obvious lust. "Yes, you are a smart young lady. You would do well."

She strolls around the desk closer to him. "I can think for myself and wear the right clothes, and bat my eyes to flirt with a man, but that's for another time."

"Another time?" he gulps.

Victoria smirks, knowing she's won. "I've got to see how things work out around here, before I can leave."

"Anything in particular?"

She shrugs. "Maybe I'll tell you...in due time." She leans on the corner of the desk, a leg on either side. Elijah eyes her hungrily and reaches out with his injured hand. She sees his mouth watering. "What did you learn?"

Desperate to change the subject, he asks, "Can you lightly rub my wrist?"

She takes his hand and sits in the chair beside him, crossing her legs in a ladylike fashion. She looks at his reddened wrist and lightly rubs it. "Maybe some lotion would make it feel better."

Elijah shifts his position. "Probably so... Lighter." She drags her fingertips along his wrist. "I learned that I want a powerful woman in my life and not one that acts like she's a victim all the time."

"Is that so?" Victoria asks, her eyes still on his wrist.

"Yes, that's so...and I have had my eye on you." Seeing her gaze, he adds, "Pete was acting like a victim and I just had to set him straight."

"You hurt him."

"Sometimes we hurt people we care about." He looks down at his wrist. "Like you hurt me. We are not enemies, Victoria, we are more than friends though." Her eyes jump to meet his. "I know your secrets, your powers, your aspirations now." Elijah moves his uninjured hand to grasp one of hers.

"My aspirations?"

"Yes, you want to enjoy, as you said, the finer things in life. And I can help you achieve that." He releases her hand and slides it along the side of her face.

She leans into his open palm.

Encouraged, he scoots her up from the chair, bringing them closer together. He shifts his hand to her neck, bringing their lips together in a tender kiss. The kiss drags on, and when they part for air, it's Victoria who leans in first, and they kiss a second time.

When they break for air again, Victoria comes to her senses and pushes out of his grasp, standing, her chest rising and falling as she tries to catch her breath. She smooths her dress down. "I'm sorry, I'm not a woman that knows what she wants. "

"That's what I'm looking for."

Victoria shakes her head. "You know what I'm looking for?" He doesn't say anything. "A man of his word. You remember the deal we made about Stephen and his release?"

Elijah evaluates the question. "Vaguely."

"Vaguely? Your memory is better than that. It was a kiss."

"I suppose you—"

Victoria cuts him off. "That's right, I've held up my end of the deal. Now we'll see if you can hold up your end."

Elijah's face begins to redden in anger, and before Victoria can take a step, he stands and steps in her direction, his hand coming up to encircle her throat and push her up against the wall. He pushes her with such force that two of the pictures on the wall come crashing to the floor.

Victoria begins to struggle, trying to raise her arms to defend herself, but Elijah presses his body to hers so she can't move them. As she struggles, she can feel his arousal through his pants.

"Life is a game, Ms. Driver, you better learn that there ain't no rules—" He shifts his right hand from her wrist over her head, his other hand drifting to the apex of her legs to rub her through her dress, "—or you'll be dead before you can enjoy it."

His eyes slowly drift down to her lips. He kisses her and Victoria finds herself kissing him back. His hand remains between her legs, and she finds herself enjoying his touch, causing her to moan.

The kiss continues...and continues, until suddenly he bites down on her lip, hard.

"Ouch!" Elijah backs away, a smile on his lips. She reached up to touch her lip, seeing the blood, red, on her finger when she pulled it away. "What did you do that for?"

"You better get used to it. I like it rough." Victoria reaches up to feel her neck as she steps away from the wall.

Elijah moves to the table with the water pitcher, pouring himself a whiskey and tossing it back. "That was a kiss. I enjoyed that. I'm convinced you satisfied your part of our arrangement now. Were you satisfied?" She is silent. "Now, we can complete the deal you talked about...how about the end of this week?"

She steps towards the chair, her mind racing. "This week?"

"Yes, I think I can get Stephen released by the end of the week." He pours another quick shot. "Would you like a drink?"

She feels her lip again. "No, it's late, I have a long way to go."

He hands her a napkin from the bar. "Here, use this." She reaches out and takes it, but he doesn't back away and grabs her hand instead.

"Listen to me, you don't have to go home tonight."

"Yes, I do," Victoria insists.

"No, listen, a bath or shower upstairs, a goose down bed, clean sheets all with a scented fragrance, and a nice long night's sleep, and breakfast in the morning. What could be better than that?" She steps away from him, thinking about his offer. "This night doesn't have to end."

She takes another step back. "It sounds like a dream, but I'm not ready for that." She takes a breath. "I've got to go home."

"Alright, just remember we talked about this before, I can protect you here, but—"

Victoria's thoughts flash back to what Slayter said earlier that night. "I need a gun."

"Where did that come from?"

"I need to be safe. Can you get me a gun?"

"Yes, but if you live here, you won't need a gun." Elijah is quickly losing his cool demeanor, upset about how the night is ending.

Victoria holds her ground and insists a second time. "I haven't got time to explain, just think about it."

"You are bat shit crazy... Is someone threatening you?"

"Men try to make advances on me, I might have to fend them off."

"You talking about me? I ain't going to get you a gun to shoot me."

She begins to step gingerly towards the door. "No, the gun ain't for you, it's for me." Tiredness sinks into her thoughts and she realizes how late it has gotten. "Never mind. I've got to go."

She steps towards the door.

"Victoria?" She freezes. "Listen, when you're in the shower in a bit...just think about me... When you're touching yourself." She doesn't respond and dabs her lip with the napkin again. At her silence, he finally realizes he isn't going to win this battle. "Alright, alright. Go check out with Seven and hit the road... Be careful."

Chapter 27

DRIVING PAST THE HIGH school, Victoria's eyes begin to droop. It had been a long night.

Desperate to stay awake, Victoria uses an old trick Jesse had taught her, cracking her front window so the chilly night breeze can rush past her eyes. It isn't the most comfortable, and it might bring on a cold, but it does the trick for now.

The empty road rushes past, Pepper's General Store completely dark. Her thoughts run over the night in her head, her thoughts constantly returning to where she can possibly get a gun, since Mr. Sweet won't give her one.

Her thoughts drift to the way he touched her. She didn't want to like it, but it was impossible to deny that she had. Mr. Sweet was unlike any other man who Victoria had spent time with, a far cry from Trevor and other boys in high school.

Luckily for her sleep-addled mind, Victoria turns the last corner and bumps up the road to her home, taking immediate notice of the lights on her front porch illuminating Hal's truck in the drive, Cebo sitting in the bed, his eyes wide.

As she parks, Cass emerges from the porch, Silva with her, and Ms. Elvie and Paulene close behind.

"What's going on? What happened?" she asks, her voice panicked.

Cebo is the one who answers. "Benjamin went missing at the Festival, and they found him about 30 minutes ago." He motions to something in the bed of the truck.

Victoria looks over the edge and sees a dark shape turned on his side next to Cebo's leg.

"Victoria, can Silva go with you and follow us to Hal's?" Cass asks from the porch.

"Sure, come on dear." Victoria motions Silva over, who is tucked in a blanket to keep the evening chill from going through her pajamas.

As she walks over, Cebo whispers to Victoria, "He's drunk."

Victoria's eyes widen. "Noooo, you're kidding." Cebo nods sadly.

Suddenly wide awake, Victoria returns to her truck and backs out of the drive, her eyes on Silva in the seat next to her, her head resting on the window. "How long have you been at my house?"

She answers sleepily, "Since the fireworks, I guess."

"So, what happened?"

"They lost Benjamin, and I had to watch the fireworks with Burn and Roddy's kids. They have been looking for Benjamin since then."

"Hmm," Victoria replies as she turns into Hal's drive, pulling up next to his truck. Cass doesn't waste any time, jumping out as soon as the truck is parked to collect the sleeping Silva from Victoria's passenger seat.

Victoria watches, and once they are inside, she climbs out and opens Hal's tailgate. "How long have you been out here?" Victoria asks Cebo.

"Going on for three hours I guess."

"Three hours?"

Cebo shrugs. "Cass said they were watching the fireworks, and no one saw Benjamin, which they thought was odd. But when Maria said she saw him around nine, and she said he was acting weird...touching her and trying to kiss her. She said she slapped him and he stumbled off. She got

Cutter involved and when Burn left, she brought Silva to our house."

Victoria shakes her head in disbelief. This does not sound like Benjamin at all. She doesn't have time to dwell on it though, because within a few moments Cass is back, rolling Benjamin over so they can carry him inside.

Cass grabs his shoulder, motioning with her head for Victoria to grab his feet. The two women pant as they carry him across the yard.

"Is he hurt?" Victoria asks, as they heave him up the porch steps.

"Hurt? No. I checked him when they found him, it was night and used a flashlight but he ain't hurt. Oh, he'll be hurting tomorrow after he wakes up. But he won't feel anything until then."

Pausing for a rest on the porch, after setting Benjamin down gently, Cebo walks up the steps. "How are we going to get him inside?"

Cass shakes her head. "We ought to leave his ass out here until morning. But he's so cute and so nice, let's try and get him to bed."

Victoria nods and heads for his feet again, Cass grabs his shoulders once more, and this time Cebo places his arms under Benjamin's midsection to give them extra lift.

Once they are over the doorstep, Cass gasps, "Drop his feet." Victoria does as directed. "Come help me with his shoulders."

Victoria walks around putting both her arms under one of his shoulders while Cass manages the other. "Cebo, pick up his feet and let's go."

They make their way up the steps, much faster now that both Cass and Victoria are heaving the bulk of Benjamin's weight. By the time they reach the bedroom, all three of them are gasping.

They dump Benjamin on the bed unceremoniously.

"Are you alright?" Victoria asks Cebo.

Cebo is still breathing heavily. "I ain't worked this hard since... I ain't ever worked this hard before." He chuckles.

Cass takes off Benjamin's shoes, followed by his shirt. "Thank you for all your help tonight, Victoria." She raises her voice, "...thanks to Cebo for finding him half underneath a building."

Victoria raises her eyebrows at that. "A building?"

"Yeah, nobody knew where to look, some were in the woods, some around the rides, some around the buildings in town, but almost no one had a flashlight...only Cebo and Cutter. We are just lucky he checked in town where he did."

"Where did you finally find him?"

Again, it's Cebo who answers, "Halfway under the feed and seed."

Cebo finally stands and Cass hands him the keys. "You take Hal's truck home tonight and tell Ms. Elvie thanks."

He drops his head and looks at the keys in his hand. "How are you getting home tomorrow?"

Cass sighs. "I'm so tired we'll figure it out tomorrow."

"I'll take them home tomorr—when daylight comes," Victoria offers, realizing that 'tomorrow' is already here.

Cass nods and gives Cebo a good firm hug. "Could you be sure the front door is locked on your way out?"

"I will." He leaves with a smile.

Cass removes her windbreaker and tosses it on the dresser. "Where's your jacket?"

"Don't wear one when driving home. I kinda count on that the cool breeze will keep me awake."

Cass shakes her head. "Kids." Cass turns to Benjamin. "It's been years, but this reminds me of my husband."

Victoria chuckles darkly. "This reminds me of work." They both giggle in exhaustion.

Silence settles over the room and it's Cass who eventually breaks it. "I'm going to check on Silva and use the bathroom. Do you think we need to make him more comfortable?"

Victoria goes to him and physically turns his face to hers. She lowers her nose to his face and smells. "I don't think he feels anything."

Cass says as she leaves the room, "Take off his pants maybe, I know I would want that." Victoria nods as Cass exits.

Victoria unbuttons and unzips his pants, fighting to roll his heavy body over so she can pull them off. By the time he is just lying in his underwear, she is panting again.

Cass comes back into the room with a wet washcloth and bowl of warm water, her nose wrinkling at the smell coming from Benjamin.

With a sigh, she begins to wash the parts of him where there is dirt from being under the building—avoiding the area covered by his underwear. Soon, the water is brown with dirt. She hands the bowl to Victoria asking her to get more from the sink.

Victoria does so, returning to the room to find Cass just sitting there next to the nearly naked Benjamin. "I'm going to go take a quick shower. Will you stay and check on Silva if she should wake?"

Victoria nods, taking the rag from Cass to finish washing him.

Cass gets to the doorway and turns, "I cleaned uh...that area."

Victoria raises her eyebrows, motioning to some dirt, "I still see some spots you missed."

"Uh huh. I'll give you a head's up when I get out of the shower." Victoria is cleaning his face as Cass disappears down the hall.

~~~

Cass finishes her shower, pulling on a nightshirt and panties. She pokes her head in the bedroom. "Did she make a sound?"

Victoria stands and hands the rag and bowl to Cass. "No. No. Not a sound."

Cass eyes Benjamin's still motionless form. "I think he's clean enough now."

"Yep. I think so. Listen, I've been up since forever, I'm going to leave you and head home. I'll see you about noon."

"Yeah, thanks for offering to take us home. We'll talk more then."

Victoria yawns. "Okay."

The two women head down the stairs and Cass lets Victoria out the front door. "Be careful, watch out for the ditches." Victoria smiles as she exits the house, starts her truck and drives away.

Cass locks the door. She turns the lights off downstairs before slowly climbing the stairs. She then turns all of the hall lights off, but leaves Benjamin's on.
~~~

Chapter 28

C ASS WAKES UP EARLY the next morning and it takes a moment for her to remember where she is and why. But as soon as she does, the memories from the night before come rushing back.

She stretches, reaching for Silva, who was sleeping next to her, only for her arm to meet the empty sheets.

Her mind jumping into panic mode, she flings the sheets back before bounding to the bathroom, only to find it empty as well. Worried enough about her daughter to forgo her own needs, Cass runs through the upstairs, peeking in each room until she comes to Benjamin's, finding him still sleeping, no Silva in sight.

Beginning to really panic, she runs down the steps, calling out her daughter's name.

"Silva!"

She turns the corner into the kitchen, sliding to a stop when she sees her daughter sitting in a kitchen chair, her knees curled to her chest.

"Yes ma'am?" she asks innocently.

"Honey, I've been looking for you!"

"Well, I'm right here."

Cass lets out a sigh of relief, her eyes catching on the mess of paper on the kitchen table. There are several letters, all open, one which Silva's eyes were currently running back and forth over.

"What are you reading?"

Silva turns her head but keeps her eyes on the letter. "A letter I found on top of the refrigerator."

Cass snatches it from her hand. "You don't read other people's mail."

She flinches. "Why? They're right up there in the open."

Cass folds the pages and puts them back in their envelope. Silva hands her two other envelopes. "You read all of them?"

"Almost, if you hadn't yanked them out of my hands."

Cass sets the letters back on the refrigerator. She sounds angry, "How did you get them?" Silva points to the chair she is sitting in and then the fridge. "Maybe you need to go back to bed," Cass suggests before starting the process of making coffee.

Silva watches in silence, biting her lip.

"We don't read other people's mail, okay? It's disrespectful."

She drops her eyes. "Yes, ma'am."

Cass opens her mouth to say something else, but she is interrupted by a knock at the front door. Silva runs toward it, her hand reaching for the knob. "Look and see who it is before you open it!" Cass calls after her.

She eases the curtain back. "It's Rein." Silva doesn't wait for her mom's approval before she yanks the door ajar. "Hi, Rein!"

"Hi Silva," Rein replies. "I came by to check on Benjamin."

"Come in. Want some coffee? I'm just making some."

She shakes her head, entering the kitchen. "No, I had some at the hospital."

"He's about naked upstairs, I put a blanket on him this morning," Silva spouts, and Rein looks taken aback, her wide eyes rising to meet Cass'.

Cass quickly corrects her daughter, "Silva, he's got his underwear on, and he's covered up with a blanket." She turns back to Rein. "Benjamin is still out. It might be better if he wakes up on his own."

She sighs. "Guess you're right. Well, I guess I'm also here to say goodbye. It was so good to see both of you. Are you leaving today?"

Cass pours her coffee and sips it. "Supposed to, around noon. Victoria offered last night to drive us back, if Benjamin can't."

"Victoria?" Rein seems surprised.

"Yeah, she was just getting home when I picked up Silva at their place." She sips her coffee. "Hope she got better sleep than I did."

"Listen, I'm going to feed Glory. Silva, you want to help me feed her?" Rein asks.

She jumps up and down. "Sure do!"

"Go get dressed and I'll clean up your mess."

She streaks off. "Thanks Rein!"

Cass calls after her, "You know what clothes you're wearing today?"

She stops in her tracks. "Can I ride Glory?"

Rein looks at Cass and lifts her chin. "Maybe, just a quick walk around."

Cass lips' twist but she allows it anyway. "Put your clothes on you rode in yesterday."

Silva agrees and stomps up the stairs. Cass briefly wonders if Benjamin will be able to continue sleeping through her racket. "Thanks," she says to Rein.

"My pleasure. That's the one thing she loves doing." Rein gathers the items Silva left on the table from her breakfast.

"What have you got planned today?"

Walking over to the sink she says, "My sister, Amber, moved out of the house and now this afternoon she wants me to help her gather up some of her clothes from her closet."

"That's nice."

"Say, while Silva and I are outside, can you look and see if Julie's got some spare bags to carry clothes?"

"I'll look and see."

Rein smiles. "You think Silva might wake Benjamin by running up the steps like she did?"

Cass' chuckles thinking about Benjamin's state the night before. "Maybe, but probably not, he was out cold. Do you need to talk to him?"

"Annie Mae needs to talk to him, kind of sounds urgent, you want me to write a note and when he gets up you—"

Cass interrupts. "I'll tell him, and the message is, 'Annie Mae needs to talk to you immediately'. And if he isn't up when we leave, I'll leave him a note."

"Thanks." Rein finishes clearing the table just as Silva returns, her footsteps heavy on the stairs and even heavier on the wood floor when she jumps the last two steps.

Cass shakes her head. "She's trying to wake him up."

Rein smiles. "You ready?"

"Yes, ma'am," Silva replies, already halfway out the door.

Rein follows her, Silva prattling on. "Did you know Gloria and Matthew are coming for a visit this Christmas?"

Cass carries her coffee cup to the back door, watching as Silva pulls on her boots.

"Where did you hear that?" Rein asks.

Cass pushes the door open to interject. "Silva, quit talking so much and let Rein tell you about feeding Glory and cleaning the stalls, and Rein tell her about you and Amber's work at the hospital."

"Yes, ma'am!" Silva says with a huff.

"Do you want to know what we do at the hospital?" she asks and Silva nods as they make their way toward the barn.

"Let's see we have about eight patients now at the hospital." She points. "You see it over there? Amber, my older sister, cooks for all of them..."

Rein's voice fades and Cass closes the door, returning to the kitchen to refill her coffee cup before walking to the window to watch, her hand absentmindedly buttering a piece of toast.

~~~
~~~

After a shower, Cass feels refreshed, and takes the time to strip the beds they stayed in and look for the bags Rein requested. She finds one and resolves to check the other bedrooms for more. She also packs up all of their belongings, checking under the bed to ensure Silva didn't push anything out of sight.

Finished with everything and ready to go, she heads to Benjamin's room to check in.

The room is cool and dim, and Benjamin is still unmoving on the bed. A bit concerned, she leans down and checks his pulse and forehead, but everything seems normal.

She grabs his arm and lightly shakes it. "Benjamin…Benjamin."

His eyes open a smidge and he groans, only to roll over and close them once again.

With a sigh, she heads to the closet to see if there are any clothing bags in this room, and though there are plenty of nice clothes, both suits and dresses, there are no clothing bags. Her eyes peruse every shelf, but though there are several expensive items, including jewelry, there doesn't seem to be any way to transport them.

Heading into the last bedroom room on the top floor, Cass finds much the same, with additional accessories, hats and scarves, piled in one corner. There are even some boxes of Madison shoes. Temptation gets the best of her and she pulls one open, a whispered "Wow" on her lips when she spots the brand name shoes. She replaces the box.

Heading back into the hall, she looks in on Benjamin one final time before heading down the stairs and out the door, spotting Silva on Glory's back and Rein pitchforking hay into the horse's corral.

Rein pauses her work as Cass approaches.

"Rein, I did what you asked, and I feel like I shouldn't have."

The young woman looks confused. "What do you mean?"

"I know it's not my place but there are like five or six full bags of clothes, shoes, jewelry, and other expensive stuff in the closets. I feel bad, like I was spying on these nice people."

Rein brushes Cass off. "Oh, don't worry, I found some small crates out here in the barn that Amber can—"

Cass interrupts. "They may be thieves."

Rein jumps at her sudden statement but doesn't seem perturbed. "No, it's okay, she's going to start a new job at the railroad when she gets back from Texas."

Cass isn't convinced. "She got enough stuff to start five jobs at the railroad."

Rein sets the pitchfork down. "Listen, I'm not telling anybody nothing about what you saw, so don't worry about anything."

"I just feel bad...dirty even... like I need to wash my hands."

Rein lowers her voice and steps closer to Cass so Silva can't hear. "Listen, some rich people got lots of nice stuff."

Cass raises an eyebrow. "Are they rich?"

Rein presses her mouth into a thin line, realizing the other woman might have a point. "No...no. The farm is going through some tough times."

"I won't say anything...for now," Cass says. "But...maybe you need to be more cautious around them."

"Okay. You're right." Rein smiles, trying to lighten the mood. It doesn't work.

Cass shivers. "We need to go. I don't feel right." She turns to where Silva is still riding Glory. "Silva!" The girl doesn't seem to notice, so Cass tries again, louder. "Silva! Get down now and get into the house."

Silva's eyes widen at her mom's tone, and she does as she is told. Cass watches as Silva returns the horse to the barn.

"Rein?"

"Yeah."

"Are you about through here?"

"I guess I am...just a couple of chores before I'm finished."

"Did you drive over here?"

"J.B. lent me his car to come over here, yes."

Cass nods, her arms crossed tightly across her body. "Would you do me a favor and go by Victoria's now and see if she can come take us home?"

"I guess."

"Thank you." She turns to leave.

Rein steps closer. "Wait, Cass, I'm sorry if I put you in a predicament. It was nice to get to know you and Silva, I'll miss you both."

"It's not your fault, it's no one's fault. It is what it is. Nice to meet you too. I'll write that note for Benjamin quickly and then we can leave." She rushes into the house just as Silva pops up at Rein's side.

"What happened? Am I in trouble?"

Rein shakes her head, leaning down to hug the girl. "No, everything is okay. Say goodbye to Glory and maybe you'll see him at Christmas."

Silva hands the horse's bridle to Rein. She leads the horse into the barn and starts to unbuckle the saddle as Silva whispers to Glory, "Glory, I love you and I'll miss you." She hugs the horse.

Rein removes the saddle and blanket and throws it over the railing. "You better get going."

"Goodbye, see you at Christmas," Silva says before she turns and runs out the doorway.

Rein solemnly leads the horse into his stall, giving him a quick brush before locking the door. Without meaning it to happen, she finds a tear is tracking its way down her face, followed by another, and another.

By the time she leaves the barn to head to the car, she is fully crying, but also furiously trying to wipe at her face so Silva won't see.

The last thing she wants to do is upset poor Silva and Cass.

Chapter 29

November 6, 1945
10:30am
On the Road, Chatham Hill, Middle Tennessee

TREVOR CRANKS THE WHEEL, his 1940s black Ford nosing into the turn by Pepper's with ease. His eyes catch on Amber, who is sitting in the middle seat, with Sadie occupying the window. Amber is dressed to impress in a royal blue skirt, gold jewelry, and matching scarf, to cover her neck scar.

Sadie is also dressed in her best, a floral blouse paired with a long beige skirt, her hair braided. The escaped tendrils of her hair blow in the afternoon breeze, a smile dancing on her lips.

"I hate this road," Amber whines as Trevor navigates the bumps.

"I know what you mean, but when do you ever come this way?"

"Walking back and forth for years...and now driving to get Paulene after work. I watch her a couple hours after school now because Cebo has started working at the hospital. Just helping out." Amber turns to Sadie. "She's a curious child though, so you may want to keep your bedroom door closed."

Sadie laughs. "I ain't got nothing to hide. Just don't let her jump on the bed...or the sofa or chair...or nothing. Tell that child not to jump on anything in that house."

"Yes, ma'am," Amber replies with a grin.

Sadie shakes her head. "I remember Trevor and his cousin would leap from sofa to table to couch to—"

Trevor interrupts. "Now, ma'am, don't tell Amber all my secrets."

Sadie continues acting like she didn't hear her son, "—It was a game to go around the room without touching the floor. Made me so mad...tore up one table like six times."

Amber interjects. "Guess that's how he became a carpenter, fixing that table."

"Yeah, he'd tear things up and then he'd fix them. You remember that nice basket I had?" Amber nods. "I got it for a present, for blankets and my sewing stuff. He stepped clear through the top of that—"

Trevor, again, tries to stop his mother from revealing anything truly embarrassing. "Now, ma'am, she doesn't want to hear about my mistakes."

"—Oh, he couldn't fix that. Your daddy tore your butt up then, didn't he?"

Trevor rolls his eyes, accepting that they are indeed discussing his transgressions. "You didn't help. You got him so riled up even before I even got whooped, I didn't stand a chance."

Amber attempts to redirect the conversation. "He turned out to be a good kid though, didn't he?"

Sadie turns her head to look out the side window. "Yeah, he's a good kid now, but don't go taking his side, can't be having that."

"Oh, no, ma'am. I wouldn't dream of it," Amber says as she peeks out of the corner of her eye at Trevor. "I don't remember you ever walking home with us this way."

"I didn't." He points down a drive across from the school. "Mr. Tate would let us go through his fields and along the creek and in less than an hour, I'd make it home."

"Wore out many a shoe, but out of sight, out of trouble," Sadie says under her breath. "He's a good kid...sorry you ain't here to see it, Bobby," she says, the last part in a whisper.

"I've done business with both of Tate's sons. I need to stop in and see Tatter before it gets too late."

"I fixed dinner last night so you can go see him this afternoon."

Trevor shakes his head, Amber misunderstood him. "No, too late, as in he's in the hospital in Madison. It doesn't sound promising."

Amber frowns. "I'm sorry Trevor, I'll pray for him."

"Thank you."

"Oh, Paulene asked if you had any horses in your barn," Amber asks, changing the direction of the conversation.

"My barn?" Trevor looks at Amber. "Did you tell her it's a storage barn? A working shop?"

"No, but she loves your rocking chairs, and I told her you built them and other things out there… She wants to look."

He thinks for a moment before answering. "I guess you can look, but there's a lot of sharp tools and stacked lumber and wood straps back there, good tripping hazards, and…maybe she can look from a distance, I guess."

"I'll hold her hand and lead her around," Amber promises.

Trevor looks to Sadie now. "What do you think, ma'am?"

"I think she can look through the window, but it's your barn."

"I'll let her hammer a nail—you never know she may be a carpenter one day… Your little helper."

Trevor and Sadie spoke almost simultaneously, "Yeah."

They all giggle. "Keys are on the side of the cupboard with all the books."

"I'll take responsibility for her," Amber promises.

Trevor turns his attention back to the hard packed dirt road, passing the school and continuing out of town. While Amber and Sadie are dressed up, Trevor's got his work pants on, though he did slip on a button up shirt.

"Trevor, you look dapper today," Amber comments.

"That's good, isn't it?"

"Yes, are you trying to impress anyone special today?" She smirks, a knowing gleam in her eye.

Trevor slows his speed and turns right off the main road, "Now,

Amber, don't you start prying. Did Sadie put you up to this?"

"I ain't said nothing. It just goes to show she's thinking the same thing I am," Sadie insists, her eyes watching the scenery roll by outside the window.

"You bitties need to leave me be and let me make my own decisions."

Amber smiles as Trevor finishes his rebuttal. Sadie leans over to whisper in Amber's ear, "More like mistakes." But she isn't as quiet as she thought.

"What'd you say?" Trevor snaps, his eyes narrowed on his mother.

"I said, if you'd ever ask me for advice, I'd give it to ya'."

"Oh, I know you would...that's why I don't ask." There is silence for a moment. "Now just out of this next bend—" He points to the right, "See this building with blocks and wood?"

"Yes."

"That's where our doctor is, Dr. Nichols."

Amber takes a moment to analyze. "You mean, you and Trevor?"

"Yeah, pretty much all the people living in this part of town come here. He's been here for ten years or so, and he's busy all the time...the last doctor got too old..." Sadie puts her hand out horizontally and starts shaking it. "He got to shaking so much he couldn't give you a teaspoon of medicine. He'd have to put it in a cup. It was so sad. Dr. Nichols started about when the other doctor started shaking." She eyes the car parked in the lot. "Looks like he's got a patient there now."

"I guess that's why I don't see any patients anymore coming to see Dr. Windsor from out this way." Amber also eyes the lot, a frown occupying her face.

Trevor studies the road as Sadie replies, "Most see Nichols. J.B. got...too friendly." Sadie looks ashamed as she admits it to Amber. "I'm sorry."

Amber brushes her off with an understanding smile. "No, I understand, people need to go see whoever they think can take care of them the best."

Trevor points. "To the left are two of the best mechanics in these parts...look at all the cars."

Amber's eyes widen. "Good golly, there're so many."

Trevor nods. "Yeah, really one guy, the other one you got to catch him on the right day."

"That's enough work for an army," Amber agrees.

"Most of 'em are unfixable or people can't afford parts."

"Hmm." Amber thinks for a moment before turning to Sadie. "Where's the church?"

Sadie points alongside the road but there isn't a building in sight. "Down here by the river. Our little church can't afford a baptismal so they built the church down here by the swimming hole."

"Just remember Amber, at Beulah, it's best to get saved in the summertime. Around here, any other time of the year, it may take only 10 seconds to dunk someone. They say, if God sneezes he'll miss a baptism at Beulah," Trevor jests, elbowing Amber lightly.

Sadie chastises her son. "Trevor, stop telling lies."

They drive a couple more miles until the wooden church finally comes into view. Amber is immediately taken by the quaint nature of the small structure.

"It's beautiful. The cross, the steeple, and stained-glass windows...it looks so holy."

Trevor and Sadie don't reply as they pull into the lot and Trevor searches for a spot. The lot is already quite full.

Sadie opens the door and slides out onto the hard pan dirt. Trevor, before exiting, looks to Amber. "Good luck today, be ready to talk." He smiles and she returns the gesture.

Sadie motions for Amber to follow her and she immediately discovers what Trevor was talking about as everyone seems to want to talk to her. Some are satisfied with just a handshake, while others seem to want a quick rundown of her whole life story. Sadie does her best to keep the vultures at bay, but by the time they climb the steps to the door, Amber is exhausted already.

The minute she steps through the wooden doors onto the crimson carpet, she freezes.

It's the church from her dream.

People are still talking to her, but she can't seem to find the words to respond besides a squeaked "hi," her mouth opening and closing like a fish as she takes it all in.

The more she observes, the more it looks exactly like her vision. The hairs on her arms and the back of her neck prickle.

She stands just like that, in awe, until Sadie says, "This is our pastor, Reverend Christopher Rockwell."

Amber's eyes blink furiously, trying to bring her mind back to reality. As his strong grip shakes her hand, she chokes out a response, "Nice to meet you."

He smiles a warm smile that Amber immediately etches into her memory.

As he turns to greet the next guest behind them, Amber looks ahead to see Sadie greeting lots of other women as she makes her way to the pews. Most look to be mothers, younger than Sadie but older than Amber, and they all have a wide crimson sash draped around their necks.

Amber resolves to ask Sadie about them later, needing to walk quickly to catch up to her, the pew creaking as she sinks into the spot next to Sadie.

The piano and organ start up, each musician pressing a few heavy-handed notes to set the rhythm. As soon as they finish their introduction, the music crescendos and a cacophony of voices join the hymn. Amber's eyes are drawn to the women in crimson sashes, who are all standing abreast and singing along.

The music is hypnotic, and Amber can't stop her foot from tapping. Something touches her hand. It's Sadie, who is also smiling with the same joy that Amber knows is radiating from her own face.

Her eyes travel the crowd, catching on a young girl in a pinafore dress with a white shirt, standing a few feet away and watching her every move. Amber smiles and waves at her, and the girl waves back.

This draws the attention of the mother, who is wearing a striped dress and turns her daughter's attention back to the choir. Amber can see now that the father is there too, as is the son, who stands on the other side of him. They appear to be happy.

The pastor makes his way down the aisle to take his position in the front of the church. His foot is tapping too as his mouth moves to the words of the music for several more minutes until the hymn ends.

"Let us pray," his deep voice booms from the pulpit. Amber bows her head.

"Dear Father..." The pastor begins, but Amber zones him out as she prays her personal prayer of thanksgiving, thanking the Lord for everything that has happened in the past few days. For allowing her to accept the good things along with the bad.

"...Amen." The pastor booms, and Amber jumps as the crowd responds with a simultaneous 'amen.'

The piano and organ start up again, this time with a tune she is familiar with, so her lips begin to move along with the choir voices. As she sings, she searches the crowd for Trevor.

It doesn't take long, as it's not a huge crowd. Amber estimates maybe 35 people total. She finds him toward the back, standing with two young men his age.

The song ends, just as another begins. Then another comes after that. Just before the sermon, the choir sings a song all on their own, allowing everyone to get settled before the sermon.

Wanting to make someone else's day, Amber reaches into her purse, enclosing something in her fist, before holding out her hand to the young girl.

The girl looks at her mom, who looks at Amber. Amber smiles. The mother dips her chin.

The young girl opens her hand, palm up. Amber drops two wrapped peppermints into her palm. Her eyes lit up. Her fingers wrap around the mints so fast it is like a Venus fly trap slamming shut on a fly. She gingerly but noisily unwraps and puts one in her mouth.

Amber watches, hoping she made a friend.

As the sermon drags on, Amber reaches into her purse a second time, again balling her fist. The young girl's eyes watching her every move. Wondering what the girl will do, Amber rests her fist on her thigh for a moment before reaching it out again.

Amber slowly raises her hand and pushes her balled fist over the wood pew. The girl places her open palm below Amber's fist, watching. Amber finally opens her balled up fist and drops her open hand onto the child's hand and clasps her fingers with the child. To hold her hand.

Not expecting this type of interaction, the child flinches, pulling her hand back, and banging her elbow on the pew. The mother doesn't say anything, smiling as the girl snuggles back into her mom's side.

Amber turns her attention back to the pastor, who is growing louder, Amber nearly jumps again when the crowd yells "Hallelujah!" Some members are more enthusiastic than others.

Amber tries to pay attention, her palm still lying up where the child left it, in hopes she would return. The child stares at the hand, but doesn't venture a finger in Amber's direction. Eventually, with an encouraging nod to her child, the mother places her hand in Amber's and interlaces their fingers.

Proud of her accomplishment, the two women stay like that for some time. Amber feels blessed. She found a friend. Moments pass until finally the mother releases her grip on Amber's hand.

Amber leaves her hand open for a few more moments.

Then Amber feels a small hand lay into her open palm, her head turning to connect eyes with the young girl. She smiles. Amber smiles back.

Maybe Amber had found not just one, but two friends.

Chapter 30

V ICTORIA SHOWS UP AS planned, with Paulene in tow. Trudging up the porch steps, they knock politely on the door.

Paulene, ever curious, peeks in the front window to spot Cass and Silva gathering their things and heading for the door.

"Morning…again," Cass sighs as they step out onto the porch, closing the door behind her.

Victoria lets out a light chuckle as Paulene hugs Silva. "Can we go see Glory and say goodbye?"

Victoria looks at Cass. "It's up to you."

Cass relents. "Five minutes."

"Yes, ma'am!" Silva hugs her mother before grabbing Paulene's hand, the two of them running around the house toward the barn.

Victoria and Cass stand in silence for a moment, until Victoria finally says, "I feel like I need some water before we head off."

"Get me a small glass too."

Victoria nods and heads for the kitchen. "Sit down a minute, you look tired."

She sinks into the kitchen chair with a sigh. "I feel tired. Yesterday, last night and this morning, it was all…" Victoria hands Cass the water, her eyes catching on the letter Cass left on the table. "I'll be glad to get back to Yaphank. I can't believe I said that. Usually, that's never been the case."

"How's your beau doing upstairs?"

Cass chokes on her sip of water. "My what?" Victoria grins as she downs half her glass. "Benjamin?" Victoria wipes her mouth with the back of her hand. Cass shakes her head. "I saw his eyes briefly open about an hour ago. Just going to let him sleep it off."

Victoria shifts in her chair. "We go whenever you are ready."

"We better enjoy the quiet before we get trapped in the truck with the two yahoos for an hour."

Victoria nods. "You answer all their questions going and I'll answer them coming back."

They look at each other and giggle. "Thanks." Cass finishes her glass and sets it down. "I didn't know Benjamin drank."

Victoria shakes her head. "I don't think he does. He's always been such a good boy."

"Maybe he wanted to act like a bad boy?" Cass suggests. "Oh, that reminds me." She gets a pencil out of a drawer and turns the note, writing.

"What'd you forget?"

"Somebody said that he kissed and was touching Maria pretty frisky before he passed out."

"All men get that way when they drink." Victoria taps her chin. "Maria? That's Cutter's daughter. I'm sure he'll have a few words with him, anyways."

Cass begins scribbling, whispering to herself, "Maria slapped you for being too forward. Better apologize, Bad Boy."

Victoria smiles. "Did you write bad boy?"

"Yeah."

Victoria wiggles her eyebrows. "Did you kiss him?"

"Kiss who?"

"Benjamin."

She leans her head back, her eyes closed. "He's half my age."

Victoria eyes the older woman. "I've learned that it can make it exciting."

"You're closer in age, what only three to four years apart?" Victoria bites her lip, Cass evaluating her for a moment before coming to the realization. "Did you?"

Victoria smiles and looks at Cass out of the corner of her eye, "Maybe more than that."

Cass slaps a hand over her mouth, shocked at the younger woman's reveal. "Dammit, Victoria." She quickly runs over the actions of the night before wondering when she would have had time. "While I was in the shower?"

Victoria beams. "You were in the shower a long time." She picks at her nails. "You can't be mad, you had more time than I did later."

Cass raises her hand to cut her off. "This is getting too spicy. Just tell me the truth."

Victoria debates for a moment. "Just one admission and that's all I'm going to say, and we need to go."

"Go on," Cass urges.

"Well, when I was taking his pants off...I might have seen something..."

Cass grimaces. "Something...or...it?"

"It," Victoria confirms, not seeming embarrassed in the least.

Groaning, Cass pinches her eyes closed. "Dammit Victoria...that was bad."

"I know."

"You don't even sound embarrassed," she accuses.

"I'm not," Victoria confirms, standing and making her way to the door. "I've got a reputation around here to uphold. Now, it's time to get you home."

Put off by their recently finished conversation, Cass can't do anything but stand and watch as Victoria heads to the barn, grabbing the girls and heading to the truck. It isn't until the girls reach the truck that Cass decides to run back upstairs for a moment, returning right as Victoria comes into the house looking for her.

"Everything okay up there?"

Cass narrows her eyes at Victoria, not saying anything until she reaches the truck and leans her head in. "Everybody ready for a trip to Yaphank?" The girls cheer.

Cass pulls back from the truck, looking over her shoulder at Victoria. "I had to get a kiss goodbye."

Victoria smiles, a glimmer in her eye.

~~~

It's a rough road back to Yaphank, the truck swaying from side to side, Cass bumping into Victoria or one of the girls every other second. Cass is running over the night before in her memory, realizing suddenly she had forgotten to ask Silva something.

"Silva, who did you stay with during the fireworks?"

Silva's smiles, her eyes bright. "Colette and Roddy."

"And who else?"

"Peaches and..."

"And who else?"

Silva groans. "You know who was there...I don't want to say his name and you get mad."

Victoria raises her eyebrows but says nothing. Paulene is equally as quiet, her eyes staring out the passenger window.

"Did he talk to you?" Cass presses, her voice serious.

"A little."

"Did he put his arm around you?"

"A little," Silva admits again.

"What did he say?"

Silva hesitates a moment. "He said that I was as pretty as you and wished we would come see him more."

Cass doesn't say anything more, trying to suppress the anger that is
~~~

bubbling in her gut.

Victoria decides it's time to intervene. "Who's Peaches? His wife?"

"No, Bernard's wife went missing a year or so ago. Peaches is the one sharing his…" Cass trails off, knowing Victoria is old enough to know what she is leaving unsaid. Switching the subject, she points out the passenger window. "Paulene, you see this next big house on the left?"

The house is run down, vines climbing up the walls and through the windows. Even from afar the girls can tell it isn't a nice place to spend time.

"Yes, ma'am."

"That's the old Kelly house. That's how the road got its name."

Paulene cocks her head to the side, thinking. "That's history, isn't it?"

"Sure is." Cass points to the old large oak tree next to the house. "There used to be a rope tied from this big tree to another across the river. Kelly and his son would pull a raft or ferry people across using the rope and that's how people would cross the river years ago. Before cars and bridges."

"That's a long time ago," Paulene thinks out loud. "It's a long way from this side to that one."

Cass nods. "Yeah, if a family lived on this side of the river and another family on that side, you can wave at each other but not really have to deal with them. Just visit occasionally. But the farther down the river you go, like where we live, the river gets wider—and the current stronger—so you can't cross at all."

Paulene connects the dots. "So where you live down here, the families can't even wave to each other."

Cass with a slight smile, her eyes far away, replies, "Yeah, down there you can't even see each other."

Victoria says nothing as the cab falls into silence, the trees growing closer to the road, the air getting darker as they block out the sun. Cass doesn't say anything more, her eyes growing sadder, her lips more drawn down, with each bumpy mile they drive. Silva and Paulene seem to notice the change in mood too, and the silence remains packed into the cab, suffocating them, for the remainder of the drive.

Chapter 31

November 6, 1945
12:30pm
Hal's House, Chatham Hill, Middle Tennessee

THE NEXT THING BENJAMIN knows, he's blinking up at the bedroom ceiling at Hal's, a chilling breeze blowing over his body from the cracked window.

He turns toward the other side of the room, noticing the door to the bedroom has been left open, the house quiet. Sitting up slowly, Benjamin tries to recall the events of the night before, but they are just outside of his mental reach. Grimacing, he gets up from bed and makes his way into the bathroom.

As he passes by the mirror, he notices that he is only wearing his undergarments, his chest completely bare. He fills a cup sitting by the sink, chugging it down quickly after using the toilet.

Once he is finished, he walks toward the stairs and calls, "Cass? Silva?"

There is no response.

He makes his way downstairs and opens the front door. Hal's truck is gone. He goes to the kitchen and goes to look out the back door, but the yard is empty. Just as he is beginning to panic, his eyes catch on a note resting on the table.

Benjamin,

Victoria and Paulene were kind enough to take me and Silva home. Sorry you didn't hear us say goodbye, but we did. Hope you get to feeling better. We had a great time. Paulene had twice the fun. Victoria, Cebo and I brought, well... carried you home after the fireworks. Silva and Paulene stayed and watched the fireworks. They loved it all. Victoria and I put you to bed. Hope you were comfortable. Maybe you can return the favor one day. See you Friday.

P.S. Annie Mae wants to see you. URGENT.

P.S.S. Maria slapped you for being too forward. You better apologize, bad boy.

Cassidy

Benjamin sets the note down and goes to the cabinet for a glass. He fills it with water and sits down at the kitchen table. He drinks half the glass of water. His eyelids batter a couple of times before he picks up the note and reads it again.

Suddenly, an idea comes to him. Not wanting to waste a moment, he runs upstairs and dresses, forgoing a jacket as he still feels a bit warm from sleep.

Once he is somewhat put together, he rushes to the barn to saddle up Glory before hopping on his back and urging him toward the main road.

Although they are already moving at a gallop, Benjamin urges the horse faster with his heels. Glory pants with the exertion, but Benjamin doesn't notice. Instead, he is focused on the free feeling that comes from riding the horse through the brisk October air.

The pair continue this pace until they reach the main road, and Benjamin spots a car coming. He slows, nodding to the driver, before picking up speed once more until they arrive at the porch of the hospital.

Benjamin dismounts at the porch and ties Glory's reins to the post before heading into the lobby to run right into Annie Mae.

"Why didn't you just call?" he gasps.

"'Cause it's too important." She signals him to follow her.

Annie Mae holds the door as Benjamin sits down in the wood chair across from her desk. She closes the door and locks it. "What happened?"

Benjamin is still breathing heavily. "I got Danny to drink at least half the bottle."

"Half?" Her eyes are wide.

He nods. "I'm just guessing. He drank from an orange drink bottle. Maybe two swallows and a moonshine bottle, maybe three or four good swallows. I don't know, for sure."

"I'm just glad Cebo found you last night."

"Cebo?" Benjamin asks, perplexed.

"Yeah, after the fireworks show, Cass and Silva couldn't find you and they told Cutter and Maria and...then they called me. So I sent Cebo."

Now it's Benjamin's eyes that are wide. "I'm sorry, I don't remember nothing from last night except Danny asking me to drink from the bottle or he wouldn't."

She puts her hand on his arm. "You drank from the bottle?"

"Yeah, maybe two sips?"

"Is that how you got drunk? Are you feeling sick?" Annie Mae walks around the desk to put the back of her hand to Benjamin's forehead.

Benjamin's stomach turns. "Well, I ain't bleeding, so I must be okay."

Annie Mae lets out a heavy breath. "I'm just glad you're alright, I'll call Sadie and tell her what you said and see what she says."

Benjamin nods. "I hope we got him."

"I don't care about him now. I've just been worried about you." Annie Mae moves back to her seat. "Go home and rest. Don't come by tomorrow. You've had a stressful weekend. Go to school." His eyelids begin to droop. "You did good."

"Thanks, can Cebo take me home?" Annie Mae cocks her head to the side, confused. Benjamin motions for her to follow him to the porch, where he points out Glory, still panting.

"This is your ride?" He nods and Annie Mae looks over her shoulder before answering. "I'll tell Cebo to pick you up at Hal's in thirty minutes. That gives you time to get Glory home." She steps down to pat the horse.

"Haven't seen you in months, boy."

"He's gotten his exercise in the last couple of days, between myself, Paulene and Silva."

Annie Mae laughs and shakes her head, still petting the horse. "Those two would wear anybody out." Benjamin doesn't say anything. "You want something to eat?" she offers.

He pats his stomach. "No, it doesn't feel right."

"Maybe you should try to drink something? Maybe milk to dilute anything that's in your stomach." Annie Mae walks to the top of the steps and turns. "Oh, Hal and Julie are coming home Saturday afternoon. Can you plan on picking them up? I think the train arrives at 3:30."

"Sure will. Could you remind me again later? My mind is messy right now." Benjamin mounts Glory.

"I will..." He turns Glory towards her voice. "...maybe you stay away from drinking after this." Annie Mae hedges.

He tries to work up a smile at her comment as he turns the horse toward the road, but he can't find the energy to do so.

Chapter 32

November 6, 1945
3:00pm
Windsor House, Chatham Hill, Middle Tennessee

AMBER PULLS UP IN front of the Windsor home in Stephen's car. The tires press the sandy soil in the large shade of two white oaks in the front of J.B's homestead. They both reach to the sky and the width of the limbs halfway up are the size of a child's body. The mammoth gifts of nature would easily reach the fireplace and front porch swing if they fell. At least those are the thoughts that went through Rein's head as she slowly swung, Amber's gaze focusing on Cheddar's head on her lap, his tongue lolling to the side.

"Where's your future husband at, doesn't he swing with you anymore?" Amber calls out as she ascends the steps.

Rein laughs and calls back, "I heard jailbird proposed, you aren't pregnant yet?" before rising from the swing to hug her sister. Cheddar barks, wanting to be included.

As they break apart, Amber notices some crates by the door. "That's enough for everything?" Amber looks towards the front door, "Hope Ms. O'Toole is okay with us disturbing her today." Rein pushes open the door.

Amber steps through, looking around the house which is no longer her home. "After all I've been through in this house... Ms. O'Toole, I can deal with her."

Rein follows her sister, pausing to grab the crates, and setting them inside the door.

"I guess I'm going to get a couple of things for me." Amber tries to convince herself to stay calm. Rein, "How many clothes do you think we should get Jennifer?" she asks, referring to the patient both she and Rein were passionate about.

As Amber's mind ciphers, Rein stands with her hands on her hips. "I've read the report Weston wrote. I think you have her farther along than I do."

Amber looks to Rein. "And with Jennifer we may have to pick up the pace."

Rein raises an eyebrow. "Why such a hurry?"

There is a pause as Amber tries to decide how much she should reveal. She finally settles on, "We need to get her out of there as soon as possible."

Rein is used to her sister's secret-keeping tactics, but presses anyway, "Again, what's the hurry?"

Amber doesn't answer, instead changing the subject. "I think we should get her five outfits." She heads for the stairs, pausing when she notices the dark fireplace. "Where's the fire?"

Rein looks into the ashes. "You've gotten more demanding and louder since you've got a fiancé."

"Thanks, maybe I've grown up."

"With Benjamin watching Hal's place and you up and moved out, the house is empty. Cora drops by and cleans and cooks twice a week. But I don't really see her."

Amber pauses her reminiscing to hug her sister again. "I miss our conversations."

"I do too. Things moved too fast." Rein hugs her back, Amber giving her a peck on the cheek before they begin to climb the stairs.

Remembering the Care Center attached to the Windsor home, Amber decides it is as good of a time as any to bring up her conversation with Cutter. "Did you hear about Cutter's mother?"

"Not everything, but it can't be good."

"It's not good, but I might be back here for a short time...to help."

"That's great... well, not great for his mother..." She trails off.

Amber bites her lip, eyeing the stairs like a mortal enemy. "It's been a long time, better hold my hand and lead the way."

Rein smiles and takes Amber's hand, gripping it firmly. They start the climb slowly, jesting with each other in that sisterly way. "How's your husband?" Amber says with a wicked gleam in her eye.

Rein laughs, "Oh, you're so funny, we've kind of headed our separate ways for the time being...and your pregnancy?"

"My husband's in jail. When he gets out, it won't be long then."

"Congratulations." Rein pats her sister's shoulder with her free hand.

"Thanks."

They reach the top and Amber turns into her old bedroom, calling out, "Martha, we're just coming in for a few clothes. None of yours, okay?"

Rein eyes the hallway warily. "Did you see her before you left?"

"Saw her and smelled her...she needs a bath, but I ain't going to tell her."

"Me neither."

The two women head into the supposedly vacant bedroom and Amber makes a beeline for the closet, picking out pants, shirts, and blouses. She removes them from the hangers and hands them to Rein, who starts to fold them into neat piles. Rein is concentrating on the clothes for a few moments, and she looks up to see Amber by her dresser, a few nightgowns clenched in her fist.

Rein observes her sister, noting the tear rolling down her cheek. Unsure of how best to comfort her older sister, she sets down the bundle of clothes in her hands and crosses the room to pull Amber into an embrace.

"What's wrong, Amber?"

She just shakes her head, the tears flowing earnestly now.

"Amber, what's wrong?" Rein pleads.

Amber hesitates, struggling to swallow over the lump in her throat, before saying, "Has J.B. ever touched you?"

Rein pulls back and tilts her head to the side, a bit confused. "Yeah, he hugs me, and holds my hand and–"

Amber shakes her head. "No. Has he touched you...down there?" She points.

Rein's eyes widen and she gasps. "No. Never! Did he...touch you there?" Amber, ever so slightly, nods yes.

Now a tear tracks down Rein's cheek, and not knowing what to say, she leans in to hug her sister once more. The only sound in the room is their occasional sniffling, until Amber finally pulls back, furiously trying to brush away the tears.

"That's good, because I asked God to allow all the tribulations to come on me and not you."

Rein also tries to dry her eyes. "For how long? The...uh...touching I mean."

"Until I left the house a week or so ago."

"And when did it start?"

Amber thinks for a moment before dropping her shoulders and shaking her head. "I don't know, I've lost track of time."

Rein grits her teeth, her shoulders tensing. "I've got to say something."

Amber reaches out and lightly grabs Rein's arm. "No. No. He won't touch you. You're too strong. I was the weak one."

This does nothing to calm the anger on Rein's face. "That's no excuse. That son of a bitch needs to suffer."

"No. No ... Suffer? No." Amber searches for a word, "Revenge? ... Maybe in a way. Vengeance? That's too harsh. Payback?" Amber nods affirmatively with determination. Rein sees a side of Amber she hadn't seen before. Wrath. Rein struggles to swallow. Amber's eyes illuminate, "But not now, it's not the time."

Rein glances at her sister out of the corner of her eye. "But when?"

"I'll let you know. He can't hurt me now. I've stood up to him. I slapped him in the hospital."

Rein raises her eyebrows, surprised at the sudden change in Amber's demeanor. "You sound like you got this figured out?"

Amber lifts her chin. "We do." She smiles at her sister, rising in confidence to return to the task at hand. She grabs a few more items and hands them to Rein.

Rein keeps her eye on her sister as she folds the clothes. "Do you want to talk about it?"

"No. I don't want to remember right now. As far as I'm concerned, it's in the past."

Rein isn't so certain. She continues observing her sister as the process of packing clothes continues, not sure how to bring up how long the process of dealing with grief is with her sister.

Finally, once there is a good pile in front of her, she says, "I think that's enough for Jennifer."

Amber backs away from the closet and points at the dresser. "Get a handful of socks out of that drawer."

Rein slides one drawer open and her eyes catch on a yellow notebook in which she had once asked Amber to write her dreams down. She holds it up. "Have you been writing in this?"

"Not since I moved out," Amber says, pointing to their piles. "Put it on top of those clothes. We'll carry it down. I need to add a couple things in there anyways."

Rein frowns, her eyes still on the journal. "Any dreams with me in them?"

"Maybe one a couple of days ago."

Rein adds it to the pile as Amber indicated, her face still clouded with uncertainty. "Are you going to let me know if they're important?"

"Three headstones, two down by a river and the other is separate like on top of a hill," Amber spits out, not seeming too worried.

Rein, on the other hand, is hyper focused on the topic. "And I'm in it?"

"I see your back, gazing at the graves, and it sure looks like your back."

Rein retrieves a pencil from the top drawer and opens the yellow notebook pages. She begins to scribble Amber's comments down, but she isn't satisfied as she attempts to concentrate, "Three...two on a river and one on a hill." Amber dips her chin. Rein eyes her sister, waiting, but the silence which follows makes her realize Amber will say nothing more. "Thanks for letting me know."

Amber smiles, unaware of her sister's anxiety. "My pleasure."

Amber steps over to the pile of clothes and begins loading her arms. Rein sets the notebook down on the bed and helps, stacking items up until the bottom of her eyes. "Oh, we forgot a belt."

Rein clicks her tongue. "No. That will not be allowed."

"Oh, right." Amber lets out a half laugh.

Rein wedges the notebook into the pile of clothing. The two women make their way down the stairs, setting the items into the two crates. The piles exceed the top rim, so Rein kneels down to adjust the piles. She picks up the notebook and holds it in Amber's direction.

"Now keep this updated. Everyday."

Amber looks discouraged. "It's painful."

Rein isn't going to let Amber slack off that easily. "You've had more pain than writing the future in this book." Amber still eyes it like it might bite. "What are some of the good dreams you've seen?"

"Oh, me seeing where I'm going to get married...a cross and lots of stained glass."

"Oh, that's nice."

"But then there's this other dream." Amber's eyes seem to glaze over. "There's a boy, maybe Benjamin?" She takes a deep breath, "He is floating on a log down the river...and I see two pairs of hands grab him and pull him up."

Rein looks up from her rearranging. "Is he alive?"

She hesitates. "I think he is... That's all I know."

Rein holds out the book again. "This is why you need to write this stuff down that morning..." She opens the pages again and adds the Benjamin comment to the book, "...so you can remember it more clearly."

Amber concedes, staring at the notebook. "I guess you're right."

Still a bit lost in her thoughts, Amber drifts over to the side table, picking up an image of her as a young girl.

Rein tucks the notebook on the crate's interior edge and follows her sister's movements with her gaze. "That is a beautiful picture. You look so young and happy."

Amber walks to the nearest chair, sinking into it with a sigh. She studies her face while holding the picture frame, tracing her face with her index finger. "I've learned to hide things pretty well now."

"Hmm?" Rein is confused.

Amber continues on, not seeming to notice. "When you go through the fireplace into the past—"

"What?!"

"Yes," Amber continues tracing the photo, "You will be leaving a note in the past."

"I will be doing what!? What will the note say?"

"I haven't a clue, you're the one writing it."

Rein shakes her head, standing up, "First you see the future, and now are you telling me you can see the past? How far am I going to go back?"

Amber smiles, focused on the picture. "Twenty years sounds like a good round number. When Hal was building this house."

Rein squints. "That's before you were born."

"Good, look over their shoulders and tell me what ma'am and daddy say."

Realizing she would indeed get to see her parents again, Rein's spirits brighten. "Okay, I'll let you know what I find."

Amber gets emotional and veers off topic. "You're my sister, we are always on the same team. Me, you, and Benjamin for life. We only got each other to depend on."

Rein agrees with her sister, moving toward the chair she is sitting in. "I've already resigned myself to that long ago. We've got a bond that is special and forever."

Amber stands and walks to the side table, placing the picture upright with its little felt leg. "Before you go in...lay this picture frame flat on this table."

"I will, did Annie Mae tell you that?"

Amber looks up to the ceiling. "So many voices, so many ears."

"I guess that means, yes," Rein says, her eyes still watching her sisters every move. "When will I go?"

"Soon."

Rein rolls her eyes at her sister's vague answer, deciding to try a different tactic. "Will I come back alive?"

"Yes, I think." Amber walks toward her sister, giving her another hug, "If I don't see you before you go. Have a safe trip and I'll see you when you get back."

"I love you too," Rein replies as she returns the hug.

When they break apart, Amber motions to the crates, now packed. "Let's get these crates to the hospital and sneak them under Jennifer's bed. I want it to be a surprise in the morning."

Rein takes a step back. "Now I know why you want to get Jennifer out of the hospital...to get her away from J.B. as soon as possible."

Amber nods. "Watch him. But say nothing until it's time. And do not let him know you know."

Rein bites her lip, clearly wanting to disagree, but in the end, she says, "Alright."

Amber turns and collects her purse. "Maybe we can use this as leverage."

Rein is confused. "Leverage?"

"Yeah, I listen to Benjamin when you think I don't." Amber leans down to pick up the first crate.

Rein shakes her head, grinning. "I thought when you said we, I thought you were talking about God."

Amber shakes her head and laughs as she watches her pick up the second crate. Once they both have their arms full, they head out the door, making their way down the steps and into the fading light of the late afternoon.

"And don't forget to write!" Rein demands.

Amber interrupts her response spiritedly, "I will. I will dammit...It's like I've got homework again."

Rein's comeback is loud, "Just scribble it down!"

Amber's voice fades, "I will...I will."

Chapter 33

November 7, 1945
11:30am
Windsor Hospital, Chatham Hill, Middle Tennessee

A NNIE MAE SAVORS THE remaining few bites of her lunch at the small table in the hospital kitchen as Haven washes up the last of the dishes.

"That was an excellent lunch, Haven. You and Cebo are doing a great job around here," she says as she walks her empty dish over to the sink and adds it to the stack.

Haven turns shyly. "Ms. Mae...I need to ask you something—or not ask but, well anyway, here goes. I've got an offer to come help at the diner, but you've been so nice to me—"

Annie Mae looks into her eyes. "Haven, I'm not going to stop you from bettering yourself. I know you enjoy cooking, and we need you around here but...who have you been talking to?"

"Amber—" Annie Mae nearly knocks over the pile of dishes in shock before realizing Haven misunderstood. "Amber? No, I mean at the diner?"

"Well, the owner of the diner, Hannah, Amber's friend, and I've spoken to someone at Jernigan's also." Haven pauses, waiting for a response.

Annie Mae is silent.

"Ms. Mae, are you alright?" she asks hesitantly.

Annie Mae's eyes look glazed over, her pupils dilated. Haven quickly grabs Annie Mae's arm, assisting her to a nearby chair. Annie Mae sinks into it, a bead of sweat rolling down her brow. As soon as she is situated, Haven runs from the kitchen to get help.

A few moments later, she returns, Ms. Elvie in tow. Ms. Elvie takes one look at Annie Mae and then snaps into action. "Ms. Mae, you need a doctor. Haven, go get Weston now." Haven does as she is told.

"I do...need..." Annie Mae tries to speak, gasping for breath.

Haven returns to the kitchen, her face flushed from all the running, Weston at her side.

"Haven, get the wheelchair, now. Ms. Mae, do you have any pain in your chest?" Weston kneels down next to Annie Mae and begins taking her pulse.

Annie Mae can't speak but she nods. Weston continues, his voice loaded with concern, "Have you been taking the pills J.B. prescribed to you?" She shakes her head.

As soon as Haven returns with the wheelchair, Weston and Ms. Elvie help her into it before wheeling her to a hospital bed. They lift her onto the bed gently.

"Ms. Elvie, get her a nitroglycerin pill."

Ms. Elvie nods, heading for the medicine cabinet. Weston pulls out his stethoscope to check her heart rate.

When Ms. Elvie returns with the pill, Weston puts it in her mouth. "Ms. Mae, put it under your tongue." She does as he asks.

Ms. Elvie props her up on a pillow as Weston asks, "Is J.B. at home?"

Ms. Elvie nods. "I'm going to call him and let him know what's happening."

Weston walks away, and Ms. Elvie brushes Annie Mae's hair from her forehead. "Ms. Mae, you look tired." Her voice is filled with kindness. "All these problems with the lawyers snooping around every other day, David, and Canine—I hope you don't mind me saying but it's the truth—it's killing you."

Annie Mae understands, her eyes watering at the revelation in Ms. Elvie's voice. She doesn't say anything, but Ms. Elvie can tell by the look in her eyes that she understands.

"Where's Amber?" Annie Mae croaks at last, her voice scratchy and uneven.

"Don't you remember? She went to visit Stephen at the jail."

Annie Mae closes her eyes and puts her arm over her forehead. Haven brings a damp cloth, gently moving her arm to lay it over her crown.

"Where's Sadie?" Annie Mae asks as Ms. Elvie begins to dab her forehead with the cloth.

"I'll go look for her right now," Ms. Elvie replies, the hurt evident in her voice at the prospect that Annie Mae prefers Sadie to herself. She stands and leaves the room, and Haven takes her place dabbing Annie Mae's forehead.

Only a few moments later, Sadie enters, motioning Haven aside as she leans over Annie Mae.

"She asked for you," Haven explains, but Sadie doesn't reply as she sinks onto the edge of the bed.

"I'm here, Ms. Mae. Right here."

Haven takes this as her cue to leave, brushing past Ms. Elvie on her way out of the room.

"Tell Amber and Rein 'I love them'," Annie Mae whispers.

Sadie just rubs her arm with her open palm.

Weston comes back, taking Annie Mae's pulse again. "Your pulse is coming back to normal. You need to see a specialist, Ms. Mae."

"Well, finally someone is talking some sense around here," Sadie says, sarcasm lacing her voice.

Weston exhales a deep breath and looks Sadie in the eyes. "I know."

"I'll check on the other patients," Ms. Elvie calls from where she is leaning against the wall, but Weston and Sadie Blue don't seem to notice as she leaves.

A few minutes later, J.B. and Rein enter the room. Weston steps back so J.B. can take Annie Mae's vital signs for himself.

"Have you seen Benjamin today?" Annie Mae asks as J.B. takes her pulse.

"You just saw him yesterday. You sent him to school today," J.B. informs his confused wife.

Dazed, Ms. Mae replies, "Are you sure? I thought he said he was coming by for lunch."

"Ms. Mae, you need to rest," Sadie Blue interrupts to insist and then turns to J.B. "Dr. Galloway insists on Ms. Mae seeing a specialist."

J.B. looks to Weston to confirm, and the young man nods.

"I'll rest when I hear good news from Benjamin," Annie Mae says, but despite the conviction in her voice, her eyes drift closed.

"Thank you, Sadie, she loves you very much," J.B. says. He opens his mouth to add more, but before he can, a commotion reaches their ears.

"It's in the lobby," Weston concludes, as he rushes out of the room, J.B. following behind. Rein takes his place at the bedside.

"We're lucky that you seem to always be here when we have trouble," Rein muses.

"Blessed."

"What?"

"Not lucky, blessed," Sadie Blue insists.

Rein nods. "Did you go to the fireworks at the festival last night?"

"No, I didn't stay that late. I came back to the hospital to help out." Sadie looks at Rein before continuing. "If you and Annie Mae don't watch yourselves, this hospital is going to take both of you out of here. You both need to step away or—"

"Or?"

"You'll die inside these walls."

Rein's eyes widen at the harshness of her words, but before she can think of a response, the noise from the lobby increases. "I better go check on the noise, you got this?"

"You know I do."

As she nears the lobby double doors, she recognizes Major's loud voice. Rein pushes one side of the door open slowly, peering into the lobby.

"I'll tell you what I know. My son is deathly ill, and it's got to do with your family!"

Rein steps into the lobby, and as soon as he sees her, Major continues yelling, "Where's your brother!?"

"Why my brother?" Rein tilts her head to the side in confusion.

"He gave Danny a drink Saturday at the fair and now he's bleeding from his eyes and ears, and even his fingernails."

J.B. shakes his head. "Benjamin, wouldn't do that. I know my grandson very well and—"

Major's eyes are red. "He ain't your real grandson and don't tell me what he won't do! I know his dad and mother, and this is Benjamin all the way!"

J.B. tries a different tactic. "What are his symptoms?"

"The doctors from town have been at my house all morning. They say it's not normal. His symptoms are not any medical illness. It's your strange and crazy powers!" He points an accusatory finger at Rein.

Just then, Benjamin enters the lobby. Before anyone else can act, Major is across the lobby, grabbing him by the neck of his shirt and pushing him back out on the porch.

Weston and J.B. rush out after them, just in time to see Benjamin twist out of Major's grip and land on top of him. Major rolls over, pushing Benjamin down against the porch.

Weston is quick to step in, wrapping his arms around Major's chest and pulling him back.

"Let me go!" Major yells, spittle flying from his lips, his eyes crazy.

Weston eases his grip. "You're a lawman, come to your senses."

Major nods, brushing himself off, realizing just how many people saw the altercation.

Benjamin scampers to his feet. "I don't believe—"

Major pulls his bully stick from his waistband. But before he can make a move, Rein uses her powers to send it flying off the porch and into the sand by Major's patrol car. Pissed, his hand goes toward his holstered pistol.

"Stop right there, don't do it!" Rein shouts.

Her threat isn't enough to phase Major, but suddenly the metal beneath his fingertips becomes blazing hot. So hot, that the leather holster begins to smoke, and Major is forced to yank his hand back.

Turning back to Benjamin, Major snarls, "Danny told me you gave him something funny tasting. Did you poison him?"

Benjamin shakes his head. "He drank the same things I did."

"You're a liar! Sunday morning he was sickly, and today he's lost weight and bleeding from everywhere!"

Realizing he isn't getting anywhere he turns to J.B. "Does Annie Mae have anything that will help him? The doctors want to send him to other specialists in Nashville—" Major eases his tone, "—but he won't last that long."

"Annie Mae is resting from an episode with her breathing. I'll talk to her and see if she has anything she would give him for his symptoms," J.B. explains, trying to calm the sheriff.

"Benjamin and I will come see Danny this evening if Annie Mae or J.B. gives us medicine to help Danny," Rein adds.

Major steps back a step and looks each person on the porch in the eye. Major points his finger and threatens, "Bring him back to good health, or I will do everything in my power to ruin your family."

"Do you want me to come over and examine him?" J.B. asks.

Major gets right up into J.B.'s face. "Use whatever powers are in this place, but if he dies, there will be hell to pay!"

He turns to leave but stops halfway down the steps to add, "I don't always wear this badge!" He takes the remainder of the steps and retrieves his bully stick. "Sometimes I am a concerned father that has to do what a father has to do." He opens his patrol car door. "I expect someone to visit my house...and it better be soon!" he threatens one final time before driving off.

J.B. turns to his grandson. "Benjamin, what have you done?"

Benjamin doesn't answer, and instead turns to the hospital door. "Let's go see if Annie Mae is doing okay." He keeps his eyes down as he enters the hospital, J.B. following him close behind.

Weston watches Major's car drive out before looking to Rein. "I hope the powers inside this hospital can fix the future. What do you think?"

"I think...I'll have to ask and I'll get back to ya'," she replies before following Benjamin inside.

Weston is alone now. He shakes his head, pulling his car keys from his pocket as he talks to himself out loud. "You should have driven away the last time you could've." He goes down the steps, goes to his car and opens the door.

Rein calls from the open door. "You coming in?"

He pauses and gives her a hard look. "I'm just going to smoke a cigarette." She nods and closes the door.

He reaches into the dash and gets a cigarette. He leans against his front bumper and lights one up. "I should get in this car and drive," He blows a puff into the breeze, "and drive so fast and so far away...and not look back..." He puffs and blows another cloud into the air and looks at the front facade of the hospital. "But...the powers in this hospital are so captivating...I can't leave."

Rein walks from the lobby, joining the crowd at Annie Mae's bedside.

"J.B., let me take care of this. I understand that he threatened us," Annie Mae's voice calls out feebly.

J.B. just shakes his head in disdain before leaving the room. Rein watches him leave before moving closer to Annie Mae.

"Benjamin, you must have been successful," Annie Mae says.

"I mixed the potion in two different drinks. I only saw him drink a little of both."

Annie Mae turns to Sadie. "How long until he passes?" Rein raises her eyebrows in surprise.

"Depends on how much he drank."

"Sounds like enough." Annie Mae can't keep the faint note of elation from her voice.

"Major thinks we are going to pretty much bring an antidote to Danny, so we could take some colored water with some more of the potion in it. If we want to be sure."

"I don't have anymore," Benjamin announces sadly.

"I think I got something at the house, in my office, that you and Rein can take to Danny just to make Major think he's getting a cure." Rein's eyes widen in surprise. She has never seen this side of Annie Mae before.

"If he drank half that bottle it would only take three to five days. At least I think so." Annie Mae turns to Sadie. "Did you make the doll?"

"It's made with burlap and straw. I sewed that piece of the red handkerchief to his backside and colored the burlap to match his clothes." Her excitement is evident in her voice. "And early this morning—" She draws her fist into a ball, "—I pounded the life out of that doll with a hammer."

Benjamin and Rein watch Sadie Blue wide-eyed. They don't quite know what to say.

"Why are we even going to his house if it isn't a cure?" Rein asks in disbelief.

Annie Mae looks unbothered. "To appease Major and make him think we are trying to help. But there is something else I want you and Benjamin to get from Danny before he passes."

Benjamin and Rein look at each other before turning back to Annie Mae, both unsure of what she could possibly be hinting at.
"So, in my office..."

Chapter 34

November 7, 1945
1:00pm
Windsor Hospital, Chatham Hill, Middle Tennessee

VICTORIA PUSHES OPEN THE door to the diner, her red floral dress blowing lightly in the breeze. Her steps are confident, and the waitress immediately waves her to a booth along the far wall.

Sliding into the red plush booth, Victoria sets her small black purse on the bench beside her, crossing her legs to show off her sleek, black pumps.

Her eyes scan the diner, taking notice of the smattering of patrons occupying some of the 20+ tables. Some are businessmen, and others are ranchers, all of their dusty shoes resting on the checkerboard floor—except for the few customers seated at the diner counter, their feet resting on the metal bar.

The waitress cuts her evaluation short. "Hello, Ms. Driver—Victoria—you don't remember me but I'm a friend of Ambers' from her church. I saw you at the Windsor Hospital when I visited her a couple of times. My name is Hannah Miller."

"Oh, yes, I remember seeing you during my visits," Victoria replies coolly, resting her elbows on the table and her chin on her hands. Hannah's blonde hair is pulled back in a ponytail, making it easy for Victoria to give her a once over. Hannah is thin, but looks good in the diner uniform which is a tight dark green dress with a cute apron tied over the front. "You working here now?"

Hannah smiles proudly, a coffee pot gripped in one fist. "My husband and I are the owners."

Victoria is surprised, but nods approvingly. "That's great."

Hannah's smile continues. "Amber spoke so highly of you as she was healing. It's nice to finally put the name to the face."

Victoria returns the smile. "Nice to meet you. I love her very much and glad you supported her on her road to recovery—" She is interrupted by the sound of a vehicle rattling as it speeds past the dinner. "What is that?"

Hannah frowns, her eyes searching the diner windows. "I'm not sure. Cars go flying by sometimes, most people are in a hurry to get out of town."

Victoria studies the now silent street. "I guess business is great. It looks like you serve the whole cattle association?"

"Between them and the railroad I have to hire more people and I'm running out of space for tables."

"That's a good thing!" Victoria looks down at her menu before looking back up at Hannah. "Can I get a water? I'm waiting for someone."

"Sure, I'll be right back," Hannah says brightly before turning away from the table and heading behind the countertop.

It isn't long before Tobin steps through the door wearing a long button shirt and dark pants, his ensemble highlighting his bulging muscles which Victoria had never noticed before. His chiseled chin moves from side to side until his eyes settle on Victoria. He gives a small wave and makes his way to the table, struggling to fold his tall 6'2" frame into the booth.

Victoria smiles at him just as Hannah arrives with Victoria's water. Tobin immediately appraises Hannah in much the same way as Victoria had done moments before. "Hello, I didn't know I was going to have lunch with two beautiful women today."

Hannah's hand, which is holding the glass of water, freezes. She eyes

Tobin warily, in shock, until the man reaches for her hand to pull her into the booth alongside him. This snaps her out of her momentary reverie, and she pulls her hand out of his grip. "No, no, no. I'm the waitress. I just came over to say hello and see what you would like to drink?"

"I'll have water and sweet tea," Tobin says, flashing her a smile.

Hannah gulps, her eyes still trained on the large man. "Would you like to order now?"

Tobin looks at Victoria. "Do you know what you want?"

"Sure...and she's the owner of the diner," Victoria adds.

Tobin gives her a look of accomplishment and smiles. "You are? At such a young age...you must be only two or three years out of school..."

Hannah blushes and Victoria interrupts, "Her and her husband." She emphasizes the last word.

Unperturbed, Tobin continues, "...Husband? You both must be so proud of yourselves and what you both have accomplished... Is your husband here right now?"

Nervously, Hannah's eyes shift as she answers, "No...he's..." She tries but can't seem to remember where he is. "...I don't know where he is, but I'll tell him...I'll tell him you are impressed."

"That's great." Tobin's eyes finally drift from hers down to the menu. "What do you recommend?"

It takes a moment for her to realize he asked her a question and she struggles to find the answer. "Well...I...the pot roast...mashed potatoes, and string beans are excellent."

Tobin closes the menu, holding it out to her. "That sounds delicious, with biscuits or cornbread?" She nods.

Victoria watches the entire exchange, smirking.

"Did you make the cornbread?"

Hannah's nods furiously before realizing the question and quickly shaking her head. "I made the biscuits."

Tobin smiles, causing Hannah to smile back. "I'll have the pot roast and all the rest and...I guess I'm having the biscuits...My name is Tobin Lopez, what's yours?"

"Hannah...Miller."

Tobin stands and stretches out his hand. "Nice to meet you, Hannah. I love that name."

She shakes his hand, still blushing. "Thanks." He releases her hand as she turns away from the table.

Victoria calls after her, "Hannah..." She turns back, a confused look on her face. "I'll have the same."

She nods, embarrassed. "Oh, yes, okay...it was nice to meet you. I'll get your order." She disappears between the swinging double metal doors.

Tobin sits down and holds his hand out to Victoria. She replies with a sneer. "You're rotten."

She places her hand in his, Tobin kisses the back of her hand, "Good to see you today, Victoria...and by the way that's a beautiful name also."

"I know of a 90-year-old grandmother named Hannah...I know your game. Charm and charisma."

Tobin's eyes flash to hers, "Aren't they the same?"

Victoria laughs. "You got charisma and—"

Tobin interrupts, "And you've got charm—" As if realizing what she had said previously, he circles back, "—you don't really know a 90-year—"

Victoria shakes her head. "She doesn't know where her husband is...I'm sorry, if I don't melt in your fingers."

He stretches his arms open. "My mama always said, 'An act of kindness will come back to you when you least expect it.' You aren't jealous of a little flirting, are you?"

"Maybe not right in front of me."

"So behind your back is okay? I'm not like that."

"You could have probably taken her skirt off and she wouldn't have known."

Tobin eyes the closed doors which lead into the kitchen. "Maybe, but I got my eye on other skirts—not hers—right now." He catches Victoria's gaze.

Victoria sips her water. "Tell me about yourself and how you got to Mooney's... Lopez? Is that like Arizona or California?"

He leans forward to look into her eyes. "I was born in Miami. I got in trouble, and we kept moving north ahead of the law. Mama tried to change me, but it didn't go so well... Tampa, Jacksonville, by the time we got to Georgia, she sent me to the army."

"Sounds like you've done some traveling."

He shrugs. "My travels had just begun...Europe, Africa...seemed like the army only goes where there's shooting. It took 'em eight years to straighten me out good. By the time I got out a few months ago, my mama had moved just outside Madison, but I'm through running for now. How about you? Tell me about your travels to Chatham Hill?"

She lowers her eyes, embarrassed to tell him she had never been anywhere. Luckily Hannah returns at that moment with Tobin's sweet tea and water. "Your order will be right up."

Tobin winks at her before turning his eyes to Victoria, who starts her story. "My story is not as extensive as yours. I was born here. My mama and daddy worked at a hospital and a farm their whole lives—we've lived here for all of it—so my travels are just beginning."

Tobin raises his sweet tea. "Here's to a new beginning." Victoria clinks her glass with his.

Once they set their glasses down, he reaches for her hand and she doesn't pull away. "You love to dance, right? You know you can travel with your dancing, right?"

Victoria had never heard that before. "How do you mean?"

His grasp of her hand tightens. "The music on the dance floor can transport your mind to Spain, to Italy, to New York City...the music can take you and your partner all over the world..." He pauses, a mischievous glimmer in his eye. "I told you once before I'll teach you to dance."

Victoria leans in. "Who taught you?"

"Every different country I have been in."

She pulls back. "Now that makes me jealous."

Tobin smiles. "We'll start when you are ready."

Realizing how close they are leaning toward each other, Victoria pulls back and sips her water. "Was that you zipping by the window?"

He looks towards the front of the diner. "Yeah, I'm military."

She smiles. "Yeah, you done said…your trouble and the army."

"Well, all that trouble I talked about was with cars, stealing them and taking them apart. My mama said it was my training…I'm a military technician. I can fix jeeps, cars, tanks, trucks, motorcycles, anything with wheels or tracks—no airplanes though—so when the war ended a few months ago, I happened to be high enough up and they gave me a good deal on a Jeep."

"I didn't get a good look, but it looked fast."

Tobin brightens, passionate about his car. "You'll love it…you've driven with your arm out the window, right?" She nods. "This is like driving with your arms, head, feet, and body out of the vehicle…you get to see the road moving ninety miles per hour right in front of your face," He holds his palm right up to his face, "And it's right there."

"Sounds like you're trying to get yourself killed."

He thinks a split second on her words. "Maybe so…but you've got to try it."

"I saw how fast you were going…we'll see." He smiles.

Hannah brings their plates out and sets them on the table. "Anything else?"

Tobin keeps his eyes on Victoria. "Victoria, need anything?"

Victoria shakes her head, not taking notice of how much smaller her portion is than Tobin's.

Tobin doesn't seem to notice either. "This looks great…be a darling and maybe get me some butter?"

"Sure, right back," Hannah replies, rushing to do as he asked.

They each pick up their knives, slicing through their pot roast. They eat quietly, Tobin eating at a faster pace than Victoria, which draws her attention.

He feels her eyes on him. "I'm sorry, this food is tasty and smells great."

"You don't need to apologize. I can just imagine what you're used to."

"Ms. Driver, you read my mind." She takes another bite. "I see you love a good meal, too."

"I do…this may surprise you, but I don't cook much," Victoria admits, a bit sheepish.

He butters his biscuit. "I believe you. Listen, if your truck needs work...I'm your man. If you need anything...I'm your man." He takes a bite of the biscuit.

She raises an eyebrow. "Where you working?"

"Madison, isn't good for me."

"Well, there's a place out the road you're on, across from Jernigan's that's got mechanics..." He nods as he chews. She points her fork, "...And back behind you, turn left at the bank, across from the railroad depot is a dilapidated house that had a mechanic but not anymore... They may be looking."

He takes a drink and looks at Victoria. "I see what you're doing. You think if I get me a job here in town then I'll be closer to ya' and I'll owe you another meal and another date...and you know what? I think it might just work."

"Just know my plan is like your mother's. Keep working and moving farther away from here and closer to New York City... I visited there when I was little. Going to make my way back again soon."

"You can get lost there... Be careful what you wish for," he warns, his triumphant mood falling.

"I'm a big girl. I think I can handle it."

"Oh, you may be right about that. I've had my eye on you since months ago." His fork scrapes the plate as he finishes off the last of his mashed potatoes.

"You have?"

"I seen you punch that man to the ceiling and walk away. You're strong and feisty...I like that. I may have to come around more often."

Victoria wipes her mouth with her napkin and lowers her voice, "You talked about if I need something...you're the man?"

"I said it, I mean it."

She casts a glance from side to side to make sure no one is listening in before she continues. "You know the rodeo I work at?"

"I do."

"There are bulls and clowns all over the place." He nods. "They'll both get me killed...I need a gun for protection."

He stops chewing, wipes his mouth, and drinks a swig of sweet tea. "I believe you... Have you been to a rodeo?"

Victoria answers by pointing her knife. "A half a mile that way, the other side of tracks when I was twelve."

Tobin nods. "I'll get you a gun, as soon as you grant me three wishes."

She jerks back, stunned by his offer. "What's this, a fairy tale?" When he tilts his head to the side she realizes he is serious. A smile begins to break out on her face. "What's the three wishes?"

"You don't sound real thrilled, by your attitude."

"I've got to be excited, too? That's four wishes, now."

He thinks for a second tapping his finger against his chin. "Okay, you may be right about that... Number one, you gotta let me take you for a ride in my Jeep."

"You promise not to kill me?"

He gives an affirmative look. "Okay, I promise... Number two, you got to give me a kiss out by my Jeep in just a few minutes."

"Today? Damn, everybody wants kisses." Tobin draws back and Victoria quickly changes her tone, not wanting to scare him off. "Maybe we should do wish two before wish one?"

Tobin recognizes her logic. "That's why you're the brains in this operation."

"Took you long enough to realize it, and wish three?"

"Promise you'll let me teach you to dance."

Silence falls over the table as she considers the proposition. "I'll get the gun before something happens, right?"

He touches her hand. "Has someone threatened you?"

She brushes him off, repeating firmly, "I need a gun, soon."

"I'll have it tomorrow night. Are you working tomorrow?"

"Yes. I'll be there."

"Then I will too." She relaxes, leaning back for the first time in several minutes, pushing her empty plate away which he takes notice of. "You ate pretty good for a girl."

"I was hungry."

"You love good food, like I do." Tobin motions to Hannah, making a sign for the check. She nods and heads for the register.

"I think we get along good together, I hope we can become good friends," Victoria muses.

"I hope we're more than good friends." Hannah approaches the table and Tobin pulls out a few bills from his pocket.

"That's good, thank you very much, come again," Hannah says, her eyes on the tip he left her.

Tobin stands and holds out his arm for Victoria who thanks Hannah one last time, "I'll tell Amber I saw you and you said hello."

"Thank you and nice to meet you, Victoria... Mr. Lopez." She nods her head to each before reaching for their empty plates.

"Did you ever remember where you lost your husband?" Victoria asks.

Hannah smiles. "Not really, but he'll be back when he gets hungry."

Victoria narrows her eyes feeling a sudden punch of jealousy and the urge to rile Hannah. "Hannah?" She turns to face Victoria. "Tobin and I agreed during lunch we are going to name our first-born girl Hannah."

Hannah smiles in a forced way. Proud of herself, Victoria turns to the door and begins walking, pulling Tobin along.

"Who's rotten now?" he hisses as they reach the door.

Victoria shrugs, unconcerned about the waitress's feelings. "At least she remembered my name." She steps outside. "Let's go see what this death trap of yours looks like."

Chapter 35

November 7, 1945
2:00pm
On the Road to the Grisco Residence, Chatham Hill,
Middle Tennessee

REIN DRIVES IN SILENCE as Benjamin stares out the passenger side window. Every so often Rein glances at her brother, shaking her head slightly in disbelief.

"I'm guessing this could go bad or even worse than that." She rubs her forehead with the back of her hand. "Try and stay arm's length from Major... How much do you think he drank?"

"If he drank all the moonshine bottle...over half," Benjamin admits with a sigh.

"Moonshine?"

"Yeah, Roddy gave me a bottle as a gift for some help I gave him at the pregnant girl's house. I mixed it along with the potion and gave it to him."

They pass the burnt hickory tree, and Rein grips the steering wheel tighter, guiding J.B.'s car along the curving road. "Luckily Cebo found you when he did and Cass, with Victoria's help, got you home Saturday night—as drunk as you were."

"Drunk?" Benjamin grimaces then explains, "I don't know what happened...I had to take a couple of swallows, both to get the poison in the bottle and Danny wouldn't drink unless I did—"

"So you took one for the team?"

"I guess I did." Benjamin cuts his eyes at Rein. "I tried to fake it, but I must have taken some in..."

"Benjamin...you were drunk."

Benjamin ignores Rein. "How did everyone get home again? All I know is what Cass told me in a note this morning. When I woke up, everybody was gone."

Rein grins. "Victoria and Paulene drove Cass and Silva home Sunday morning. Cass had to get back to the hospital."

"How do you know all this?" Benjamin asks, turning to look at his older sister.

"I came by Sunday morning to say goodbye, and check on you and Glory. I wanted to make sure you were still breathing."

Benjamin wrecks his brain, trying to remember anything from that night, but it was totally blank. "That shine knocked my ass out." Benjamin hesitantly asks, "Who undressed me and put me to bed?"

Rein is quiet as she doesn't really want to say. "I guess you could say it was a team effort."

Benjamin runs a hand through his hair in embarrassment, but he doesn't say anything.

"Oh, by the way, I want to tell you something and don't tell a soul," Rein says as she directs the truck over the steel bridge. "I found a cast iron pan in Hal's barn with the initials RAW and VD etched on the bottom."

Benjamin's eyes widened. "Annie Mae's magic worked...after all this time..."

"I guess so. I ain't going to ask Hal about it, he'll ask questions I don't want to answer."

"Well, I'll be damned! You goin' to tell Annie Mae?" Benjamin asks.

"I already did."

"I've found out something about Hal and dad since I was at his house this last week or so." Benjamin admits, letting out a hesitant breath. He hadn't planned to tell his older sister this information so soon, but it seemed like a good time.

"Michael?" Rein questions in shock.

Benjamin nods, his mind flashing back to his time in the closet at Hal's. "I saw some papers with large sums of money in some bank accounts in New York City."

"You think Michael and Hal hid some of the missing money from years ago?"

Benjamin doesn't say anything, the look in his eyes saying it all, "Like you said I don't want to ask Hal questions because—"

Rein interrupts. "He'll know you know," she surmises.

Benjamin nods a second time. "In the back of my mind, I've been wondering what Michael and Alex...Well, mom and dad are doing now."

Rein quickly corrects him. She elongates as she pronounces, "It's Alexandra." Benjamin smiles. They both laugh then Rein returns to Benjamin's question. "Like two alley cats landing on their feet, I'm sure."

"Might make them easier to find," Benjamin whispers, before adding, "If we ever want to, that is."

"Let's keep these secrets amongst ourselves," Rein says and Benjamin agrees, watching the road as Rein maneuvers the car toward Major's house. "Amber told me yesterday I am going to go into the fireplace hearth...into the past."

"Are you afraid?"

"If I go in, something bad has happened...I told Annie Mae and Amber and now you...I'll lay down Amber's picture frame on the side table flat on the table, then you know where I've gone."

"Aren't you worried about getting back?" Benjamin asks.

Rein replies immediately, "Amber told me I would be coming back alive."

"Good luck," Benjamin replies to Rein's surprise.

Rein's voice gets choppy. "Amber told me something that may change how we feel about our childhood...but she's got to tell you, not me. It's big."

"How big?" he questions innocently.

"Big enough that it made me feel like it's time to act as an adult."

Benjamin shakes his head. "I've poisoned a man and now I'm going to visit him and lie to his face about getting better...Don't you think I already feel grown up?"

Rein looks at him out of the corner of her eye. "I guess you have a point."

It is silent for a moment.

Then Benjamin breaks the heavy quiet, "And I am enjoying it all...except getting drunk."

As Major's house comes into view she turns to Benjamin one last time. "You know this ain't going to turn out good. There could be a fight. If he lifts a hand, I'll be forced to use my powers."

"I understand."

Rein pulls the car underneath a tree, putting it in park. "Just remember we have to trick him."

"I know," Benjamin agrees, but Rein can tell by the tone of his voice he isn't quite sure how they will do so.

Benjamin and Rein are interrupted by the barking of Major's dogs as they run up to greet the car. Popping open his door, Benjamin uses his foot to push one away as it tries to force itself into the car.

"We ain't got out of the car yet!" he yells as if the dogs could understand.

Rein ignores them. "Do you have the bottles?" Benjamin nods a quick yes, and the two begin to climb out of the car. Although they sounded ferocious before, the dogs back up as the two step out from the vehicle.

She takes his hand in hers. She looks into his eyes as they make their way to the door. "Do you want to go see Michael?"

"Maybe... If I do, I'll let you know first." He pauses, his eyes climbing to the second story of the home. "Do you want to go?"

Rein immediately knows who he is talking about. "Hell no."

Benjamin squeezes her hand in understanding. He quickly releases his grip and says, "Annie Mae said he is going to look...like a bloody mess."

As they approach the house, the door swings open, and Major steps out onto the porch.

"Get in and get out," Rein says under her breath before waving at Major, a fake smile plastered on her face.

"You got a cure?" Major snaps.

"We brought something we hope will work," Rein explains as they climb the steps.

Major's face is stoic, his hands on his hips. "That don't sound promising."

"Annie Mae says if this doesn't work then she can't help," Rein clarifies.

"Tell her, if he ain't healed, then I'll put my gun belt back on, and she can expect a visit real soon."

Rein and Benjamin don't say anything as Major holds the door open for them and directs them upstairs. As they walk up the stairs, their eyes are drawn to Elliott and an older couple, the three of them sitting in the large front room.

"Is that a doctor?" Rein asks.

"No, doctors don't help. They're just some friends," Major explains cryptically.

At the top of the stairs, Kathleen materializes, bloody rags gripped in her hands. Her eyes water, but she doesn't say anything as she moves past the trio.

"Mrs. Grisco," Rein greets her, but the woman only responds with a hard glare.

Major leads them to the room where Danny is lying on a bed, his hands, fingers, and head bandaged. A nurse is there, leaning over his thin form. While he was once burly for his age, Benjamin can see he has clearly lost weight. His eyes and ears are covered with white eye pads and Benjamin suspects he doesn't even know they are there.

"Let's see what you got. He's dehydrated and don't want nothin' to drink," Major explains.

Benjamin reaches into his side pocket and pulls out two bottles, handing them to the nurse. She rolls them over in her hands, noticing that one has an eye dropper and the other has a twist top. "Ms. Mae, says three drops in his eyes and ears every hour for the first twelve hours then every three hours after that." The nurse retrieves a pad from the nightstand and writes the directions down.

"The bigger bottle, she says, give him two tablespoons every hour for the first six hours and then two tablespoons every four hours," Rein adds, pointing to the bottle with the twist top.

"When will we see some improvement?" Major raises an eyebrow.

"Annie Mae says if you don't see any improvement after 24 to 48 hours, then she doesn't have the answer."

Major cuts Rein off. "That's bullshit."

Before Rein can retort, Danny Boy moans. The nurse sets the pad on the bed and tilts Danny's head up, placing a straw in his mouth so he can sip water before twisting the top off of the larger bottle.

"Rein, help her," Major demands.

"Danny...you gotta take this medicine," the nurse says in a low voice to Danny Boy.

Rein helps the nurse lift Danny's head so they can pour a spoonful of medicine into his mouth. She follows with a couple of spoonfuls of water.

"When did he get sick?" Rein asks Major after Danny has swallowed the medicine.

"Saturday night, late...when he got home from the fair."

"Can he talk? I guess he can hear," Benjamin asks as he looks at Danny's bandaged head.

"For now."

"I want to talk to him alone," Benjamin insists.

"Alone?" Major is skeptical.

"Yeah, alone. You know we have an edge," Benjamin says, hinting at the fact that he plans to use magic on Danny.

Major raises his eyebrows. "You see he's growing old right in front of us."

"Alone, or it won't work."

Major relents.

"Okay, but tend to him, or I'll throw your ass down the steps."

"Yes, sir," Benjamin agrees.

Major reluctantly goes to the door. "Nurse, let's let them be for a time." She stands and follows Major out the door, closing it behind them.

Benjamin goes to Danny's bedside and takes his hand like he is greeting him. He then sits on the bed. "Rein, stroke his arm as I speak to him."

She does as he asks. "Danny...imagine in your mind that Amber...yes, Amber, is here...she's worried about your condition, Danny...she is here now, caressing your arm and wanting you to think about being together with her...for a long time."

Benjamin continues in a monotone voice, "Danny..." Benjamin clenches down on Danny's hand still gripped in his own. For a moment all is still, then Danny flinches. Benjamin has Danny under a type of hypnosis. Rein jumps a bit in surprise. Danny's lips twitch at their edges as if he is trying to smile. "Danny...Relax. Imagine lying on a blanket in a wide open field and Amber is by your side. Rest your eyes. Can you speak to this beautiful creature lying beside you? Say 'relax sweetheart,' say it Danny," Benjamin urges.

Danny's voice is cracked and broken, likely from dehydration. "Sweetheart, relax here beside me."

"Danny...now imagine a cool breeze blowing over the field." Benjamin takes the pad from the bed and waves the pages over his face to create a breeze. Danny's arms and shoulders relax. "Danny...your sweetheart knows about her picture you have—" His eyes rise to meet Rein's as he continues, "Danny...she wants to know where it is so you can hold it."

Danny turns his head toward Rein as she begins a whisper, "Sweetheart, where is the picture?" She waits for a quiet moment. "I want you to hold the picture to remember me by...where is the picture?" Danny's lips move. Rein leans down to his lips and turns her ear so she can hear the quiet words. "The book?" she asks, trying to clarify the words she can't quite hear.

"Sweetheart...where's the picture?" Danny's lips move, and Rein's ear is close. "In the book?" She nods to Benjamin, and he looks toward Danny's desk.

Rein continues stroking his forearm as she watches Benjamin search the desktop for a book of some sort.

Benjamin searches every book on his desk. There's nothing. He opens the drawers on each side of the desk, setting all the books from the drawers on the desktop. He turns each book upside down and dangles all the pages open, looking for anything that resembles a picture.

Rein turns back to Danny. "Danny…are you saved? Do you know the Lord?" Benjamin stops for a split second, but Rein nods for him to continue as she asks, "Do you believe in Jesus and ask forgiveness for your sins?"

Danny's grip tightens on Rein's hands, just as something falls from the book onto the disheveled pile of books. It's the exact picture they were looking for. Benjamin quickly starts shoving the books back into the drawers, stuffing the image in his pocket.

Major enters just as Benjamin does so, his eyes following the movement. "What did you just put in your pocket?"

Rein stands, releasing Danny's hand. "We got Danny into a more relaxed state. Hopefully, he can heal easier."

Major looks at Danny, noticing his even, deep breathing. "Well, at least he is resting peacefully. Did you heal him?"

Rein steps towards the door. "We are going to quietly leave and give him time to heal," she replies, avoiding Major's question. Benjamin follows close behind her.

Major isn't fooled and asks again, "Is he healed?"

"We gave him peace. It's up to the Lord now," she says, her voice firm.

Major turns to Benjamin. "What did you put in your pocket?"

Benjamin puts his hand deep into his pocket, feeling the folded picture. But he also feels a scrunched-up piece of paper. He quickly pulls out the paper, showing it to everyone. "It's the paper Annie Mae gave me with the directions on taking the medicine."

He holds the paper out to Major, who snatches it as Rein and Benjamin make a quick beeline for the door.

Major follows them out the door and watches as they reach the bottom. "Tell J.B. and Ms. Mae I'll be by soon and give them an update."

They nod, exiting through the door and running past the barking dogs to the car. Rein climbs in, starts the car, backs up, shifts it into drive, and stomps the gas.

Benjamin looks behind them, watching as the dogs give chase. "Well, we got what we came for...What's with the Lord stuff?"

"Amber will ask, so this way I got something to tell her." Rein takes a deep breath. "What you did to Danny back there...Ms. Elvie told me awhile back that Daddy had a power like that."

Benjamin looks at Rein, but he doesn't say anything. Neither does Rein, and they are silent the rest of the drive home.

Chapter 36

November 7, 1945
4:00pm
Sadie Blue's House, Chatham Hill, Middle Tennessee

AMBER AND PAULENE SIT side by side on the piano bench, Amber explaining scales to the younger girl. Just as Paulene attempts her first scale on her own, the phone rings, a jolting sound through the peace of the afternoon.

Rushing to the phone, Amber picks it up with a breathy, "Hello." She pauses. "Yes, this is Ms. Blue's residence. I am a close friend of Ms. Blue, Amber Windsor. I'm living here now. Can I take a message?" A longer pause. "Yes. I believe Trevor knew of Mr. Tate's condition."

Paulene walks over to stand by Amber, concern clouding her eyes, but Amber isn't distracted from the call. "Yes, I'm sorry. I'll give this message to Trevor and Ms. Blue." She pauses again and Paulene can hear a voice on the other end but can't make out what is being said. "I'll pray for you and your family during this time of need and pain. I'm sorry for your loss, there's nothing sadder than losing a family member." She motions for Paulene to return to the piano as she finishes the conversation. "Good afternoon."

With a sigh she returns to the piano, finding Paulene's large eyes swimming with moisture and fixated on her. "Is Mr. Tate alright?"

Amber shakes her head. "No, sweetheart, he lost the battle at the hospital, and he passed. Did you know Mr. Tate well?"

Paulene's lips turn down at the corner. "He talked to me before I left school almost every day and I looked for him when I didn't have anyone else to talk to."

Amber reaches her arm around the younger girl, pulling her close. "I'm sorry." Realizing the piano bench isn't the most comfortable, Amber stands, guiding Paulene to the couch. "Was he a teacher?"

"He kept the school clean." Paulene sniffles. "He is a good friend, and I want to see him tomorrow."

Amber hugs the young girl tighter. "I'm sorry Paulene, the Lord wanted to see him in heaven right now. He was in a lot of pain, and it was time for him to go to heaven."

Paulene is crying in earnest now. "Why do good people die so early?"

"I don't know, sweetheart, I guess God wants to see how the rest of us reacts to his passing and to his close family."

"Can I go—" She stops and rubs the back of her hand under her nose.

Amber eases Paulene to the side. "Let me go to the kitchen and get you a tissue and a glass of water."

She returns a moment later, handing both to Paulene and once she had made use of them both, she envelops the girl in a hug again. After letting the girl cry for some time, she decides to make a suggestion. "Let's take a walk, Paulene, in the fresh air. And maybe go check out the barn out back. I haven't seen what's in the barn yet myself."

The two girls stand, Paulene shuffling her feet as Amber leads her to the back door and helps her into her coat. After slipping on her own, Amber opens the back door, a chilly breeze immediately inviting itself in the home.

"Ms. Amber, can I hold your hand, please?"

"Of course, dear," Amber replies, closing the door behind her and taking up Paulene's hand.

They make their way to the long, skinny, wood frame building,

Amber's eyes catching on the rough cut slats running vertically around the entire exterior. The barn was once painted gray, but it was many years before and the paint is now chipping in places. There are two windows on either side of the door, the wind making an odd sound as it bounces off the metal roof.

Letting go of Paulene's hand, Amber pulls the key ring from her pocket and starts trying each key. It isn't the first or second key, but the third clicks into place without issue. Amber pushes open the door, ushering Paulene onto the hard dirt floor before pulling the door closed behind them.

It's dark in the barn with the door closed, and it takes a moment for Amber to feel around the seam of the door for a light switch. Even when she does find it, and flips it on, the two lightbulbs aren't nearly enough to truly illuminate all of the shadows lurking in the corners. But they can see the rows of projects Trevor has been working on.

Amber steps toward the first one in awe. "Paulene, do you believe this!"

Paulene makes her way forward slowly, eyes on an unfinished wood chair. Although it looks a bit rough, Paulene sinks into it before Amber can stop her. She rocks back and forth.

"Paulene, you know you might be the first one to sit in that chair," Amber observes, a smile growing on Paulene's face as she comes to the same realization.

Paulene grows bored quickly, and moves on to the next chair, which is less finished, touching the uneven wood surface. Amber chuckles.

Paulene stops. "What's so funny?"

"You've got sawdust all along your backside," Amber admits between chuckles.

Paulene quickly tries to slap the sawdust from her backside but can't quite reach. "Let me help you. Turn around." Amber brushes her hand lightly over Paulene, removing all of the sawdust.

Once she is clean, Paulene heads further into the barn, running her hand over an unfinished table.

"Be careful. If it's not sanded you may get splinters. I'm partially a nurse but you might not want me digging them out," Amber warns her.

Paulene continues running her hand over it, unconcerned. "I'll let mama get it out." She then moves on to another table to do the same motion.

Amber shakes her head. "Paulene, come here a minute. Stop and come here."

Paulene freezes and turns slowly. She walks back to Amber, begrudgingly. "Listen, Paulene, Trevor, said we could come in here, but there are dangerous things in here we could get hurt on. Now I'm going to take your hand, and we are going to walk a circle around here to that back door and back up here before I let you go on your own. We can't run in here. Okay?" Paulene nods and takes Amber's hand.

She begins their walk around. "You see there are saw blades and screwdrivers and there's a sanding machine, I guess, of some kind." They walk around a scrap pile of all different lengths of wood. "See if you get too close to this pile you could trip and fall and hurt yourself. How would I be able to explain that to Ms. Elvie?"

Paulene thinks before answering, "You wouldn't be able to. You'd be in big trouble."

"You're right, big trouble and I don't need that." Paulene agrees and grips Amber's hand tighter. "Let's walk this way and get back to the front door." Paulene nods and starts skipping along. "You see all that stacked wood?" She nods again, as Amber steps on the edge of the piece of wood. It flips over on its side. Paulene jumps. "See if you try and step on this wood, you'll go down."

As they finish their circle and near the door, Amber spots a counter with drawers. They head that way, noticing that there is an attached desktop littered with bolts and screws. "See all those nuts, they match up with one of those bolts." Paulene steps towards the tray, sits on the stool, and begins to dig through the pile.

Glad that the girl is busy with a seemingly innocuous task, Amber drifts further down the counter, eyeing the tools hanging on the wall before pulling open drawers out of curiosity.

One drawer has sandpaper and drill bits, while another holds nails and a hammer. The final drawer she pulls open strangely has a voodoo doll she vaguely remembers spotting in the house before.

Confirming that Paulene is still busy with a glance over her shoulder, she swoops up some nails and a hammer. "Paulene, you want to hammer some nails?"

Paulene nods, her eyes dancing with excitement.

Stopping by the wood pile, she brings all the supplies to the desk. At the sight of her approaching, Paulene's eyes grow wide. Amber sets up the wood, hammer, and one nail. "Let me show you."

Amber holds up the nail. "This is a roofing nail, Hal and Cebo use these all the time. You hold it between your fingers first and you lightly tap it like this, and it will stand on its own. And then you tap it like this and then again harder and it will sink like it's supposed to."

Paulene nods in excitement and reaches for the hammer. Amber hands her a nail as well. "You hold it like this." Amber nods. "And tap it ever so lightly."

"Yes."

Paulene hits the nail and it barely sinks into the wood. She strikes again, misses and then strikes a third time, bending the nail.

"Well, you got the nail in. It isn't pretty but it's in," Amber observes. Paulene, meanwhile, has a smile from ear to ear. "You try a few more, I'm going to be right here...and if you hit your finger then you're doing it wrong."

"I watched daddy do it," Paulene explains while reaching for a second nail.

"You practice and be careful." Paulene agrees and Amber drifts back to the counter, her hands drawn to the drawer with the voodoo doll. She pulls it out, holding it in her hand.

Studying the doll, she runs her fingers over the stitching and button eyes. She turns it over and sees the red piece of handkerchief. The sight of it sparks a flame in her memory but she can't recall why.

She stares at the doll a while longer, eventually closing her eyes. When she does, it all comes rushing back. She has felt this cloth before.

Heart beating fast, she lays the doll on the counter, her mind flashing back to that summer afternoon when she was slammed onto the table in her home by the devil.

At some point, during her flashback, she apparently grabbed a second hammer, which is now lined up with the doll nose. Without thinking, she taps the nose lightly. Then again. And again. And again.

Until eventually, she is pounding the doll on the countertop with all her might, the sound of the metal colliding with the wood ringing in her ears.

"Amber."

She doesn't stop.

"AMBER."

"AMBER!"

Spinning around, Amber finds Paulene behind her, eyes wide. "You're scaring me."

Suddenly remembering where she is, Amber spins back to the counter, sweeping the doll and hammer into the drawer with one movement, slamming the drawer back into place. She turns back around and reaches for Paulene.

Panting and afraid, Paulene steps just out of Amber's reach.

Trying again, Amber takes a step forward.

Paulene steps out of reach, her foot catching on a rough edge, sending the girl tumbling.

She reaches out to catch herself, her soft hand meeting the sharp edge of unfinished wood, slicing open her palm. Blood begins to flow down her light skin, dripping on the floor.

Jumping into action, Amber snatches her arm and practically drags her to the counter, wrapping the wound in a rag she found. Applying pressure as she has been taught, she quickly leads the girl from the barn into the house. Paulene, scared, is crying the whole way.

Pulling the girl over to the kitchen sink, she rinses the cut in cold water, replacing the dirty rag with a tea towel from the counter. Paulene continues crying as Amber increases the pressure on the wound.

"Paulene...Paulene, it's going to be alright," she promises.

Paulene nods, but the tears keep coming as Amber dabs the wound, applying even more pressure. "Hold this while I go get some ointment to put on your cut." Amber heads into the bathroom, grabbing a tube of ointment and returning to lightly apply it to Paulene's wound. After it is applied, she wraps the wound delicately with a bandage, taping it into place.

Paulene inspects the bandage. "Ms. Amber, do you think it'll leave a scar, like on your neck?"

Amber draws her into a hug. "Let's hope not, sweetheart, let's hope not."

Chapter 37

November 7, 1945
9:00pm
Mooney's Bar, Outside Chatham Hill Township,
Middle Tennessee

VICTORIA SHOVES HER WAY past another intoxicated man, stumbling as she nearly falls into the lap of another. There's a lively band on stage tonight, though the lead singer can barely remember the words in his own stage of intoxication. Finally giving up, he stops singing, letting the band continue to play as he jumps off the stage into the crowd.

Booze flows freely, the dim lights of the club illuminating the numerous campaign posters dotting the walls. Not that it matters now, as Elijah had announced a few hours earlier that Kieffer had won. He is now the new Coweta County District Attorney. As such, the next round had been on the house, which is what started this loud rambunctious party. Although Elijah had covered that one round, Victoria knew for a fact that the patrons were currently repaying him tenfold.

Victoria finally makes it to the bar, coming to stand next to Jesse, who looks just as annoyed. "Seven, I can't keep up with the orders, they are getting the beers and drinks off my tray before we get to the person who ordered the drink.”

Seven smiles at Victoria, yelling, “Put your trays behind the bar and just walk around and try and keep the peace.”

Victoria looks at Jesse, who shrugs, and they do as Seven suggested, heading to the front door to get some air.

Other people had the same idea, however, as the hallway to the porch is so packed Slayter and Boots can’t even eject the unruly patrons from the bar.

As Victoria nears the front door, a hand grabs her wrist and pulls her towards the dance floor. She tries to pull away, but there is nowhere to move away to, as the crowd immediately swallows any available space. She’s still trying to figure out how to escape the hand when she runs right into Tobin’s chest.

Her eyes trail up his body to the smile occupying his face.

“Glad to see you. I didn’t know if you could get in. I’m glad you did,” Victoria says with a smile.

“Let’s dance,” Tobin whispers, though the two of them can barely move with the number of bodies on the dance floor.

“Okay, but just ‘til the song ends.”

Tobin shrugs as he tries to spin Victoria. “I can’t hear any music. We’ll dance until we get evicted.”

Tobin smiles and pulls her close and Victoria wraps her arms around his shoulders. The two rock awkwardly back and forth in the limited space until Victoria sets her head on Tobin’s chest and whispers, “You got something for me?”

He nods.

Pleased, the two continue dancing until the musicians finally stop and begin packing their instruments. With one last glance at the dance floor, Victoria motions to Tobin. “Follow me.”

Tobin grabs her hand and follows her past the bathroom toward the kitchen, constantly dodging couples and men who are standing in every inch of available space. When they arrive at the kitchen door, Victoria pushes against it, only to find it won’t move.

"I can't open the door," she says to Tobin who immediately pulls her aside and uses his large form to push.

As soon as the door opens a crack, Walter shouts, "One minute!" Scuffling comes from the other side of the door before it swings open. Walter motions them to enter, closing the door behind them and pressuring the chair up against it. A big man Victoria has never seen before sits in the chair, effectively keeping the door blocked.

Victoria shakes her head. "Walter, this is the worst I've ever seen!"

Walter nods, brushing sweat off his brow, as Victoria grabs Tobin's hand and goes into the locker room.

The minute they are alone in the locker room, Victoria sinks down to sit on a crate with a huff, and Tobin follows suit. Both pant from the effort it took for them to enter the kitchen.

Despite being two closed doors away from the dance floor, they can still hear drunken yells and cheering from time to time. It isn't until Victoria finally catches her breath that she realizes she is still holding Tobin's hand. She drops it immediately. "When did you get here?"

"About 30 minutes before the speech." Tobin pulls out a pack of cigarettes from his pocket, offering one to Victoria. She declines. Snatching the eagle lighter from his front pocket, he lights the cigarette, blowing the smoke of the first puff toward the ceiling.

Victoria grimaces. "I wouldn't date a man that smokes them things."

"The military taught me three things: cigarettes, cards, and guns."

Victoria watches him take another puff. "What have we got going here?" She motions to him with her finger, then herself.

"What do you mean?"

"I'm not the marrying type, or the steady girlfriend type...I'm more day by day, take a chance girl."

His eyes peruse her face, a smirk on his lips. "I figured that out a while ago." He takes another puff. "Has anyone threatened you?"

Victoria twirls a piece of her hair between her fingers. "Yeah, a couple of guys up your way roughed me up...it's been a month or more. One hit me with a gun, but I got the upper hand." Tobin raises his eyebrows. "They might be pissed...And you can't trust a man, you know?"

"Listen, you can't trust a woman, either." Tobin counters as he shifts his weight towards her. "Ms. Driver, sounds like you got moxie."

"What's that?"

"Well, you said you got beat on with a gun, you survived, and you knocked an asshole's head to the ceiling, and walked away...what I'm asking is, if I attacked you right now, could you defend yourself?"

She stands, facing him. "You do what you think, mechanic?"

He smiles. "That's moxie, right there. Now sit down and let's talk a deal."

She crosses her arms. "Deal?... Is this like your wishes?"

"No. No...I got other skills that I'll show you one day, when I know you better."

This causes her to raise an eyebrow. "How do I know I can trust ya'? And know that you're not a con man?"

He draws back, shocked by her words. "I'm offended by that, you hurt my feelings."

"I hope it'd take more than words to hurt your feelings." Victoria smirks, not fooled by Tobin's antics.

"You're right, I am pretty thick skinned, besides you're going to be holding a gun soon, you do what you think best..." She nods. "... you're special and I don't want to lose you...all I ask is that you take me along with you when you go."

Victoria studies Tobin, pensive. After a while she motions her chin to his pocket. "You got a cigarette?"

His eyes brows raise, but he obliges, lighting it for her with his eagle lighter.

Victoria begins to pace. Her heels clacking against the wooden floorboards. Tobin watches in silence.

"Crack that window over there," she says at last, motioning to a small two panel window in the corner, Tobin does as she asks then returns to sit on the crate once more. "How do you get paid? For helping me, I mean."

A saccharine smile spreads across his features. "You're smart and beautiful, money will come to you easily when you get your roll on...I just want to be on your train."

"Okay…" She blows another puff of smoke, apprehensive.

"Do you know what you are sitting on?"

Tobin tilts his head, trying to see the words on the crate. "Alcohol, I guess."

"No…look." He stands, opening the crate he is sitting on to pull out a bottle and hold it to the light. "Does it scare ya'?" she asks.

"No, what you got on your mind?" Victoria takes another puff.

"Let me do some ciphering…and I'll let you know."

"Ciphering? Is that like counting?" Victoria scrunches her nose, her mind turning.

"Yeah, counting money…let me talk to some people and maybe we can get a business going."

"I always wanted to be in business," he muses.

"You can talk a good game. You know how to use that gun?"

"I can make a living with a gun if I need to." She considers a moment before holding out her hand toward him. "It's a deal."

He grasps her hand in his, giving it a firm shake, "Now, I'll watch your back while I'm here. Just give me a head's up if you see them out-of-towners."

"Will do, but after talking with you, we might search them out."

Tobin nods. "Sounds good…I'll wait to hear from you." He tilts his ear toward the ceiling, silence reaching his ears. "Sounds like the rodeo is calming down."

"It does, don't it," Victoria agrees. "Let's go get my little sister."

He pulls open the door for her. She passes him by, and he falls in step behind her. They weave their way through the kitchen and out to the back lot. "Where'd you park?"

"Back row along the side," Tobin confirms, his eyes jolting every which way into the dark and shadowy corners.

"There's usually a shotgun in the shadow at the corner," Victoria says, trying to reassure him.

Tobin doesn't seem to hear her, pulling up his pant leg up to reveal a small gun. He pulls her behind him, checking around each corner as they make their way around the building to his Jeep.

Once they are both inside, he unlocks his glove compartment. He reaches in and pulls a revolver out. "It's a .38 special. It's common for the police to carry now and the military, it's pretty accurate."

"Is it from—"

Tobin interrupts, "Now, don't ask me a question, unless you want an answer. Remember the answer could be dangerous."

Victoria's mouth snaps shut. Tobin holds out the gun, handing it to her barrel pointed down.

"Have you shot a gun before?"

"Not as much as you," she fibs.

"Why don't we do some practice tomorrow afternoon before your work hours?"

"Okay, but I don't work tomorrow. Got off to watch my sister. I'll shoot and then head home. Meet you at the bridge at 2:00?"

"I've got a place we can go...here's the bullets for tonight." She takes four bullets from his outstretched hand. "Go put them in your truck under the seat. While you're shooting tomorrow, I'll make you a place to hide the gun and make it easy to get to. Now go."

Victoria doesn't argue, rushing over to her truck to stow the gun and bullets in the glove compartment. After snapping it shut, she glances around briefly to ensure the coast is clear before running back to the Jeep.

"That should give you a little comfort tonight," Tobin says, leading her back to the door of Mooney's.

"Did you go by and check on a job yesterday?" she asks Tobin.

"I did, told them I'd have to think about it..." She raises her eyebrows at him. "Besides, I work for you now."

She stops. "I don't have anything in the works, right now."

Tobin shrugs, unconcerned. "Maybe I'll take one of them jobs to stay out of the way a bit, until you hear about something."

"That's a plan."

"Okay...now let's see if we can get back in." He turns toward the back door, apprehension clouding his face.

"Walter," Victoria calls through the door, "Let me in...and I vouch for Tobin."

Tobin smiles as they hear shuffling on the other side of the door, leaning in close to whisper, "How about let me get one of them wishes crossed out by driving you in my Jeep to the shooting area."

"Sounds like a plan."

"What if our deal doesn't turn out like we want?"

They hear the sound of the lock turning, but just before the door opens, Victoria leans into Tobin and gives him a quick kiss. Her eyes alight with mischief. "I've got a gun now... What is it they say, 'shoot first and often'?"

Chapter 38

November 8, 1945
7:00pm
Windsor Hospital, Chatham Hill, Middle Tennessee

T HE EVENTS OF THAT day run rampant through Rein's mind as she stands at the sink, staring wistfully out of the back window of the hospital. While it is sad what is happening to Danny Boy, that is the consequence of the type of evil he had been involved in perpetuating.

She glances over her shoulder to notice Weston examining Mary as she lays in bed. He finishes the examination then walks to the cabinet to collect her medication.

"Are you planning to go to Boston for the holidays?" she asks as he shakes out a few pills into his hand.

"I haven't decided, but I am leaning towards a trip...or at least a change of scenery."

"Change of scenery?"

He locks the cabinet and raises an eyebrow at Rein in answer.

"Will you return?" she prods.

"I most certainly will," he promises before heading back to Mary's bedside, pausing to talk to Rein, "Why? Would you be surprised if I jumped ship?"

Rein shakes her head sadly. "I'm sorry, but I'm surprised you haven't already."

"Are you trying to run me off? Because what you are implying about my character, or lack thereof, maybe you don't know me at all." He turns away. "Ms. Windsor, I have a patient who needs tending." She watches as Weston helps Mary take the pills.

Once he is finished, he rises and heads back in Rein's direction. She thinks maybe he will say something more, but he passes her by in favor of sharing hushed whispers with Ms. Elvie.

He senses Rein's eyes on him, and walks back toward her after he is finished giving Ms. Elvie instructions. "Are you trying to fire me, Ms. Windsor?"

"No, not today. But I did see you with your girly friend the other morning." Rein crossed her arms over her chest.

"You did? You're up mighty early." Weston seems surprised.

"Don't want to miss anything." Rein presses her lips into a thin line.

He smirks. "Are you jealous?"

"Jealous?" Rein looks around and realizes that many of the sets of eyes in the room currently rest on her and Weston. "If you have a minute, could you follow me, please?"

Weston follows her to J.B.'s office. Rein closes the door behind them.

She turns to Weston. "No, but you have taught me to be forward and direct, so I might as well say that I've heard you are planning to leave at the beginning of the year."

The smirk is knocked right off his face. "Yes, I will have completed my obligation with Dr. Windsor. There is nothing to keep me here after that," he admits.

"Nothing? What about your lady friends at Jernigan's?" she snaps.

"Those lady friends do not do festivals well," he replies, anger lacing through his words.

"You might think me a child, but I have to learn sometime." Feeling brash, she moves closer to Weston, pressing her lips to his. She only intends to leave them there for a moment, but Weston's arms come around her back, holding her in place.

Their lips move together as one, and there is something so addictive about the feeling. Each time Rein thinks that Weston will release her and stop the kiss, his arms only grip her tighter.

She isn't sure how long they kiss, but eventually they break apart, both gasping for breath.

"I'm sorry, Weston—" She starts to apologize.

Weston cuts her off. "No, I must apologize, I shouldn't—"

Rein puts her fingers against her lips. "No, I'm sorry, but that didn't feel right."

Weston is quiet. Rein walks toward the door, but turns back, her hand resting on the doorknob. "I'm sorry, Weston, but that was not what I was expecting. It wasn't fireworks, or anything special, I'm sorry."

Weston grabs her arm. "Rein, you are not a child. You are a woman, and you found an answer that we both have been searching for."

"Both?"

He grabs her by the shoulders, "Listen, Rein, I have grown fond of you, and I didn't know until this very moment where we stood, but I know now."

"I understand. We can continue to be good friends," she concludes, leaning in to give him a warm hug.

"Rein, you are a brave woman, and I have witnessed a very powerful spirit in you. We will eventually part, and when we do, I will never forget these times we have shared. And when you get accepted by a college up North, I'll help you get a leg up in your studies when you arrive."

"Thank you, I hope to get the courage to leave, I mean…"

"When the time comes, you'll know," Weston promises her.

"Mr. Galloway, you have patients" she jokes, turning back to the door and pulling it open.

"Thank you, Ms. Windsor, and by the way, the woman the other morning, she has connections with our troubles with these lawsuits," he explains.

"So, you're ahead of the game?"

He shakes his head. "I'm learning a lot from her." He pushes past her, turning toward the patients, only for Annie Mae to step in their path.

"Weston, J.B. says you got some information about Danny's condition?"

"Yeah, my friends—" Weston looks at Ms. Mae, "—at City Hospital, say Danny is dehydrated, has lost 30 pounds, is bleeding from his eyes, mouth, ears, and fingernails. He is on his last days. None of the doctors can seem to find what's wrong."

Annie Mae raises her eyebrow. "And what did you tell them?"

"I told them that I thought it sounded like stomach cancer, but I didn't know the exact cause."

Annie Mae nods in approval. "That's good," she says before walking toward where Burn is helping Mr. Solomon into bed.

Burn looks up at Annie Mae as she approaches. "Ms. Mae, you got something on your mind?"

"Burn, do me a favor, if you would please?"

"Anything, Ms. Mae," he promises.

"If you got a gun in your truck, would you bring it into the hospital for the next day or two?"

"You expecting trouble?" Burn tucks Mr. Solomon under the blanket before turning his eyes to Annie Mae.

Annie Mae's eyes look troubled. "Major's son is sick, and I think he's going to blame me."

Burn, sadly, understands. "I'll go do that right now." He leaves the room, presumably heading for his truck.

Next, Annie Mae's eyes turn to Cebo, who is currently changing the bedding on one of the patient beds. "Cebo, I appreciate you helping out, you have been a great help—"

Just then, she is interrupted as Major bursts through the door, an invalid Danny clutched to his side, blood dripping down onto the floorboards with each step. Annie Mae can tell by the odd angle he's being held at that he isn't conscious. Without waiting for permission, Major drops his son into the bed that Cebo had just finished preparing.

"Ms. Mae, the doctors have no answers for his condition but I'm sure you do, so I ain't leavin' here 'til he's cured." Major puts one hand on his holster, the other on his hip.

Annie Mae's eyes are steel, as she stares at Major, but she motions with her hand for Weston and Rein to help. They immediately rush to the bedside, helping arrange Danny so he is more comfortable.

Major starts ranting again, but Annie Mae finds it difficult to focus on his words as she notices Canine's nose twitching, his features transforming before her eyes as he lays tied to his bed.

J.B. also notices and begins inching his way toward the gate without alerting Major.

Burn happens to re-enter the hospital at that moment, quickly stuffing the gun into his waistband at the sight of an irate Major. Canine's features have now fully transformed, his hair longer than before, his sharpened canines poking out from the corners of his lips.

Annie Mae says, "Take him back to the hospital...he ain't welcome back here. You've got these patients all riled up." Major's eyes turn to the other patients, their eyes full of fear.

Rein grabs a basin of water and begins trying to clean Danny's wounds, but she finds the more she cleans, the more he seems to bleed. She is interrupted by a snapping sound as Canine breaks loose of his restraints, coming to stand at the fence.

Canine no longer looks like a human. His body is completely covered in hair, and his shoulders are hunched. There is foamed saliva dripping from the corners of his mouth as he opens it and lets out an animalistic roar.

Before anyone can do anything, Canine attacks the nearest victim. He rips down the fence with a single movement, knocking it onto a shocked Major.

Not interested in anything but the blood, Canine charges toward Rein, his eyes fixed on the bloody rags in her hands. Thinking fast, she drops the rags and tries to run, but she is too slow, and Canine's claws sink into her shoulder near her neck, causing her to collapse.

Canine sniffs the rags, but instead of focusing on them, his head turns toward the hospital door, only Burn standing in the way. Quick as a whip, Canine changes tactics, running toward Burn.

As if by habit, Burn pulls the gun from his waist, training the barrel on the creature running toward him. Just as they think he might be too late, a BANG echoes through the hospital.

The bullet goes into Canine, but it doesn't slow him down. He knocks Burn to the side as if he weighs nothing before pushing out the hospital front doors and running off into the darkness.

Burn tries to chase after him to fire another shot, but by the time he reaches the doors, there is no creature to be seen.

Major, who has finally regained his wits enough to push the fence panel off of him, pulls out his weapon, and follows Burn, reaching the front door shortly after, swinging around madly as his eyes search the dark for the animal.

Headlights illuminate the two men as David pulls into the parking lot, stepping out of his truck.

"David, Canine's escaped. I'm going to call Cutter, and you go get PaPaw's dogs," Major shouts, waving at him to get back into his truck.

"I just saw PaPaw in town." David seems a bit shocked at the new development.

"Get both his dogs and bring them here. I'll talk to Cutter to bring him here as well."

With a nod, David climbs back into his truck, throwing it into drive and speeding off into the darkness.

Major races in and makes a beeline for the phone.

Annie Mae knows that her worst fears have been confirmed. She turns to where Ms. Elvie and Burn are helping to try and calm the patients, some of which are distraught over the events.

"Burn, please take Ms. Elvie home right now." Burn nods as she continues, "Ms. Elvie, go hug Paulene and don't let her go tonight. Go now—GO!" Burn and Ms. Elvie exit quickly. Ms. Elvie turns back toward where Cebo is helping J.B. work on Rein, but Annie Mae shakes her head. "I'll tell him, just go!"

Once they are out of sight, she turns to where J.B. is trying to help

Rein. He has pulled her shirt away from her shoulder and has Cebo pressing clothes over the deep wounds as he prepares to clean them with antiseptic.

"Cebo?"

Cebo turns toward Annie Mae but before he can answer, J.B. cuts in, "The cuts are deep and jagged, she needs stitches."

Annie Mae looks at Rein. "Let's leave it open for a bit since it was a...dog?" Annie Mae bites her lip. "I might have to use something from under the stairway, in my office."

J.B. knows she means a potion and nods. "Call Benjamin and let him know about Canine, that he may be coming his way."

Annie Mae nods. "I'll call." As she turns to leave, she remembers why she had called for Cebo, "Cebo?"

"Yes, ma'am?"

"Burn took Ms. Elvie home," she explains quickly, "And as soon as you are done, please head home as well."

Cebo nods and Annie Mae resumes her path to the phone, only for Major to step through the door before she gets there.

"I've called Cutter, he's going to lead a posse out and try to hunt down Canine, or whatever, and kill him. I got dogs and every able person with a gun to meet here." He looks at Annie Mae. "Cutter's going to be in charge of the search. I'm going to be here and watch you cure my son. I ain't leaving here—like I said before."

Annie Mae turns away from Major, biting her lip. Figuring it would be a good time to get some air, she steps out onto the porch. She sees splatters of blood trailing from the front door down the steps. Of course, it's then that the reinforcements show up, as two vehicles come tearing up the drive, one a police car with sirens roaring.

Remembering that she, too, had a call to make, she quickly hustles inside and picks up the phone. As she is finishing up, Burn reenters the hospital. Annie Mae waves him over.

"You still got the gun?" Burn nods in affirmation. "Let me have it." She holds out her hand.

"How about if I put it back in—"

She interrupts, "No, I might need it later, besides you don't need it back with the patients."

He reluctantly hands the pistol to her open hand. She takes it and opens the cylinder, checking to see if it's loaded, before clicking it shut, noticeably neglecting the safety. She slides the gun in the large pocket in her hospital apron.

Burn watches, his eyes meeting hers when she's finished. "You put a bullet in that evil creature, right?"

"I got him point blank."

She nods as she walks towards the office door. "I might have to do the same later to another evil creature."

Burn follows her as she leaves the office. "What about the patients?"

Annie Mae doesn't seem fazed. "I'll be sure I'm too close to miss."

They re-enter the patient area and Burn closes the door behind them.

Chapter 39

November 8, 1945
8:00pm
The Driver Household, Chatham Hill, Middle Tennessee

VICTORIA AND PAULENE ARE sitting on the couch, eyes trained on the fire roaring in the fireplace, when the sound of a truck door slamming interrupts their thoughts. Paulene jumps up and goes to the window to see who it is.

"It's mama."

Victoria quickly rushes to the door, pulling it open for her mom.

"Are you children okay?" Ms. Elvie asks, breathless. She gives Paulene a quick hug and sets her pocketbook down on the small table by the door.

"Why ya' home so early?" Victoria asks, confused.

"Canine escaped—" Ms. Elvie gasps, "—he turned into—" She pauses, noticing that Paulene is listening. "Paulene, would you go get me a glass of water from the kitchen?"

Ms. Elvie waits until she is out of earshot to continue. "Major brought Danny to the hospital covered in blood. Rein tended to him, and I guess Canine went wild over the blood and rags and like last time—you saw—he turned into a dog, no, a wolf creature, half man and half—"

Her voice comes to a halt as Paulene returns with the water. She grabs the glass and takes a long sip before sinking onto the couch. Victoria sits beside her, but before she can say anything, Ms. Elvie jumps up and goes to the front door, checking to be sure it is locked.

"Paulene, are you through with your homework?" Paulene nods. "Then go get ready for bed."

"But mama, it's too early!" Paulene protests.

Ms. Elvie insists. "Go get ready for bed."

Paulene lets out a groan but does as she is told.

Ms. Elvie beelines for the back door, checking the lock. She steps to the sink and gulps down the rest of the water, setting the glass down hard. Victoria follows her mom, waiting for her to say more. "That madman, or animal, was last running towards Mr. Hal's...or *here*."

Victoria's eyes widened. "So he could be close. Where is Cebo?"

"He stayed at the hospital. I saw the sheriff had men gathering there to start a search, so they'll be around tracking through the woods."

Ms. Elvie walks down a hallway, turning into the first bedroom. Victoria follows watching as her mother goes to the closet and reaches up to the top shelf. When she pulls her hand back, Victoria spots the revolver clutched in her hand. She quickly checks to see if it's loaded before walking past Victoria to the living room and setting it on the side table.

"Mama, Cebo is safe and we are safe now," Victoria tries to reassure her mother.

Paulene comes in and sees the gun on the table, her eyes excited. Ms. Elvie reaches for her younger daughter, enclosing her in a tight hug. "Mama, what happened? Why are you scared?"

"Well, a patient escaped from the hospital and the men from town are chasing him down. I'm sure they will catch him soon."

The sound of barking dogs reaches their ears, breaking through the peace of the night. Ms. Elvie grips Paulene tighter.

"I see you got your necklace on," Victoria says to her sister, trying to be reassuring.

"Just to be on the safe side," Paulene whispers.

They all listen to the chorus of dogs barking until it grows fainter.

"I just wish I had told Benjamin to make us all one," Paulene says.

Ms. Elvie smiles slightly. "Sounds like they have chased him away from here." She looks down at Paulene. "Paulene, would you do me a favor and let's turn in a bit early tonight, okay?"

"I'm not sleepy," Paulene protests.

"You go lay down for ten minutes. Here, I'll come read you a story," Ms. Elvie bargains.

"Alright," Paulene agrees reluctantly before heading into her bedroom, her mother following her.

Left alone in the living room, Victoria walks to the window, looking out into the dark night. Although she knows her mother will hate it, she slips on her shoes before unlocking the door and stepping out onto the porch.

She tilts her ear, able to faintly hear the dogs barking still, combined with the sounds of the trees swaying in the wind. Victoria walks to the edge of the porch, spying the light from Jimmy's small house through the trees. The house far across the field, which belongs to Hal, is dark.

"Child, get in here."

The sound of her mother's voice stops her thoughts in their tracks and Victoria reluctantly steps back into the house, closing and locking the door behind her.

"Did you get her to sleep?" she asks.

"No, she asked me about the gun. She's so keyed up. I read her a story, hopefully that settled her a bit."

The two women are silent for a minute before Victoria voices the thoughts that were swirling in her mind while she was on the porch.

"Mama, you know about the powers around the hospital. You've been telling me about the pit, the blood must have set the demons loose—"

"They boarded over the pit," Ms. Elvie's voice is adamant.

Victoria shakes her head. "Walls don't stop demons, mama. Remember at one of those gatherings at Ms. Mae's?"

"What one?"

"Annie Mae's past and why she had to leave up North. They ran her out of town, and they killed her husband."

"Who killed her husband?" Ms. Elvie doesn't remember this story at all.

"The town did."

"I don't remember, how did they do it?"

Victoria shrugs. "Maybe it was one of those late nights between Ms. Mae and Sadie. I overheard them talking about spells and demons and one of her close friends was burned alive."

Ms. Elvie thinks for a moment. "It must have been to Sadie 'cause she ain't told me about her past. I just remember her and the three kids hiding outside of town. She told me she was hiding from the soldiers, and that they killed her husband."

"It wasn't soldiers," Victoria replies, "It was because she was a witch and has powers. I heard it was clubs, swords, and...pitchforks and such,..they killed him with."

"I heard about burning witches but that was 200 years ago."

"Mama, you've seen the powers that Annie, Rein, Amber and Benjamin all have. I guess, somehow, her powers have passed down to them."

It's Ms. Elvie who turns to shake her head. "My guess is it was Annie Mae and their dad, Michael, combined with their mother, who also had powers."

"Is that what you heard?"

"No, but I vaguely remember their mother was English."

Victoria says her next words with caution. "I'm afraid of their powers, well not afraid, but, yeah... afraid." She sighs. "I just don't know why I was able to fight off Canine a few weeks ago."

Ms. Elvie looks out the corner of her eyes, wanting to change the subject. "Maybe it was the potion you drank that almost killed you."

"Maybe, but—"

Ms. Elvie cuts her off, "Oh, Canine cut Rein's shoulder near her neck with his claws—"

She is interrupted by the sound of heavy footsteps onto the front porch. Ms. Elvie stands and reaches for the gun.

"Elvie? Elvie?"

"Cebo, is that you?" Ms. Elvie puts the gun down and opens the door as the out of breath, sweaty man stumbles into the open room.

Victoria grabs Cebo's arm and helps him to the couch. "Did you run the whole way?"

He tries to catch his breath, panting between words. "Ms. Mae said for me to go 'cause of some dream."

"It was a vision she had several weeks ago," Ms. Elvie explains.

"She wouldn't say the details, said you'd tell me?"

"All she told me was she saw Paulene draped over a firewood pile," Ms. Elvie says with a sigh.

"That's it?" Cebo can't believe he ran the whole way here for that.

"Yeah, I pressed her, but she says that's all she saw."

"Was she alive?" Victoria asks.

"Again, she wouldn't say."

"You girls go to these meetings at Ms. Mae's, Victoria about dies, and tonight I see with my own eyes the evil powers that possess that hospital...what else do you girls know?" Cebo's eyes darted between his wife and daughter.

Both are quiet for a moment. "I don't know but your daughter has powers that might protect us," Ms. Elvie admits at last.

"My daughter?" He turns to Victoria. "What powers you got?"

"Nothing special, just when I get overwhelmed, my mind just does things that—I don't know—things I'm not aware of," Victoria explains, embarrassed.

"Seems like a lot of 'I don't know'...well, we're all safe right now. Where's Paulene?"

"Put her to bed, she saw the gun and she got jittery."

Cebo's eyes are drawn to the gun still sitting on the table. "Well, Cutter has five or six trucks with guns and dogs chasing this evil creature down and hopefully they kill it. I ain't going back to that hospital." He stops mid-sentence to take a deep breath. "I don't know, guess I'll go clean up and I'll check on Paulene." Cebo stands and moves the gun to the center of a larger table more central to all. "Victoria, could you make me a bite to eat?"

Victoria stands but Ms. Elvie stops her with a hand, heading to the kitchen herself after her husband ducks into Paulene's room.

Left alone on the couch, Victoria begins thinking out loud in a hushed voice, "The only way Rein and Amber got their powers were from their mother or dad." So how did she get hers? From Cebo? From Elvie? From... Her mind wanders and her eyes peruse the framed pictures on the wall. She notices younger pictures of her, and Paulene, and two family pictures taken over the years, her eyes catching on the crocheted image nested between all the pictures.

She reads out loud quietly, "I can do all things through Christ who strengthens me. Philippians 4:13."

Victoria's thoughts are interrupted by a distant yell.

Chapter 40

November 8, 1945
8:20pm
The Driver Household, Chatham Hill, Middle Tennessee

R USHING TO THE DOOR, she yanks it open to see Jimmy's roof is on fire. Her eyes widen as she yells, "Mama!"

Without thinking, she runs out the door, across the porch, and down the steps.

Ms. Elvie comes rushing to the door, Cebo on her heels. They too, quickly make their way toward the burning house.

Ms. Elvie hears a faint voice behind her. She turns to see Paulene a step or two off the porch. She yells, "Paulene, get back in the house!" Paulene freezes a moment as she sees the blaze in the distance. Ms. Elvie sees in the lone porch light the silhouette of Paulene standing in the doorway.

She steps a few feet closer to watch Victoria outrun Cebo through the tall pines and oaks and the scattered underbrush. Victoria has to high step the tall grasses and clumps of briars. She sprints with heavy pants for a good minute or so. As she nears the cabin, her hands raise in the air and sweep her arms towards the burning roof. As she does, the topsoil of a barren patch in the woods rises up, flies through the air, and like a blanket, settles across the part of the roof that is ablaze.

A figure emerges from the door, stumbling and falling to the ground. Cebo races past Victoria, checking on Jimmy.

Victoria's eyes search the woods and listens, feeling that something about the situation is off. But she hears nothing. Her eyes turn back to the fire which is now just a few tendrils of smoke rising through the layer of dirt and floating to the heavens.

Ms. Elvie screams violently, "ULYSSES!" Victoria and Cebo look towards their house. Cebo's heart drops.

Both begin to dash home, "Paulene! Cebo!" Ms. Elvie's voice reaches their ears from within the house.

As moments pass, they reach the porch, Ms. Elvie comes out onto the porch, screaming desperately, "Paulene's gone." Ms. Elvie goes around to the side of the house and screams with all the energy she has into the night, "Paulene!"

Victoria runs onto the porch, broken glass crunching under her feet. Confused, she looks up, only to see the porch light, which was on earlier that night, has been shattered.

She turns back to see her parents searching desperately for Paulene.

"She's gone! Someone took her!" Ms. Elvie rants.

Taking matters into her own hands, Victoria runs into the woods, toward the road. "Paulene!" she shouts, before listening for a response.

She doesn't hear anything other than the wind in the trees, but her eyes are drawn to a faint red glare, similar to taillights glimmering in the darkness. She rushes back to Cebo and Elvie. "I think I see something."

Without waiting for a response, she rushes to her room and grabs her keys, running out the door.

"Want me to go?" Cebo calls after her.

"Ain't got time," she yells back, already halfway in her truck.

Cebo quickly runs inside, grabbing the gun before running to Victoria's truck and tapping on the window. She rolls it down.

"Take this."

She grabs the gun and tosses it on the seat beside her before flooring the gas. Cebo jumps into the bed of her truck. Fishtailing the truck around curves to the main road Cebo holds on for dear life, as she keeps her speed as the vehicle crosses the wooden bridge.

She's so focused on the road, and going quickly, she doesn't notice when the gun slides out of the seat and wedges itself alongside the door.

From the bridge she sees headlights coming from Yaphank. Stopping at the intersection just past the bridge, she slams her truck to a stop, stepping out and standing in the path of the truck.

As the truck slams on its brakes, Victoria notices it is Pepper's truck. Cebo jumps to the ground. "Girl, you're driving crazy." She lets out her breath as Benjamin steps from the cab, Mr. Pepper following closely behind.

"Did you pass a car or truck coming from this way in the last couple of miles?" she asks in a rush.

Benjamin answers, "No. We haven't passed anybody in the last ten minutes, why?"

"Somebody has grabbed Paulene from the house. I saw lights headed this way."

Benjamin looks back at Mr. Pepper before heading toward Victoria's truck. "I'll go with ya'! Cebo, could you take Mr. Pepper to the hospital? He's sick."

Cebo agrees quickly. "Yeah, you go with Victoria!"

As he gets in Victoria's truck, the gun falls out. Benjamin anticipates it and quickly shoves it into the glove compartment. In a panic, Victoria yells at her father, "Cebo, call Major—" She climbs into the driver seat, "—or Cutter and tells them somebody snatched Paulene five minutes ago and they headed towards Burn's! Tell him to go by the house and talk with mama."

"I will!" Cebo calls back as Victoria speeds off.

"Did you see who grabbed her?" Benjamin asks as they merge back on the road.

"No—" She tries to take a couple of deep breaths. "Someone set fire to Jimmy's roof and while we were all helping Jimmy, they snatched her from behind us."

"Could it have been two people?" he asks.

Her eyes are searching left and right as she speeds down the road only slowing at each turn.

"When Cebo calls Cutter I'm sure he can send some of the searchers this way. The dogs showed Canine crossed the river, so all the searchers are headed back to the hospital." He notices Victoria's hands are shaking. "Do you want me to drive?"

"I need you to look for my sister, please, just look," Victoria snaps.

Benjamin's eyes scour the darkness for any sign of the young girl. "Turn down here, I see something stopped."

Victoria hits the brakes and slides into the turn. She spots a stopped vehicle off the road, but as they get closer, she can tell it is rusted and abandoned. "Dammit." She revs the engine, turning back to the road.

She pushes the truck to its limits until she comes to a fork and is forced to stop. She rams the gear shift to neutral, her head slamming onto the steering wheel.

Sensing her distress, Benjamin slides over to Victoria, resting a comforting hand on her shoulder. Without saying anything, Victoria releases the steering wheel, turning to Benjamin, her tears wetting his shoulder.

"We're the only ones looking."

Benjamin rubs her back, knowing she might be right. "Listen, let's go towards Burn's. It's a straight shot and we can make good time."

She nods and he feels her grasp tighten around his arm. "You drive," she relents.

"Okay." He gets out and walks around to the driver's door while she slides into the passenger seat.

"Let's go," she begs, "Please."

"I'll drive as long as you want me to," he promises as he noses the car back onto the road.

Victoria nods, brushing away her tears, her eyes searching the darkness as it rushes by. Benjamin is driving a bit slower than she was, and he stops at the next fork.

Victoria points. "Turn that way...I thought I saw something."

"But they could circle around by Sadie's or head on through to the pavement," Benjamin says, causing new tears to well in Victoria's eyes. He grimaces. He had spoken before thinking.

They turn around a bend and see a car's headlights coming towards them. As it nears, Victoria opens the compartment and draws the revolver out, just in case.

Her hands are shaking as she raises the gun and points towards the approaching car.

Benjamin, out of the corner of his eye, sees the gun, his breath hooking in his throat. Using his magical eyesight, he sees through the car, realizing it's a husband and wife—no threat to them. He raises his hand, using his palm to push the gun down just before the car stops alongside theirs. Victoria's hands are shaking.

"Excuse me sir," Benjamin leans out the window, "Have you passed any vehicle since you've been traveling this road, say, in the last fifteen minutes?"

The man in the driver's seat replies, "No, we've only traveled for ten minutes or so, we haven't passed anyone."

"Thanks." Benjamin nods his head, watching them drive off before turning around, flooring it, and passing them. He turns down the road toward Burn's place, slowing as they get closer.

"You know where Burn lives?" Benjamin asks.

Victoria gets quieter. "It's been a couple of years but yeah, I think I could find it again."

"I'll drive there, and we'll turn around..." His voice slows and his words fade out, "...and I'll turn around." He corrects himself.

Victoria leans forward, gun still gripped in her hand, seeming to search the darkness for something. "I think his drive is over this hill and a half mile on the left."

Just as they are approaching the last of the road to Burn's house, Benjamin slams on the brakes. "Want to go back to the bridge now and see what the others have found?"

She nods, silent.

He makes quick work of the turn, pulling back out on the road. Victoria, the adrenaline leaving her blood, begins to feel sleepy and moves to sit closer to Benjamin, seeming to forget the weapon still clutched in her fist.

As her eyes droop, Benjamin covers her small hand with his, slowly prying the gun from her grip while keeping his other hand on the wheel. Once he manages to extract it, he sets it on the dash.

They spend the rest of the drive in silence.

Chapter 41

November 9, 1945
7:00 am
Windsor Hospital, Chatham Hill, Middle Tennessee

PARKING HAL'S TRUCK IN front of the hospital, Benjamin climbs out. Under the circumstances and with no sleep, he momentarily enjoys the colorful sunrise view.

His enjoyment doesn't last long though, as he takes in the view of the ambulance parked in front of the hospital steps, and the fact that the parking lot has several more cars than it usually does.

Making his way up the steps, a cool breeze brushes past his neck, only to continue on to gently rock the rocking chairs occupying the porch. Cheddar walks over to rub against Benjamin's leg, and he gives him a quick pat before proceeding through the hospital doors.

The hospital lobby is quiet this morning, Benjamin heads into the patient area, only to stop dead in his tracks at the sight of a huddle of people around one particular bed. His eyes catch on a sobbing Mrs. Grisco, and Major, who is patting her arm. Annie Mae and Weston are also there, their heads lowered.

Before he can step forward, J.B. appears from his office, and motions back through the door Benjamin just passed through. Benjamin nods in understanding, exiting quickly and heading into Annie Mae's office in the front.

As he sinks into the wooden swivel chair, Benjamin lets out a breath and runs a hand through his hair. He is exhausted, after ten hours of looking for Paulene. They still didn't find anything, and despite how tired he is, Benjamin wishes he could continue looking.

Thinking he will just rest his eyes for a few minutes while he waits for J.B., Benjamin lays his head on his arms on the surface of the desk. He closes his eyes, just for a moment.

~~~

Annie Mae watches Major's back as he kneels bedside Danny's bed. A white sheet has been placed over Danny's shriveled face by Dr. Weiss, to hide the blood streaks.

The last two hours have been brutal, waiting with bated breath as Danny's breath slowed, until it finally came to a stop.

Kathleen Grisco hasn't let go of her fisted grip on the white sheet since it was placed there. Dr. Weiss, who came just as things took a turn for the worse a few hours before, leads Major away from the group, his vest and suit pants clean only because he wore a doctor's coat when he first arrived. It has since been tossed in the trash. He speaks with Major in a faint whisper, "We must take Daniel back to the hospital for autop—observation."

"Why is his body so bruised all over? It looks like he was beaten with a rod." Major can barely control his emotions as he mutters the words.

"Usually blood clots or some disease—"

"No," Major interrupts. "He didn't have nothing. He was a healthy boy."

Dr. Weiss smiles sadly, trying to reason with him. "Let's get him checked out and to City Hospital. I'll know more then." He pats Major on the arm. "We'll get you a report, I promise."

"You do that!" He points at the bed where the remnants of his son lie,
~~~

"But I know what really happened here. He's been poisoned. There ain't no snake bite or disease do this to a kid and the person or persons will be—" Kathleen begins to sob louder. Major pauses his tirade to help escort his wife to the lobby.

Dr. Weiss walks over to J.B. and speaks with him quietly, before taking one last look at the corpse and leaving. J.B. steps towards Annie Mae and takes her arm. He leads her away but she stops abruptly, her head turning to watch Major as he exits.

"There is nothing else we can do. It's been a long night for all of us. Go home and get some rest," J.B. tells his wife, "Burn and Weston will be back just after daybreak."

Annie Mae nods and heads for her office. She is startled to find her grandson asleep at her desk, but thinking fast, she closes the door behind her, the click of the knob waking Benjamin.

"How's Rein?" he asks, sleep muddling his voice.

"She's been stirring all night with a fever, and she's been drifting in and out of consciousness. The jelly I put on Rein's cuts hopefully has stopped any infection," Annie Mae explains in a low voice.

"Amber told us she didn't want to leave her, but you sent her to comfort Ms. Elvie."

Annie Mae nods. "I did. Was she any help?"

Benjamin leans forward as Annie Mae sits in the other chair in the office. "She was there for only about 20 minutes or so."

Ms. Mae leans back and lifts her eyebrows. "What happened?"

"First ten minutes were okay, but Victoria and Ms. Elvie kept grilling Amber about Paulene, and her whereabouts, and accusing her of withholding information about what she knew about the firewood pile."

"Oh, Lord, I thought I was helping, sending her over there," Annie Mae groans.

"They tried to pin her down and she finally told them about the barbed-wire around her neck and—"

"Barbed-wire? I didn't see any barbed-wire."

"Well, when she started telling them about a shadow dragging her along, oh, then, then, they stopped asking questions…" Benjamin rubs his forehead with the back of his hand. "I tried to stop their insults."

"Insults?"

"I had to get her out, or away from them. Ms. Elvie was yelling that she hoped one day that Amber would know what they were feeling. Amber left in tears. I sat outside with her until she calmed down."

Annie Mae looks at Benjamin. "Thank you for that. I should go check on Amber."

"No, Trevor came back from searching and we got her home."

"Maybe I should—"

Benjamin cuts her off, "That was hours ago. She's got Sadie to help her."

"But she should have a mother for that."

Benjamin looks straight into Annie Mae's eyes, his voice firm, "Like I said, Sadie is there for her."

Annie Mae knows Benjamin is right, as she isn't technically her mother either. "I guess you're right. God, I sent her to the house earlier to get the medicine from under the steps, she told me she didn't want to go back in that house, and I told her that Rein needed the medicine, and she was the only one who could go."

"She's a big girl now," Benjamin says, sounding wise beyond his years. "She's grown up in the last few weeks or so. She's stronger than she used to be."

"Tell her I'm sorry."

"I will," Benjamin says, then pauses before asking his next question. "I guess Danny's gone?"

She looks at him, "Yeah. He was a mess…if he had suffered in private, I'd been fine, but so, so many people watched him suffer…that was something I didn't think of, even as a nurse. My heart screamed so loudly in my chest when Kathleen came—" She puts a hand on her face, "—and she brought Elliott."

"Elliott saw?" Benjamin gasps.

"Oh yeah, Major made him watch Danny spit up blood and everything."

"Well, it is finished," Benjamin says, knowing it won't erase Elliott's last memories of his brother. "Oh, I want to tell you something that I've never told anyone...it's a secret."

"What is it?" Annie Mae asks.

"As I talked to Cutter tonight, I just thought it might help with all these girls being attacked, I told him that there were three shallow graves in the backwoods at Yaphank."

"He needed to know that," Annie Mae assures him.

"I've seen 'em, and told him not to say nothing to Major but if he could do anything, the doctor down there probably could help."

"Ain't a secret anymore."

"Guess not, but I had to say, it may help with things..." He shakes his head, "...but they're going to know it was me who said."

"Cutter's a good man." Annie Mae reaches over to pat his hand. "You were right to do so."

"I guess. I told him I could meet him down there when I go to make my next delivery." He is about to say something more but is interrupted by the sound of heavy footsteps outside the office door.

The door slams open, nearly breaking off its hinges, and Annie Mae and Benjamin jump to their feet as an enraged Major steps into the office.

He doesn't say anything, he simply reaches for his revolver.

Knowing this moment was coming, Annie Mae reaches for her own gun, pulling it from her pocket and pointing it at Major. He freezes in shock.

"I think I want Benjamin to come with me to my office for some questions," he demands.

Annie Mae's hand is steady. Benjamin's eyes go between Major and Annie Mae.

"You don't need to point that weapon at me. There has been a murder, and someone needs to be accountable, justice needs to be served."

Annie Mae just grits her teeth. "Listen to me, Major. Sometimes the

Lord works in mysterious ways, and sometimes all of us don't quite understand, but right now, justice has been served. You need to take your ass home and comfort your family and let everything rest for a while, do you understand? If you want to talk to Benjamin, see me first." Major notices that Annie Mae's hand is quivering.

"It's been a long night," Major says, his hand moving toward the doorknob.

J.B. creeps up behind Major. Annie Mae shakes her head. "J.B., I'll be right with ya'. As soon as the sheriff leaves." J.B. steps back.

Major turns and steps back into the lobby looking at each of them in turn. "I might have a few questions for all of ya'."

Without another word, he leaves the hospital, the door sneaking shut behind him.

"He's gone," J.B. says to Annie Mae, as she lowers her gun to rest it on the desk.

"Check again," she insists.

J.B. goes to the front door, looking through the window to see Major's police cruiser pulling out and heading down the road, away from the hospital, dust billowing in his wake. "He's gone," he assures her, his eyes drifting to the now empty desk. "Where's the gun?"

"I got it. Don't worry, I'll hold on to it for a while." She takes a deep breath. "J.B., please go check on Rein...and Jeremy, too."

He nods. "Jeremy's condition is getting worse."

"And Nina is back there, isn't she?"

He nods again and leaves as Annie Mae turns to Benjamin. "Why don't you go wash up and sleep here for a while in one of the hospital beds, just for tonight, well, for this morning." He hesitates. "I insist."

"Yes, ma'am." He begins to leave, but just before he does, he turns to hug Annie Mae. "Thank you. Love you."

She hugs him tight. "Watch your back. You might need to carry a gun for a while, do you understand?" she whispers in his ear. "Love you." Benjamin nods and steps towards the door. "Remember a while back I said you need to watch out over the girls."

"Yes, ma'am?"

"Well, you need to watch out over the girls," she reiterates. "Take the bed next to Rein. We moved Jeremy to the far side...pray for him. He's not improving."

"Nina about wrestled him to the ground begging him not to go. But he was as stubborn as ever to go search for Paulene when everybody else was going...I should have just drove off." Benjamin's voice is thick with guilt.

"You can't blame yourself. He's a good man. Now go get you some sleep."

He nods with a slight grin and leaves the room. Annie Mae lets out a breath and taps her side apron pocket with her open hand.

The coolness of the metal is comforting beneath her fingers.

Chapter 42

November 9, 1945
1:00pm
Windsor Hospital, Chatham Hill, Middle Tennessee

BENJAMIN NOSES THE CAR over the rickety bridge and stops just past the patrol car. Stepping out of the vehicle, his boots thump on the hard packed dirt. He pulls his thick coat tighter across his front, the afternoon wind proving to be quite chilly as he approaches the patrol vehicle.

"This is frustrating." His breath freezes in the air, coming out in white puffs.

Cutter lays down his clipboard beside him and motions for Benjamin to step back so he can exit the vehicle. "You think this is frustrating? Become a lawman...every person through here hasn't seen anything that night. It's like she vanished into thin air."

"I don't have to tell you that there are exits—"

Cutter interrupts, "I know. I know. Did you see PaPaw and the dogs?"

"Yeah, you said they were walking towards the main road to the pavement towards Madison. They are about a mile past Canaan Branch along Gaddy's Pond. So I searched all the secondary drives and deer trails...behind them." Cutter unrolls a map, setting it on the hood of the car, and Benjamin points as he speaks, "I drove up these roads but some of them just ran into open fields and old logging roads. I'd hate to say I searched when I might miss something."

Cutter makes a mark in each spot where Benjamin points. "I got two more teams of dogs coming this afternoon...I told them to meet me here."

"Good idea."

"Victoria is tore up. She's been driving her truck and some friend of hers...some military guy in all the backwoods. They're my best search team. But she looks ragged and ain't slept since you and her chased the taillights yesterday."

Benjamin shakes his head, his eyes searching the trees. "She doesn't want to face her mother."

"I guess, you're right." Cutter folds up the map and tucks it into his pocket.

"I saw Hal's truck pass with Cebo and Ms. Elvie. It is so sad."

"Can you tell me your story about that night?"

Benjamin's eyes grow wide and he swallows audibly. "Am I a suspect?"

"Hell, Major wants you in the office right now to question you about poisoning his son. And about something you told Maria, now Paulene has been snatched, and you are throwing up info about graves at Yaphank. I could probably question you myself for an hour or so." He pulls out a notepad and pen from his pocket. "Start with Canine's escape and your whereabouts?"

The wind whips the pages of the notepad as Benjamin begins, "About 6:30 or after, I got a call from Ms. Mae about Canine's escape and he may be headed my way. Got Hal's rifle and looked outside the house and the barn—" He shifts his weight and stomps to try and warm his feet, "You've seen Canine. He probably ran past Hal's before I was called. Didn't hear or see anything."

Cutter scribbles something. "Hal out of town?"

"Yeah, he and Julie have been to Houston to see the kids for about two weeks. Going to pick 'em up Saturday afternoon."

Cutter nods. "Continue."

"So I went to the hospital where the search party was gathering. Then you saw PaPaw's dogs take off across the field toward Hal's place, so Mr. Pepper and I drove down Kelly's Ferry a long ways but saw nothing. Then Mr. Pepper was coughing so bad I had to turn around and take him back to the hospital. And when I got to the bridge Victoria drove by and me, well, we tried to chase down some taillights...but we didn't have any success."

Cutter taps the pad with his pen, thinking. "I talked to J.B. this morning...Mr. Pepper's probably got pneumonia. Nina is distraught and still angry that Jeremy left the store that night."

Benjamin stomps some more and rubs his hands together. "You know how he is. Somebody's in trouble he's going to help."

"Yeah, but you can't run into this weather at his age."

Benjamin thinks over the last few minutes of their conversation, suddenly remembering something Cutter said earlier. "What's this about Maria?"

"She said you and her had a plan to have Danny meet some girl."

"She told me about some girl that fancied him, and I was going to get Danny introduced to her. Maybe get him a girlfriend, but she dumped him before they were introduced."

Cutter raises his eyebrows. "What piqued my interest is I didn't think you and him were friends?"

Benjamin tilts his head from side to side. "I guess not, but it's good to try and get on his good side...even if it is hard to see. It may help down the road."

"Help?"

"Me, I guess." He shrugs. Danny was a well-known bully in Chatham Hill.

Cutter is not convinced. "And you gave Danny a swig of the moonshine...as friends?"

"Like I said, trying to get on his good side."

"Hmm." Cutter returns to his notepad. "And where did you get the moonshine?"

"Found it sitting on a barrel."

This piques his interest. "Where was this barrel?"

"Behind the feed and seed." His reply is quick.

"So close to where Cebo found ya'?"

"I don't remember that."

"No, I guess you wouldn't." He jots down on a pad. "You were behind the feed and seed and happened upon a bottle of 'shine...a coincidence?" Benjamin nods and Cutter narrows his eyes, "You know what I've learned as a lawman...I don't believe in coincidences."

Benjamin clenches his teeth together.

"You don't have a guess who left it?" Cutter pries.

He tries to brush the obvious accusation off. "I don't know the moonshiners around here...but I do know what it smells like."

"And you thought finding a bottle on a barrel means you could pass it to your friends?"

He shrugs. "Thought he might enjoy it."

Cutter stares, not buying it. "And did he enjoy it?"

"I drank it, too." Benjamin presses, rubbing his hands together and breathing on them.

"Yeah, not as much...I don't know if I believe you, but I talked to Amber and her I believe."

His sister's name on the officer's lips are a surprise to Benjamin. "What did she say?"

"I'll tell you if you need to know. It's still a police investigation."

Silence settles between the two men, the cold air making it seem heavy.

"I apologized to Maria for my rude antics the other night," Benjamin confesses.

"She's sixteen and is a bit gullible."

"I'm the same age."

If Cutter is surprised by this, it doesn't show in his demeanor. "Why don't you stay away from her for a while? Her being a material witness and all."

"Yes sir, but we are in some of the same classes in school."

Cutter flips his notebook closed, slipping it into his pocket. "She says you aren't in class half the time anyway. I guess all your family troubles. Or is it special treatment?"

Benjamin isn't sure how to admit the full truth, so he says, "The teachers give me some leeway."

"I don't think I should give you leeway, do you?"

Benjamin steps back. "My family didn't ask for all this."

Cutter's eyes darken and he crosses his arms over his chest. "You might have a hard time convincing me of that... Just don't talk to her, you hear? I may have a few more questions. On Sunday—"

Benjamin cuts him off. "I've just got to go to Yaphank Sunday for a delivery for Peppers. I feel like I owe the Peppers that."

Cutter's posture relaxes a bit at the caring tone Benjamin uses as he talks about the Peppers. "What about the afternoon?"

"Yes, sir, I'll be there," he agrees.

"Any comment on the missing girls at Yaphank?"

"No, sir, just talk to the doctor down there. Keep it quiet, though, please," Benjamin pleads, not wanting trouble for Cass or Silva.

"Keep it quiet, you say? You sure do have your hands in a lot of trouble, son." Cutter shakes his head.

"She was at the Festival, Cassidy, the doctor, was the girl looking for me with Cebo and Victoria."

"Wait a minute, the thirtyish, black girl I needed to talk to was in town the other night and you don't say anything until after she leaves town?"

"Sorry," Benjamin apologizes sheepishly. "But to be fair she left while I was sleeping so I didn't have much say in the matter."

Cutter peers closer, his eyes judging Benjamin. "Whose side are you on?" Benjamin opens his mouth, but Cutter keeps talking. "I tell you what, Sunday afternoon while you're making this delivery you tell her to come to the Chatham Hill Police Department and see me, Cutter, and I'll take her statement... I think you owe me that."

Benjamin tries to picture how that news is going to go over. He grimaces but says, "I'll tell her."

Cutter isn't about to have Benjamin brush him off. "Or I'll drive my patrol car down there with my lights on and have her picked up and brought in for questioning...is that quiet enough for ya'?"

He nods. "Yes, sir."

"I have talked with the search party participants, and I am working on some leads."

"And have you found out anything?"

"Can't tell you." Cutter opens the door of his patrol car, displaying his intent to leave.

"I guess I better go check and see how everyone is at the hospital." Benjamin looks toward J.B.'s car but doesn't move.

"You know what the hardest part of my job is?" Benjamin watches him. "My mother needs help and...who's telling me the truth...who's lying, do you know what I mean?"

Benjamin doesn't say anything.

"Word of advice, son. I've never seen Major this angry. Be careful."

"Yes, sir." Benjamin turns away before pausing to turn back. "Mine and Amber's prayers are with your mother."

Cutter watches him warily. "Tell Amber to pray for me, too."

He nods and starts the car, watching Benjamin return to J.B.'s car before driving away.

~~~

Benjamin nearly turns into Annie Mae as he is crossing the hospital lobby and before he can head into the back, she steers him into her office, motioning for him to sit down as she closes the door.

She crosses her arms and gives Benjamin a look. "Are you listening?" He nods. "Saturday afternoon, 3:30, pick up Hal and Julie at the train station."

"Yes, ma'am, I'll be there...except—"

She unfurls her arms, interrupting, "What, say it, haven't got time, or what?"

"I left Hal's car at the shop for Julie when they left town and I'm sure that she wants me to pick her up in it."

She rolls her eyes. "Go talk to Amber in the kitchen, right now, and see if she can take you tomorrow, we don't have time here."
~~~

Benjamin stands but doesn't leave. "Just talked to Cutter about the search for Paulene."

"How's it going?" Annie Mae moves around the desk to look for something in a drawer. "No one's found anything?"

He shakes his head, his expression grim. "He asked me about the moonshine and Maria, but I didn't tell him anything new."

She stops her search to set her eyes on her grandson. "Okay, this isn't going to end well."

"Is that what your vision shows?"

"No, it's a mother's fear."

Benjamin doesn't know how to answer so he changes the subject. "How're Rein and Mr. Pepper?"

"Rein is doing…" Annie Mae exhales heavily and sits on her desk. "She has a slight fever and some redness and swelling but she—we are going to leave the wounds open. J.B. and Weston decided not to stitch her up 'cause…" Annie Mae turns away.

"What? I want to know!" Benjamin is impatient.

She turns back, searching for the right way to word what she has to say. "There is a strange ooze coming from her cuts, both of them on her back shoulder. They're both six-inch-long cuts, deep and irregular. We decided we just need to let them drain out."

Benjamin's eyes widen. "I need to see her right now." Without waiting for her response, he jumps up from his chair and runs back into the patient area. Annie Mae follows Benjamin the best she can. He skids to a stop right by Rein's bed.

Rein is awake, trying to sip her water, both J.B. and Weston at her bedside. All three sets of eyes turn at Benjamin's arrival.

Without context he says, "Burn it out of her."

"Burn her? How is that going to help?" J.B. wonders if his grandson has finally lost his marbles. Annie Mae, "Listen to him, he might have a point."

With a determined look, Benjamin said, "No, you and Weston need to perform surgery and cut all the skin out around the wounds. If we let the wound close…she will die. That evil, that spirit Canine left behind, it's an infection and it will turn her wound black. Then it will spread throughout her body, and she will die. It will kill her."

J.B. tries to calm his grandson, "I don't think—"

"J.B., Weston, you have seen the evil inside Canine. Remember, Weston, how his hair blackened the field outside. He has left his marks inside my sister. Annie Mae remembers the story of the body parts buried at Orleans in the bogs." Weston's eyes widened. "It's the only way to save her," Benjamin insists.

"He's right," Annie Mae says from behind Benjamin, surprising everyone that she is agreeing with this option. "It might be our best option. It's got to be done. J.B. if you don't agree, step aside and let Weston do it."

Benjamin turns to Weston. "Please save my sister." Weston looks between Benjamin and his grandparents, indecisive. "Weston, I know you care for her. If I need to call Amber or Victoria or Sadie or pray myself, I will. It must be done soon."

Weston turns to J.B., determination filling his voice. "J.B., we must cut the disease out."

J.B. shakes his head, still skeptical. "We could be doing more harm than good."

"I'll assist. Burn is here." Annie Mae steps closer to the beside. "Dr. Galloway, you must be the lead surgeon. We have faith in you... J.B., you keep an eye on Jeremy." She turns toward Burn, who came over at the sound of his name. "I'll get everything ready for surgery. You two get her wheeled into the operating room, now."

Chapter 43

NINA SITS AT REIN'S bedside, brushing a few stray hairs from her sweaty brow. Rein's eyes move, but they don't quite open as she fights the last remnants of the medication from the surgery. Although Rein is the one who was just cut open, Nina looks quite disheveled herself.

Nina continues to touch Rein's arm gently, until the young woman finally comes to. "Rein, I'm taking Jeremy to City Hospital and trying to get him more help. I might not see you anymore."

Rein makes a sound, her eyes drifting closed of their own accord.

"You left a note in my safe under my counter at the store, I guess over fifteen to eighteen...twenty years ago." Her voice is at a whisper. "Anyways, after twenty years I'm sick of carrying it around, so I'm going to put it under your pillow." She slides the folded note into Rein's hand and slides her hand under the pillow. "Now, it's out of my hands."

Looking up, Nina sees Burn waving at her. "I'm being called...I've got to go. I've watched Annie Mae throw her potions in that fireplace for years, you'll figure it out…I didn't listen and Jeremy's sick. You do what you have to do."

Nina stands, rushing from the room, just as Rein's fist opens, releasing the note. She tries to grab it again but she's too sleepy…

~~~

Cebo arrives at the hospital a few minutes later. Benjamin has given the Drivers the use of Hal's truck the next morning after Paulene's disappearance. He thought that was the right thing to do. Cebo parks off to the side because an ambulance is pulled up to the hospital stairs. Ms. Elvie comes into view, her scarf whipping in the wind. Cebo moves to stand next to her.

"Nina, we heard Jeremy wasn't doing so well." Nina grimaces at Ms. Elvie's words. "I'm sorry, I know that there will be good news just right around the corner."

Nina nods, saying nothing at first, as the woman pulls her into an embrace. Not even a minute later, the ambulance workers swing open the hospital doors, Jeremy on a stretcher between them.

"I decided that with all the commotion going on around here, I'm going to get him moved to City Hospital," Nina whispers at the sight of her husband.

Ms. Elvie pats her friend on the shoulder, showing her support. "Whatever you feel is best, that's what you should do."

"If you need me, you know where I'll be."

"What about your store?" Ms. Elvie asks, realizing too late it's the last thing Nina needs.

Exhaustion clouds Nina's features. "Benjamin has the key and he has to load deliveries. Find him and tell him I said to let you get whatever you need."

Elvie and Cebo both give her a thankful look. "We will and good luck."

Nina chokes out the words "You too," she says as she follows the stretcher into the back of the ambulance, nearly stumbling on the front hospital steps.
~~~

They watch her go, Annie Mae stepping forward from where she had been watching the exchange.

"Ms. Elvie, I'm sorry for—"

Ms. Elvie interrupts, "I'm sorry, too, but we can't stay long. We got some errands to run and we gotta get back to the house for an update from Officer Cutter. And it's Friday—"

"Of course—" She motions to the door. "—Step into J.B.'s office and we'll get you taken care of."

Cebo and Ms. Elvie share a look before following her through the hospital doors. "I'm going to check with Mr. Willis," Cebo says, watching his wife duck into the front office before heading through the doors into the back of the hospital.

The first thing he sees is Rein struggling to sit up with her bandaged shoulder. He rushes over to help her.

Rein tries to smile but it comes out more like a grimace as she gets into a sitting position. "Hello, Cebo, good to see your radiant face around here today."

He looks her over. "Are you getting worse? I'm sorry, but you look more bandaged today than yesterday."

"Weston cut open my wounds and dug out the infection, it feels like it hurts worse today... it has a burning sensation."

Cebo replies, "I'm sorry to hear that."

Rein pauses for a second, looking for the right words. "I love you and Ms. Elvie...and I would do anything to help just..."

Cebo is at a loss for words. "I love Elvie, too...I know you got powers, but if you can just make a miracle happen, that's all I can ask."

Rein sighs. "I wish Amber was here. She would know what to say."

"We've already talked... It didn't help." Cebo shakes his head. "Ms. Elvie and I have had our hearts torn out and stomped on, we cannot be hurt any more than we are." Rein's eyes tear up. "Do you know where Benjamin is?"

Rein, still a bit groggy, thinks for a moment before answering, "I believe that Amber took him to pick up Julie's car in town, they should be back in ten to fifteen minutes, why?"

"Ms. Nina said he could help us with our grocery shopping, he's got the keys," he explains.

"You're right, he's been in and out every day, with Mr. Pepper getting ill." Rein lets out a breath as she realizes just how much has happened over the previous months. "I hope to move to the Care Center at the house tomorrow…I got to get some different scenery."

"I think we're all needing different scenery these days." Cebo stands and turns away from the bed, picking up his coat. "If you see Benjamin come in, will you grab him and hold on until I get back."

"Yes, sir, I will. Where will you be?" Rein agrees quickly as Cebo makes his way toward the door.

"Gonna talk to Bernard."

Emerging from the patient area, Cebo finds his wife waiting for him, just as Burn enters the hospital. "What's the news?"

Ms. Elvie shakes her head, her lips warbling as she tries to maintain her composure. "It's all bad. Cutter is searching the area with a bunch of dogs and a handful of friends are looking. They don't know where else to look, they've checked everywhere already." She gets a tissue from her purse and dabs her nose. "I don't know what else to do."

Burn takes her hand. "I can see you've been thinking."

It's Cebo who answers. "We have…Elvie might not come back if Paulene doesn't come out alright."

Ms. Elvie blows her nose. "I told her neither of us will be back until we find her alive." Cebo puts his arms around her shoulders, trying to comfort her. "I've got some choice words for the Lord if you see him, Mr. Driver."

"Now, Elvie."

"I told Ms. Mae that with all this power around here, none of the powers were used in my direction."

Burn is taken aback. "You said that to Annie Mae?"

"I did, and I made sure she heard me clearly."

"I've had my men looking for Paulene out around my house," Burn promises, trying to do all he can to help the situation.

Cebo nods. "Thank you for that, we appreciate it." He looks up from their conversation to see Benjamin standing at the door, only for him to disappear a blink later. Cebo squints. "Well, I'll see you whenever," he says to Burn, his voice more uncertain than it had been the moment before.

Ms. Elvie doesn't seem to notice her husband's confusion. "And I'll see you...or the Lord, whichever is brave enough to step up." Burn hugs Ms. Elvie quickly before they part ways, Burn heading to the patient area and the Drivers leaving to their car parked in the hospital lot.

~~~

Amber is driving Stephen's car, Benjamin sitting silently in the passenger seat. When they arrive at Pepper's, he steps out, Ms. Elvie and Cebo stepping out of Hal's truck as well. Ms. Elvie's eyes zero in on Amber right away.

"Ms. Windsor." Her tone is anything but friendly, and all four of them are immediately on edge.

Amber turns. "Yes, Ms. Elvie?"

"I just had words with Ms. Mae about what we had words about at my home."

Amber sighs. "I was hoping we would have come to an agreement about my gift."

Ms. Elvie snorts in disdain. "You call it a gift."

"I actually call it a burden...but I and only I have to wake and sleep or wake and dream...do you know what it is like to regret closing your eyes to sleep? It ain't no fun." Amber's face is stoic, though her emotions are rolling like a wave in her gut.

Elvie begins trembling, "Yes, Ms. Windsor, I understand the burden—" Her voice gets louder, "—I don't want to sleep, I don't want to dream, I don't want to breathe, or talk, or see, or touch..." She lets out a breath, "...or remember what my life was like a few days ago. I want to blank everything out...and time to stop... But it won't."

Amber can feel her heart breaking and moves to stand in front of the distraught woman. "Yes, I understand how you feel, but we must learn to forgive or we all will die."
~~~

"Well, Amber, I haven't gotten to that point yet. So I ask you to wait outside until I finish inside the store. Not enough time has passed... I don't want to even look at your face."

Amber raises her eyebrows but concedes, "I'm sorry to hear that. I will do as you ask."

"Thank you. I knew you would understand." Ms. Elvie pushes past Amber, her voice lacking sincerity.

Amber turns to Benjamin. "I'll wait for you in the car."

Benjamin unlocks the store, allowing Cebo and Ms. Elvie to cross the doorstep before locking the door behind them, ensuring the closed sign is still in place. "You got a list?"

Ms. Elvie holds up a torn piece of paper. "I've scribbled a few items but it's mostly memory. Let me walk around and it will be quicker. Cebo can follow me with a basket. He shouldn't be long."

Benjamin agrees and the two begin their shopping, Cebo needing to unload the basket twice so Ms. Elvie can fill it again. Once all their purchases are on the counter, Cebo calls for Benjamin, "We're ready."

Ms. Elvie, always impatient, begins inputting the purchases in the register on her own. Benjamin raises his eyebrows. "You've done this before?"

She clicks her tongue at his foolishness. "You forget, I've lived around here most all of my life. I have done this job before. A long, long time ago. I'm about finished."

Benjamin watches. "You are a very special woman. We are all fortunate to have you in our lives."

"Benjamin, you might be the smartest—" She stops, suddenly remembering something. "There should be a box right there at your side, would you be a dear and come load these groceries?"

"Yes, ma'am." Benjamin does as he is told.

"—while you may be the smartest boy. Mr. Driver, there, is the smartest man."

Cebo grins.

Benjamin carries the now full crate to the door of the store. "I believe you may be the smartest woman in my life. What do you think, Cebo?"

"I know you're right. She tells me that all the time," Cebo agrees as Ms. Elvie opens her purse and begins taking out bills. After counting them, she slips them into the register, making the amount on the ledger behind the counter.

"Give the box to Cebo. We will see you later, Mr. Windsor." Benjamin hands the crate to Cebo, pulling open the door for both of them to exit before closing and locking the door behind them.

Cebo puts the box into Hal's truck.

"Cebo, keep the truck as long as you want," Benjamin shouts from the porch, motioning to the truck Cebo is driving.

Cebo nods. "Thank you."

Ms. Elvie stops at Amber's window calling through the glass, "Amber, I will see you when the time starts up again. I will let you know when that is."

Amber, not wanting to argue, dips her chin and says, "Yes, ma'am."

Ms. Elvie lifts her own chin. "I fear it will be painfully long."

"Yes, ma'am," Amber agrees for a second time, remaining stoic until Ms. Elvie finally loses interest, climbing into the passenger side of the truck. She tracks their movements in the rearview mirror, watching the dust billow behind them as they pull onto the road and towards their house.

Chapter 44

A S BENJAMIN HEAVES THE sheets from Jacob's old bed, stuffing them under his arms to join the other set there, he turns and looks out over the fields, frowning. Turning back to the task at hand, he peruses the bed, his eyes catching on the various wrinkles. He had attempted to make Jacob's bed the night before, but it looks different. Giving up, he walks by Hal and Julie's room next to set the pile of clean, folded sheets on their bed. Benjamin has decided that he would rather hear that he didn't make the bed rather than that he did it wrong.

The grass and trees are swaying harshly in the breeze. As he ducks into Julie's car, he briefly considers grabbing a gun from the house before leaving, but in the end, he decides against it. He's just picking up Julie and Hal from the train station.

Climbing into the driver's seat, he remembers school that morning, and the somber mood which seemed to be dwelling inside every student. News of Paulene's disappearance had spread, whispers of the other odd deaths over the course of the year passing from ear to ear.

While everyone hoped Paulene would be fine, they knew there was a chance that she was the next victim of the killer that had been plaguing the area for several months.

Benjamin was a good student, plus the cutest and most popular boy in the school. His attendance was really never questioned by anyone, not even when he left early as he had today. All the teachers loved him, and he brought an extra smile to their faces whenever he was able to attend classes, and when he wasn't, they understood.

Benjamin had eyes for the girls, but Maria caught his eye most of all because of her fashion sense and the way that their conversations were honest and challenging. He made it a point to talk to her every day, and he was currently kicking himself about treating her badly the night of the festival.

Although he's a bit too early to pick up Hal and Julie just yet, Benjamin decides to run some errands, stopping first by the hospital to drop off the dirty sheets.

When he enters the hospital, he is surprised to see Annie Mae's office door closed, and he heads directly to the back. He is happy to see Rein up and about helping with the patients, along with his other sister Amber. Amber motions to Benjamin that she wants to talk to him. He nods before swinging by the laundry room to drop off the sheets.

Sadie Blue is there, loading sheets into the water.

"You come to say hello?" she asks without turning around, recognizing Benjamin from the sound of his footsteps.

"I did and I brought you a present," Benjamin jokes, dropping the bundle of sheets from his shoulder.

"I don't want it now, save it for Christmas," she jokes back before answering seriously, "It'll cost you a hug."

Benjamin walks to her side and as she leans in. He gives her a hug. "You work too cheap, Ms. Blue."

"I know, now go tell Ms. Mae I need a raise."

"Maybe I will."

Sadie Blue turns around, a serious look on her face "Don't get me in trouble, you hear."

"I hear. These are not mine. They are Julie's. I'll come back and get them later and get them back to her."

Sadie Blue points to a shelf off to the side of the room. "I'll put them on that top shelf just for you. She does have extras, right?"

"Yeah, I got them straight, for now. I see Rein up and around or at least awake. How's Amber working out?" he asks.

"Great. She's doing all the cooking and cleaning. I love having a new daughter, she's a hard worker. And she loves playing that piano. It's like a free concert every night."

"Has she heard about Stephen?" Benjamin asks as Sadie Blue stirs the water.

"Amber said tomorrow."

"Tomorrow? That's great!" Now Benjamin is the one smiling. He's happy that his sister will get her beau back. "We will have to have a big celebration."

Sadie quickly holds up her hand. "No, not big, small like two people—Do you understand."

The smile falls off his face. "I do, as long as Amber is happy, we all should be happy." He glances out the window to see the sun sinking in the sky. "I have got to go pick up Hal and Julie. See you later."

He gives her another hug as she shifts linens into their correct pile. "Filthy, you ain't changed them for two weeks, I can tell."

"Thank you, love ya'."

"I know you do." He leaves, giving one last wave as he heads back to the patient area.

Amber approaches him, following him out into the lobby. "I heard the good news about Stephen, tomorrow's the day," he says as soon as they are out of earshot.

"Supposed to be, the Lord hasn't steered me wrong before." She tucks her blond hair behind her ear. "Oh, I got something to tell you," She glances around to make sure they are alone before continuing, "I had a dream about a kid standing in the middle of a dirt road and you are in great pain."

Benjamin raises his eyebrows. "And?"

"That's it, that's all I saw—oh, then I saw darkness."

"Like nighttime?"

She thinks for a moment. "No, like a buried coffin darkness."

His eyes widened, but he knew better than to ask for anything more. "Thank you, I'll carry a gun."

She shakes her head. "Maybe go with someone. Are you going to talk to Rein?"

"No, I've got to get Uncle Hal and Julie at the train station, why?"

"No big deal. She just wanted me to tell you that she plans on moving to the Care Center in the morning." She leans in and gives him a kiss on the cheek. "Thank you for helping the other night."

"I'm your brother."

She smiles at his words, before her face clouds with worry once again. "Remember—take somebody along."

He nods in agreement before heading out of the hospital and back to Julie's car.

Amber enters the laundry room with a proud smile on her face. "Sadie, have you seen Jennifer today?"

Sadie turns. "I did. I had to look twice, she got some of your old clothes on?"

Amber grins enthusiastically. "She does, and I put the cushioned chair beside her bed, and she seems to be sitting in it instead of lying in the bed."

"Did she ask for any—"

Amber interrupts, "No. I thought of what I would like and...I think I need to get her some books too. Maybe a picture book and some reading books."

"Don't get too far ahead of yourself, but yes she would like that."

Filled with enthusiasm, Amber is undeterred. "I saw Rein talking to her and I think she was trying to tie her shoes."

"Be careful, she may walk out of here soon," Sadie warns, though it is clear that she is secretly happy about the developments as well.

"That would be a blessing. I'll run that by God tonight and see what he says."

Sadie turns back to the wash, gasping as Amber encloses her in a hug. "Is everything okay?"

Amber looks somber. "God's not going to like what I did this morning...He'll let me know tonight."

Sadie frowns. "Sounds like he's giving you regret right now. What did you do?" Amber drops her head. "That ain't going to help."

Amber shakes her head but begins to explain, "When I woke up early this morning, I mean early, before Trevor got up, with my night clothes on, I put my shoes on, got the keys and went out to the workshop."

Sadie furls her brow. "What pray tell did you go out there for?"

Amber drops her head again, "I pounded the straw doll with the hammer til I broke a sweat."

Sadie gasps, "You did? You're going to catch a cold, being so bitter out there. And I expect God saw everything?"

"He did."

"Did you get it out of your system?"

She nods. "It's flatter than a pancake. I beat all the straw out of his head."

Sadie sighs, but she knows Amber meant well. "I expect I'll bury that doll and see what God has in store for me."

"Tell him it was for me," she pleads, her eyes big.

"I will, except he already knows."

~~~

Benjamin drives past the burnt hickory, remembering how he needs to go to Yaphank tomorrow, which he has pushed back two days because of Paulene's disappearance, but he is just so busy. He has never regretted this trip before, but he's got to tell Cass about what Cutter told him. It won't go over well and that alone is causing him to grimace, though he looks forward to seeing Cass and Silva again. He plans to try to make the journey every Friday in the future, when possible.

As he drives by Pepper's store, he notices that he still has plenty of time before he has to collect Hal and Julie.
~~~

Danny Grisco was supposed to be buried today. Benjamin wonders if there was a large crowd and decides he has a moment to stop by.

With a turn of the steering wheel, he makes his way over the river bridge, parking just off the road so he can peek through the trees at the crowd surrounding the burial plot along the riverbank.

He's surprised to see a large crowd of over fifty people gathered along the river's edge. Halfway up the gentle slope is the cemetery spot Danny is to be laid in.

Benjamin thinks about the poison, and he wonders if he can truly be held accountable for what he did. It's not like he shot or stabbed him, and he even drank some of the poison himself, and he was still alive.

He hears a car door close behind him. It's Mr. Strickland.

"Hello, Benjamin, let me guess, you weren't invited?" Mr. Strickland, the newspaper owner, steps to stand beside Benjamin.

Benjamin is surprised by the unexpected guest, but answers with the cool tone he is known for, "Mr. Strickland, how are you? I'd guess you got a notice?"

"Well, since I put it in the paper, I knew about this sad event. I'm doing well, myself. I've noticed my presence gets people jittery so today I'll keep my distance."

"I guess so."

The cool breeze blows Mr. Strickland's long jacket. "I'm sure you've read the news about Danny in the papers. Would you have any comment on the poor lad's death?"

Benjamin looks into Mr. Strickland's eyes, before looking back at the crowd, "Nothing lasts forever, except music and memories."

"True, and death?"

"Maybe so," Benjamin acquiesces, "I imagine all evil must die, better it sooner than later."

"You wouldn't want to live forever?" Mr. Strickland asks, his voice steady.

Benjamin ponders for a moment. "I don't need to worry about that. I need to worry about tomorrow."

"You don't know how right you are. Tell me something I don't know."

"Thanks for keeping Amber's name out of the papers." Benjamin thinks for a moment, "You know, I sense you seem to know more things about me than I know myself. Any comment?"

"In due time, young man. You wouldn't believe me if I told you everything I know."

Mr. Strickland's voice is full of mystery and intrigue, which piques Benjamin's interest. "Try me," he says with confidence.

"Life's a game, son. Patience is a virtue. I like you, Benjamin, wish I had a son like you, I'd enjoy life more, maybe one day we can be friends."

"We are friends, Mr. Strickland, just not confide-everything-we-know friends."

Mr. Strickland stares at him a moment before answering, "Just remember, your closest friends can be your worst enemies."

"That sounds like a warning."

"It is."

Benjamin sizes up Mr. Strickland's smile. "I heard Stephen might get released tomorrow."

Mr. Strickland steps back. "Now, that is news. I know the new district attorney was close to finishing all the paperwork, but I hadn't heard about a release date."

"Don't print anything," Benjamin adds quickly, "I heard it second hand."

Mr. Strickland's eyes appraised him for a moment before answering, "I'll drop by the jail this afternoon to see if I can put it in Sunday's edition." He pauses before changing the subject. "How much more school you got? Two years?"

"Little more. I'll be sure to come see you."

"Be sure you do."

Benjamin steps towards his car. "Got to go to the train station."

"Yeah, pick up the folks," Mr. Strickland replies, Benjamin can tell the smile on his lips is fake.

"You know all about everything, don't you? Even about Hal, and my father?" Benjamin watches Mr. Strickland's eyes turn toward him again.

"I got to save some stories for later. Oh, by the way, the train pulled in early, even before I drove up here."

"It did?" Benjamin hustles to the driver's door. "Got to go!"

Mr. Strickland steps up to Benjamin's open window, "Any other headlines for the paper?"

As Benjamin starts the car and shifts it into gear. "To be continued."

Mr. Strickland steps away, watching Benjamin as he drives off, coat still billowing in the wind like a bad omen.

Chapter 45

November 10, 1945
3:30pm
Railway Depot, Chatham Hill, Middle Tennessee

THINKING HE IS LATE, Benjamin speeds to the train station, his mind full of what Mr. Strickland said. He clearly knows more than he is letting on.

As the train depot comes into view, sure enough, the train is already there. Benjamin slams the car into park, and hustles into the depot. His eyes quickly spot Hal, who is dressed in a brown suit, his eyes skimming a newspaper. He stands as Benjamin approaches.

"I didn't recognize you. Are you a politician now? I haven't seen you wear a suit even to church."

Hal shrugs. "I just feel different when I get away from Chatham."

"I see you do, you dress like a rich man. How are the kids?"

"Doing great. Feels good to spoil 'em. Where have you been?" Hal glances behind Benjamin as if expecting someone else to be there.

"Thought I was on time. How long have you been waiting?"

"About 20 minutes or so."

"Where's Julie?" Benjamin's eyes search the nearly empty station.

"She's talking to the people in the railroad office. She's got news from what she's been doing for the last two weeks, and she's got to tell somebody."

Benjamin shakes his head.

Hal motions to the trunks across the room. "You grab the bags, and I'll go see if I can peel her away from the socialites."

Benjamin grabs two bags, loading them into the car before returning for the last one. Hal still hasn't appeared with Julie, so he leans against the car to wait.

After ten minutes, Hal escorts Julie down the steps and across the lot. Benjamin gives Julie a hug before helping her into the car. As he does, he takes notice of her new dress with a matching handbag, pearl necklace, and new rings. She also has a hat that is pinned onto her hair.

"Sorry, I was late," Benjamin apologizes as he climbs into the driver's seat.

"That's okay, I could still be in there talking." Julie has a smile on her face.

Hal rolls his eyes. "You couldn't have been talking about the trip still."

"No, we were talking about the job offer."

Hal's head snaps to the side in shock. "The job? I thought you were dead set on not taking a job down at this smelly place."

"Well, they offered me good pay."

"Good pay? You were only in there for a few minutes." Hal is surprised. Benjamin keeps quiet.

"I know. We talked fast."

"Are you thinking about taking the job, and what job are they offering?" This is the first Hal has heard Julie say anything about a job at the train depot.

"It's in the accounting department. And yes, I am. I need to get out of the house and spread my wings. I told them I would start next week."

"Houston sure changed ya'," Benjamin comments, almost as shocked as Hal.

"Changed me? I guess it did. I got out and saw the world, you can't do that by sitting at home."

"When were you going to tell me about this?" Hal demands.

Julie doesn't seem bothered. "I tried to talk to you on the train, but you were too busy reading and pacing."

"I guess I missed that part of the train ride." Hal rubs his forehead.

"You did," Julie says matter-of-factly. "You missed over two days and countless hours of conversation."

Hal raises his brow. "Maybe you can repeat what I missed on the train when we get home?"

"Maybe...I doubt it," Julie replies.

The car fills with silence as they pass the jail. Benjamin decides it is time to catch them up on what happened while they were away. "Canine escaped and Paulene got kidnapped."

"We heard down at the station. Any news?" Hal replies, still looking at his wife with questions in his eyes.

"No, not yet. We searched all night...but nothing still."

"That poor child," Julie says sympathetically.

Benjamin continues, "Cebo has your truck. Victoria thought she saw taillights head towards Burn's...the night Paulene was taken. We drove all the way to Burns drive, but we didn't see anything." He takes a deep breath. "So Cutter has had PaPaw's dogs searching in that direction. And Victoria and a friend of hers from Mooney's has been searching nonstop all the roads. She ain't giving up. I told Cebo to use your truck as long as he needs it."

Hal agrees. "Sure. Sure. As long as he needs it."

"And Danny got sick and died. They are burying him down at the cemetery by the river, right now. I stopped by on my way here."

Hal nearly chokes on the air he is breathing. "Oh my God...How did it happen?"

There is a brief pause as Benjamin turns by Pepper's. "The coroner isn't sure. Might be a disease, he said."

"Sounds like it was sudden," Julie says as she stares out the window at the scenery passing by.

Benjamin continues, "Oh, it was...and one other thing I think you should know, Uncle Hal—"

"This doesn't sound good," Hal groans, interrupting his nephew.

Benjamin isn't bothered by his interruption. "Cebo's working at the hospital now...full time."

Hal shrugs, surprising Benjamin with his nonchalance. "I knew that would happen... Just not this soon."

"Ms. Elvie is so tore up, I don't think she will work there again...her and Ms. Mae don't see eye to eye anymore."

Julie sympathizes, as a mother herself. "I like Ms. Elvie. It's going to take a while before—"

"So it's just you and me then, kid," Hal interrupts for a second time, talking over Julie.

Benjamin's eyes darted between the two of them, not sure which conversation to continue. In the end, he decides to answer Hal. "Well, with school and helping the Peppers, I'm not sure—oh that reminds me, Jeremy's at City Hospital with possible pneumonia. It doesn't look good. So Peppers is kind of closed. I got the keys so—"

Hal nearly chokes at the information. "Good God, I wish you would have called me... It sounds like we should have stayed in Houston with the kids." Benjamin turns the car down Hal's drive. "It looks like I need a heart to heart with J.B., and we need a serious talk about the farm."

Benjamin stops the car in front of their house. Julie jumps out of the car and heads up the steps, pausing by the door, "Got the keys?"

Benjamin hurries up the steps. "Yes, ma'am." He lets her in the house. "Glad to have you back." He holds open the door for Julie, remembering that he dropped off the sheets. "Took the sheets to Sadie Blue. The spares are on now and she'll bring 'em back when they're clean."

"Thank you, Benjamin. Things are going to change around here, a new life, a new world." She disappears into the house as Benjamin turns to help Hal with the bags.

"And Paulene was kidnapped? Cebo and Ms. Elvie must be devastated," Hal says as they unload.

"They are. I think it was probably someone searching for Canine. Cutter has been collecting names and comparing stories of that night, but I don't know what has become of it. There were so many people looking, cars and trucks going every which way, I don't know how he can make any sense of it."

"What did Major do?"

"Nothing, he was at the hospital with Danny. Cutter has been doing all the work."

Hal shakes his head. "Let's get the bags in and I'll change and go check on Cebo."

"Yes, sir."

They grab the bags and head up the steps. "And Canine?"

"The dogs chased him to the river, but they lost his scent down towards Kelly's Ferry, where we shot at the wolves a few weeks ago." Hal nods. "The hunters say he crossed the river, and his trail was up the riverbank into the mountains."

"He may still be running in those mountains."

Hal shifts the bag to the opposite hand and holds the door open for Benjamin.

"Looks like Julie's glad to get back."

"Yeah, who would have believed? She's been like a different person since she left Houston."

"Maybe, that's a good thing...change can be good sometimes, Hal," Benjamin says as they set the bags inside the door. "Oh, I changed some bed sheets, so Julie may need to adjust and fix them her way." Hal looks around the house, probably looking for Julie, "I also saw a small mouse run through the upstairs, under the dresser and into your closet. I chased him, but I put everything back right."

Hal is quiet in thought.

"Julie looks elegant, maybe her hair changed or she's wearing a new dress," Benjamin comments, as Julie passes through the room to the kitchen.

"You know, she's gotten younger, I guess, she's acting like before we got married." Hal's eyes also follow Julie's form.

"That's a good thing, isn't it?"

"I don't know if it's a good thing or not... Time will tell. I just hope I can keep up with her."

"Well, if you don't, she'll leave you behind."

"Good thing I got my good looks," Hal says proudly, as he runs a hand through his thinning hair.

"Like I said, she'll leave you behind."

Hal scoffs, before looking at Benjamin. "Need a ride?"

"Yeah. If you're going to check on Cebo."

"I am."

"I'll check on Glory and tell him you're back...I'll wait out front. I'm glad you're back," Benjamin says, giving his uncle one last hug before slipping out the door.

Chapter 46

November 10, 1945
MIDNIGHT
On a Mountain, 15 Miles Outside of Chatham Hill,
Middle Tennessee

CANINE'S NOSE IS RAISED to the air as he tracks through the mountain laurel, passing blackberry briars and rock ledges. His heart rate is elevated, piqued by the smell of his own blood. Pausing, he raises his ear to the wind, searching for the telltale sound of barking dogs.

Luckily, they've been quite a while now, which is good because his body wouldn't survive this punishing pace forever.

Although it's midnight, his eyes have adjusted easily to the darkness, dilating so he can see everything—all of his wolf-like senses aroused. He knows now that he is smarter than a human being. Humans lost their ability to think a long time ago, when they invented cars and indoor plumbing.

Wolves are family oriented. They kill for their family. They hunt for their family. They live for their family. And they sacrifice for their family. Humans don't care about anything but themselves. A wolf will get a mother bear to chase him so a family member can steal her cubs. Humans hunt for sport. Wolves hunt for survival. Humans have no instincts.

The short thoughts puncture Canine's brain, causing his energy to fade as he slowly shifts back into his human form, aptly named Jack Singletary. He looks down to see his own blood seeping out of a hole in his side. He's a mess, and a quick look behind him confirms he's been leaving a blood trail for hours. He stops to rest by the rock outcroppings abundantly strewn along the steep slope.

The sound of small animals rustling in the underbrush reaches his ears, and he worries the sound could be a bear. Canine had no fear, but Jack is another story. Unlike Canine, Jack isn't a predator; Jack is a victim.

As the change completes, Jack's night vision fades, and he realizes he can go no further in the inky darkness. Exhausted, he sinks to the floor, laying his head back on the leaves and light dusting of snow. His breathing slows.

The moon is shrouded behind the clouds, giving them an ethereal glow. Although he can't see well, Jack lifts his wrist, looking for any sign of the restraints which held him prisoner in the hospital. The remnants of one strap circle his left wrist.

The sound of a howl pierces his ear drum, but Jack can't run anymore tonight. His legs ache.

A second howl follows closer still.

Jack blinks, and when he opens his eyes again, it is much darker than before. Did he fall asleep during his blink? He doesn't know for sure.

A branch snaps to his left. He can hear the sound of the river rushing by. He closes his eyes again.

Behind his eyelids plays a rendition of his soldier days. He's back in his uniform, in the trees, waiting silently for the enemy.

The hairs on his arms stand on end as he listens intently for the sound of their movements. Their faces might be camouflaged, but it's no use because their helmets reflect the moon beams, revealing their location.

His mind snaps back to the present. These enemies aren't wearing helmets, so he needs to attack them before they see him.

He lets his animal instincts take over, his mind swirling. With a lurch, he jumps, aiming for their vulnerable necks. He can clamp his jaw down easily on a throat, ending the enemy before it ends him.

His mind clears for a moment. His mouth is empty of the enemy. That was a flashback.

A twig snaps again. It's not the wind stalking him.

He must attack before he is ambushed.

Letting the spirit take over, he bares his teeth when the sound of a growl comes from the underbrush. It's a low, guttural growl. He sees a set of eyes glowing yellow in the dark night.

It's a wolf...no, two...no, three, no...

His senses relay that he has invaded their territory. This is their den. His body starts to shift, only to pause. Is he Jack or Canine right now?

The metallic scent of blood reaches his nose, coming from the wolf's chops. They must have just had dinner, if the blood dripping down their maws is any indication. Jack scents the air, is that fellow wolf blood he is smelling?

Regardless, the scent takes over his features, his eyes glossing over and his teeth sharpening. The change has won again.

As his hair grows longer, his feet and legs begin to grow stronger and larger. The wolf pack in the underbrush isn't happy, their growls growing as the change progresses.

When he is halfway wolf, they step from the shadows, closing in on their prey.

Canine's mouth and teeth are fully wolf, and they ache with the need to feed. Without thinking, he turns and pounces on the nearest wolf, his teeth sinking into the supple neck of a young, and aggressive, pup.

The blood pools between his lips, the burning in his throat is receding, but he needs more.

So consumed with bloodlust, Canine barely notices as the teeth of the pack mates sinks into his legs, his side, and his foot. Although he changes tactics, trying to fight off the pack with his claws, the pulsing pain of their bite is overpowering.

He makes a mistake, exposing his underbelly. As a result, he releases his mouth, letting go of the wolf. Before he can make another move, a different member of the pack clamps their teeth on Canine's neck, his breath beginning to flow out.

His energy cannot thrive without air and immediately fades as another wolf takes a bite from his face. He barely notices as yet another begins to attack his chest in earnest.

The wolves, by this point, are in a total frenzy, like a group of piranhas attacking a small meal. Canine is exposed and defenseless now, as more and more of his innards are exposed. He has lost this battle.

Reverting back to his human mind, he tries to yell for help, but it is no use. Sound cannot pass through his open neck. He tries to shift back, but it is too late. Jack tries to take one final exhale as his soul officially leaves the earth, the munching of wolves providing background noise as they feast on what remains of the man. Canine will never be seen again.

The pack continues its onslaught until they become tired and confused, the adrenaline of the hunt fading. A young pup snaps a few fingers as a souvenir, only to lay them on the ground a few feet away. Celebrating, the adults in the pack bark and yip as they leave the corpse to rot.

Turning away from the mess that was once a possessed man, the wolves are happy and content, glad they have eliminated the threat to their pack—thanks to their basal instincts.

A light fall of snow and rain begins to spatter the trees, creating a chilling calm. The pack leaves, there is nothing more for them here.

As soon as the wolves are out of sight, the scavengers know it is their turn to enjoy a meal. Silence is a beautiful sound. It is still and peaceful for several minutes or so.

After some time, opossums emerge from the bushes. Their noses sniff out the pungent odor of a dead animal. They snatch pieces to feed their young. While worms and maggots come up into the body from beneath. Vultures will wait until daylight, but they will eventually take their piece.

From the maggots to the possums and the wolves, all have a right to use what is left of Canine for survival. It's their right. It's their instinct.

It's how they survive.

Chapter 47

November 11, 1945
1:00pm
Pepper's Truck, Yaphank Compound, Middle Tennessee

B ENJAMIN PARKS PEPPER'S TRUCK in front of the small Yaphank hospital. It's colder here than in Chatham Hill, and a heavy layer of snow dusts the ground.

Exiting the truck and heading inside, Dutch's eyes follow his form through his truck windshield. He is parked around the corner, just out of Benjamin's sight.

When Benjamin enters the hospital, Cass looks up from her paper only to stumble back in surprise, as she wasn't expecting him, before quickly giving him a hug.

"I didn't get a chance to thank you for helping me get back to Hal's from the festival. I had a wonderful time with you and Silva, 'til then," Benjamin whispers in her ear as they embrace.

Cass leans back, making eye contact with Benjamin. "Oh, Victoria and I enjoyed, I mean, struggled to put you to bed."

Benjamin's mouth turns up at the corner in amusement. "You sound like you maybe had too much fun at my expense."

"You were, in medical terms, falling down drunk. We had to get you comfortable before we left."

"Well, I woke up the next afternoon with only my shorts on," Benjamin says, jesting with her.

Cass turns to write something down on a notepad. "Is that so? I don't remember."

"Victoria probably doesn't remember either, I guess."

Cass laughs. "She's got a very...let's say...eccentric imagination."

He's fully smiling now as he replies, "Eccentric? I wasn't in any danger, was I?"

Cass smiles back. "Not danger, you were in good hands."

"I did survive," Benjamin surmises as Cass peeks around to spot Pepper's truck.

"I see you delivering to Hamel. Wrong day, isn't it?"

The smile immediately falls off his face as he remembers why he is here. "Paulene was taken from her home last Wednesday night."

Cass gasps. "Oh, no, not Paulene. What happened?"

"A patient escaped from our hospital and during the search, someone set fire to Victoria's next door neighbor's house, and as everyone paid attention to the fire and the search, someone snatched her away. She's gone."

Cass stares at Benjamin open-mouthed, the panic evident on her face. "I need to go check on Victoria."

"Victoria and I drove all the way to Burn's house that night. But we didn't see anything... The sheriff and everyone has been searching every day since, but it doesn't look good." Benjamin looks down at his feet.

"Maybe she'll turn up," Cass says, trying to keep things positive.

"Like I said, it doesn't look good," Benjamin reiterates. Cass turns away with a sad look on her face. "Silva hasn't seen any more new graves, has she?"

Shocked, Cass slaps Benjamin with her open hand. She recoils her hand across her mouth. "Don't talk like that." Tears form in her eyes. "I'm sorry, but I don't want to think like that."

Benjamin rubs his face where she slapped him. "I told a deputy from

Chatham named Cutter about the graves I saw down here, and I told him to ask for you if he were to come down and that I would come with him if need be."

Cass shakes her head, lowering her voice, "Oh, Lord, trouble is coming. If anything happens or we disappear overnight, we'll either be dead, or just running."

"Running? Who will you be running from? The killers?" Benjamin is confused by her outburst.

"No one knows who the killers are, that's just it." Cass looks over her shoulder to be sure no one is listening in on their conversation.

"Where are you running to?" Benjamin asks.

"Up north or out west. We will run until nobody knows who we are."

"You don't need to talk like that," Benjamin argues with her, leaning in close.

"Why, we got to stay alive. You may have told the wrong person." Cass' voice is clouded with panic.

"I trust the person I told, it's everybody around him, I don't."

Cass looks stressed. "All we got around here is family and we don't trust any of them."

Benjamin quickly thinks about what Mr. Strickland had told him on the roadside. "You tell Silva about Paulene—I know I can't."

"I will, somehow," she promises.

"And ask her to look for—"

Cass stops him. "You go out right now and look for graves yourself. I ain't asking her to do that. You're sick, I think it's time for you to leave."

Benjamin turns back to the door. "I'm sorry for what I said, but Victoria needs a friend. Sorry the news wasn't better, but you had to know."

He takes a deep breath. "One other problem, the deputy I told about the graves wants you to come to town and make a statement."

Cass looks at Benjamin with concern. "No way. I ain't putting our lives in jeopardy."

"I'm on your side. Come see Victoria and when you do, I'll get the deputy to meet us somewhere out of sight and just tell him what you know. That's it."

"How can I trust you? You've put both our lives in danger." Cass turns away from Benjamin, clearly angry.

"Look at me," Benjamin demands. "Besides my sisters, you and Silva are the only ones I care about more than myself. So let's do the right thing and I promise everything will be alright."

Cass shakes her head. "You're too young to promise. If you see me at your door..." She searches for the words, "We'll be either running or trying to fight the devil... You need to leave, please."

He drops his head and turns. "I'll save my hug for the next time I see ya'." Without another word, he rushes out to his truck, throwing it into gear.

Benjamin drives along the river's edge, grimacing as he pictures Silva's face when Cass tells him the news about Paulene. He's so engrossed in his thoughts that 30 minutes later his mind comes back to the present and he isn't exactly sure where he is.

Navigating the truck around the next bend, he sees a teenage boy standing in the middle of the road. He slows the truck to a stop. It's Elliott.

He briefly considers going around him but instead decides to inch the truck forward until the bumper just brushes Elliott's leg. What Amber told him the day before comes to mind and he grabs the gun from the glove compartment, holding it on his thigh.

"Get out of my way, Elliott!" he shouts out the cracked window.

Elliott doesn't say anything. His chin is high, his lips pressed into a thin line.

"I'll run over your ass! I swear!" He yells again.

Never one to lie, Benjamin steps on the gas, just enough to push the boy over. The truck rocks as it climbs over his body. Benjamin steps on the brakes and puts the truck into park. Benjamin waits a few moments and then climbs out. He leaves the keys dangling in place.

His eyes scan the dense brush at either side of the road, the gun clutched tightly in his hand. Lifting the gun, he walks around to the front of the truck, keeping it trained on Elliott's unmoving form in the roadway.

He notices that Elliott is laying on his side in the road, facing away from Benjamin. Benjamin inches closer—

BANG.

The sound of a gun firing reaches his ears just as he feels an intense pain in his side, causing him to drop the gun. His hand reaches up to grab his side, as he falls forward.

He opens his eyes, not realizing he closed them, reaching for the gun, but he only manages to push it under the truck. His vision is blurred.

Then everything goes black.

~~~

Major and Elliott stand over the motionless body, a small pool of blood blooming on the hard roadway. Nodding at his son, Major returns to where his patrol car is parked behind the brush, driving it over to Benjamin's body.

Elliott helps him load Benjamin into the trunk, before they both climb in and drive off.

They drive for several minutes, until finally Major pulls over, opening the trunk to drag Benjamin's body out. It is just Major and Benjamin now, Elliott staying in the passenger seat of his patrol car. Major sets his broken body on a rock outcropping before grabbing a hickory walking stick from the patrol car's trunk.

"I knew I was saving this for a special occasion," he says with a grin before turning back to an unconscious Benjamin. He tears off his shirt.

THUD.

The walking stick comes down hard on Benjamin's back, creating a long red welt.

THUD.

Another welt.

THUD.

Benjamin's skin tears and becomes bloody.

"I hope you suffer like my son," Major hisses.

THUD.

THUD.

THUD.
~~~

A few strikes hit Benjamin's head, breaking his skin.

Major has begun to work up a sweat. He's lost count of the number of lashes, and Benjamin's blood runs down his face.

Major is exhausted but satisfied. His son has been avenged.

He stops long enough to go to his trunk and retrieve a dirty rag. He uses it to try and clean the blood from himself and the walking stick, but soon the rag is soaked in blood and no use.

Shrugging, he removes a short-handled shovel from his trunk and digs a shallow hole off to the side of his car, tossing in the rag. Brushing the dirt back in place, he tosses the shovel back in the trunk before slamming it shut.

Returning to Benjamin's body, Major rolls him off the rock, allowing the dirt to embed in his skin. Blood pours from the wound in his side, as well as from his back. There is even a small stream coming from his mouth.

Major looks out over the river and leafless trees. He is parked near the river, and a few feet away is the cliff over the river. The highest point, in fact, where the drop is over 100 feet. He looks up, the lights of Windsor Hospital barely visible in the setting sun.

"Benjamin, I know what you did, and I figured you would want to be buried on a hill overlooking your house. Well, this is your final resting place, so enjoy it down there."

Motioning to Elliott, the boy exits the car to help his father move the body. The two of them lift Benjamin, straining under his dead weight. The move toward one of the many caves dotting the landscape, nearly slipping on the large amount of bat poop near the opening of the cave. With one final heave, they release the body. As Benjamin's body falls thirty feet, Major hears a thump or two as it lands in the dark.

"Good riddance," Major hisses.

The sound of Benjamin's body hitting the cave floor wakes some of the bats, who are none too happy about being awoken before it is fully dark.

Major is unbothered by the bats flying out of the cave. "Stephen won't need to speak any words over your body. You'll never be found."

He motions to Elliott and the two get into his patrol car and drive toward town.

Benjamin groans. The feeling of hitting the ground woke him, and now everything in his body hurts.

Unable to lift his head, Benjamin observes what he can of the cave from where he is lying. He senses and recognizes it immediately, it's where Annie Mae sends him to get bat parts for her potions.

Benjamin can both feel and see the blood leaking from his body, along with the feeling of something landing on his neck...probably a bat.

It's the first of many, and soon he is sure there are several bats resting on his neck and back...and they are hungry.

Benjamin closes his eyes as the bats begin to bite him. They swarm him as it's been too long since they had a good meal.

He prepares to take his last breath, his finger twitching as his eyes drift closed.

Chapter 48

November 11, 1945
2:00pm
Windsor Hospital, Chatham Hill, Middle Tennessee

CUTTER MANEUVERS THE PATROL car up the hospital drive, his eyes following Cheddar, who is running alongside the vehicle. Pulling the car into the parking area, he steps out, putting his hat on his head as Stephen steps out from the back seat.

Eagerly watching for their arrival, it doesn't take long for Amber to bound down the steps into Stephen's arms. Cutter looks away as Stephen leans down to kiss Amber.

J.B. and Annie Mae step out onto the hospital porch, glad to see their granddaughter happy. Sensing the commotion, Rein also exits the hospital to stand next to Annie Mae and watch as Stephen and Amber continue to embrace.

"Major wanted you to know all his paperwork has been cleared and he's a free man." Cutter announces as he makes his way up the porch steps.

"Thank you, Cutter, for bringing him by." Annie Mae says with a small smile.

"Well, I thought it's the least I could do. I told Stephen on the way over here that I hope he has no hard feelings towards the department, we were just doing our job."

Annie Mae nods. "I know you were not responsible for the last few weeks, but someone should be."

"Well remember, if Amber would have told us what happened then—"

Annie Mae cuts him off, "I understand. And where is Major?"

Cutter looks at Ms. Mae. "Oh, Major wanted me to tell you that he wanted to be here, but he had an appointment to go question a suspect for a recent crime in the area."

Annie Mae's eyebrows rise. "Question someone? Did he say who?"

"No, he left before lunch," Cutter replies, looking over his shoulder to see Amber and Stephen still in each other's arms.

Annie Mae turns to J.B. and then to Rein. "Where is Benjamin?"

It's Rein who replies, "He was supposed to make a delivery for Peppers down at Yaphank."

Annie Mae is nervous, and she can't explain why. "Cutter, will you do me a favor and wait here a minute while I call Nina?"

"Sure," he replies, watching as Annie Mae disappears into the hospital.

Rein turns to J.B. "Do you know what's going on?"

J.B. looks anxious but just says, "Benjamin."

Sadie comes hastily out the front door onto the porch. She is waving a folded-up paper. "Ms. Amber! Ms. Amber, you have got to read this right now." Amber and Stephen briskly walk along the back of the parked cars. She takes the note from Sadie, the paper crumpling in her fist as she reads.

Amber turns to Rein. "Rein, tell Annie Mae I'm gone for the rest of the day. I'll see her tomorrow."

Rein nods, watching as her sister and Stephen climb into his car, driving off down the dirt road toward town.

Rein looks at J.B., going back to their previous conversation. "That's it? Just Benjamin? You don't know any more?"

J.B. shakes his head. "We don't talk much anymore, since well...I don't know."

Rein touches the bandage on her shoulder, not sure what else to say.

Before she can follow that thought further, Annie Mae rushes back onto the porch. "Cutter, please go down towards Yaphank down Kelly Ferry Road and drive until you see Benjamin."

Cutter is surprised by her demands. "What did Nina say?"

"She says Benjamin is in serious trouble and needs our help, NOW!" She points to his patrol car. "Use your siren."

Not needing anymore prodding, Cutter hustles to his car and drives off, siren blaring.

Annie Mae turns to Rein. "Rein, go get the keys, we're going to follow him." Then she looks at her husband. "J.B., pray we find Benjamin before Major."

Rein returns with the keys and the two women make their way to J.B.'s car, pulling out before the dust from Cutter's patrol car has even settled.

"What did Nina say?" Rein asks, as they pull onto the main road.

"He's gone to Yaphank. Major threatened to take Benjamin into custody the night Danny died, but I had a gun and told him to leave Benjamin alone. He believes Benjamin killed Danny."

Rein understands, pressing the gas pedal down harder. But as they turn the bend on Kelly's Ferry Road, they see Cutter's patrol car stopped in the middle of the road. Beyond his patrol car is Pepper's truck, the driver's side door hanging open.

Putting on the brake, Annie Mae and Rein step out, neither voicing the fear they are both feeling.

Cutter holds up a hand. "You ladies stay back." Cutter has his gun out and is circling the truck. As he does so, a glint of metal catches his eye, and he leans down to retrieve the gun from under the truck.

He holds it up, and Annie Mae screams. "Oh, God, please help my boy."

Rein notices Cutter's gaze. "Cutter, is there blood?"

Annie Mae is in hysterics. "If you follow Major's steps since lunch, you'll find my boy!" she shouts.

"Why do you say that, Ms. Mae?" Cutter asks over his shoulder.

"A mother's intuition."

Cutter rolls his eyes, but Annie Mae can't see since his back is still turned. "Rein, take Ms. Mae back to the hospital and let us do our job."

Rein starts trying to guide Annie Mae back to the car. "Call Major on your radio and find out where he's at, right now, please!" she begs.

Deciding to appease her, Cutter does just that, but there is no response.

"Check the woods, please!" she shouts even as Rein almost has her in the car.

"We will. I got back-up officers coming," he replies, watching as Rein starts the car and turns around, heading back to the hospital.

As soon as they are almost out of Cutter's sight, Annie Mae shouts, "Stop!"

Rein stands on the brakes, and as soon as the car is near a stop, Annie Mae climbs out.

"Cutter, come see what I just found!" She calls.

He puts Benjamin's gun in his car and walks towards the women. "Is it someone?"

"No, just evidence of an ambush." Annie Mae points to the tire tracks which lead into the underbrush.

"Cutter, Major ambushed my boy and has probably—"

He cuts her off. "Why do you keep saying Major?"

Rein looks at Annie Mae and thinks about what she is about to say, "He threatened Benjamin the afternoon Danny died at the hospital. You'd have to ask Major about his evidence, but I think he's delirious from his son's illness."

Cutter is quiet, his mouth agape.

"This is Major's patrol car and he's gone," Annie Mae adds.

The sound of a distant siren breaks the silence. Cutter turns to Annie Mae. "You all go home and I'll drop by when we find something out."

Annie Mae nods in agreement bleed she and Rein climb back into their car, driving toward the hospital once more. It isn't until they cross the bridge that they come in contact with the other patrol car. It's not Major.

"Ms. Mae, you think Major got to Benjamin?"

Annie Mae doesn't answer. "Oh, God, help him, Lord," she whispers.

It isn't until they pull up at the hospital that Annie Mae remembers the conversation she had with Benjamin the day before. Her hand flies to her mouth.

"What? What are you thinking?" Rein demands.

Annie Mae is struggling to breathe as the realization sinks in. "I'm thinking about what Benjamin said. Ms. Elvie told Amber something the night Paulene was taken."

"What did she say?"

Ms. Mae's eyes are downcast. "I hope one day you'll know how it feels to lose someone close."

Rein swallows.

The two women sit in silence for a minute, until Rein finally helps Annie Mae out of the car and to her office, Weston and J.B. coming to help.

Annie Mae waves them off. "I need some time to think and rest. Please, go help in the back."

Weston and J.B. leave, but Rein lingers. "What do I need to do?"

"I would say find Major, but I don't want to lose another child." Annie Mae takes a breath. "Pray, Rein. Pray for your brother."

Rein nods, leaving the office and closing the door behind her.

Annie Mae sits at her desk and sobs for several minutes. When she finally has no tears left, she rises from her seat and heads to the lobby telephone dialing Sadie Blue's number, where she is sure she will find Amber.

Amber answers after the third ring.

"Amber?" Annie Mae's voice is fearful. "You and Stephen get home alright?"

"Yes, I'm fine." Her response is curt.

Annie Mae lets out a shaky breath. "I just wanted you to know I love you and I'm glad Stephen is back home with you. I didn't get a chance to speak to you before you left."

"Thanks" is her only response.

Annie Mae figures she might as well ask. "Amber, have you talked to Benjamin lately?"

"Yes, yesterday," comes her response through the line.

"You did? What did you tell him?" Annie Mae listens patiently as Amber describes her dream, her hopes dying with every word. "That's all?"

"Yes," Amber replies, clearly wanting to get off the line.

"Will you do me a favor tonight?" Amber doesn't answer, but Annie Mae continues anyway, "Dream about Benjamin tonight and let me know what you see, okay?"

"I'll try," Amber promises.

"Okay, I'll see you in the morning," Annie Mae says. "Get here when you can, okay?"

They say their goodbyes and Annie Mae hangs up the phone before returning to her office and closing the door. She sits behind her desk, laying her head on her forearms.

Benjamin has to be okay. He just has to be.

She can't lose him.

Chapter 49

November 11, 1945
5:00pm
Windsor Home, Chatham Hill, Middle Tennessee

W HEN REIN OPENS HER eyes, it takes a moment for her to remember where she is, her gaze focused on the roaring fire. It doesn't take her long for the reason behind her nap to come to the front of her mind, the sadness seeping back in as she realizes that she was not disturbed from her nap by the phone ringing. A chill suddenly snaking down her spine, she rises from the couch to set her shoes in front of the fire to warm.

Not wanting the fire to die until they are nice and toasty, she quickly grabs a poker to stoke it, the motion causing her shoulder to ache. Glancing back at the lumpy couch she realizes it may not have been the best idea to nap there. She should have headed to the Care Center instead.

At the thought of the Care Center, she realizes that she should check it out, ensure that it's ready in case Cutter's mother needs it. Walking quietly, she passes Annie Mae and J.B.'s room, pausing as the sound of running water reaches her ears.

J.B. must be bathing, she thinks, quickening her pace so she won't have to talk to him.

Passing through the Care Center, she notices that it is well set up before entering the ensuite bathroom to dab a little water on her face. It isn't until she has dabbed a few times that she notices the odd smell of smoke and soot clinging to her clothing.

Wrinkling her nose, she sniffs her shirt to confirm her fears. *Yes, everything smells like smoke.*

Without delay, she slips off her current clothes, noticing the blood seeping through her bandage. Since she is already in the Care Center, she decides to just change her bandage as well, replacing it with a clean one, tossing the old one in the trash.

Satisfied that she is now clean, she slips on a new set of clothes, and heads back into the Care Center. Though she had planned to stop in the kitchen, she feels her eyes getting heavy and decides she will lay down in the Care Center and rest her eyes, just for a few minutes...

~~~

Tap. Tap. Tap. Rein's eyes crack open a sliver to look for where the sound is coming from. She rubs her eyes and sees Annie Mae's face framed in the glass. Rein springs out of bed and unlocks the faded white wooden door.

As she opens it, her grandmother explains, "Oh, child, I forgot my keys. Have you heard anything good?"

The cold breeze follows her in, and Rein closes the door quickly to keep it out. "No ma'am, phone hasn't made a sound."

Annie Mae's lips press in a thin line, and she makes a bee line for the pile of dirty clothes Rein left on the floor. "Cutter came by and there isn't any good news...either." She gathers up the clothes, commenting, "These smell like Weston when he's tried to smoke his worries away." Without waiting for Rein to answer she heads for the entry to the main house. "Cora's coming by Tuesday to cook and clean. I'll put these in the washer for her."
~~~

Rein suddenly remembers the conversation she had with her sister earlier. "Oh, I invited Amber to come by. I better get ready."

Annie Mae raises one eyebrow. "Maybe Amber will have seen something in her sleep."

Rein follows her, spotting her shoes aglow on the hearth. With a smile she slides her cool socks into her toasty warm shoes, relishing in the warmth. She sits to lace them up as J.B. comes from his bedroom, his eyes on the waning fire.

His gaze narrows, but before Rein can inquire, he's walking toward the front door, opening it and allowing the cruel fall breeze to scurry in. Rein wants to close it, but before she can, J.B. is back, his arms laden with firewood.

Annie Mae takes a seat in the chair, watching as her husband tosses the pieces of wood into the flames, the wood gobbled up in seconds by the hungry tendrils.

J.B. says nothing as he takes a seat in his rocking chair, pulling out his pocketknife. The flames forgotten, he pulls a small piece of wood from the stack by the fireplace and begins to whittle.

He strips the darker outer skin first, until its color changes from nearly black to light brown. He caresses the stick gently, never forceful, the shape forming beneath his knife, slivers hitting the ground at a rhythmic pace.

Annie Mae is hypnotized by the random pattern, her eyes following his knife's every motion. "Major is pissed at all of us...especially me. His behavior has turned irrational."

J.B. brushes it off, his eyes focused on his art. "He's just grieving, any father would do the same."

Rein shakes her head. "He has threatened us in front of several people—"

Annie Mae interrupts, "He doesn't care about what anyone says."

The sound of a car door slamming brings their conversation to a halt, but J.B. doesn't make a move to answer the door, his eyes still on the project in his hands. Rein heads to the window, pulling the curtain back to see Major's patrol car. Major has maneuvered his patrol car just far enough back from the front of the house for Rein's eyes to focus on him. Whether it is the setting sun, the curtain interference, or the shade of the oaks, Rein jolts at the surprise. "It's Major."

Annie Mae stands, and Rein turns her attention back to the window to see that Major isn't making a move to approach the house. Rather, he is just standing there by his open patrol car door, several paces from their porch, staring. His right hand is at his side.

Never one to be intimidated, Annie Mae cracks the front door shouting, "Major?"

When he doesn't respond, J.B. hesitantly sets aside his project to follow his wife to the door. As she pushes open the screen door as well, the wind is suddenly silent.

J.B. looks at Major.

Annie Mae studies Major.

Major stares at Annie Mae.

Then Major has his rifle barrel pointing directly at Annie Mae's chest.

BANG.

Her heart is pierced with a piece of lead, her weight drooping down like a sack of potatoes. Her eyes are open, but she is already gone.

Rein is frozen in shock at the window, unable to move.

J.B. jumps at the sound of the shot, his eyes immediately finding his wife's lifeless body, wedged between the screen door and the door frame.

In shock, he runs to his bedroom, getting the rifle from behind the door.

When he returns to the front door, Major is still by his car, his gun still raised and pointed at the Windsor home.

J.B. raises his gun, just as Major fires a second shot.

BANG.

Rein is right there, moving J.B. out of the path of the bullet. He slows a moment and kneels to steady his aim.

BANG.

J.B. watches as his bullet misses, striking the headlight of the patrol car with an explosion of glass.

BANG. BANG.

Two simultaneous shots. Major's bullet whizzes over J.B.'s head, striking the upper outside corner of the door frame.

Then, J.B. falls toward the front porch. His body lays almost parallel with Annie Mae, their fingers nearly touching. His rifle bounces a step or two away.

Rein slowly turns her head to see Frost's shadow lowering his rifle from his position in the kitchen, darkness filling the space behind him. Rein steps quickly back out of sight.

Major steps around his door and approaches the scene. His steps are long and slow...each one deliberate, as if he is in no hurry. His pace picks up as he mounts the porch step, his eyes finding his deputy heading his way through the house.

They both enter the living room, looking around bewildered.

"Didn't you see the girl?" Major's voice is gruff.

Frost scratches his head in confusion, his eyes darting from left to right. "I thought I did...but she ain't here."

They look behind the couch, and the chair. They checked the window she had peeked through. Frost even touches the stones of the fireplace, ensuring there was no hidden door.

But it was no use, Rein was gone.

After completing their searches, they look at each other and shrug before heading back toward the door, stepping carefully over the bodies.

With Frost's rifle barrel aiming towards the sky, he bounds down the porch steps. "I'll call it in," Frost says, leaning into the patrol car to use the radio.

Major watches, a grin playing on his lips. He notices the broken headlight as he climbs into the car, but nothing can upset him today. As the two men close their doors and make their way out of the drive, Major turns to Frost. "Let's swing around and head down towards the hospital and squelch any trouble from Burn."

Major accelerates, but they don't need to go far until they spot Burn carrying a rifle and Weston with a pistol by his side.

Swinging the car to a stop, Major opens the door as soon as the brake is engaged, training his pistol on the two men, pulling a paper from his pocket, and yelling, "I presented an arrest warrant for Annie Mae and J.B. They opened fire on us. We returned fire and well...other officers are on the way and the ambulance is on the way, too."

Burn grinds his teeth together. He wants to argue, but he knows he is at a disadvantage so instead he says, "You killed all of them?" His eyes have a red sheen to them.

Major ignores his question and raises his pistol. "Both of you need to drop your weapons."

Burn looks at Weston, but he knows he's in a precarious spot. He pauses for a moment, trying to calculate a way out of this situation, but eventually he relents and drops his rifle.

Weston drops his gun, his eyes wet. "Did you shoot Rein, too?"

Frost shuffles forward and gathers both weapons. "She wasn't there."

Weston raises his eyebrows, and Burn returns the look, turning to ask Major, "Can we go check on the injured?"

Major's eyes shift. "No...it's too late. Let the other officers do their jobs."

Weston doesn't buy it for a moment. "You shot an old man and woman?" His doctor training starts to take over and he moves to disobey Major's orders.

But Major steps in Weston's way, his gun raised to Weston's chest.

Burn sees what's about to happen and calls, "Dr. Galloway, you can't do anything for them now..."

Major shakes his head. "J.B. shot at us...we just returned fire."

Weston lowers his head and backs up a step.

Burn steps forward, laying his hand on Weston's shoulder as he leans in to whisper, "We're too late...between Amber and Rein let's not give up hope."

Major's eyes shift between the two, but he doesn't seem concerned. "You both get back to the hospital and we'll let you know when we finish our investigation."

Weston looks to the house, his mind filled with questions he knew, for now, would remain unanswered.

Chapter 50

November 11, 1945
6:00pm
Windsor Home, Chatham Hill, Middle Tennessee

A MBER NUDGES STEPHEN'S CAR off the road and toward the
Windsor home. Her mind is overloaded with worry over her vision
about Benjamin, and the fact that she hadn't seen him in a while, and as
such, she doesn't notice as her car rolls over Major's broken glass headlight
left in the Windsor front drive.

It isn't until she puts her car in park, climbing out of the driver's side
door that she spots the screen door ajar, and the two bodies lying there.

Her breath stops, her hand gripping the door tighter as her eyes dart
from side to side, checking for danger.

Once she is sure there is no one lurking in the shadows, she tosses her
purse onto the roof of the car and runs up the porch steps. Kneeling down,
she checks for Annie Mae's pulse first, frowning when there is none to be
found, before moving on to JB.

She sits back on her heels, the silence of the house all consuming. Her
mind briefly flashes back to her attack just months before, immobilizing
her momentarily.

When she is finally able to regain control of her mind, she pushes the thoughts to the side, remembering her sister. "Rein? Rein are you in there?" she calls.

There is no response.

Carefully picking her way over the bodies and rifle on the front porch, she enters the house, her eyes snagging on the overturned furniture. "Rein?" Then, with desperation, "Please answer me." Her eyes search the room, but there is no sign of her sister.

With a sigh, she leans down to pick up the fire poker, which is laying across the wooden floor, when she spots it. The picture frame on the table by the fireplace is laid down flat.

Breath frozen in her lungs, she slowly steps toward the table, her fingers shaking as she reaches for the picture frame and stands it upright. It's her...in the church.

She pushes the first framed picture aside, to see a second picture of her beneath, the edges curled, as if the photo had been rolled.

Without thinking, she sinks into the large chair where Annie Mae had sat just a few minutes before, a tear rolling down her cheek. Rein had done it. She had gone into the fireplace and left the signal as promised.

Noticing that the firewood in the fireplace is haphazardly placed, she uses the poker to move the logs back into a pile, wondering if it was Rein, or the person who had killed J.B. who had left the logs like this. Then she stirs the embers, the fire once again roaring to life.

With a sigh, she sinks back into the chair, the rolled-up photo clutched to her chest. The sound of a siren tickles her ears. Her eyes drift closed.

"Dear Lord,

My trials and tribulations have caused me anguish and sorrow. Thank you for allowing my sweet sister to give me this present. It's a sense of freedom from one of my enemies. The gift you have bestowed on me is glorious and has had me wretchedly unhappy and uncomfortable. I have prayed in the past that all Rein's and Benjamin's atrocities be placed upon my body and soul. But I am weak and vulnerable. Please give me the strength to hold my head up and face the fears. With you by my side we will be victorious... Thank you for Stephen and the life soon to be...And Lord..."

Amber's hand raises and points at the door as her voice grows louder.

"...help me understand that those bodies on the front porch ain't supposed to be there—"

She takes a deep breath.

"In Jesus name. Amen."

Amber stands with a firm grasp of the rolled-up photo and walks to the front porch, wiping her tears with her sleeve. She steps between the bodies that once were Annie Mae and J.B., her eyes catching on the rifle lying nearby.

She looks down to J.B.'s side, gritting her teeth as a thought edges into her mind. She lifts her leg up and kicks J.B. hard in his rib cage. The body moves a smidge.

"Thanks for the strength...forgive me Lord."

The sound of the siren grows closer. Not sure what else to do, Amber heads for her car, tucking the rolled-up picture in her purse.

Starting the car, she heads to the main road, but before she can turn, she spots Hal's car, heading directly for her. Stomping on the brakes, she waits until he skids to a stop along beside her, his window rolled down, before rolling her own.

"Amber am I too late?" he pants, fear clouding his eyes.

Amber presses her lips together, her eyes red from crying. "I called you an hour ago and you said you were headed this way with your gun, what happened?"

Hal lets out a breath, running a hand through his mussed hair. "Well, if you must know, Julie's been excited for her new job and the trip, so much good news lately. We got a little frisky this afternoon. And I lost track of time..." Hal looks up and sees the emergency vehicles behind him. "Am I too late?"

Amber's eyes are cold as she answers. "We all lose track of time... I'll know better next time."

Hal swallows, but as the vehicles stop behind him, he realizes he has to continue on to the house, and he does so without bidding Amber goodbye.

Amber watches as the ambulance and patrol car turn into the drive, following Hal's vehicle to the house. Then she looks both ways and turns right onto the main road.

She reaches over and pats her purse, the rolled-up picture contained within. It was safe...for now at least.

To Be Continued...

ACKNOWLEDGEMENTS

I wish to acknowledge those who supported and encouraged me during the daunting process of penning my third book in series.

First, my wife Debbie, who was beside me for the entire journey. Additional thanks to my other encouragers: Renee, Wes, and Anne. Also to my friends at B&G: Sydna, Lan, and Blake—thanks for giving me the confidence to move forward on this project.

Hope E. Davis is a spectacular ghostwriter that has worked diligently to bring the characters of 'Bleeds For Life' to fruition. I am more impressed with her prolific wordsmithing, effortless flow, and great value for her services. Thank you for your due diligence and hard work. It has been essential in bringing 'Bleeds For Life' to life.

Next is Sarah Lemcke, my editor and interior book designer at 'All in the Edit'. She was recommended to me by another author and I'm so glad I took their advice. Thank you for your several weeks of twisting and turning our words into a gem. Your technical insight has given me an assurance that this book will be enjoyed thoroughly by the reader.

Lastly, Victoria, my book cover designer at Victoria Cooper Art. Thank you for your beautiful images and bold artwork. You were prompt, diligent, and patient with me as we took the time to perfect the designs.

Thank you all.

ABOUT THE AUTHOR

I was born over 65 years ago in the state of Georgia. I lived in a dozen different houses in 5 different states all before I graduated high school. I had to learn to make friends during my family's travels, but also had to learn to say plenty of goodbyes.

My dad taught me what hard work looked like, while my mom taught me all about creativity. I pulled from my experience with both as I found my passion in construction stationed mostly out of Atlanta. I worked for 45 years at many high-profile jobs: the new ballpark for the Atlanta Braves (Truist Park), the Georgia Aquarium (both the dolphin and shark exhibits), several hospitals, and many office buildings as far away as Boston.

I have a passion for golf, and I'm sort of a handyman around the house. I'm retired and loving every moment of it. It gives me more time to write. They say everybody has one good book in them. For the last ten years or so in my life I've watched movies; old and older ones, which gave me something very valuable: ideas. Ideas that are so strong that I have to put them down on paper. In the last five years I have assembled a team of individuals, all strong women, that have the passion to help me bring this story to life.

I've written this series, *Bleeds For Life*, with the hope that you'll see pieces of our own fears and struggles reflected in its characters. The people of Chatham Hill face many of the same challenges we do—loneliness, despair, the fear of others and of ourselves, and, yes, the heavy weight of regret.

Maybe, just maybe, a few good-hearted souls will join me along the way. If you do, I truly believe you won't regret it. Well...I pray it never comes to that.

Thank you for your time and enjoy.
Godspeed,

Rik Jones

RIK JONES

rikjonesauthor.com

ALSO BY RIK JONES

BUTTERFLY BLEEDS

BLEEDS FOR LIFE

BOOK ONE

MOONSHINE BLEEDS

BLEEDS FOR LIFE

BOOK TWO